Halloran looked across his desk at Frank Kurowski, who was on loan to the crime commission to catch crooked cops.

"I think we've found the right candidate to turn around—our guy's name is Tommy Sloane. Thomas Patrick Sloane, age thirty-six, thirteen years on the police force. A real one hundred percent swinger. A typical New York wise ass cop. Knows everybody. Owners, bartenders, maitre d's, they all kiss his ass like he's the commissioner. Pisses away money like water, real comedian around his pals, keeps everyone laughing. Married, never goes out with his wife. In New York, anyway. Supposed to own a big home in Whitestone.

"Has a beautiful girlfriend, name, Constance Ward. Works as an executive in a big advertising agency. They practically live together in a co-op on East Seventy-fourth Street and York Avenue. Drives a neat BMW, good foreign car. I have no idea who pays for all this—the co-op, car, big house in Whitestone—but this guy lives pretty good.

"But now the good part of the scenario. This guy's getting real careless. He's a lead-pipe cinch to tail. Drinks a lot. Maybe that's why his guard is down."

Halloran sat back in his broad leather chair. "Good work. Super. No question you are on the right track. This guy Sloane looks very vulnerable…"

BIG TIME TOMMY SLOANE

JAMES REARDON

ST. MARTIN'S PRESS/NEW YORK

BIG TIME TOMMY SLOANE.

Copyright © 1987 by James Reardon

All rights reserved including the right of reproduction in whole or in part in any form.

Published by arrangement with Freundlich Books, 212 Fifth Avenue, New York, N. Y. 10010.

Library of Congress Catalog Card Number: 86-31957

ISBN: 0-312-90981-0   Can. ISBN: 0-312-90982-9

Printed in the United States of America

First St. Martin's Press mass market edition/April 1988

10 9 8 7 6 5 4 3 2 1

To All The Good Cops in The Big Cities,
The Small Cities,
The Big Towns, The Small Towns—
Watch Your Ass—It's a Jungle Out There

BOOK ONE

THE LEO P. QUINN FUNERAL HOME stood somberly on the corner of one of the lower numbered streets bordering Queens Boulevard, about two miles short of the Queensboro Bridge, an ancient and famous span that led directly into the bright lights and promising joys of midtown New York City. The Home was in an enclave of the borough of Queens called Sunnyside. Sunnyside was truly a neighborhood, one of the endless number of neighborhoods that had sprung up to form the great city. The residents of this ethnic compound were in equal ratio either Irish or Italian, with a smattering of Jewish storekeepers and Greek restaurant owners.

The funeral home, or the wake house, as it was usually referred to, was a two-story red brick building with a jet black canopy over the entrance proudly bearing the name of the owner, by now the third-generation Leo P. Quinn. As you walked in the front door there was a large foyer and on adjacent sides were comfortably furnished sitting rooms off which were two large chapels, or wake rooms, where the bodies of the recently deceased lay. The dead ones rested peacefully, usually in expensive coffins, inevitably surrounded by dozens of glorious floral arrangements with cards prominently attached attesting to the deep affection and anguished sympathies of the donors.

It was more than a coincidence and only fitting that a bar and grill, Ed McGrath's Chop House, flanked the Leo P. Quinn Funeral Home on the Queens Boulevard side. However, the only chops ever sold in Eddie McGrath's saloon were the duplicate slips Buster O'Brien, the neighborhood bookmaker, gave to his players as receipts for whatever horses they had just given him bets on. The action took place in Buster's headquarters, the stoveless kitchen of McGrath's Chop House.

Paddy Sloane, first-grade detective, Manhattan Main Office squad, stood at the bar drinking Canadian Club whiskey. He was surrounded by a half-dozen old pals commiserating with him over the death of his wife, Helen, who lay in a genuine mahogany casket in the right-side wake room next door.

"Give us all another drink, Paulie, set the boys up again," said Paddy as he pushed the change of a hundred—a residue of fives and tens scattered across the bar—towards the bartender. Paddy's eyes were bloodshot slits from booze and weeping and all he could manage to say in return to each murmur of condolence from the crowd surrounding and drinking with him was, "Poor Helen, Jesus Christ almighty, poor Helen. Dead, dead, dead! Jesus, God, she was only thirty-nine! Why? How in the name of merciful Christ could you take her away from me so young?"

Paddy had been home to Helen and his two kids only once in the last three years. Now, half-drunk, standing at the bar, he was drenched in remorse. His cronies just patted his back and quietly sipped their fresh drinks while the tears rolled down Paddy's cheeks.

Head down against his chest, he silently brooded. Why in the name of Jesus Christ did I ever leave Helen and the two kids, Rosemary and Tommy? Why the hell did I ever fall in love with that long-legged bitch of a night-club dancer and leave my beautiful family? But as Paddy sipped his drink he rationalized his bitter situation. A man needed sex, didn't he? And poor Helen, sickly ever since little Tommy was born, frightened to death of becoming pregnant again, always pleading a headache or some goddam ailment, continuously refused him, pushed him away. He inwardly seethed with rage at his fate and

4

wanted to bang his head against the fucking bar and banish the Irish guilts that were eating his brain away.

Paddy slowly raised his head, emerged from his tortuous reverie.

"One more drink, Paulie, and give the boys here what they want. I have to leave now and go in and see my poor Helen, God bless her."

A murmur of sad approval greeted this tearful lament as the boys reached for their fresh drinks.

Helen McElroy Sloane, dressed in baby blue, her favorite color, looked beautiful even in death as she lay peacefully in her casket at the center of the extreme end of the wake room, almost like a fairy princess lying in state, with her lovely face encased in her soft, blond, curly hair. The physical debilitation of her final, lingering illness had been miraculously reversed by the skillful and seasoned ministrations of Leo P. Quinn the third. A two-foot statue of a robed Jesus Christ was mounted on the wall above her casket, arms outstretched, as if imploring Helen beneath him, "Get on with it, come up to me in Heaven."

A mass of floral pieces lay on both sides of the casket and straight chairs stretched row by row from the middle of the chapel to the rear wall. Some easy chairs and sofas flanked the casket at the front of the chapel. At half past seven in the evening the wake room was just beginning to fill. Rosemary Sloane, age nineteen, with her mother's lovely face and a bit too-heavy figure—her father's heritage—was standing at the side of her mother's bier, dutifully kissing relatives and dear friends as they arrived. The newcomers would then kneel before the casket, tears welling in their eyes as they recalled how gracious Helen was, what a wonderful person she was, how beautiful she looked, even in death. They then said their brief prayers for her quick ascension into Heaven and took their seats in the straight chairs in the back of the room.

Tommy Sloane, age fifteen, curly-haired and stockily built, sat in the easy chair nearest his mother's casket. He was too grief-stricken and numb to stand. He occasionally stole a covert glance at his dead mother's face and had all he could do to choke back the tears and sobs that had wracked him almost uncontrollably since her death two days before.

Tommy looked up gratefully at his sister, Rosemary, who had her steady boyfriend Billy Walsh at her side to give her aid and comfort as she greeted the mourners of her beloved mother. Billy, just out of the Marine Corps, was working as an apprentice steam fitter, and Tommy knew that they planned to marry as soon as a decent interval of mourning elapsed after their mother's burial.

Tommy stood up respectfully as his father approached him and proceeded to hug him to his breast. He involuntarily shrank away as the stink of whiskey almost suffocated him.

"Oh, Tommy, my boy, what a crime to lose your mother so young. She loved you more than life, Tom, you know that. Be brave, keep your chin up, son, we'll make it, everything will be okay," Big Paddy sobbed.

He left Tommy, turned, and crushed Rosemary in his arms, both of them wailing. There wasn't a dry eye in the wake house and a cacophony of muffled sobs arose from the middle rows of chairs as one and all tearfully witnessed the fatherly embrace.

Only young Tommy Sloane's eyes were dry. Where the hell was my big windbag old man when we needed him the last year when Mama was dying inch by inch? Sure, he sent home plenty of money, but what the hell difference did that make? Besides, who the hell knows how much money he made in his fucking Broadway detective squad?

Tommy had been to visit his father and his live-in sweetheart only once since Paddy deserted their flat in Sunnyside. He was astonished at the grandeur of the fancy apartment the old man and his whore—as all the immediate family referred to her— resided in on East Sixty-fifth Street in Manhattan. Fuck him, said Tommy to himself, as he sat grimly watching Big Paddy put on his horseshit wake-house act.

Ten o'clock, closing time, mercifully arrived. Paddy Sloane stood tall, with his arm around Rosemary, saying tearful good-byes to everyone who came up to the coffin to pay their last respects. Tommy looked at him, shook his head in disbelief.

The phony sonofabitch is acting like the number one father of the year.

Tommy quickly escaped from the funeral home and walked the few city blocks back to the middle-class development where they lived. He wanted to be alone, to think about his mother, to remember how she tried to protect him when his father was looking for an excuse to beat the shit out of him.

To Tom, the next day was unforgettable, to be remembered all his life. The funeral service, the incredibly clear voice of the soprano singing the Mass a capella, filling the crowded church with the ethereal, sad, but beautiful funeral hymns. When they arrived at the nearby cemetery the graveside prayers of the priest were all a blur to young Tommy Sloane. His heart was breaking through every minute of it, but he went through the motions stoically, choking back each sob.

His sister Rosemary was beautiful and brave throughout the entire burial ordeal. Big Paddy Sloane clung to Rosemary and cried his heart out the entire route, the pangs of guilt churning inside him and exposing to his naked inner self what a worthless no-good sonofabitch he really was.

The funeral over, the family, relatives, and close friends repaired to a spacious restaurant on Queens Boulevard where the traditional Irish postburial feast took place. The whiskey flowed, Helen McElroy Sloane was toasted towards heaven to a fare-thee-well, drink by drink. Paddy Sloane, with a half-dozen Canadian Clubs under his belt, soon regained his composure. After a few hours of drinking and eating the crowd finally dwindled down to Rosemary, her sweetheart Billy Walsh, Grandma McElroy, Tommy, Paddy, and a few of his ever-thirsty cohorts. Finally even they left and the funeral party was over. Paddy peeled several hundred dollar bills off a fat bank-roll, and the family walked back a couple of blocks to the Sloane apartment.

Paddy made himself at home in the apartment just as if he had never left. He fixed himself a drink, turned to the assemblage, and said, "Well, where do we go from here, now that Mother's gone? What's going to happen to you two kids?"

Rosemary spoke up. "Dad, Billy and I are going to be married sometime during the summer. Mother knew about us, was crazy about Billy, and I'm sure you approve of him."

Paddy said expansively, "Sure, Rosie, sure, Billy is a fine young man. Of course, you two have my blessing."

He arched his eyebrows, gave Billy what was supposed to be a stern, yet comical look, and said, "You'll take good care of my little girl, won't you, Billy? She's the only one I have now."

Billy Walsh, struck mute by the great man's blessing, nodded dumbly. He was still very much in awe of the first-grade detective with the big reputation among the union guys and top-racket guys in the city.

Then came the bombshell, the question young Tommy sensed was inevitable, but the thought of which terrified him.

"And you, Tommy, you'll want to come live with me and Linda. There's no use kicking the shit under the rug. We have a nice place, as you know, and we'll fix the den into a bedroom for you. I'll send you to Loyola School up on Park Avenue with the Jesuits, maybe they'll knock some learning into that thick head of yours."

Tommy stayed mute, too scared to answer. Grandma McElroy rose to the rescue.

"Leave Thomas alone, Pat, he'll finish the school term here at Bryant High and stay with Rosemary until she gets married. Then he can come out to my house in Middle Village and live with me. He can transfer to Bishop Molloy next year. It's not far away and it's a wonderful school, the Brothers are fine teachers. You can surely afford it the way you throw hundred-dollar bills around."

Paddy said, "But Grandma, the boy needs a father. I realize I've made some mistakes but I want to make a home for him, sincerely."

Grandma McElroy was as overpowering as her daughter Helen had been docile. She emigrated from Ireland to a job as a domestic when she was fourteen years old. She married a New York cop at eighteen, had Helen when she was twenty. Shortly thereafter, McElroy the cop was shot dead trying to abort a stick-up. She raised Helen from the age of two and never had a really poor day.

Grandma looked hard at Paddy Sloane.

"Now tell me, Paddy, just what the hell kind of father do you think you've been? Go back to New York to your fancy flat and your red-haired whore, Paddy Sloane. I'll take care of my grandson, Thomas, and that's the end of it. You just send me his tuition money. That's all we'll need."

Big Paddy blinked a few times, his face reddened, he started to speak, strangled on the words and shut up. He sipped his drink thoughtfully, looking Grandma dead in the eye, shrugged his shoulders and finally said, "I guess you're right, Grandma. New York City is a tough place to raise a kid."

And that was that!

Tommy Sloane breathed a sigh of relief.

In early June the school term ended. He received his term marks. From average to bad, but he couldn't care one shit less. So long, Bryant High School. He had passed English, history, and civics. He flunked algebra and Latin resoundingly.

Rosemary Sloane and Billy Walsh were married in July and settled into the Sloane apartment in Sunnyside. As per schedule, Tommy moved to his Grandma's house in Middle Village, another of the many neighborhoods in beautiful Queens.

Through the persistent entreaties of Grandma, with a possible boost from Big Paddy, Tommy was accepted in the fall term at Bishop Molloy High School, a nearby Catholic school administered by the Christian Brothers Of Ireland. His acceptance was subject to the condition that he repeat his sophomore year. He was rejuvenated by the change in neighborhood and school, and he loved living with Grandma. He formed quick friendships with a number of guys his own age. Contrary to his previous hatred of anything academic, he loved Bishop Molloy.

Tommy had turned sixteen in early summer, a while before school opened, and had started to grow enough to appear almost lean in contrast to his early stockiness. Paddy Sloane sent Grandma the tuition money as promised, as well as ten dollars a week spending money, a stroke of fortune Tommy had never received while his mother was alive. He grinned to himself and reasoned that his old man must really be suffering the pain of the Irish guilts to cause such a sudden burst of generosity.

Tommy, a good, solid schoolyard player as a kid around

Sunnyside, tried out and made the junior varsity basketball team. He loved playing the game, especially when they played rival junior varsities in the preliminary before the varsity games. The cheering, the crowds, the burst of applause that rewarded a good shot—he ate it all up. He had only recently begun to chase girls and when they played co-ed schools he surreptitiously appraised each rival cheerleader as he took his warm-up shots. During these games he went all out, driving for balls, scrambling, scratching, giving every extra strenuous effort to impress the long-legged little devils who danced and clapped along the sidelines. He managed to date a cheerleader for every away-from-home game—an all-time Bishop Molloy school record.

But school and the arduous regimen of studies were something else. Tommy just couldn't seem to grasp the mysteries of algebra and Latin. At the end of the first semester, in mid-January, he failed both subjects and was declared ineligible to play basketball for the junior varsity. He was heartbroken. When school resumed in the beginning of February, he started to lose interest altogether. He was truant much of the spring term, forging Grandma's name to excusatory notes, doing things he despised himself for.

The school term ended, his marks a disaster he adroitly concealed from Grandma, he made the most momentous decision in his young life. Knowing he would not be welcome back to Bishop Molloy in the fall, he decided to take the advice of the posters he saw on the subway every day and join the United States Navy and see the world. His seventeenth birthday came, he discussed the idea with Grandma, and with a big hug of encouragement from her, plus a flood of tears, Tommy went over to downtown Church Street in New York City and enlisted in the navy. His commitment was for four years.

Tommy was sent to Great Lakes Naval Station, off Lake Michigan, outside of Chicago, for his training period. He enjoyed every working minute of the navy and as part of his training was induced to embrace a study curriculum that would eventually give him a high school equivalency diploma. On completion of his training at Great Lakes, Tommy was sent to

San Diego Naval Base in California. In due course he was assigned to a destroyer as an apprentice seaman, gunner's mate.

The navy was a whole new world to Tommy after the sidewalks of Queens. He loved the laughs and camaraderie among his shipmates, the firm but polite officers, the ship plowing through the rolling blue green ocean, serene under starry, breathtaking Pacific nights, the moon huge and brilliant. But so far there was one vital thing missing—girls. Girls, a major omission in any seventeen-year-old kid's life. And at age seventeen, regardless of how much he bullshitted his fellow sailors, Tommy Sloane was still a virgin. He put on the act with his buddies aboard ship—probably as they did—that he was an experienced lover, a regular Queens Casanova, but he knew in his heart that he was still cherry, never had the earth-moving experience of a good fuck.

After a three-month training mission at sea, Apprentice Seaman Thomas Patrick Sloane returned to San Diego Naval Base. He was bronzed from the Pacific sun, blue-eyed, curly-haired, five feet eleven inches tall, and weighed one hundred and seventy pounds. He was given a week's shore leave and one hundred dollars pay in advance.

The most idyllic part of San Diego to a young sailor is its proximity to the sensual delights of the bordellos of Tijuana. Tommy crossed the border in a taxi with a couple of his shipmates and while maintaining a super cool exterior for their benefit, inwardly he was almost dying in anticipation of his first piece of ass. The next few days were a maze of blonds, brunettes, redheads, black stockings, garter belts and cold beer.

When he finally woke up alone in a tiny hotel room he was the happiest and the best-fucked sailor in the United States Navy. He was in such a state of ecstasy he didn't mind his throbbing hangover.

Now an experienced lover, man of the world, the Irish Cary Grant, Tommy embarked on his naval career and steadily rose through the ranks. The next two years were spent in the familiar navy routine. His destroyer visited many ports in the Pacific on its training cruises but the ones he loved best of all were Pearl Harbor and Honolulu. He was crazy about Hawaiian girls and the lush tropical climate, savoring every minute of his shore leave.

Tommy was proud when he at last was awarded his high school equivalency diploma. The navy brass had insisted that he take both shore and correspondence courses when at sea, and once they shunted algebra aside and substituted Spanish for Latin, Tommy's natural intellect asserted itself and at last he became a full-fledged high school graduate.

He sent his sister Rosemary his treasured diploma for safe-keeping, and wrote her and Grandma McElroy long letters telling them how happy he was in the navy. He knew deep down how proud they would be to learn of his intellectual feat, that he wasn't such a dumb shithead, after all. He briefly toyed with the idea of writing to his father but quickly discarded it for fear that it might seem as if he was kissing his old man's ass. He hadn't heard a word from Big Paddy in over two years. Just as well. He knew through Rosemary's letters that Paddy had retired from the Job, that he had not been well. No wonder he thought, all that booze has got to catch up to you sometime.

About a month later he was ordered to report to his C.O.'s office. He was a lieutenant commander, a real nice guy, a Naval Academy graduate.

"Sit down, Sloane, I have some bad news to tell you."

"Yes, Commander."

"Oh, shit, Sloane, I hate to tell you this but I must. Your father passed away yesterday. We had a call late last night from your sister, Mrs. Walsh, right?"

"That's right, sir." Tommy was stunned; the old man was one of those big strong guys you figure will never die. Still, he didn't feel an iota of sadness, not a speck of grief.

"You can have a week's leave, Sloane, and I'll arrange a pay advance for you."

"Thank you, sir, but I'd prefer not to go to his funeral. To be honest, sir, I never got along too well with my father and I'd just as soon let it go at that."

The C.O. raised his eyebrows, looked a little quizzically at Tommy and said, "It's purely up to you, Sloane, and I respect your decision. But please wire your sister and express your intentions. If you want, so as not to hurt her feelings, tell her you can't get leave or some excuse like that. Okay, Sloane, again, I'm sorry, but I guess I know how you feel. Don't forget to call or wire your sister. You can go now."

They both stood up and the C.O. reached out and shook Tommy's hand. A nice gesture. Tommy called Rosemary and gave her a bullshit story about not being able to get away, but he knew deep down that she didn't believe him. The next day he went to Tijuana, visited a couple of whorehouses, had about twenty beers, and put his old man out of his mind.

The time rolled by and in time Tommy became a full-fledged gunner's mate, as well as a crack shot on the pistol range at San Diego Naval Base. He had shunned both submarine duty and engine-room training while at Great Lakes and instead opted for the gunnery sections on deck. He couldn't seem to get enough of the heaving seas and the salt air that filled his nostrils with a sharp fragrance. Tommy Sloane had found his niche.

He was keenly aware that he was a bit claustrophobic as a kid. Scared shitless when his old man locked him in a dark closet, apprehensive in an elevator, glad he lived in a walk-up apartment house. His early fears had been documented in his psychological tests at Great Lakes, where he had confessed his dread of close places to the psychiatrist who then recommended he be assigned above decks.

And now, when at sea, he loved to stand on the scrubbed-clean deck breathing in the heavenly blue Pacific skies. He reveled in the salty sprays that sprang from the sea over the rails of the destroyer as he stood watch behind them during the hot, sunny days. His mind wandered as he gazed across the endless span of blue green ocean and he contemplated his future. What would it be like, what did the world have in store for him? He was an orphan, now. He smiled ruefully. What would he do when he left the navy?

Maybe he would never leave the navy. He was happy here. Nice bunch of guys. Always showered, shaved, clean as a whistle. Always fifty or sixty bucks in his pocket, and best of all, the finest chicks in the world to come home to after a few months at sea. A sweet life, Tommy often said to himself as he lay back on his bunk and meditated on his good fortune.

The days, weeks, months, and another year passed quickly and Gunner's Mate First Class Thomas Patrick Sloane was a bonafide three-year veteran of Uncle Sam's navy. He was the lead gunner of a group of four in an enclosed turret on the deck of a destroyer. The magazine was fed automatically and the guns were guided by radar, so that each man had his own specific, technical duty to master. Tommy felt like Captain Horatio Hornblower in charge of the gun crew. He had occasional moments of apprehension about the close quarters during target practice, but with the laughing and joking among the four-man gun crew his anxieties were quickly allayed.

The social turmoil and internecine warfare in the Republic of Korea soon exploded into civil war between the North and South zones. The United Nations, led by the United States, fearful of a takeover of South Korea by the Soviet Union or even Communist China, was soon drawn into the war to aid the South.

The Korean War was a predominately land-based conflict, but patriotic fervor still accounted for a huge increase in naval enlistments and soon the San Diego Naval Base was teeming with future admirals.

Tommy Sloane, seasoned navy veteran, was assigned to shore duty as a gunnery instructor. Korea also renewed a dormant patriotic urge among the civilian segment of America, and soon enlisted-men's clubs proliferated throughout the country, staffed in the main by volunteer women. San Diego Naval Base soon had its share and the clubs began to thrive with dances, U.S.O. entertainers, and, of course, loads of pretty young girls.

Tommy at one time or another had crushes on various girls but sooner or later he tired of them or they got on his nerves. Up to this point in his life he had never experienced either the agony or ecstasy of being in love. If he had a special date, which was seldom, as he preferred to take his best shot with whomever was available, he turned on all his charm to get laid. If he failed in his pursuit of the ultimate happiness, there were always the sultry, olive-skinned whores of Tijuana, a short sprint away.

14

At a dance one steamy Saturday night, Tommy was introduced by one of his pals to a lovely, reserved, dark-haired girl named Justine Brooks. When he first danced with Justine she was incredibly firm but slender, and fitted into his arms as if she were molded to him. Tommy flushed, felt a tremendous rush of tenderness towards her, almost overwhelming in its intensity. He also immediately got a giant hard-on.

The blissful couple finished their dance and as Tommy walked off the floor with his left arm around Justine he slyly took his sailor's hat out of his right-hand pants pocket and attempted casually to mask the straining bulge in front of his tight-fitting navy bell-bottoms. He bought a couple of soft drinks and they engaged in the same easy banter that two young people of opposite sexes engage in when they first meet and mutually feel the indescribable thrill of a strong animal attraction.

"You dance just great, Justine."

"Thank you, Tommy, you're a regular Fred Astaire, yourself."

"I guess I should be. All guys from New York are supposed to be good dancers, you know that," he casually bragged.

"Really, Tom, you're from New York? How wonderful," Justine said excitedly, now really impressed.

"Right in the heart of the big city, sweetheart," Tommy lied. Queens was an outpost of New York City, but still part of it, so Tommy privately consoled himself—it was only a small white lie.

"Gee, Tom, you're the first fellow I ever met who came from New York," Justine said, now really taking in his curly hair, blue eyes, and tanned, strong face. "No wonder you're so smooth. I heard all about you New York guys." She laughed, a light, lovely laugh, revealing even, white teeth.

Tommy looked at her, sipped his Coke and joined in the laughter. Christ, I could be crazy about this kid. He was slowly relaxing, his hard-on had finally subsided.

"Where are you from, Justine?"

"Right here in San Diego. My parents are divorced. My father lives in Los Angeles and my mother is a secretary right here at the naval base. I just finished business school and I work as a secretary in an insurance agency here in town. That's my story, Tom. Tell me about you."

"Well, as you can see, I'm a near admiral." They both broke up laughing. He finally composed himself. "Seriously, I'm in my fourth year in the navy. Both my parents are dead and I only have a married sister and my grandma to account to, but Grandma's pretty tough. But tell me, do you have a steady boyfriend?"

"I'm free, single, and I never even thought of having a steady boyfriend until a couple of minutes ago," she said and winked at Tommy mischievously.

"That's great, Justine, 'cause I'm going to see a lot of you, I hope."

Justine squeezed his hand, kissed him on the cheek, and said, "I hope so, too, Tom."

And so began the romance of Tommy Sloane and Justine Brooks. As the weeks went by the love affair flourished and he courted her as gallantly as a knight from King Arthur's court romanced his dream princess. They had some torrid love scenes in Tommy's car and at Justine's apartment when her mother was out, but she steadfastly clung to her virginity. Defying all odds, wonder of wonders, Tommy remained temporarily celibate. Swollen, painful testicles and all, he renounced the dark-skinned lusty whores of Tijuana and turned away the blandishments of the ever-ready sailor groupies who flocked to the U.S.O. dances, panting to have their thighs parted to enhance the fighting abilities of the United States Navy.

Tommy and Justine were in love. Tommy met Justine's mother, became great friends with her, charmed her out of her shoes. But she was reluctant to give her blessing to their marriage. She approved of Tom, but frowned on Justine's marrying him while he was still a sailor, probably remembering her own brief and unhappy marriage. Fortunately, it was only a few months until Tommy's four-year enlistment was up, so they decided to wait it out.

Their courtship was a happy one and they made their marriage plans with the imponderable hopes of the young. They planned to marry in San Diego and move to New York directly after their marriage. Their honeymoon would be a cross-country trip in

Tom's battered 1948 Ford. They would settle in Queens near Rosemary and Grandma and figured that neither would have trouble getting jobs in the booming economy.

The great day, like all great days, finally arrived. Tommy was mustered out of the United States Navy in the morning with a pocket full of money and Justine's mother had all the plans made for the wedding in the late afternoon. Two of Tom's closest buddies and two of Justine's best girlfriends, together with Justine's mother, made up the wedding party. The justice of the peace was swift and sure in overseeing their exchange of wedding vows. The ceremony over, Justine's mother arranged a little party at a nearby Italian restaurant with plenty of good wine and champagne. At last, they took off for New York amidst a million tears, hugs, and kisses.

The first night they stopped at a motel about one hundred miles east of San Diego. They made love almost as soon as they locked the motel room door and Tommy was stunned, then delighted, by the ardent and almost insatiable desires of Justine. They both reached orgasm simultaneously in a couple of minutes and a few minutes later Justine was smothering him with kisses and groping him and pleading with him to make love to her again.

Justine, at last satiated, fell asleep in Tommy's arms about midnight. He looked down at her face, her mouth slightly open, snoring softly, and thanked his lucky stars he had saved all those bangs the last few months or he would be dead right now. The next day they continued their trip and through the ensuing ten days made love leisurely at what seemed like innumerable anonymous little motels across the country. The great lover from New York, at first a little abashed and shaken up at Justine's intensity, prevailed over all and soon their lovemaking was as harmonious as the galaxies in outer space.

That is, until their last stop, just outside Harrisburg, Pennsylvania, off the Pennsylvania Turnpike. They had driven about three hundred miles through a driving rain and Tommy was very tired when they checked into the motel. They had a beer and a hamburger in the motel restaurant and returned to the room. Tommy undressed, brushed his teeth, and hopped into bed. He fell asleep almost immediately and never even felt Jus-

17

tine crawl into bed next to him. He awoke suddenly, as if out of a bad dream. He sat up in bed and saw Justine at the far end of the bed. She was crying, very softly. He pulled her to his chest.

"What's the matter, hon, did you have a bad dream?"

"No, Tom, it's nothing, go to sleep."

"What the hell do you mean, it's nothing? What are you crying for?"

"It's nothing, go to sleep."

He grabbed her roughly.

"Now tell me, for Christ sake, what the hell is the matter? Why are you crying?"

She hugged him fiercely.

"Oh, Tommy, you didn't make love to me this morning and now tonight you went right to sleep on me. You don't love me any more."

"Oh, Justine, you're crazy, baby." He pulled her to him and kissed her lips, her breasts and made love to her wildly until she finally pushed him away, exhausted. She immediately fell into a deep sleep. He lay there, exhausted, too, but couldn't resist a smile.

They were more in love when they arrived at Rosemary's house than they had ever thought possible. The homecoming was fabulous and Justine was hugged and kissed as much as Tommy. Rosemary, her two-year-old son, Billy, Jr., Billy, and Grandma threw them another big party at Grandma's house, inviting a lot of old friends and all remaining relatives. The booze flowed and Tommy was treated like a returning war hero although he insisted that he never heard a shot fired in anger. According to custom, Justine and Tom received enough cash in the envelopes thrust upon them as wedding presents to enable them to rent an apartment in the Woodside neighborhood of Queens and to make a generous down payment on the furniture for it.

They only stayed in Grandma McElroy's house about a week when they both got jobs, the new furniture was delivered, and they moved into their own apartment. Justine landed a job as a secretary in a major insurance company just over the bridge in

Manhattan. Billy Walsh, Tommy's brother-in-law, now a full-fledged union steam fitter, got Tom a job with a small non-union construction company. Justine's salary was fifty dollars a week, Tommy's salary eighty-five dollars a week. They were both ecstatic at their good luck, and rolling around in their new-found wealth.

The first year in Woodside they added little decorative effects to their apartment with any extra money they had and they were both very proud of their new home. They seldom left the house at night except for an occasional movie or a visit to Rosemary or Grandma. Justine proved to be a neat house-keeper and an exceptional cook, so they rarely ate dinner out. Tommy ran into some old school and boyhood friends once in a while, but never went beyond having a few beers and coming home early.

The same routine continued into their second year of marriage and Tommy began to grow a bit restless. He was making good money, with plenty of overtime, but he couldn't foresee a future in pushing a wheelbarrow, bricklaying, or banging nails into two-by-fours. The one bright aspect of the job was the friendship he developed with an Italian guy his own age named Vinny Ciano. They had a mutual bond in that both of them had cops in their families, Tom a two-generation inheritor with Grandpa McElroy and Big Paddy and Vinny from his uncle Rocky. Like Grandpa McElroy, Vinny's uncle Rocky was also shot and killed in the line of duty.

They laughed and joked with each other with the easy familiarity of New York street kids, calling each other "stupid Irish mick" or "dopey guinea bastard" whenever one or the other made a trivial mistake.

Vinny Ciano was from Little Italy in Manhattan's lower East Side. He was the kind of a kid everyone liked, a kid who would stop a stickball game on the street to run over and take a heavy bag of groceries from an old woman and help her up the flights of stairs to her tenement flat. Nobody in the game would have dared to make a remark about the temporary halt in play, because weekends and summers since the age of ten he worked as a helper on his father's ice truck.

He graduated from a public high school on the lower East Side and a couple of years later he joined the army, probably to get off the ice truck. After seeing some thankfully brief but heavy action as an infantryman in Korea, he was finally released from the service with a well-healed bullet hole in his thigh, a Purple Heart and a Silver Star. Through some family friends he got the construction job that placed him next to his new pal, Tommy Sloane. Side by side, pushing loaded wheelbarrows, hauling bricks, carrying sections of two-by-fours—working their respective balls off.

Vinny was a bachelor and, like Tommy, an orphan. He lived with a married sister and her husband and kids in a nice one-family house in Astoria, another of the many neighborhoods in Queens. Knocking off work early one sultry summer afternoon, Tom and Vinny stopped at a small bar near the Queensboro Bridge to have a few beers. They tipped glasses for good luck and Vinny said, "Tommy, have you ever given any thought to what the hell you intend to do with your life?"

"I hope not keep working on this goddam construction job, that's for sure."

"Well, can't you see? That's why I'm asking you. What the hell else have you in mind, you stupid Irish prick? Rob a bank? Kidnap Henry Ford? Become the president?"

"Christ, Vinny, I really don't know. Eventually become a steam fitter, I guess. My brother-in-law Billy Walsh is trying to get me an apprentice card in the union. They make good money, you know."

"Yeah, I guess they do, Tom, but I'm tired of all this manual labor shit. It seems like I've been breaking my balls working hard since I was a kid. I'm getting out of these fucking overalls and work shoes as fast as I can."

"Well, then, what the hell are your future plans? You intend to be a top wop mayor like that bullshit artist Fiorello LaGuardia, or one of the big mob bosses in Little Italy you're always bragging about?"

Vinny looked at Tommy and laughed.

"You know, Irish, you're hot shit, you really are. You kill me."

"Well, tell me what the hell is on your scheming, Italian, alleged mind?"

Again Vinny laughed, then took a long swallow of beer. He put his empty glass on the bar.

"This will really kill you, Tom. I'm going to be a cop, or at least I'm going to take the test for the cops."

"You're what?"

"A cop! A flatfoot! But only for a while. Then I'm going to be a first-grade detective in the homicide squad."

"You, a cop, I can't believe it. Of course we talked about it enough, so you know my old man was a cop. In fact, he was a first-grade detective."

"I know that. We go over it every time we have a few beers. And your grandfather was shot and killed just like my uncle Rocky. What the hell have you got against being a cop? You'd make a damned good one, I bet."

"I really don't know. I guess it goes back to me and my old man always being on the outs that turned me off cops."

"If you ask me, that's a stupid way of looking at it. Fuck your old man, he's dead and buried. You have a new wife, soon maybe a couple of kids, your own life to lead. Worry about your own future—fuck all your old man hangups."

"What the hell is making you so conscious of your future all of a sudden? And what's all this cop bullshit out of a clear blue sky?"

"Listen to what I have to say, Tom, and keep that Irish kisser closed for a few minutes. When I was a young kid working on the back of my old man's ice truck, our route was all around police headquarters on Center Street, right off Broome Street. About three blocks from where I was born and raised. I used to go green when I saw those big Irish bulls standing together outside police headquarters, their new hats pushed back on their heads, their hands in their pants pockets holding back their new topcoats over the top of their asses. Whenever we stopped for a red light I'd look them over and I knew that in their left-hand pocket was the bankroll and in their right-hand pocket was the gold shield that got them the bankroll.

"There were crap games, card games, horserooms, book-makers, and number guys all over the fucking neighborhood where I came from. And these same bulls with their hands in their pockets were as thick as shit with the big wise guys around Mulberry Street. I saw it with my own eyes every day in the week. You see, Irish, you get the picture? Or by chance did you think your old man got all his fucking money from the Salva-tion Army?"

Tommy just sipped his beer, taking it all in. He shook his head, then said, "You sure get windy with a few beers in you, Vincenzo?"

"All right, keep listening. I understand there's a cop test scheduled anywhere from nine months to a year from now. My brother-in-law, Tony, works for the city and he gets the *Civil Service Leader,* so I read it every week. From what I understand the applications for the police test will be available in about six months. What do you say, Tom, let's both of us put our appli-cation in. What do we have to lose?"

Tommy knew that his old man made plenty of money, or "scores." And what about the fancy apartment Big Paddy had where he lived with his girlfriend, Linda? He thought about the way his old man would casually throw a hundred-dollar bill on the bar. Still, the idea of being a cop repelled him.

That was all that was said between the two of them about the idea of taking the police test until about six months later. It was the middle of winter; Tommy and Vinny were working to-gether on a very cold, dark, windy day. They were both shiver-ing, freezing their balls off. They were waiting to get their wheelbarrows filled with bricks to haul to the third floor of the small office building their crew was constructing. They couldn't shake the icy air that ripped clear through their outer gar-ments to their bones. The wind whistled through the steel gird-ers and barren framework of the building shell.

It was just getting dark when they finished work at four thirty and they walked swiftly through the icy, shadowy streets to the nearest oasis, George O'Neil's bar in Maspeth, another neighborhood of Queens. It was one of Vinny and Tommy's favorite places, with a mixed bag of construction guys, white collar guys, pretty girls, good juke box. While cheerful and noisy, it was always in good order under the smiling supervision of Big George himself.

Jackie the bartender greeted them with, "Hiya, guys, the usual beer?"

Vinny said, "No, thanks, Jackie, tonight is a Scotch on the rocks night. And quick, please, we're freezing our nuts off. Black and White for me, Cutty Sark for Tommy.

"Tommy, here's what I have to say. Don't interrupt me, just listen. Remember I told you about my brother-in-law I live with, the guy in civil service. Anyway, he brought home two applications for the police department test next summer, one for me and one for you. Whadda you say? Take a shot with me, you'll never regret it."

"Christ, Vinny, I'm not sure. I still have the reservations I spoke to you about originally. You know, how I never got along with my old man, and how much I resented all that cop bullshit I had to listen to when I was a kid. Besides, my brother-in-law Billy has practically assured me that he'd get me a card in the steam fitters."

"Shit, Tommy, you want to be a peasant and live in overalls and work shoes all your fucking life? You're a good-looking, bright guy. Take a shot. If you get a break you might wind up in plainclothes or become a detective. Look at all that shit that went on in Brooklyn a few years ago and all the dough those guys must have made."

"They made a lot of money, so what? How about the poor fucking cops who killed themselves? How about the poor bastards who are still doing time upstate? Christ, I feel sorry for those guys."

"So do I feel sorry for them. But that's their tough luck. And you gotta admit, they were just plain stupid. They had the world by the balls and began to think they had a license to steal. Overconfidence, that's what buried them—overconfidence. They were untouchables! Untouchable my ass, no one is. If we get on the Job and ever get a crack at plainclothes we profit by their mistakes. Low profile, salt the cash away, live quietly. No fancy clothes, beautiful show girls, big homes. Not like those silly bastards in Brooklyn."

"That's easy to say, Vince, but I watched my old man and the way he lived, watched some of the bulls he worked with. Once you get a taste of that fucking cash it goes first to your head, then to your prick, and you become a high roller like every other cop who makes a buck. I'm glad my old man never got nailed. Much as I hated him I'd have died if he ever had to go to the can."

"Maybe you're right, Tom, but I still would like one crack at the big time. I'll see how I can handle it when the opportunity comes. Meanwhile, tip my glass and promise me that you'll at least file the application for the cops."

Tommy looked thoughtfully at the glass of Scotch whiskey on the bar in front of him. He was full of self-doubt, but he hated to incur the wrath of his pal, Vinny. He turned, looked searchingly into Vinny's eyes, picked up the fresh Scotch on the rocks, tipped his glass and said, "Okay, you wop sonofabitch, I give you my word, I'll go along with you."

"That's my boy, Irish, you'll never regret it."

One more drink for the road brought a long conversation as they mapped out their bright careers as members of New York's Finest. Slightly drunk, the two future police inspectors at last went their separate ways home. Tommy, to his wife, Justine, and Vinny to his new girlfriend Connie's house. Justine took the rather startling news with her usual equanimity—noncommittal, no skepticism.

Tommy went over to Vinny's sister's house the following Sunday and together they filled out the voluminous applications for the police department test. They gave the filing fees and the finished applications to Vinny's city employee brother-in-law and he personally placed them in the proper hands. At his urging they both enrolled for night classes at Delehanty Institute, a mid-Manhattan prep school for many varieties of civil service hopefuls. Delehanty's was a pain in the ass to travel to at night after a hard day's work in construction, but the course shed plenty of light on what to expect in the forthcoming test.

The middle of the following summer the great day arrived. A mild, sunny Saturday morning. Tommy and Vinny took the police department written examination along with about twenty-five thousand other applicants for the Job. All the aspiring cops, divided into huge groups in alphabetical order, took the test at the same time in public schools scattered throughout the city.

The test finished, they rendezvoused at an appointed bar to have a few beers and to discuss the vagaries of their morning ordeal at great length.

"I didn't think it was so hard, did you, Tommy?"

"I'm not quite sure, Vince, you're a little more cop oriented than me. I'm sure you dug in and prepared yourself a little more than I did. But honestly, I think I passed, or at least got enough answers right to be able to take the physical."

"Geez, I hope so, Tom. Wouldn't it be great if someday we become partners? First in a plainclothes squad to get the dough, and then in the homicide squad when we're nice and fat."

"What's with you all the time with this homicide squad shit? You got some idea of becoming the Italian Sherlock Holmes?"

Vinny laughed. "Now, Tom, you and I and a million other guys know the gambling laws are a lot of bullshit. You only get into that to make a little cash. But someday I want to be a homicide dick and grab some of those bastards who kill kids or old defenseless people and see their balls fry in the electric chair. Every time I read about one of those murders I get a knot in my belly. And now those stupid fucking judges and politicians are trying to outlaw capital punishment. What a lot of stupid jerks. In a few years you'll have to carry a machine gun or ride around in an army tank in New York."

"You're right, Vinny baby. The new New York City slogan—a Doberman pinscher attack dog in every home and a shotgun next to the bed. You remind me of something funny that happened when I was a young kid. My old man came home with a couple of his partners. They were really flying, celebrating all day, laughing it up like you couldn't believe. I finally found out why they were so happy. He worked with a detective named Tommy Mason, a real Wyatt Earp. Tommy used to keep his detective special on the night table next to his bed. It always scared the shit out of his wife but he insisted on it. This one night when both of them were asleep, Tommy, a light sleeper like all cops, hears a noise and wakes up. Out of the corner of his eye he spots this big nigger opening up the bedroom window off the fire escape. The guy only has the light from the courtyard to guide him, but so does Tommy. The burglar starts to go for the dressing table in the bedroom where the money usually is. Tommy reaches over nice and easy, aims right across his poor wife's belly, and shoots the big fuck right in the side of the head. It turned out to be the sixth guy Tommy whacked out."

"He shot him dead?"

"Dead as a fucking mackerel. Scared the living shit out of his wife though. She almost had a nervous breakdown, my sister Rose told me."

"Gee, I love to hear stories like that, it restores your faith in good cops."

Six weeks later they both received the good news, the notice to prepare to take their physical examinations in three weeks. The top combined scores of the written and physical tests qualified to make the list for the Job, and usually everyone who made the list and survived the character investigation was appointed a policeman.

The physical test was a combination of agility and strength. A mile run against the clock was also a vital part. Tommy and Vinny were both good athletes, hard as rocks from heavy construction work, so the physical test was a breeze for them. They settled back to await the final results, which were to be published in the *Civil Service Leader*.

The crisp early autumn weather made it a pleasure to be working outdoors. During their lunch hour and a few times a week after work over a few beers they discussed their future in the Job. Vinny brought his girl Connie over to Tommy and

Justine's a couple of times for dinner and they were crazy about her, a lovely, quiet, Italian girl. And smart, a Marymount College graduate.

Vinny confided in Tommy that he planned to marry Connie the following spring. He was a bit reluctant to discuss her too much with Tom, but one day over a beer he mentioned casually that she was the daughter of a big shot, a connected guy.

Tommy, wise in the ways of the street, knew that Connie's old man was probably some guy high up in the mob. He couldn't care less, didn't give a shit. He'd gone to school with some Italian kids, played ball with them, whose fathers were reputedly mob-connected. They were always real nice kids and that's all he cared about. Besides, he was crazy about Vinny, knew how level-headed he was, knew it would be a wonderful marriage for both of them.

In the early fall the list for the Job was published. Vinny came out one hundred and eighty-seven and Tommy six hundred and seventy-six, both now certain to be appointed shortly.

Vinny went into the Job in the early fall and Tommy four months later. In the interim they saw each other rarely.

When he did get to the police academy, Tommy took to the routine like the proverbial duck to water. After breaking his ass for four years in construction work and coming off a recent, bitter winter, he couldn't believe his present good luck. Rookie school was a snap. Getting paid for working out in the gym three or four days a week, playing basketball or touch football almost every day, it was like Bishop Molloy High School revisited.

Unfortunately, there were also some dark sides to the police academy. There were the endless, boring lectures at the academy and the goddam gray uniforms that gave Tom *agita*, a word he learned from Vinny meaning heartburn. But he reasoned that everything couldn't come up roses and endured the endless sessions stoically. He admitted to himself that the lectures were valuable in some ways, getting him acquainted with some semblance of police work and a cop's duty to the public. Still, the constant, incessant theme was corruption, corruption, corruption—the pitfalls and lures leading to corruption.

*   *   *

The infamous Harry Gross bookmaking scandal of 1950 had
had the effect of a direct atomic bomb hit on the Job. There
was a vast reshuffling of the various squads, great turnovers of
executive personnel, constant changes still going on several
years later. In his heart—and from his conversations with
various rookies and some cops, he knew he wasn't the only
one—Tommy felt the whole Gross thing was a lot of shit. A big
publicity stunt by that witch-hunting, headline-grabbing, bullshit judge from Brooklyn, Sam Leibowitz. As a fellow rookie,
Sy Friedman, called him—a disgrace to the Jews.

Tommy and every other hip guy knew that the same old shit
was going on, bigger and better than ever. He had seen with
his own eyes bookmakers operating all over Queens where he
worked and lived. A numbers guy had come around the construction job every morning to pick up the daily play from the
guys. What a lot of horseshit to hear these sanctimonious lieutenants constantly lecturing on corruption. Particularly a windy
lieutenant named Fenihan. The word was out that Fenihan had
never walked a beat.

Why don't they legalize all this bullshit and get it over with?
Then cops could get on with the real purpose of being a cop.
Well, he would silently meditate while the honest lieutenant
droned on—what about the robber barons of the late eighteen
hundreds? What about the court of Julius Caesar, the lords
of England who seized the lands of Ireland. That was real corruption! He grinned, the lords of England. What was that
poem he liked so much that he read in English class in San
Diego? I got it—he grinned again—"The Charge of the Light
Brigade." "Theirs not to reason why, theirs but to do and die."
But he had no intention of riding into the valley of death. He
intended, if he ever got the shot, to grab as much money as he
could from gamblers and wise guys. And he knew that ninety-
nine percent of the rookies in school with him felt the same
way.

Almost to a man Tommy's fellow rookies were army or navy
veterans of the Korean War, where crap games and card games

were as common as the dangerous weapons they handled. The young cops were products of the ghetto, the lower middle class, or middle middle class. Most of them had learned how to play the various card games and how to shoot craps at approximately the age of ten. They were mostly of Irish and Italian descent, with a substantial number of Jews and a smaller number of blacks and hispanics. This was probably due to the ill-conceived educational procedures of the era, because while many of the minority groups aspired to become policemen, few had the necessary educational tools to overcome the seemingly insurmountable barrier of the written examination.

By and large, they were all products of the streets. The streets of New York City, where you grew up in a hurry, and survival was a lesson to be learned very early in life. These rookies from New York City just plain didn't give a shit about the bookmaker or number guy on the corner, or the card or crap game in the social club down the block. As kids, most of them were delighted to run an errand once in a while for one of the wise guys, who always tipped generously. And so they listened politely, yawned, and shrugged their shoulders. They silently reasoned, so some poor guys got caught and went to prison as sacrificial lambs. Too fucking bad. Not me, I'll never make the same mistake. Not me.

The months rolled by and graduation from the academy loomed on the horizon. The main topic of conversation among the rookies was about their forthcoming precinct assignments. The connection for the coveted precinct was known in the Job as the "hook," the catalyst or the connector was known as the "rabbi". The rabbi was usually a relative in the Job who was living very well and could secure a desirable precinct to start in. With his old man dead and buried, Tommy didn't have a soul in the world to turn to.

Fortune smiled. Tommy asked Justine to call Vinny and ask him and Connie for dinner. They arrived a couple of nights later and greeted each other with an avalanche of hugs, kisses, and slaps on the back. It had been a couple of months since their last visit and Tommy couldn't resist a big grin when he put down a Scotch on the rocks in front of Vinny. He raised his own glass to him and said, "Good luck, officer, I really missed you."

"The same, Tommy."

The girls were in the kitchen chatting away and Tom leaned over to Vinny and said, "All right, how are you doing over in the Seventeenth? Give me the scoop, wop."

"Tommy, I love it, nice bunch of guys, good bosses, great people in the precinct. You eat the best and the restaurants are glad to have you. If you want to take your girl or your wife to hear some jazz or great piano there's a hundred joints to go to. They welcome you with open arms. There aren't too many bookmakers, but there's a dozen after-hour places that have gambling in them. Tom, you'd never believe these joints until you see one of them. Plush is the word, man, plush. There's lots of legitimate shit you make a buck on, guys staking you for what you have to do anyway. I'm grabbing a couple of hundred a month extra and it's only going to get better. I already made a couple of horseshit collars—a purse snatcher and a guy driving a stolen car. I'm trying to connect up and get into a radio car. Okay, that's me, what's with you?"

"As you probably know, I'm getting out of the academy in a couple of weeks and I'm naturally concerned about where I wind up."

"Come on, you don't think I forgot you 'cause I haven't seen you lately. I told you my future father-in-law is a nice guy, well connected with some top brass in the Job. The hook is in, pal, you're all set for a good Manhattan precinct. That's where the action is, Tommy baby, good old Manhattan."

Tommy couldn't resist a grin as he sipped his drink and looked Vinny over. He marveled at how good he looked. Older somehow, very confident, sure of himself, dressed beautifully in a well-cut navy blazer, white button-down shirt, dark gray-striped tie, gray slacks, and gleaming black loafers. A collar ad.

Tom raised his glass. "For Christ sake, leave a little money in New York, will you, please, so there's some left for the starving rookies when we get out of this goddam rookie school."

Vinny laughed and reached over and grabbed Connie, who had just come in to announce dinner, and kissed her hard on the lips. She broke away and held his head in her hands, looking at him like he was the Italian Robert Taylor.

Vinny pulled her next to him and said, "Don't worry, Tommy, some day some guy is gonna write a song and call it, 'New York, New York, it's a wonderful town,' and you know what? He'll be dead right."

"Yeah, Vince, it will probably be some musical-minded cop in the Seventeenth, and he'll play it on the new Steinway he just paid cash for."

"Listen, enough cop bullshit. You two are coming to our wedding, right?"

"We wouldn't miss it for the world. But what about this formal attire requested horseshit? You mean Justine in a long gown and me in a tuxedo?"

"Even the Irish have to wear a tuxedo once in a while besides St. Patrick's Day, when the Irish shitheads are roaming all over New York boozing it up at the fancy hotels and bars in their rented suits."

Graduation day finally arrived, a sunny cheerful day in late spring. The mayor made his usual eloquent speech from the steps of city hall, welcoming the five hundred sturdy young rookies to the ranks of the Finest. Justine had taken the day off and she and Tom's sister Rosemary were among the throng of relatives, friends, and little kids who watched and listened proudly, with glistening eyes, as their loved ones were sworn in to uphold the laws of New York City. What a great day!

Shortly after noon the festivities mercifully ended. The crowd broke and the rookies were besieged by their mothers, fathers, wives, and kids, who enveloped them in tearful, proud embraces. Justine and Rosemary were no exception as they smothered Tom with affectionate hugs and kisses. Tommy was overjoyed at finally being rid of his hated gray rookie uniform. He was dressed in his summer uniform—a light blue shirt and darker tie setting off the navy blue of the Finest. It had seemed to him that he wore the rookie gray every waking minute of his life the past few months and he was overjoyed at his own image now that he wore blue. A real cop. Tommy decided to celebrate the occasion by taking Justine and Rosemary to lunch at a fancy Italian restaurant on Mulberry Street.

Tommy walked tall, smiling at passersby who gave him and his uniform a cheerful and respectful smile back. Justine loved the Old World atmosphere of Little Italy. Somehow, when Vinny mentioned the name it always seemed somewhat sinister, but now she was enraptured. The only thing bothering her about the walk was that Tommy kept looking, or trying to look, at himself in every storefront mirror they passed.

The restaurant was large, dimly lit, and the air had a delicious aroma. It was fairly crowded, but Tom had made a reservation and the maitre d' greeted them cordially and led them to a rear table. There were mirrors all along the walls on both sides and Tommy shadowboxed in each mirror as they walked behind the maitre d', almost overcome by the splendid sight of himself in the navy blue of New York's Finest.

Justine, right in back of him, whispered fiercely, "Tom, will you please stop looking at yourself or else you're going to go ass overhead over one of these tables of people."

Fortunately, they reached their rear table without incident. Once seated, Tommy had all he could do to hold in his laughter.

"I'm sorry, Justine, really I am. I just can't get over how beautiful I look."

Rosemary good-naturedly calmed everything.

"Don't worry, Justine, wait until some Puerto Rican up on a roof throws a bucket of shit over him, then we'll see how beautiful he looks."

Justine laughed and said, "You're right, Rosie, that's what he needs, a big bucket of shit to hit him and reduce the size of his swelled head."

That got another big, happy laugh. They ordered fancy Italian dishes and a couple of bottles of good wine and ate and drank with what could only be described as gusto. Despite all the kidding, throughout lunch, Rosemary couldn't take her eyes off her brother, handsome as a movie star in his blue uniform.

Rosemary's eyes misted over.

"Oh, Tom, wouldn't Daddy be proud of you today, seeing you in uniform like this."

Tommy's face clouded over with anger.

"I bet he would be proud, Rose, but maybe he's up there in Heaven, looking down and thinking I finally amounted to something," Tommy lied through his teeth.

"Oh, Tom, I hope so, he always loved you."

Tommy nodded, thinking, he sure had some fucking way of showing it if he did.

The festive luncheon was finally over. Rosemary grabbed the check from Tommy's hand. The brand-new cop, full of good food and good wine, hailed a taxicab and they rode to Queens in style. The cab driver was so astonished he nearly fainted when the young, uniformed cop paid him and gave a two-dollar tip.

Two nights later Tommy reported to the ancient red brick building on East Ninety-sixth Street that would be his second home for the next few years. He arrived, dressed in his uniform, about an hour early to await his first twelve midnight to eight in the morning tour of duty. He was a bit apprehensive, but his four years of naval training had toughened him enough to face the perils of New York streets, so he was high on anticipation of his new role. He recognized a couple of other guys from rookie school and they all shook hands a little nervously, meanwhile remarking on their good luck in landing a spot in such a busy precinct.

Roll call began at 11:45 p.m.

A tough-looking, pot-bellied sergeant, who looked as if he'd cut off your fucking head if you looked cross-eyed at him, was the Boss. About ninety men were lined up in rows of ten directly in front of him. In a surprisingly mild voice he said, "Okay, men, first I'd like to welcome the new rookies to the ranks of the good old Twenty-third. Raise your hands when I call out your names. Austin, DiNapoli, Quigley, McGowan, Sloane. Now all you old veteran and would-be veteran hairbags out there, remember when you were rookies and shitting in your pants your first night tour—keep your eyes open for these kids. Radio cars, on the alert, no goofing off tonight, keep a constant watch on these kids. And that means all night long. Enough said. Here's the roll call and take out your memo books and on the way out copy down all the alarms on the bulletin boards."

Tommy's foot patrol post was on Third Avenue between 96th Street and 103rd Street. It was still a nice, well-kept neighborhood, with a few Irish bars, a couple of small Italian restaurants, and a few all-night Spanish *bodegas*. He walked his first tour alertly, like a barefoot Cajun kid in rattlesnake country. The first couple of hours passed without incident. As the hour got later and the bars emptied, a couple of drunks stopped and tried to break his balls a little, but he good-naturedly, quickly sent them on their way. About three o'clock, just before his third ring into the station house, a swarthy, medium-sized Italian guy approached him.

"Hiya, officer, you new on the post?"

"Yessir, brand-new. First time out, to tell you the God's honest truth."

"First tour, that's great. Good luck. What's your name, officer?"

"Sloane."

"I mean your first name."

"Tommy."

The dark-skinned guy stuck out his hand.

"Stevie, Tom, Stevie Maselli."

Tommy reached out, shook his hand, and felt something nice and crisp passed into his palm.

"Hiya, Steve."

"Okay, Tommy, it's a pleasure. We run a blackjack and poker game always on Third Avenue around here. We switch around, see, but it's usually in a flat over one of these stores. We've been here for years, no problem. Okay, Tom."

"I'm not here to piss on any parade, Stevie, fine with me. Nice meeting you."

Steve disappeared into the darkness as fast as he had appeared and Tommy walked casually down to the next corner to look at the goodie pressed in his right hand. A five-dollar bill, a fin, lovely, lovely. May this be the first of a long line of green bills that stretch through the sad visage of Abraham Lincoln, through Andrew Jackson, through Ulysses Grant, to the coveted one of Benjamin Franklin. At odd moments he had studied the stern faces of all these famous men, and he concluded that he liked the face of good old Ben Franklin on a hundred-dollar bill the best of all. Then he grinned, right now good old Abe Lincoln feels pretty good next to the three bucks I left home with tonight.

As he walked the dark, deserted streets he thought about the lectures of honest Lieutenant Fenihan, the fearsome foe of corruption. "First you take a deuce, then a fiver, then a tenner, until you take your first hundred. Then you're a tool of the slimy gamblers, a crooked cop." He smiled. Well, I skipped the deuce and grabbed my first fiver. Bring on the hundreds. Up your own tool, lieutenant. Christ, his wife probably played bingo at the Catholic church a couple of nights a week and the lieutenant probably played cards with the boys at the Elks every Friday night. That gambling is okay, right. Tommy shook his head. What a horseshit world!

And so life began in the good old Twenty-third. By the time he had finished his three different sets of tours, twelve to eight, eight to four in the afternoon and four to twelve midnight, Tommy had quickly assimilated into the rank and file. He was accepted by the men and the bosses, and, being an apt pupil, swiftly learned the stratagems and nuances that made a good cop. He ate in the good restaurants, which were pleased to feed the cop on post and learned the coops where it was safe to rest his weary feet for an hour or so during the bleak periods of early dawn. He knew the card-game operators, the big number guys, the bookies, the after-hour places. And he learned the pitfalls. Don't be too hungry, don't break anybody's balls unnecessarily. He learned not to make an arrest unless it was something serious. Break up fights and drunken arguments with gentle persuasion. If the combatants got too belligerent, give them a whack on the ass with the nightstick. That quickly quelled some would-be cop fighters.

Fortunately for the citizens of New York City, this was not all that police work consisted of. The cops were earnest in law enforcement of the heavier crimes. Muggers, stick-up guys, rapists—beware. There were also school crossings to maintain to assure the safety of young children, occasional plainclothes decoy crime patrol duty, office payrolls to guard, and what seemed like a million domestic squabbles. There were also traffic infractions, drunken drivers, and another hundred or so ballbusters that make for never a dull day in the average New York patrolman's life, especially in a teeming jungle like the Twenty-third Precinct.

He soon settled into the routine of foot patrol, quickly adjusting to the change in hours and using his two days off to swim and work out at the Y.M.C.A. He felt good about his hard, firm body and was determined to keep it that way. Justine, as well, seemed to adjust easily to the new mode of life. She always either personally served him a hot meal or had one prepared, which he only had to heat in the oven to enjoy. He often mused how lucky he was. What a great cook. What a sweet girl. He grinned a bit, what a great lay. He was unconcerned about still not having a child. He never used a contraceptive and he was positive Justine wouldn't know how a diaphragm worked. But he knew deep down that he was getting restless, tired of the same old shit when he got home. Constant television, an occasional movie. He had developed an appetite for books while in the navy, but only read when he was home alone. When Justine was there he thought it too impolite to retire to the bedroom to read and leave her alone to watch her beloved television.

Tommy's present state of ennui was relieved by the approach of Vinny and Connie's wedding day. He rented a tuxedo and all the accessories in a store on Queens Boulevard that advertised formal attire for all occasions. Justine bought her first evening dress in a shop only a block away. The wedding was scheduled for five o'clock on a Saturday afternoon and they were lucky to make it on time because Tommy couldn't stop admiring himself in the bedroom mirror. Only Justine's sharp voice and a yank on his arm got him out of the apartment and on their way before the mirror cracked in rebellion.

The nuptials took place in Our Lady's Chapel in St. Patrick's Cathedral. Only the immediate families and a cluster of close friends were at the ceremony in the small chapel. Tommy was impressed by his first visit to the vast, archaic, overwhelming beauty of the elegant gothic cathedral. St. Patrick's, he thought, pretty fancy for a young cop. He chuckled, especially a young wop cop.

The wedding over, a million hugs and kisses exchanged, no taxicab even necessary. The reception was at the luxurious Waldorf-Astoria Hotel, only two blocks away.

Tommy and Justine mixed easily into the cocktail party that preceded the main reception. Neither of them had ever before been exposed to anything so lavish, but as Tommy looked around at the heavy-set *paisanos* and their equally heavy-set, jewelry-laden, buxom wives, he figured they weren't too much out of their class. As he circled about the room drinking his tall Scotch and water he introduced himself and Justine to several of the other guests. He invariably caught more than a mere handshake and hello—rather a close scrutiny—as he explained that he was a fellow cop and a close friend of Vinny's. He chatted briefly with a stocky, middle-aged guy named Angelo.

"Yeah, you're a cop, too. Why, that's nice. Vinny's a great kid, right. Charlie's a lucky guy to get him in the family. He was brung up good, too, comes from Prince and Mulberry. A good family, his father was an iceman."

Tommy nodded sagely, careful not to say too much, but couldn't resist.

"Oh, really, an iceman. The way Vince carries himself he looks like he comes from landed people."

"Oh, yeah, you're right, Tom, they landed here from Sicily just like most of the other guys or their fathers here at the wedding."

Tommy kept a straight face, shook hands again with Angelo and went over to the bar with Justine to get fresh drinks. Waiting for his refill he surveyed the room. Jesus, Vince, you've come a long way, from the ice truck to the Waldorf-Astoria. He spotted Vinny in the center of the room, dressed in white tie and tails, looking like a member of the Italian nobility. Only his oft-broken nose keeping his features from being classic. His already dark skin deeply tanned from the summer sun, thick black curly hair, strong white teeth.

Connie was clinging to him for dear life. Looking up at him with adoration. Tommy grinned again as he sipped his drink. Vinny swore to Tom he had never laid Connie, was saving it for their wedding night. Wait until she gets a load of that Sicilian *schwantz*. Jesus, she'll never let him alone. Tom remembered the first time they went for a swim together at the Queens Y.M.C.A.—Tom, with the voyeur in him inherent in every locker or shower room guy in the world, surreptitiously sized up Vinny's cock. Tom, no shrinking violet himself in the cock department, sadly concluded that Vinny's was larger. Oh, Concetta, darling, will you be a happy *signorina* in your honeymoon suite tonight. Or a stone fucked-to-death *signorina*. Tommy laughed out loud.

"What's funny, Tommy?" said Justine.

Tommy snapped out of his Sicilian Stallion reverie, put his arm around her, smiled and said, "Nothing, hon, something funny just struck me, that's all."

The cocktail hour over, the crowd was ushered into the main ballroom where they were assigned to numbered tables of ten. There was an eleven-piece orchestra on the stage directly behind the raised dais where the involved members of the wedding party were seated. For the dancing pleasure of the honored guests, the leader quickly announced and then led his troops into a vibrant Cole Porter medley. Everything—the fine peach linens, the silver, the wine goblets, the band—everything was in such good taste, so elegant, it was like a movie set. Tommy and Justine felt ill at ease for a few minutes, but happily were seated at a table with members of the younger group. All dark, slick-looking Italian guys with slim, dark, slick-looking Italian wives. Everyone introduced themselves and their table was soon ringing with the laughter of conviviality. Tommy felt that he got a pretty good once-over from a couple of the guys when he mentioned he was a fellow cop with Vinny. But he figured, what the hell's the difference—I must be okay or I would never have been invited.

The party was going great guns. Everyone drinking, dancing, singing, laughing. After about two hours Vinny and Connie finally got over to their table. Connie, in a long, white satin gown and a gorgeous picture hat, was a beautiful bride. Her dark, flashing eyes and jet black hair were set off by the white background of her clothes. She carried a huge white bag—the same fabric as her dress. After she and Vinny finished getting all the hugs and kisses at the table all the young guys put envelopes in the bag. Tommy, out of the corner of his eye, noticed that the bag was crammed to bursting with white envelopes.

With a sickly smile he whispered to Justine, "Gee, honey, we only sent them an electric toaster for a wedding present."

"Don't worry about it, Tom, they'll love it."

Vinny came down to the end of the table, kissed Justine and gave Tom a big hug and kiss.

"How are you doing, Irish? You see the way the high-class Italians live!"

"Pretty fancy, baby. But don't forget, wop, you gotta deliver the ice tomorrow down in Mulberry Street before you go on your honeymoon."

They walked across the room and Vinny waited respectfully on the fringe until a good-looking, gray-haired, husky guy finished talking with a group and caught his eye.

"Pop, I want you to meet my pal. The Irish kid I spoke to you about. Tommy Sloane, say hello to my father-in-law."

They shook hands.

"Pleased to meet you, Tommy. Vinny tells me you're doing well up in the Twenty-third."

"Yessir, Mr. Mattuci."

"Call me Charlie, Tom, and someday soon when Vince gets back we'll have a drink together. I've got a lot of friends up there. You'll take good care of them if they mention my name, won't you, Tom?" He said as he gave Tommy a playful poke in the ribs.

"You bet, Charlie. By the way, thanks for your help in getting me into the Twenty-third."

"Forget it, kid. Just be a good cop."

They talked a bit further and Vinny finally waltzed Tommy over to the bar where they ordered fresh drinks.

"Well, Irish, tell the truth. What do you think?"

"Vincenzo, it's the nicest wedding I've been to since I was personally invited to Princess Grace and Prince Rainier's wedding.

"Outside of too many guineas being here, it's still a great wedding. Tell me, seriously, am I the only Irishman in the whole setup?"

"Are you kidding? There's a whole table of Irish guys from the waterfront over there on the left. And don't look now, but just to my right, the big, good-looking guy with the gray hair— that's the famous Inspector Tom Devine from downtown, the chief inspector's office."

Tommy gave a sly glance to where Vinny indicated and emitted a low whistle.

Flying high from the whiskey, they both howled, laughing, finished their drinks, and sadly had to part. Vinny to resume the boost with Connie and Tom to rejoin Justine and his table companions. The great night wound down to a close and on their way home to their flat in Queens, their arms around each other in a taxicab, Tommy said, "What a difference from our wedding, right, Justine?"

"Oh, Tom, it was a wonderful party, but I loved our wedding day. I'll never forget it and I love you twice as much ever since."

Tommy squeezed her hand contentedly and Justine pulled his face down to hers, kissed him hotly and, probed the inside of his mouth with a searching tongue.

Tommy made his first arrest after about four months on the Job. He had broken up fist fights, kicked some wise kids in the ass, peacefully settled a score of domestic battles between husbands and wives, given about a dozen summonses for traffic infractions, but never anything serious. A cardinal rule of the Twenty-third was not to arrest anyone for any horseshit beef, to smooth it out, as the bosses would say.

He was working a twelve midnight to eight in the morning shift. It was a brisk evening with the first chill winds of autumn swirling along Third Avenue. By now, he was becoming a fixture along his Third Avenue post and all the shopkeepers and bar owners warmly greeted him by name. Hiya, Tom. Hey, Tommy boy, how're you feeling, kid?

He was getting tired, dawn was just coming up, the eerie

gray light breaking over the silent sidewalks of New York. Only an occasional car disturbed the silence as it sped up Third Avenue. There was a Greek coffee shop on the corner of Ninety-eighth Street and Third. It was one of his favorite stops to help break the monotony of street patrol. He greeted Chris and Pete—as usual secretly wondering if Greeks ever christened their kids with any other names—and ordered coffee and a ham and egg sandwich. There was only one other customer in the place, a well-dressed, middle-aged, apparently half-drunk guy. Tommy looked him over and figured he had just finished getting laid. Why the hell else would he be up here at this hour of the morning in this shithouse part of town?

Tom put his hat on the stool next to him and loosened his winter uniform blouse at the neck for comfort. Waiting for his coffee and sandwich, he idly looked out the far window of the restaurant and to his astonishment saw two big black guys with a wire coat hanger working on the side door of a long, expensive-looking Cadillac. He abruptly got off the stool and with his hand motioned everyone to remain quiet. He buckled up his blouse at the neck, put his hat on, grasped his nightstick firmly, and took up a position outside the restaurant entrance where he was almost totally hidden from view. The two thieves finally raised the inside car door lock with the clothes hanger and proceeded to empty out three large suitcases from the rear of the car. Another guy up in a flat somewhere getting laid. Probably snoring his ass off, forgetting all about his valuables in the Cadillac. But not on my post, you two bastards.

He walked like a cat diagonally across the street and the two thieves were slapping each other on the back and laughing so hard at their unexpected good luck they never heard him come up on them. He swung his nightstick and whacked the guy outside the car over the head and he went down like he was shot. The other guy had leaned into the car to see if they had overlooked any more loot. He was rewarded with a smash across the back of his knees that almost jackknifed him. The force of the blow caused him to bolt upright and he hit his head hard against the upper steel part of the door. He flopped out of the car moaning, not sure which part of his body hurt worse, his head or the back of his legs. Chris, Pete, and the half-bombed

41

society guy were outside the coffee shop marveling at Tom's efficiency, chuckling with the glee that legitimate, hard-working guys have in the apprehension of lawbreakers. Tommy handcuffed the two black guys together and called out to Chris to call the precinct for a radio car.

A radio car pulled up within a minute or so and the two car thieves were piled into the back seat and Tom crowded into the front seat for the ride back to the station house. The two radio car cops congratulated Tommy and kidded him a little about the two black guys moaning in pain in the back seat, but Tom only smiled. The sharp, brief experience of combat was exhilarating, like winning a basketball game in the last few seconds with a spectacular shot. He felt great.

In the days that followed, Tommy's first arrest turned out to be even more significant when it was learned through fingerprints that the two guys had long records, one a parole violator with a history of violent crimes. He received a police duty commendation for the arrest and he was peacock proud when the captain pinned the small green bar decoration on his uniform above his police shield.

The months rolled by and Tommy made a couple of more good collars. He found out quickly that most crimes are committed late at night, when the city sleeps. He seldom went into the coop at night when doing a twelve to eight. If he did, it would only be for an hour or less to get the blood coursing through his veins after a couple of hours of walking numbly through the icy blasts of winter winds.

One of the late night patrolman's duties is to try all the locked doors of the stores, bars, and restaurants on his post to make sure that they are secure. Doing a twelve to eight, about two o'clock in the morning, he tried the door of a jewelry store on Third Avenue between Ninety-eighth and Ninety-ninth. The door opened immediately, no burglar alarm went off. It was pitch dark. There should have been a dim light. Smart pricks. Something up and they know what it's all about. Tommy drew his gun, knelt on the floor against a jewelry showcase, not exactly sure if anything was to happen. In a tense, but controlled voice, he said, "Okay, you couple of cunts.

Come out from behind the counter with your hands up or I swear I'll shoot the first fuck who makes a bad move."

He heard a swift, shuffling noise at the far end of the store and thought he detected a low whisper. The hair on the nape of his neck stood up under his uniform hat. He fired a shot into the ceiling of the store. It sounded like a cannon shot in the close quarters and a rain of plaster exploded, accentuating the bedlam.

"Jesus Christ, don't shoot, please don't shoot, we're coming out."

"Crawl out on your bellies, you two cocksuckers, crawl out. One wrong move and you're dead."

Out crawled two white guys on their hands and knees, arms outstretched as Tommy snapped on the store's main light switch. They looked to be in their late twenties—one Irish and one Italian guy, it turned out later. They sprawled face down as Tommy handcuffed them together, all the time pointing his big .38 revolver at them like a modern-day Wyatt Earp. Once he had them handcuffed, he kicked them hard a couple of times in the ass and they winced with pain and groveled on the floor. He then called the precinct from a phone on the store counter for radio car assistance.

Another good collar. After the precinct-house detectives finished kicking the living shit out of the two of them, they confessed to fifteen burglaries in the area. The station-house bulls found a generous load of swag in the Irish guy's apartment. As Vinny would say, a typical Irish shithead. The wop's apartment was jim-clean.

The captain pinned another bar on Tommy's uniform, above his shield, and the grateful jeweler gave him a Bulova watch. He finished a day tour about a week later and one of the detectives from the precinct squad came up to him, shook hands, and invited him down the block to an Irish joint for a drink. He had a package with him.

"That was a nice piece of work, Sloane, a real good collar."

"Thank you, Matty, I just lucked into it. I tried the door once and it was locked tight. I don't know what the hell made me try it again, but I'm sure glad I did."

43

"That's being a good cop, kid. Here's a present for you, a reward for your good work." He handed Tom the package.

"Gee, thanks, Matty. What the hell is it? It's pretty heavy."

"It's a beautiful movie camera, Tom, part of the swag we nailed in that Irish prick's apartment. Don't worry about it. We turned most of it in, but we keep a little for the boys. The insurance companies have all the fucking money in the world, so we only clip them a little bit."

Tommy thanked Matty profusely and over another drink confided in him how much he wanted to become a detective. Keep up the good collars, you'll make it, kid. Tommy felt that he was being slightly bullshitted, but they parted great friends. On his way home in the subway, fondling his present, he thought, not bad. Another commendation, a Bulova watch, and a sweetheart of a movie camera. Not bad, at all.

The next really good collar Tommy made was almost by accident. It was an especially raw winter afternoon in the early part of March. One of those days where you look at your watch every five minutes, wondering when the goddam tour is going to end. If ever. He was rarely inclined to have a drink when he worked, but on this day tour he almost froze to death on a school crossing post so he decided to stop at an Irish bar on Third Avenue to have a couple of Scotches to warm up and stay alive. Feeling great again, with a couple of whiskeys in him, he left the bar and walked along the avenue a couple of blocks towards Ninety-sixth Street and the station house. It was about half an hour before quitting time. He began to feel an uncontrollable urge to take a piss.

He turned off Third Avenue at Ninety-seventh Street and walked a short way up the block to the office of a real estate broker he had become friendly with. The office was located on the ground floor of a six-story apartment building. He shook hands with the boss, waved to the secretary, and hurried to the back to use the bright and shiny bathroom. He relieved himself and thanked them kiddingly for the use of the facility, telling them they just saved his life.

He let himself out the office door into the apartment hallway. He was just closing the door when he heard a piercing scream echo down from the stairwells above him. The broker and the secretary heard the scream and came to the door looking terrified. In a low voice he told them to call for a radio car and he bounded up the stairs. As he reached the higher floors he went gun in hand, more slowly, very, very quietly. At each floor he gave a brief scan for some signs of struggle. Nothing. His senses were on fire, something was dead wrong. At the sixth floor an old woman was peeping out of her door, saw Tommy and pointed straight up with her left thumb. There was a short staircase to the roof. He looked up—the goddam stairwell door to the roof was ajar. Thank God. He took the steps two at a time, and gun in hand, stepped out on the roof. He almost threw up at what confronted him.

About ten feet to the left, pants below his ass exposing dirty woolen underwear, big sweater on, was a heavy-set, dark-haired guy fucking a young girl who appeared to be about twelve years old. The kid's head was rolling back, her eyes were closed, a dirty rag was stuffed in her mouth, and the white cotton stockings on her outstretched legs were covered with blood.

The rapist was bobbing up and down on top of the little kid, humping away, so intent in his pleasure he never heard Tommy approach. Tommy put his gun back in the holster, grabbed his nightstick, amazed and nauseated at the scene. The rotten bastard never heard Tom nor anything else for almost a week. Tom hit him a shot over the head with the nightstick that reverberated over the tenement roofs all of six hundred feet away to Second Avenue.

Tommy kicked him a couple of times in the ribs for good luck and left him lying in a pool of his own blood. He removed the rag from the little girl's mouth, felt her pulse, which was rapid but good, picked her up in his arms and began to carry her down the stairs. He met the two radio car cops who had responded to the call on their way up and told them to go back and call an ambulance for the little girl right away. Don't worry about the prick who raped her, he's out cold. They got the little girl, who was still bleeding but now conscious and weeping softly, into the first ambulance that arrived.

The second ambulance attendants removed the rapist from the roof and Tommy was pleased that he slid off the stretcher a couple of times on his journey down the narrow stairway, once bouncing down about ten steps before he stopped on the landing. When they finally loaded him into the ambulance he looked like a major war casualty.

The guy was booked in absentia with some identification found on him, and the excitement subsided. Tommy's uniform was covered with the little girl's blood. The guys in the station house pieced together an outfit for him and the captain dispatched a radio car to drive him home to Queens. He gloried in the handshakes and congratulatory pats on the back from his fellow cops, but the big moment was when the captain himself and the detective squad commander took him into the captain's private office and poured him a big drink of Scotch. Another great day—another great step in his quest for the elusive plainclothes duty or the detective bureau.

Tom was subdued, exhausted, almost nauseated during the ride home in the radio car. He couldn't shake the awful memory of the raped little girl from his mind. The stench of blood still filled his nostrils. He was very quiet and the cop driving him respected his privacy, empathized with his harrowing experience, and kept his mouth shut except to ask for an occasional direction to his apartment.

Subsequent events proved Tommy's rapist had committed six other rapes in the surrounding area. The collar was a big one, and Tommy received a full commendation for it, now a brightly colored green bar to go over the others pinned to his uniform coat above his shield. Tommy had only to appear in court once when the rotten bum recovered from his fractured skull and two broken ribs. A tough judge sentenced him to fifteen to thirty years. Tom wished the fuck got the electric chair.

He got five days off with pay from the captain as a reward for his excellent police work. He had accumulated some other time off through court appearances so he put together a week's vacation in Florida to help beat the remainder of winter on the freezing streets. During his ten months in the Twenty-third he had stashed away about fifteen hundred dollars, which he kept hidden in the folds of a dress shirt in one of his bureau drawers.

Justine arranged a week off and never questioned him about the expense of the plane fares and the fancy hotel where they stayed in Fort Lauderdale. They swam in the ocean every day, went to the horse races at Gulfstream Park a couple of times, drank plenty of wine and whiskey, and made love enough times to make Tommy measure himself in the hotel steam room. He was sure he was shrinking. He loved the luxury of Florida, the good restaurants, the balmy weather, the rolling Atlantic Ocean. Someday, baby, we're going to live like this as a steady diet. And please God, don't make it too long before I get my shot.

The trip on the magic carpet was over too soon, but on the plane home Tommy realized that he had more-or-less erased the ugly image of the big rotten prick raping the little girl from his mind. Not completely. But at least the picture was not in his thoughts every waking hour and three or four nights a week in his dreams. His cold-sweat dreams, he called them. He also decided to make a big move to get into plainclothes work or the detective bureau. He rested his head back in the plane seat and thought about Florida, and all the good things his ill-gotten money had afforded. Ill-gotten my ass, someday I'll get my crack at the big time. He looked tenderly at Justine in the seat next to him, her eyes closed, her breathing soft. He covered her hand with his protectively. Someday, baby, I'll dress you in mink and put diamonds on your fingers and pearls around your neck—Vinny came into his thoughts.

Back from Florida, back to work, back to reality. Tommy had the dark Irish skin that tans easily and he dressed carefully in navy slacks and shirt, with a white crew-neck sweater to accentuate his tan. He was greeted with a round of handshakes and slaps on the back from all the guys, everyone telling him how great he looked. As if he didn't already know from a half hour's study of himself in the bedroom mirror. His first tour on his return to the Twenty-third was a four to twelve. He was pleased to find his uniform, freshly dry-cleaned and pressed, hanging in his locker, thankful not to find a vestige of the little girl's blood on it. No bill for services rendered. The tailor said that it was an honor to clean the uniform of the cop who caught the dirty fucking rapist.

The rape collar received quite a bit of publicity and his picture had appeared in the *Daily News*. As he walked his post the first day back he could barely walk a hundred feet without someone coming up to him with an outstretched hand and a kind word.

That's what we need, Officer Sloane, more good cops like you, then the city would be safe again. Just doing my job, what I'm paid for, Mrs. Kelly, Mrs. Ryan, Mrs. Rivera, Mrs. Jones, Mrs. Vitale, Mr. Rubin, the jeweler. Petey Mulligan, the bar owner, thank you, thank you. Nice of you to say that.

About seven o'clock, Mike, the real estate broker, came up to him on Third Avenue. He shook hands with Tom and said, "You look terrific, Tom. What a tan. How was Florida?"

"Paradise, Mike, just plain paradise. I hated to leave. I hope Heaven is just as nice when I get up there." He laughed.

"You're going straight up on the express, Tom, especially for catching that kid fucker on my roof. Look, that's what I want to see you about. I have someone in my office wants to meet you. Come on, walk down the block with me."

They walked the short distance to the real estate office and when Mike opened the door Tommy saw a dark-skinned, obviously Hispanics, middle-aged couple standing inside.

"Tommy, these nice people are the parents of the little girl you saved. They're Puerto Rican and hardly speak any English, but they wanted to thank you personally so I promised to bring you together with them."

The father had tears in his eyes as he reached out and fervently clasped Tommy's hand and the mother was sobbing as she came up and embraced Tommy. Tom was visibly moved, tears rushing to his eyes at this touching display of emotion. He was bewildered by the torrent of Spanish words that were hurled effusively at him, but faintly detected a thank you and knew that God was being importuned freely. *Gracias, señor, vaya con Dios.*

Mike stepped between them and interpreted.

"They're telling you how thankful they are for saving their daughter's life. The little kid's name is Isabel. Isabel Gonzales.

She is coming home from the hospital in a couple of days and she's all right. The mother, here, wants to give you a present."

"No, no, for Christ sake, Mike. I couldn't take anything from her. Explain, please, it's part of the Job."

The mother caught the negative expression on Tom's face, turned to Mike, and spoke rapidly in Spanish.

"She says it isn't much, but it's from her heart. Now please, Tom, unloosen the collar of your uniform blouse and let her give you her gift or you'll break her heart."

Tommy shrugged, loosened the high neck of his winter blouse and bent his head towards the mother—she smiled through her tears and placed what he knew was a scapular around his neck. She reached up, buttoned the neck of his blouse and kissed him on both cheeks. After another brief outburst of Spanish they again embraced him and finally left him and Mike alone in the office.

"You know what she put around your neck, Tom?"

"Sure, it's a scapular. A lot of guys I played basketball with in Catholic school wore them all the time."

"You know what she said when she put it around your neck?"

"Of course not. How the hell would I know?"

"She said, 'Now you wear the Sacred Heart of Jesus Christ, no harm can come to you.'"

"I sure hope she's right. I guess little Isabel wasn't wearing her scapular when that bastard raped her."

"Little girls don't wear scapulars, Tom."

"Oh, I see. Just the guys need them, to avoid getting their fucking heads cut off around here."

"You're so right, Tom. What a neighborhood this is turning into. But I thought it was a nice gesture by her and that you'd get a kick out of it. Mr. and Mrs. Gonzales are two really good, hard-working people. Have two other kids. Only here about a year from Puerto Rico and this has to happen."

"That's life, Mike, my man." Tom started out the door and turned. "By the way, how come you speak such good Spanish? I always thought you were a purebred wop."

Mike laughed. "Half-wopee, half-spananee, Tomaso, my

amigo. My mother came from Barcelona in Spain. I learned Spanish when I was a little kid. Thank God. You're dead in any business if you can't speak the fucking lingo up here."

His celebrity status now fully established, Tommy walked his post with even more of his usual authority. By now he was a fully confirmed, veteran, tough cop. He remembered the mental note he had made to telephone Vinny, finally reached him, and made a dinner date for the following week. The meet was set for seven o'clock at night at a restaurant designated by Vinny. It was called Joe & Rose, on Third Avenue and Forty-sixth Street in the heart of New York's opulent East Side.

Vinny was at the bar when he arrived, having a drink with the owner, a stocky Italian guy named Freddie. He whistled at Tom as he introduced him to Freddie, who ordered fresh drinks.

"You look great, Irish. What a tan. Where did you stay?"

"The Yankee Clipper. Right on the beach in Fort Lauderdale."

"Pretty good for a poor Irish cop, right, Fred?"

Freddie laughed, and after a bit of cops and robbers conversation led them to a large, comfortable booth in the rear of the restaurant.

"Enjoy yourselves, fellows—eat and drink up. Have whatever you want."

The restaurant had a good solid look about it. Mahogany bar, richly carpeted floors, tasteful paintings. Not flashy, real nice. And that wonderful, nose-tickling aroma of fine Italian cooking.

"Don't tell me we're on the arm here, Vinny. This looks like a bosses' place."

"You're right, Tom, the captain likes to eat here, so it's kind of understood that the men give it a wide berth. But I happened to do Freddie a good favor last week and he invited me and my wife in for dinner. Connie had to go see her mother and spend the night, so I figured I'd bring a good-looking fag like you for my date."

They both laughed happily, delighted to see one another after their long separation.

"What'd you do for Freddie?"

"One night, a week or so ago, about nine o'clock, Freddie called the station house and asked for a radio car. Nothing heavy, he explained to the desk sergeant, just some ball-breaker raising hell in the place. He gets top courtesy, so bang, it goes right over the air. I was riding in the sector radio car that covered this part of town and we responded immediately. My partner stayed in the car in case something serious came over the air. I walked in and there's this big fuck with a nice load on screaming at this sharp-looking chick, turned out to be his girlfriend, and scaring everyone around him shitless.

"I give him the old take-it-easy pal horseshit and he wants no part of that. He's bombed and he's spoiling for a fight. Still, he's not quite sure whether to take a swing at me or not. I'm not sure either. But the more diplomatic I get the tougher he gets and he finally lets a roundhouse right go that would have severed my gorgeous Italian head. I was on the alert, knew he was going to let one go. I ducked underneath and when he missed he lost his balance and stumbled along the bar. As he turned to square off again I hit him a shot with my stick across his kneecap and he screamed and folded up like the big bag of shit he really was. I was mad then, so as he's holding his knee I jammed the butt end of the stick right up his belly and he doubled up and puked all over the floor. The big prick was finished, *finito*.

"We threw him in the car and locked him up in the precinct for a few hours until he sobered up. Turned out he was a married guy, living in Connecticut, and fucking around with this broad from his office. In the advertising business around here. He probably played football in college and thought he was tough. I heard later that when the desk sergeant let him out of the cell without booking him that he was the happiest and most contrite ex-fighter in the world."

Tommy laughed. "Good boy, wop, the new Rocky Graziano. And for that kind deed we eat free tonight. You're beautiful!"

They ordered another drink and their dinner, and kept up a running conversation of cop talk. Their wives' health and general well-being was glossed over, and their main topic, between mouthfuls of delicious veal marsala and ziti in red sauce, plus generous gulps of red wine, was the Job.

"How often do you get the radio car?"

"Not as much as I'd like, but from what the clerical guy tells me it won't be long before I become a steady man in a car."

"You know, Vince, I've yet to do my first tour in a radio car. The only ones I seem to get a ride in is when we take some guys I just bagged back to the station house."

"Well, stay loose, Tommy, don't be impatient, your day will come. I have to hand it to you, you've made some great collars."

"I guess I got lucky, Vinny. What about you? Big connection, your father-in-law. What about plainclothes or the detective bureau?"

Vinny wiped his mouth clean with a white, linen napkin, pushed his empty plate back, leaned across the table and in a low, conspiratorial voice said, "Tommy, he's a great guy, a real sweetheart. He's not into any heavy shit any more. Connie's his only kid and he's crazy about her. My mother-in-law, Maria, just had her breasts removed. Cancer. He never says too much to me except to hint that he'd like me to leave the Job in a couple of years and take over some of his operation. He wants to go to Florida with Mom and stay there for as long as she lives. He loves to play golf and he's not too crazy about the way the city's going—think's it's on the down. I keep telling him to get me a rap at plainclothes but he keeps saying to be patient. Not to rush, learn how to be a good cop first."

"That may sound logical to some old-timer, but you and I know that you learn how to be a cop by the time you finish your first three sets of tours. You better learn or you're dead. By the way, Justine mentioned that Connie called to say you two are moving to Manhattan."

"Imagine, I completely forgot to tell you. We got so involved in cop bullshit we forget to talk about anything else. She's right. We're moving next month to East End Avenue between Eighty-second and Eighty-third Streets."

"Hey, that sounds nice. Expensive?"

"A little bit. Three hundred and fifty a month for a two-bedroom flat."

Tommy was incredulous. "Three fifty a month? Christ, Vin, you don't take home that much a month."

"I know, I know, but don't get excited. Connie makes a hundred a week in her job, and have you any idea what we got from the boost at our wedding?"

"Not the slightest idea. Don't remind me. I hope the fucking toaster we gave you is working. It didn't fit in the boost bag."

Vinny laughed. "It's beautiful, Tom. I think of you and Justine every morning when I put my whole-wheat bread in. Seriously, we got a small fortune. My father-in-law took twenty-five thousand of it, added twenty-five of his own, and put it in AT & T stock for us. What a nest egg, right?"

"That's really super," Tommy said, without a trace of envy as he leaned across the table and grasped Vinny's hand.

"So you see, Irish, the high-class Italians are living pretty good. When you come to our New York apartment for a visit I'll make sure the doorman properly pronounces your name over the intercom."

"Doorman? You sure stepped in shit, wop."

Another big laugh. "But we're going to love living in Manhattan. Connie went to college at Marymount here in the city and loved it. I love working in the Seventeenth Precinct, love the whole atmosphere. I can walk to work on nice days, no more long subway rides to Brooklyn. It's a thing I always dreamed of when I was a kid down on Mulberry Street, Tommy, baby, a real fancy flat on the upper East Side."

"It's great. I'll never forget when I was a kid how impressed I was when I visited my old man and his girlfriend, or the whore, as all the family called her. They lived in this fancy joint on the upper East Side that made our Queens flat look like shit."

Tommy paused, was going to say something about his old man, changed his mind, and said, "Well, we've been eating, drinking, and bullshitting here for three hours. I have to do an eight to four tomorrow so let's drink up and split. Thanks a million, Vince, and keep whacking the shit out of those would be cop fighters and make sure it's in a fancy joint like this so we can eat on the cuff."

They thanked Freddie, the owner, for the great dinner, hugged each other goodbye outside the restaurant and hailed separate taxis, Tommy to go over the Queensboro Bridge to home and Vinny to go over the Brooklyn Bridge to good old Brooklyn.

The days, weeks, and months rolled by with only the usual incidents to mar the routine of foot patrol. Ambulance calls for accidents, strokes, heart attack victims, store doors to try at night, school crossings, payrolls to guard, and the unending domestic quarrels that always disgusted Tommy. By now he had developed the attitudes and cynicism that seemed built-in among his fellows in the Job. It was almost like the cops against the world.

He hated the stink of piss and shit that invariably pervaded the embattled flats. Above all, he felt sorry for the little kids. Scared to death, eyes bulging with fear as they crouched down in corners to avoid the wrath of the combatants, the wife sometimes as drunk as the husband. He was swift and brutal if the drunken husband insisted on a fight. A nightstick across the kneecaps usually squelched the belligerence immediately. If it persisted, he'd grab him by the neck, drag him out the door, and throw him down a flight of stairs. Fuck them, he'd always think, they should be going to Riker's Island instead of a warm station-house cell for the way they beat and scared the living shit out of their kids. It never occurred to Tommy that maybe his vicious attitudes were related to the childhood beatings he had endured at the hands of a drunken father.

Another phenomenon that began to disturb and harass New York cops was the emergence of neighborhood street gangs. The Hispanics hated the blacks and the hatred was returned in full. The ghetto kids in the teeming flats above 100th Street banded into gangs. The Spanish Savages. The San Juan Shadows. The Black Serpents. All sorts of sinister-sounding names. The boys, with a slight nucleus of girls, were anywhere from ten to eighteen years old. They were invariably led by a swaggering young gorilla decked out in headband, Levis, and a denim top bearing the insignia of his rank and particular gang. The street gangs declared specific areas their own turf and waged war if their turf was violated. Even minor incidents resulted in bloody reprisals of vengeance. The kids usually came from large families that lacked a father in the home. They stayed in abandoned flats used as clubhouses and were not missed if they never came home to roost. Their poor mothers were so busy scratching to feed their other kids and striving to keep a roof over their heads that they never knew who was home.

When they weren't fighting the blacks, the Spanish gangs fought each other. The Puerto Ricans against the Colombians, the Cubans against the Dominicans, and if tired of inter-Hispanic warfare, back to the blacks, their common enemy. At their inception they only committed petty acts of theft, stripping parked cars at night, breaking into cars, stealing whatever they could from local stores. Most of these crimes were the province of the radio cars that patrolled the side streets. But as their strength in numbers grew they branched out into stick-ups and burglaries. They also began to prey on local storekeepers, to shake them down for protection money. The legitimate people of the ghetto hated the street gangs. The cops and detectives knocked the piss out of the gang members, especially the gang leaders, whenever they had the slightest excuse.

Tommy had very little trouble with the street gangs as they tended to form a bit north of his post, up past 103rd Street where the neighborhood worsened. But he knew from his street informants and station-house talk that a couple of youth gangs existed within the confines of his post and he consequently kept an eye and an ear open for any sign of them.

One night about eight o'clock, end-of-summer shadows darkening an early September sky, an elderly Spanish man walked up to him as he stood idly talking to local friends on Third Avenue between 102nd and 103rd Streets, the beginning of what the precinct cops called Little Puerto Rico.

"Officer, come quick, please. Bad fight going on 'round corner. Two kids, knives. Bad, bad."

"Where? Lead the way." Tommy pushed the old Puerto

Rican ahead of him. They hurried to the corner of 103rd Street and the old man pointed down the block about one hundred feet away to a big crowd that was gathered under a street light. Tommy ran down the block, pushed his way through the crowd of onlookers and in the middle of the street saw two young Hispanic kids, squared off in fighting poses. They were stripped to the waist, had traditional headbands, traditional long, gleaming, steely knives in hand, and were warily circling each other.

Tommy walked towards the two knife fighters, paused to rap his nightstick sharply on the cement street, and with a loud, authoritative ring to his voice said, "Okay, *amigos*, break it up. Drop those fucking knives on the street. Right away."

The two sweat-glistened gladiators stepped back in surprise, momentarily stunned. The knife fighter on his right, about seventeen or eighteen years old in Tommy's quick appraisal, bared white, fanglike teeth and said, "Stay outta dis, cop. Fuck off, I'm gonna cut this motherfucka's head off."

No use being diplomatic with this animal. Tommy used the oldest cop ploy in the world. He raised his eyebrows exaggeratedly, pointed his nightstick at the tough talker in front of him and said, "You take this guy, Paddy, I'll handle the other guy." Pure bullshit.

The young tough turned his head to face his new imaginary foe and crash, Tommy cracked him over the head with his nightstick and only a slight moan escaped his lips as he slumped to the street. The crowd gasped, pulled back in shock, a women's scream rent the air at the sudden violence. The second knife fighter stood his ground uncertainly, unsure of what to do, trying to maintain his macho image in face of his gang members gathered among the crowd surrounding the scene. He was on Tommy's left, about ten feet away. He said in a quivering voice, "Why you do this, man? You fuckin' cop, you slug him for nothing, we only playin'. I get you for this."

You'll get me for this, thought Tommy, you'll get me, you spic piece of shit. Playing, eh. One minute you're going to cut your pal's heart out and now you're going to cut out mine.

His voice, nice and easy. "Okay, Juan, Jose, Rodriquez or whatever the fuck your name is, drop the knife. Right now, drop it. You wanna fight with knives, go back to Puerto Rico or go down by the Harlem River. No knife fights on my post, you got that straight? Be good, now, drop it."

The kid looked uncertain, stepped back a few feet, glanced around the crowd. No other cops in sight. He then advanced towards Tommy, knife hand outstretched.

Tommy circled, back of his left hand out as in a boxer's lead, right hand firmly gripping his nightstick. He hadn't initially drawn his gun because of the crowd. Now it was too late. He circled to his left, the kid leaped forward and with a sudden thrust caught Tommy on the back of his left hand with his knife. Tommy fended him back with his nightstick as the sudden, electrifying pain enraged him. He feinted with his bleeding left hand, pulled it back as the kid leaped forward again and whacked him with the stick across the wrist of his knife hand. The blade flew up in the air and clattered to the street as the astonished kid grabbed his broken wrist and screamed in agony. Not for long. Tommy, now ice-cold and furious, seething with rage at the pain and challenge to his badge, quickly took the knife fighter out of his misery with a shot over the head with his stick that dropped him senseless in the gutter.

A radio car pulled up almost simultaneously. Tommy meanwhile had pulled a large bandanna handkerchief out of his uniform pants pocket and wrapped it around his bleeding hand. The two radio car cops quickly dispersed the crowd. It's all over. Go on home. Get off the street. Break it up.

"Jesus, Tommy, you're hurt bad, you're white as a ghost, you're bleeding bad."

"I'm okay. I'm cut, but not too bad."

"Good work, Tommy. Don't worry, we already radioed for an ambulance."

The ambulance, sirens shrieking, arrived in a couple of minutes. The three casualties were piled into the back and speedily rushed to the emergency room at nearby Metropolitan Hospital. Tommy received five stitches in his hand to close the wound and the two knife fighters were taken to the intensive care unit, still unconscious.

The duty intern finished sewing up Tommy's wound, silent throughout the painful process. He finally said, in a halting, angry voice, "My God, Officer Sloane, did you have to use such force on those boys, to club them so hard? I'm sure the X-rays will show they both have fractured skulls."

The captain's private office a couple of days after the knife fight debacle.

The precinct clerical man tapped on the frosted glass upper panel of the door, put his head in and said, "Captain, there's a Mr. Nestor Sanchez to see you." In a lower voice he added, "Sharp-looking spic, looks like a lawyer."

"Okay, Bobby, send him in."

A well-dressed, slim, mustached Hispanic in his early thirties was ushered into the captain's office.

"Captain O'Connell, pleased to meet you. My name is Nestor Sanchez."

The captain arose from in back of his desk, scenting trouble. He reached out and shook Sanchez's outstretched hand.

"What can I do for you, Mr. Sanchez?" said the captain, in precise, carefully modulated Manhattan College tones.

"Captain O'Connell, as you can see from my business card, I am a lawyer. I also head up the newly formed Hispanic Aid Association of New York City. The purpose of our organization is to protect the civil rights of the rapidly growing Spanish population of our great city. We have several objectives in mind. The foremost are mandatory bilingual instruction in the public schools, equal employment opportunities, and, what takes the most precedence, the end of all forms of police brutality."

The captain's face reddened. A definite warning signal. He replied, "I agree with your lofty aims, your high ideals, Mr. Sanchez, I agree completely. Now that you've introduced yourself and stated these lofty aims, what is your reason for requesting a private interview with me? Or perhaps it's only a social call?"

"A little more than that, Captain, in fact, a whole lot more. There are two Puerto Rican boys still in intensive care in Metropolitan Hospital. Both of these boys have fractured skulls and one boy has a fractured wrist, as well. I'm here to make a formal complaint against the police officer responsible for this piece of brutality. I believe his name is Officer Thomas P. Sloane."

The gentle tones of Manhattan College were giving way to the harsh voice of New York's Irishtown, birthplace of the good captain.

"For your information, Sanchez"—no more Mr. Sanchez—"the two wild animals you're talkin' about have been indicted by a grand jury on two counts. Felonious assault and attempted murder of a police officer. Both charges are bad felonies and some of your fellow Puerto Ricans were witnesses for the people in the grand jury. Now how does that strike your ass?"

Nestor Sanchez was visibly startled by this bad piece of news.

"What? Indicted? I can't believe it. Two young boys?"

The Irishtown voice was in high gear.

"Yeah, indicted, Sanchez, and going up to fucking Sing Sing. Two young, innocent boys, my ass. They're two goddam rival gang leaders engaging in a knife fight in the middle of a street in my precinct. Officer Sloane orders them to stop, to put down their weapons. This in front of about fifty witnesses. Sure, they stop, then decide to go to work on Officer Sloane, to cut him up in little pieces. Ever face two guys with knives, Sanchez? Scares the shit outta you. To go on, one of the young boys knifed Sloane in the hand and caused a severe wound and if he wasn't a good, tough cop he'd be dead today. Little boys, some fuckin' little boys. You tell me you head this here Hispanic Association, then do me and all New York cops a favor. Tell them New York City isn't San Juan or Bogotá or wherever the fuck your constituents come from. Let them go back to where they came from if they want to roam around in gangs, have knife fights on the street when they feel like it, or try to scare the shit out of every honest, hard-working Puerto Rican that lives here." The captain was redder than ever, breathless when he finished. The smoke was coming out of his nostrils as he looked across his desk at Mr. Sanchez.

"But Captain, I still protest. The use of unnecessary force by Officer Sloane was uncalled for. These two young kids might never be the same."

"I told you once, kids, my Irish ass. Animals they are—with a capital A. What the hell would you do if some wild-eyed animal came at you with a six-inch dagger? Again, Sanchez, you'd probably shit in your pants like the rest of your civil rights bullshit artists."

"That's no way to talk to me, Captain. I'm an attorney charged with protecting the rights of the Hispanic people of this city."

"Good. Great. Stick with your idea. But make sure you protect the good, honest Hispanic people, not the scum of the earth that migrate here from some Caribbean country where they get shot for looking cross-eyed and expect us to support them on welfare and let them break any law that suits their needs. That's my speech for the day, Mr. Sanchez, and now get what you have to say off your chest and get the hell out of my office."

"Captain, I'm going further with this. If necessary to the mayor's office. I think the way you're handling this matter is an insult to my people. We are pushing a coalition of responsible black and Hispanic people to form a civilian review board to inquire into just such matters of police misconduct as what I'm here for. You'll hear further from me about today. Good-bye, Captain O'Connell."

The harassed captain sat back in his chair, emotionally exhausted. Christ, I only ask the Lord to let me stay in this job until they make me an inspector. More of these bullshit spics coming in to argue with me and I'll never get there. He picked up his desk phone, dialed his clerical man. "Bobby, forget that. Yeah, he's gone. Sure he left in a huff. Forget about him. Listen, what tour is Sloane working?"

"Just a minute, cap. He's off two more days. Starts a four to twelve day after tomorrow."

"Good. Put this on my calendar. Tell the roll call sergeant I want to see him in my office before he turns out. Important."

Roll call over, the alarms noted in his memo book, Tommy was about to leave the station house and take his post when the duty sergeant tapped him on the shoulder.

"The captain wants a private audience with you, Sloane. You didn't shake down any of his old pals, did you?"

"Not me, sarge. You know me. Honest Tom, honest as the day is long. Never took a dishonest nickel."

"Only fives and tens, right. Get in there."

Tommy composed himself. What the hell was this all about? He was too apprehensive, the captain was a nice guy. He smiled, thinking of Buddy Hickey, a fellow cop. The house intellectual. Had a masters degree in English literature from Fordham University, but somehow decided to be a cop. Hickey always called O'Connell Captain Metaphor, also known as Captain Simile. Be prepared for a lecture, Tom. He braced up and knocked on the captain's door. The response was a gruff "come in" and a second later he stood a bit nervously at attention before the great man.

"Relax, Sloane. I don't have you in here to break your balls. How's your hand?"

"Fine, thank you, Captain. They took the stitches out yesterday. The police surgeon says it's healing fine."

"Good. I'm glad to hear it. Now, Tom, the reason I have you in here is because some spic lawyer came to see me to make a complaint against you. You know, about those two young punks whose heads you busted last week."

"What else was I expected to do, Captain? In response to a citizen complaint—you know all that. It's in my arrest report. And all true, every word of it."

"I know, I know, you're right, Sloane, but the Job is changing. These spic and nigger politicians are getting stronger. Now the latest is, they're trying to form a civilian review board or some shit like that. Imagine, to review police brutality. How about the reverse, their hostility and brutality to cops, especially some of their junkie cocksuckers."

"You're absolutely right, Captain."

"Anyway, Sloane, I've been going over your record since you arrived here as a rookie. You're turning into a helluva cop, a good man, some damn good arrests."

"Now, Sloane, listen carefully to what I have to say. To repeat, this fucking Job is changing, and for the worst. Nobody moves off the corner when the cop on post approaches like they did when we were kids. They're all defiant now. They don't know how to read or write, but they all know their fucking rights. They escaped from the dictators in the Caribbean and the rednecks in the South where they used to get locked up for taking a piss. Now they're up here in New York and think they're supposed to get away with murder. Now Sloane, watch your ass. I know that you want to climb the ladder in the Job and I'll help you any way I can. But in the meantime, take it easy with the nightstick, for your own good. For Christ sake, you're leading the league in fractured skulls."

Here they come, the metaphors and similes. Prizefight ones were out. Football ones weren't yet popular. Baseball was the in game.

"That's right, Tommy, you're the league leader. Six fractured skulls in less than two years. Not to forget four fractured kneecaps and three or four fractured arms and wrists. The orthopedic surgeon's man of the year.

"So, Tommy, that's it, the end of my speech. Please, use force only when necessary. Give those goddam gang kids a whack in the ass with the stick. Or better yet across the back of the knees." He smiled, remembering. "That's the way we took the fight out of them in the old days. If they wanted to keep on being tough, Bellevue Hospital was their next stop."

He stood up, the signal that the interview—or dressing down—was over. He walked around the desk, put his arm around Tommy and said, "Again, Tom, you're a good cop. Keep being one, just exercise a little more restraint. Okay, you can go to your post now."

Tommy left the captain's office with all the wise man's words of wisdom and admonitions on restraint of force creating doubt. He patrolled his post that late afternoon and into the night in a very subdued way. He acknowledged the cheerful greetings of all his friends and business people along Third Avenue, but not in his usual carefree, effusive manner. He didn't want to stop and talk for more than a minute or two, and shook off the Irish bar owners, refusing the occasional drink he often had to break the monotony of patrol.

What the hell kind of inferno was the Job turning into? The captain was a nice guy. He knew from station-house gossip that the captain had been through the mill. He had been a cop a long time, had risen through the ranks—foot patrol, plain-clothesman, detective bureau, desk sergeant, precinct lieuten-ant. Above anyone, he was aware of what it was like out here on the street. Or worse, in a radio car.

You had your .38 caliber revolver, your nightstick, and your steel-butt loaded leather blackjack in your pants pocket. That was it. Your tools against the world. Of course, you were as-sured by the saintly lieutenants of the police academy that you wore the shield of New York City, the sacred shield that auto-matically gained you the respect of the citizenry. He mused on this tenet of the learned guardians of the academy and shook his head, his face breaking into a sad grin. The kind of shit that was arriving in human waves to settle within the confines of the Twenty-third Precinct would happily spit on his shield, his pseudosymbol of authority. For Christ sake, they'd even shit on it if they weren't afraid to get their brains knocked out.

Tommy shook his head, smiled ruefully, what the hell's the sense of getting all pissed off about the Job. This is what the Job was turning into, but in his heart he knew he still loved the Job. He looked at his watch. Time to have a drink. Cheer me up. Ho, thank God, Petey Mulligan's bar was just down the street. What a coincidence! A couple of nice Scotches and a chat with good old Petey will calm me down.

The brisk, cool breezes of autumn days and nights soon gave way to the bitter cold and slush and snow of winter. Tommy hated the winter weather, the freezing days and insufferably cold nights. But there was one solace of winter he, and all other Twenty-third Precinct cops, were thankful about. The Arctic blasts kept the criminals off the streets and huddled about their kitchen stoves. The crime rate in the Twenty-third fell pre-cipitously during the winter. Game called on account of cold weather, remarked the sagacious Captain O'Connell as he read the declining weekly crime reports.

Tommy decided the best way to avoid the tortures of foot patrol in winter was to arrange his vacation plans to start the beginning of March. It was a simple enough request, as most of the guys with more seniority opted to vacation during the balmy days of summer. Justine arranged her vacation to coincide with his, and they decided to spend two weeks at the Yankee Clipper Hotel in Fort Lauderdale, Florida, where they had spent a glorious week the previous winter.

Tommy had saved almost all the money he made on post during the last year, so the expense was no problem. The fives and tens he grabbed added up, and he was just as diligent in his collections as he was in enforcing the law in what he perceived to be important directions. As time passed his attitude was reinforced by his equating the graft with honest money he and every other cop was entitled to. The card games, crap games, number guys, bookmakers, after-hour places, and the victimless, slightly shady other enterprises did not seem terribly illicit to him. As long as he received his five or tenner and they kept their premises peaceful he couldn't care less.

Tommy, like most cops, gave plenty of thought to the situation. His take-home pay was one hundred and fifty-five dollars every two weeks. Justine made almost as much money as he did. Granted, there were generous pension benefits and medical provisions to enhance his miserly pay. Still, how in the name of Christ could a cop live decently on such a meager salary? And so his rationalization was simple: the two or three hundred a month, or whatever, that I grab is in some small way a reward for the dangers I face, for all the shit I have to put up with.

The impending vacation only two weeks away, Justine was bubbling over with anticipation. Tom smiled and nodded his head reassuringly as she described her shopping trips and her excitement about going away. He found himself evaluating Justine more, developing a slightly hesitant analysis of their marriage. He knew that in many ways he still loved her; he had never cheated on her with another woman. She was a good person, an excellent cook, an immaculate housekeeper. They still made love four or five times a week and Justine was as passionate as the steamy days of their honeymoon. But to Tommy, making love to her had become almost perfunctory.

Most times when they were making love he was extremely tender, very conscious of her hot, insatiable desires. He would fuck her interminably through her series of orgasms, while he often faked coming himself. At last drained, she would push him off her exhaustedly and almost immediately sink into a deep sleep. He would hold her in his arms and listen to her snoring gently against his face, her breath sweet as the scent of fresh roses. As she lay there he thought about their life together, past and present.

He was only going up in the world, right to the top. He was convinced of that. He had always imagined Justine at his side when he reached his pinnacle, but he admitted to himself that recently she was beginning to bore him. Little things she did got on his nerves. He attributed his feelings to a natural reaction after five years of marriage. He had often noticed a similar indifference to their marriages in some guys he knew. He wasn't exactly apathetic, but as the years rolled by he became acutely aware of how their tastes varied in numerous ways.

He had developed a love for reading, a thirst for knowledge that he had so assiduously avoided in his formative years. But he could only indulge his passion when he was home alone, because when Justine was home the television seemed to glow and blare constantly. She knew all the serials, all the shows, and would inevitably fill Tommy in on what he missed when patrol duty prevented him from enjoying the cornucopia of thrills and laughs emanating from the tube.

He looked at her sleeping beside him and shook his head. I guess I never gave it much thought because I loved her so much, but let's face it—Justine isn't too bright. I suppose she's smart enough working around her insurance company, gets a good pay raise every year, but as far as I know she's never finished reading a book. I offer to take her to the theater, she only wants to see a musical. I get a big kick out of foreign movies, she can't understand why, hates them. God forbid I put on a night baseball or football game and deprive her of her shows. Murder in the first degree. But the most disconcerting thing of all was Justine's recent addiction to bowling.

Bowling. Ugh! I love to keep in shape, but for Christ sake, you keep in shape swimming and playing handball, not in some asshole bowling alley filled with cigarette and cigar smoke. He grinned. Besides, she's beaten me every time we attempted that stupid, fucking game. Forget bowling, leave it to the morons and the Polacks. He kissed her cheek, patted her ass, turned over, and went to sleep.

Tommy braved the winter winds as New York turned into Anchorage, Alaska, and prayed for the days and nights to hurry by so that they could be off to sunny Florida.

Sometimes it seemed Justine was almost reluctant to go away as her fascination with bowling increased. As much as he despised the sport, he was happy for her, pleased to have her out and mixing with her bowling groups just as long as he wasn't included in her plans. Often, after a daytime eight to four tour he would take the subway downtown to the Grand Central area where she worked and treat her to dinner in a Chinese restaurant. Dinner finished, Justine would give him an absent-minded kiss good-bye and gleefully hurry off to join her insurance company co-workers at a nearby bowling alley in one of their fierce biweekly matches.

Florida was three days away. To Tom's dismay the subject of bowling was apparently to be the main topic of conversation for the evening. Throughout dinner Justine chattered about her improvement, her teammates, and other facets of the matchless sport. He nodded in bored assent and silently finished his dinner. He excused himself and went into the living room to read the evening newspaper to see how many people got killed in New York in the last day.

Kitchen sparkling, dishes done, Justine appeared in the living room. She didn't snap on the television set immediately as she would ordinarily do. Tom looked up from his newspaper and was surprised to see her sit in a chair opposite him.

"What is it dear, something on your mind?" Putting aside his newspaper.

"Tommy, love, do you mind if I ask you a serious question? I need some advice."

Puzzled, his brow creased. "What's up, babe, something bothering you?"

She laughed, happily. "Oh, no, not that serious, silly. It's just this. The guys and the girls at my insurance company decided to form a bowling league." She beamed, her voice rising excitedly. "You know, a real match play league. Beautiful prizes at the end of the season for the winning teams, big bowling banquet to give out the prizes, you know, things like that. Real competition. What do you think?"

"Hmm, I understand. That sounds great. But, sweetheart, what is it you want to ask me?"

"Well, Tom, wait'll you hear this. All the teams are getting their own bowling shirts. Real, beautiful shirts. White silk material."

Tom sat back in his chair, nodded his head. No shit. I can't believe it. Is this my wife? Bowling shirts! Be nice to her, she sounds really sincere.

"Gee, Justine, I think that's great. But you know how little I know about bowling. What is it you want to ask *me* about bowling shirts?"

Justine frowned. "Tom, I don't think you even paid attention when I told you, but I'm now in the fiduciary department secretarial pool."

"That's right, I forgot. What the hell is that? What does it mean, fiduciary?"

"It's the trust department. You know, like estates, wills, things like that."

"Honest. That sounds like a very interesting part of the company." He laughed. "Maybe you'll be able to handle my estate. Seriously, what's your question?"

Proudly: "Tommy, I want you to know that I've been elected captain of our team and I have to come up with a name for us. Preferably, a name to reflect our particular department. You're good at that stuff, think of a name."

"Wow, you're elected captain, babe, that's great! Beautiful. Okay, a name, let me think a minute. Fiduciary department, right? Let's see, how about the Fiduciary Phenoms?"

"Hey, Tom, that sounds fine. But just a minute, don't you spell phenom with a P?"

"That's right, sweetie, P-h-e-n-o-m. What's wrong with that?"

"To be honest, I'd like a name that starts with an F, to like rhyme with fiduciary. You know, like the Fiduciary Favorites."

"Fiduciary Favorites, you gotta be kidding. That stinks. What about the Fiduciary Fillies?"

"Oh, Tommy, c'mon, be serious. I know a filly is a female

horse. You're just being a wise guy 'cause some of the girls you met from my office are a little bit heavy."

Tommy laughed. "Don't be silly, honey, a filly is also a word for a very attractive young girl, just like you. Go ahead, look it up in Webster's dictionary, right over there in the bookcase."

Justine crossed the living room and removed the massive dictionary from the bookcase. She thumbed through the pages for a couple of minutes, located the word, and broke into a big smile.

"Oh, Tommy, I love you. You're absolutely right, the definition fits. Wait till I tell the girls tomorrow. Give me a big kiss."

Justine leaned over, put her arms around him and kissed him deeply. She squeezed him tight and probed his mouth with her tongue. He flushed with heat, got the message, bounced up out of his chair and followed her into the bedroom. Their clothing was cast aside and they were both naked in seconds, and in a few seconds more they were on the bed making love. The suddenness of the whole act, the urgency of Justine's mouth, caught Tommy by complete surprise. Agreeable surprise. He had had a long day, was very tired, never had an inkling that he would be deep inside Justine at nine o'clock at night. But the unexpected burst of passion, the sheer abandon of Justine, turned him on and got him so excited he made love to her twice within an hour without losing his erection. Justine came at least five times. He felt like Superman.

Moaning gently, satisfied at last, she kissed him pristinely on the lips, a sign that her passion was finally spent. She pushed Tom off her, sighed, turned, and was asleep in thirty seconds flat. Tommy, by now accustomed to her reaction after one of their more torrid love scenes, put his hand on her head and kissed her tenderly on the eyes. Not ready for sleep, he switched on his tiny bedside reading lamp and took a magazine from the night table.

He read for a few minutes, but couldn't really concentrate on the article he had started. He put the magazine aside and switched off the lamp. His eyes were heavy, but he was still so stimulated by the wild lovemaking he wasn't yet ready for sleep. A bit drowsy, a bit wide awake. He laid back, head on a pillow, to contemplate life. He wanted to think. Especially about Justine.

In spite of her shortcomings I guess I really love her. Christ, she's a wonderful lay. Her back was to him. He reached over and tenderly felt her small, firm ass, his favorite night time resting place. She was everything a good wife should be. But why the hell aren't we having any kids? He thought of Vince and Connie, already proud parents of a baby boy. Maybe we both should go to the doctor's and get tested. Christ, maybe it's me shooting blanks! God knows we make love enough. He grinned in the darkened bed as he remembered that last week at the Y.M.C.A., he had measured his height. He was still five feet eleven, thank God. His fears of shrinking from screwing too much were not justified.

His eyes began to droop, he was just entering the subliminal stage of exhaustion, ready for deep sleep. He smiled, thought about Justine and her bowling team, patted her ass. Captain of the team. Give a rousing cheer for our captain. Bowling shirts. He was too knocked out to condemn them in his mind. He patted her ass again. The Fiduciary Fillies. Why I just fucked a Fiduciary Filly, the captain of the team. Twice. What a headline for the *National Enquirer*. HERO COP FUCKS FIDUCIARY FILLY TO DEATH. Found in alley. Bowling alley. Tom fell sound asleep.

Vacation time. Tom held Justine's hand as the plane took off from nearby LaGuardia Airport and felt like he was flying to Heaven instead of sunny Florida. No more pugnacious drunks, no more freezing my ass off, no more listening to a million bullshit complaints from the citizens of New York—who pay my princely salary. I'm on my way to Heaven for the next couple of weeks.

Heaven was the Yankee Clipper Hotel in Fort Lauderdale. How Tommy loved it. He embraced the surf and sun like a baby porpoise. He arose early every morning, careful not to awaken Justine, slipped on swimming trunks, t-shirt, and sneakers, and walked miles along the ocean beach, slipping off his t-shirt as soon as he was clear of the hotel. His walk finished, he took his sneakers off and dove into the pounding surf and swam and lolled around the ocean for thirty or forty minutes. He lay on the sand until he was almost dry, went up to his floor through the rear hotel entrance, awakened Justine, and had a late breakfast. What a life. Heavenly!

Justine would have a brief swim in the hotel pool, as she feared the big waves and strong undercurrent of the ocean, and they would dress and explore Fort Lauderdale and the adjacent cities in a rented car. They visited all the places of interest and had lunch at a different, elegant restaurant every day. By sheer coincidence—Tommy wondered skeptically—they found a sprawling, brand-new bowling complex. Justine was exuberant. Now she could have a secret practice session every day and sharpen her skills to a degree that would make her worthy of the captaincy of the Fiduciary Fillies.

Tom passed on this splendid opportunity to learn the elusive art of bowling, preferring to sit outside in the car and read a paperback. One day, while Justine was honing her bowling skills, he was too preoccupied to read and decided to go for a walk. A short distance from Justine's beloved bowling alley he found a thirty-two-court tennis complex. He watched the players on the various courts from behind the high screen and quickly concluded that this was a game he would enjoy. He knew a little about tennis from television and newspaper and magazine accounts, but always figured it was a rich man's game. Right at the far end of the complex was a Quonset hut with a sign above the door—GENE WILSON—PROFESSIONAL.

Tom walked over to the hut, found the pro inside, and within five minutes he bought a new tennis racket and signed up for six tennis lessons. A new love was born. His lifelong preoccupation with being in good physical condition and natural athletic ability quickly asserted itself and he took to the game so easily that he amazed the pro. Once he learned the proper grip and the stroke technique, forehand and backhand, he would rally with the pro for minutes at a time without an error. When his lesson series was finished, Gene, the pro, congratulated Tommy on his excellent progress and extracted a promise from him to continue playing tennis when he returned home. There was slight need for that, as the tennis bug had bitten deeply, and Tom resolved to become as good a player as possible. The long-legged, bronzed beauties bounding around the complex in their short shorts added an extra dimension to his fascination for the game.

The days flew by and vacation time was coming to a close in a few days. It had been invigorating for both of them. The long walks along the beach, the daily ocean swim, the newly acquired tennis skills for Tommy, the sharpening bowling skills for Justine, the relaxed but often scorching sessions of lovemaking at night. It was truly idyllic.

But an unexpected highlight was still to come. The experience meshed perfectly with his burning ambition for future riches, with his inner feelings that surely someday he would be in the big money. A couple of days before they headed back home, a young couple they had just met, also guests at the Yankee Clipper, suggested that they take an inland waterway cruise on the pleasure yacht that sailed every day from Bahia Mar yacht basin, almost directly across from the hotel.

It was a four-hour cruise, cost ten dollars apiece, and in retrospect Tommy figured it was the best ten dollars he ever spent. He stretched out in a canvas beach chair on the top deck of the yacht, sipped a tall, icy Tom Collins, and quietly observed how the rich live. The yacht cruised through the inland canals. Every ten minutes or so a yacht, equal in size or larger, would pass them going south, its approach heralded by a honking of horns. Tom turned from his chair and looked over the side as the luxurious yachts motored by. He cringed as his fellow horde of sightseers waved and shouted to the disdainful guests on the other yacht. Even the white-uniformed crew and mess attendants barely acknowledged the greetings of their fellow seafaring peasants.

What impressed him even more were the lovely houses and occasional story-book mansions that rose on either side of the canals they sailed through, particularly as they reached the Boca Raton area on to the incredible homes of Palm Beach. The spacious lawns dotted with luxuriant foliage, the bright colors flashing in the morning sunlight, the predominantly Old World Spanish architecture defining the magnificence of the mansions, the sheer beauty of it all, absolutely captivated Tommy. So this is how the rich live. Someday I'm going to be rich, he thought, for perhaps the hundredth time.

He was a little sad at leaving Florida, but as he sat in his window seat on the plane and gazed out at the cloud formations beneath him he realized one certain obsession that consumed him. He had to make some money, real money, to live in style. He had gained a further sense of luxury as each day passed in Florida. He determined to become a good tennis player, proficient enough to be able to hold his own at the better clubs he would join or be invited to play at. He grinned. A sport worthy of princes and kings. Let Justine do the bowling for the two of them, the sport of peasants, he concluded.

The chill winds of winter soon blended into the exhilarating breezes of spring and life was once more livable in the good old Twenty-third. The advent of spring brought a new and more concrete hope to his dream of the opulent life. He had just finished a nice, easy, trouble-free eight to four when one of the sergeants in the station house informed him that the captain wanted to see him right away.

He knocked on the upper glass portion of the door to the captain's office.

"Come in."

"Officer Sloane, Captain, you wanted to see me."

"Oh, Sloane. How are you, Tom? You look great, have a nice vacation?"

"Wonderful, Captain. I love Florida."

"Who the hell doesn't? Okay, Tom, here's what I want to see you about. I'm assigning you as a relief man in one or the other of the sector radio cars. From all reports you've done a good job on post, made some crackerjack arrests, and I think you'll do well in a car. You won't be steady in a car for a while, but you'll get at least two or three tours a week. What do you say?"

Tommy beamed. "That's great, Captain. It'll be a new experience. I'm sure I'll love it and I'm sure you won't regret it."

The captain extended his right hand, Tommy shook it en-

72

thusiastically and left him as happy as the day he got married. A radio car at last. Break out the caviar and champagne.

A few days later Tommy was given his first assignment in a radio car. To him, even though it was only as a relief man, it was still a step in the right direction, the direction to plainclothes duty or the detective bureau. He soon began to ride in the radio car almost every tour, but as a relief man, almost never with the same driver. He was soon deployed to sectors of the precinct he never knew existed. It was a real treat for him to be finally off the narrow confines of Third Avenue and to explore a different segment almost every day or night he worked. A couple of tours among the luxury high-rise apartments along Fifth, Madison, and Park Avenues. A couple of tours among the sleazy tenements of the transplanted Puerto Ricans along San Juan Hill. A couple of tours, the best and most lucrative, among the streets of uptown Little Italy.

The radio car in a wildly busy precinct like the Twenty-third was an earthshaking experience for a relatively young cop like Tommy. The action was so furious and time-consuming that the tours seemed to pass almost before they began. There were enough domestic squabbles, traffic accidents, gang fights, ambulance calls, aborted stick-ups, muggings, and burglaries to more than fill the tour of a radio car cop.

Worst of all were the D.O.A.'s, dead on arrivals. Usually the stink emitted from a three-or four-day-old body would cause a neighbor to call the precinct and report it. There were all types of dead bodies to greet you on a D.O.A. call. Old people of both sexes who died of natural causes, people who lived barely above the poverty level and whose lives ended in relative anonymity. There was the shock, the heartbreak, of the young D.O.A.'s, some in or barely out of their teens, dead of drug overdose and abandoned by their fellow users. There were the brutally mutilated murder victims and others dead of gunshot or stab wounds. Sickening, but still exciting.

Tommy, after an especially gruesome discovery, privately thanked his rookie school training, where periodical visits to the city morgue and mandatory presence at medical examiner's autopsies were required. He often grinned when he thought about how some of his fellow rookies had reacted to a particularly gory D.O.A. He remembered how some of the rookies vomited, a few even fainted, when the medical examiner sawed across the body's head, or blandly sliced down and spread open a midriff with a long, gleaming, surgical knife and the bloody guts spewed out. Cops not only needed strong minds and strong physiques, they surely needed strong stomachs.

Tommy worked several tours in the radio car with a veteran cop named Ray McCann, a nice, easygoing guy that he soon took a great liking to. Ray had been a plainclothesman in the main office police commissioner's squad that covered the entire five boroughs of New York City. The P.C.'s squad, as it was called, was one of the juiciest plums in the Job. Unfortunately for Ray, and a lot of other guys, he had been put back into uniform as a result of the Harry Gross scandal. Ray loved the Job, lucrative or not, and he was just as good a cop driving a radio car as he was a P.C.'s man. He was a good-looking, bright guy, about ten years older than Tommy, and they hit it off instantly. Ray always requested Tom when his regular partner was off duty.

He was understandably quite reticent about the good old days, as he referred to his years in the P.C.'s squad, but occasionally, in the quiet, eerie morning hours of a late tour just before dawn, they would stop the car outside one of the after-hour clubs, get a couple of large paper cups filled with Scotch and soda, park alongside the East River and discuss the vagaries of the Job. Some of Ray's anecdotes were hilarious, but the best story of all, one Tommy would never forget, concerned a D.O.A.

Ray explained to Tom that when he was first reassigned back in uniform to the Twenty-third Precinct he was subjected to much good-natured kidding about his alleged wealth after six years in the P.C.'s squad, which supervised the enforcement of vice and gambling throughout New York. He took it all in stride, always with a big smile, and soon proved himself a tough cop and quickly became well-liked by the guys. After a few years of street patrol he was assigned to a radio car and quite often was partnered with a loud-mouthed pain in the ass named Seifert.

In Ray's words: "Tommy, this prick Seifert never let up on how rich I must be. He'd always be moaning, oh boy, if I only had the shot you had. What a lucky bastard you are. He'd go on the whole goddam tour in that vein until I was tempted to wait for him after work, take him somewhere, and whack the piss out of him. Then came the night. The night of nights.

"Seifert and I were doing a four to twelve, cruising along First Avenue on the upper East Side, when we get a call over the air to proceed to an address in our sector. Possible D.O.A. We drive to the specified address, which turns out to be a run-down tenement house on East One Hundred and Eighth Street. The Puerto Rican super meets us and explains in broken English that he had no key. He said the tenant was a nice old guy nobody had seen in nearly a week and the smell coming from the flat was terrible. We go up to the apartment and terrible was the understatement of the year. I swear, Tom, the stink was enough to overcome an elephant. We put handkerchiefs to our noses and kicked the door in. I walked over to the windows and knocked the glass out with my stick to let some fresh air in. In a few minutes the air cleared enough for me to look the scene over.

"The poor old guy lay on a living room couch with the swollen blue face and expanded belly of a guy dead five or six days. But, Tom, stink and all, I didn't miss a trick. A P.C.'s man's wife buys nothing but the best and I spotted the furnishings in the room as really good shit. What the hell is this old guy with such fine furniture living in a shithouse building like this? I motioned Seifert to come close and said, 'Get rid of the super and the nosey neighbors. Let's have a good look around, something's fishy here and I don't mean the stink. This poor old dead guy looks like he might have a pretty good stash around this flat.'

"Seifert clears the super and the neighbors out of the flat, giving them some bullshit about calling the homicide squad and not disturbing any clues. Always a good line, remember that, Tommy. Anyway, to continue. I immediately hit the most logical place, the bedroom closet. Right off I find a couple of bankbooks, a manila folder with some stock certificates, and bingo, in the rear on the floor, a laundry bag filled with dirty shirts ready for the chinks. I grab a few shirts off the top and there it is, bundles of hundred-dollar bills, the whole bottom of the bag. I've got a grin on my face from ear to ear. I yell to Seifert, 'Come here, baby.' He comes in, looks into the bag of cash and nearly faints. Honest, Tom, he gets white as a sheet. I said, 'Come on, let's whack it up, it looks like there's over fifty grand here.'

"The yellow prick says, 'No, no, Raymond, we'll get nailed for sure. It's too much money. Please, please, leave it as it is.'

"I can't believe my ears. I look at this stupid bastard, all the time crying about the score he'd make if only he got lucky enough to get a shot at plainclothes. Right in front of his kisser stares maybe thirty grand as his end and he's too chicken shit to take it.

"I said, 'Are you crazy or something? C'mon, give it a count. I'll watch the door.' He says, 'Wait here, please, I'm calling the sergeant.' I just gave him one of my tough guy looks, waited until he left the bedroom and then I stashed a bundle of hundreds under my belt, even below my heavy undershirt. To make a long story short, the sergeant came, another square john prick himself. You know, take a five or ten but scared stiff when he saw thousands. Anyway, everything got turned in except the gorgeous five thousand that gave me an itch on my belly beneath my winter underwear. Lovely, lovely itch. The total was close to fifty grand, plus the bank books and stocks, altogether over two hundred thousand. All turned over to city property clerk's office. Would you believe it? And from what I later heard, never claimed by anyone. It turned out the poor, or rather rich, old guy was retired from the telephone company, loaded, no relatives. He'd lived in the same house forty years ago when it was a solid Irish and German neighborhood. Everybody was nice to him, so he never bothered to move out.

"Nobody even missed, even questioned me about the five grand I nailed, not even a murmur."

All through Ray's story Tommy's brain was whirling. Oh, baby, if it were only me.

"Ray, what about Seifert?"

"Tom, at the end of the tour I waited for him to get dressed and took him aside. I told the chickenshit bastard that if he ever even mentioned plainclothes to me again I'd kill him with my bare hands. He never opened his mouth to me again and now he's been transferred out to the sticks somewhere near his home. It's where he belongs, out with the cows and the chickens. Now, Tommy, isn't that one helluva story?"

"Jesus Christ, Raymond, that wins the prize. I only hope and pray we get the same kind of break some night."

"You know the old saying, Tom, lightning never strikes the same place twice. But you're a good kid, Tom, a good cop, you'll get your shot."

As the months passed by, Tommy spent almost two thirds of his tours in a radio car and he loved it. Radio car patrol had many severe demands, but it also had its share of generous rewards. The restaurants, bars, and gamblers were as kind and hospitable as Las Vegas hotel keepers. He soon settled into his new routine. In his own private estimation, his take from all sources was by now approaching respectability. About four to five hundred a month. Uptown Little Italy was the daddy of them all, with the Italians being very liberal to the protectors of their gambling, after-hour clubs, and other enterprises. There was always something happening in the Twenty-third, something exciting to make the days and nights pass. Each partner he worked with had another tale to tell, and no matter how horrifying the experience, they always made it sound funny.

He quickly blended into the mainstream of the precinct and made several arrests with a variety of radio car partners, but nothing startling. Possession of a deadly weapon, stolen cars, car break-ins, attempted premises break-in, all soon usually broken down by overworked young district attorneys into misdemeanors by the time-honored court process of plea bargaining. He was required to spend many days in court on these cases, usually with drawn face and rumpled uniform as he waited for his case to be called. Sitting in court, disheveled, needing a shave, he never failed to eye carefully the plainclothes cops in the courthouse. Except for the occasional guy who had worked in disguise in a decoy unit, the rest of them dressed like affluent young stockbrokers. Three-piece dark suits, tweed or cashmere jackets, button-down shirts, striped ties—neat as pins as they laughed and joked among themselves. Tommy wasn't envious of them. Good luck, boys, good luck, all the luck in the world. His face would break into a big grin—someday I'll be there with you, boys, in my fancy dark suit, Brooks Brothers shirt, and Countess Mara tie. I'll be there, you guys, count on it.

Tommy gained experience with each tour in a radio car. He drove through the streets, or sat by the driver's side, always on the alert, his eyes scanning the streets relentlessly. He searched, indeed he ached for the big arrest that would bring him to the attention of the top brass. The collar that would vault him into the spotlight whose bright rays would spring him on the golden path to plainclothes duty or the detective bureau. He loved the Job, loved the camaraderie of the men he worked with, but he chafed at the tedium of year after year of uniform duty.

The balmy days and star-kissed nights of spring soon dissolved into the heat and stifling humidity of New York's summer. Tommy enjoyed the hot weather. Now thoroughly enamored of tennis, he played every chance he got. When his days off fell on weekends, he took off with Justine to the beach at Rockaway, on Long Island, the last outpost of the New York Irish. His sister Rosemary and her husband Billy had rented a summer place and Tommy and Justine were always welcome, along with what seemed like a hundred other friends and relatives.

Somehow there always was a place to sleep after a night of drinking in the Irish bars, where it was a thrill to hear the singing waiters, or occasional talented customer, go up to the piano and in clear tenor voices sing the beautiful songs of Ireland. They sang of the valleys, the hills, and the many martyrs. They sang of the men and boys called to war against the bloody English, of the men and boys hung on the gallows, bravely walking to their grisly fate. They sang of Kevin Barry,

Robert Emmet, Wolfe Tone, young Danny Boy—and they sang the love songs of Tralee and the sad songs of County Down. Oh, thought Tom, it was wonderful to be Irish in Rockaway on a summer Saturday night. Justine, hair now tinted red, readily acknowledged being Irish, adding, with a big laugh, "By injection, of course!"

The summer flew by and Tom kept in shape playing tennis, working the kinks out of his body put there by the narrow confines of a radio car. His game soon reached the point where he felt that he was outgrowing the public courts, so he decided to join a private tennis club. A friend he had met at the Queens Y.M.C.A. the previous winter proposed him for membership in a tennis club in Bayside, one of the more affluent neighborhoods on the outskirts of Queens.

He was quickly accepted in the club and in short order signed up for additional lessons from the club professional. Like everything else he pursued—handball, swimming, pistol shooting—Tommy became obsessed with mastering tennis. After a lesson he would volley against the wooden practice wall for hours at a time. He soon played well enough to be invited into as many friendly matches as his schedule permitted. He made no secret of his profession, freely admitted he was a cop. It amused him that none of his fellow tennis club members seemed to have any feeling of superiority one way or the other about his being a cop. He soon found out that the only thing tennis players cared about was how well they played, or, in a doubles match, how well their partners played.

He kept a low profile around the club, very polite, very quiet. When in a match, he played intensely but never displayed any signs of temper, even though he often felt suicidal after hitting an easy shot into the net, or too long, or too wide. He was invited to play in some mixed doubles matches and very soon discovered that there were plenty of available women—single, divorced, married, players of other things beside tennis—to connect up with at the conclusion of a match.

Tommy was more than conscious of his firm, tanned body, curly hair, fine teeth, rough good looks—as were the racket-wielding nymphets he played with. Oh, Tom, good shot. Gee, Tom, you played beautifully. He would smile shyly and thank them. They would question him about his being a cop. Isn't it terribly dangerous? Oh, God, I'd be frightened to death! Again he'd smile, maintaining a certain mystique about his status—discussing it very little, intimating by his apparent reluctance to talk about it that he was on some secret mission, only concerned with solving the most baffling crimes. He would grin to himself. These white-clad assholes would never go uptown beyond Seventy-ninth Street, so they'll never see me wearing a uniform.

Justine grew just as fascinated with her bowling as Tommy was with his tennis. She now bowled with a local church group as well as the Fiduciary Fillies and regaled Tom with the stupendous bowling feats of herself and her teammates. One evening, when they were at home together for a change, she chattered on as she prepared his dinner while he sat at the kitchen table having a drink. Tom nodded his head in approval and smiled as she discussed her bowling exploits, although it was boring him to death. He observed her carefully as she talked and decided that she was changing—not too much, but changing, nevertheless. He had liked her hair dark, and while he was too polite to say it, he thought her new, tinted red hairstyle was unbecoming to her. Her features seemed to be getting sharper, losing the appealing, soft roundness of his early years with her. To his further surprise, she didn't require or look for as much sex as he was accustomed to, seemingly satisfied with making love one or two times a week.

He thought about that for a moment while he sipped his drink. He grinned. That was it, bowling. He'd reluctantly been persuaded to go with her a few days ago to watch her bowl in one of her local church league matches. She was as jumpy and nervous beforehand as a rookie making a World Series start. She would slowly approach the foul line of the glistening alley, ball in hand, like a predatory tiger, speed up and release the ball with left foot rooted firm at the line and right leg arched back in the air. When she made a solid hit she would jump up, legs together, right fist clenched upward to the bowling gods. Strrr-iiike—ooh, ooh, baby. Could a strike cause maybe a mini-orgasm? He almost laughed out loud, just caught himself, realized he hadn't absorbed one word of what she'd been saying the last few minutes, and got back into the conversation very easily. Oh, really, babe, that's great, and what about next week's match?

Dinner finished, Tom was about to leave the table and go into the living room and read. Justine said, "Just a minute, dear, I'd like to ask you a question."

Tom sat back in his kitchen chair. "Okay, hon, what's on your mind?"

"Well, Tom, the church I bowl for is Catholic, St. Sebastian's. I was born a Catholic but after mother got divorced we never went to Mass any more."

"So, I was born a Catholic and I haven't been to Mass in years."

"Anyway, every Sunday while you were working days I went to Mass with the girls on my team. To be perfectly honest, I really enjoyed it. I didn't understand everything, but the music, the choir, all the, you know, pageantry, gave me a great feeling."

"Well, I guess that's what religion is all about. It gives you a great feeling!"

"What I want to say, Tom, is how about us going to Mass together?"

"No good. It's not for me."

"Are you an atheist?"

"Justine, an atheist denies the existence of God. I'm an agnostic."

"What's an agnostic?"

"You know, it's like the jury's out. You're not sure of anything. You don't believe in any formal religion like the Catholics, Jews, and Protestants."

"You'd prefer to stay that way, not to know if there's really a God or not?"

"Sometimes I can't believe you. You go to Mass a couple of times and now you're St. Theresa. For Christ sake, you do what you want to do, let me do what I want to do. Let's end this conversation right here, okay?"

Subdued, Justine said quietly, "Fine dear, I'm sorry if I offended you, but you have no objection if I go to Mass?"

Expansively, arising from his chair, Tommy answered, "Of

course, not, sweetie, and make sure you pray for me." He leaned over and kissed her.

In retrospect, Tommy often felt it was God-ordained, or at least foreordained, that after the first conversation about religion he had had with Justine, fate, or chance, dictated the events that led to his first marital indiscretion. At least, in one of his rare moments of guilt, he consoled himself that it was inevitable. Whatever caused it—God, fate, or chance—he knew one thing. He loved every minute of it.

He went to the club shortly after noon, changed into an old warm-up suit and volleyed against the practice wall for a couple of hours. In short order he was slamming the ball really hard, the ball ricocheting back off the wall almost as hard as it flew off his racket. In his mind he was playing Pancho Gonzales in center court at Wimbledon, rallying relentlessly against the wall, when he mis-hit a shot. He muttered a couple of curses and started to chase the errant ball.

A well-pitched female voice said, "Tommy, I've been watching you for ten minutes. I never saw anyone practice so intensely. You know something, you're getting to be a real good player."

He looked up in surprise. "Oh, hi, Barbara, thanks a lot. I'm sure as hell working at it."

He smiled, wiped the sweat off his forehead with a soggy handkerchief, and took a good look at Barbara. Bronzed and beautiful. Dark brown, long legs accentuated by white short shorts, cropped dark blond hair, brown eyes, great, simply great tits. He waited for her to speak. Her full mouth was half open, she looked eager, really ready. He hadn't been a sailor for four years for nothing. The recognition factor.

"Tommy, we need a fourth, how about it? Joe McHugh and his wife are looking for a game. Why don't you join us, we'll be partners."

Partners? My life is at your disposal, my love.

"Super, Barbara, just wait until I wash up and put on some fresh clothes. Okay!"

"Great, Tom, and please, stop calling me Barbara, it sounds so formal. Call me Bobbi like everyone else does."

"Yes, Bobbi, dear. See you in a flash."

Tom hurried to the locker room, stripped out of his sweat clothes and jumped into the shower. He soaped himself and began to sing as the shower sprayed his body. "When Did You Leave Heaven?" He grinned, jumped out of the shower, toweled himself off, sprayed some Right Guard under his arms, splashed a bit of aftershave on his cheeks, and dressed quickly. He donned a pair of white shorts and a pink alligator shirt. He looked himself over from every angle as he combed his hair in front of the washroom mirror. He threw a kiss at his image and sang out, "How's everything in Heaven, that's all I want to know."

On the way to the far tennis court to join Barbara, better known to the Bayside world of tennis as Bobbi, he jogged his memory to recall what he knew about her. He was positive he had never played with or against her, but he remembered having a drink with her in the club lounge a couple of weeks back in the company of several other members. Barbara, forget Barbara, dummy, it's Bobbi. That's it, Bobbi, with an i—Bobbi, Bobbi Schuyler. I got it! How could I ever forget? I guess she looked so unattainable—tall, light green dress, a dream—probably, hopefully, divorced.

Joe McHugh and his wife were nice people but not very good tennis players. Bobbi was one of the better women players so it was more of an easy workout than a real match. Tom and Bobbi played well within their game to keep it interesting and the match lasted about an hour and a half. The stakes were a round of drinks, and after finishing their drinks and thanking Bobbi and Tom, the McHughs left, saying they had to get home to the kids. They were the only couple left in the club lounge.

They sat quietly in the low-slung easy chairs, a tall Rum Collins in front of each of them, at ease with themselves, pleased with each other, serene in the sense of physical well-being a player feels after a couple of hours of good tennis. Bobbi leaned closer to Tom, sipped her drink, and said, "You know something, Tom, you're a pretty nice guy. I mean the way you acted on the court today. We could have killed the McHughs out there, but don't think I didn't notice how you took it nice and easy and kept the ball in play to give them a good work-out."

"C'mon, Bobbi, it's only a game, none of us will be champs. Why take it so seriously?" He said modestly, giving her a shy, country boy grin. He took his glass, tipped it against her glass. "Good luck, babe." Christ, she was gorgeous.

"Good luck, Tommy, dear. But honestly, Tom, wait until you're around the club a while and you'll understand what I'm saying. Most of the guys around here like to show off their game and blow everybody off the court. The big, macho image. They're ridiculous, some of them, the way they carry on, playing every game like they were center court at Forest Hills."

"Now, take it easy, Bobbi, I'm not that good and the McHughs weren't that bad."

"Oh, c'mon, Tom, they weren't in our class. I recognized right away that you were trying to keep the match interesting and I went along with the act. They were absolutely delighted we only beat them six-three, six-three."

Tom took a long swallow of his drink, looked his partner over carefully. She was still a bit flushed from the tennis, had just a slight beading of perspiration across her upper lip, but otherwise she looked, well, she looked—oh shit, there goes that song spinning around in my head again—"When did you leave Heaven, how did they let you go, how's everything in Heaven—" Jesus, speak up, dum-dum. He found his voice.

"If they're happy about the match, I'm glad. Joe McHugh's a helluva nice guy and she seems great. Besides, he bought us a great drink."

"You're right, they're a wonderful couple." She took a long pull on her drink. "M'mm, you're right, Tom, a great drink. Tastes fantastic—listen, enough tennis talk. Tell me about yourself. The word is out. You're a New York cop. Is that right?"

"One hundred percent right, Bobbi, one of New York's Finest."

"Gee, a cop, it must be a terribly exciting job. Are you some sort of detective?"

"Not exactly," he lied glibly. "I'm in all sorts of undercover things—decoy units, anticrime patrol—things like that." He consoled himself. Only part bullshit. He was, after all, into anticrime. He suppressed a grin. Most crimes. Anyway, real ones.

Bobbi shivered. "Ooh, sounds scary, and you're such a cleancut, nice-looking guy. Gosh, you don't even look like a cop or act like a cop. Anticrime—sounds so dangerous. How can you stand it?"

"That's the idea in a nutshell, Bobbi, anticrime guys are not supposed to look like cops. At least not the stereotype cop the public pictures. You know, big, heavy-set, menacing looking. That's why guys like me get picked for the anticrime detail. Our looks are deceiving and even the criminals don't recognize us so easily." He was really pouring the bullshit on now, warming up to the task, noticing that her lips had parted again, her tongue flickering snakelike across them, her brown eyes dancing. He motioned to the waitress with raised hand, signaled for another drink. The waitress pointed to the tall glasses, the same? He nodded. Tommy, boy, this is getting real interesting.

The drinks arrived. They tipped glasses good luck again and both took generous swallows, the sweet rum drink loosening their tired muscles and inducing the delicious euphoria that accompanies the first couple of ice-cold tall ones. He sighed. Beautiful, beautiful. Then came the inevitable, the direct question fired by all would-be lady district attorneys, the searing question, the shot that's fired around the raunchy world of singles bars and tinseled cocktail lounges a thousand times a day, all year long.

"Are you *married*, Tommy?"

"Doesn't everyone get married?" He parried the question deftly, lowering his eyes as if the mention of it wounded him. Buying time to frame his answer, time to bullshit her further. She laughed happily at his hangdog look—his apparent misery had taken him off the hook. "Doesn't everyone get married. Tom, that's rich. I sure did, twice."

Eyebrows raised. "Twice? Really? Tell me about it."

"Tell you what, Tom, let's finish our drinks and shower and change. We won't go to a restaurant, we'll go to my house. We'll have a couple of drinks there and I'll whip something up out of the fridge for dinner. Is that okay with you, or do you have some clandestine police operation you're involved in that you must report for?"

He smiled, nodded his head, thinking, only the fucking radio car with that old pain in the ass, Charley Malloy, as my partner. He shook his head, with the same hesitant smile.

"You know something, Bobbi, you're actually clairvoyant. I swear, you must have some of that gypsy mind-reader blood in you. I do have a heavy job I'm assigned to about midnight. It's a must, a stakeout. There's been a bunch of stick-ups recently in East Harlem and we have a lot of men deployed up there to nail these two bums who are having quite a picnic." He lied easily, looking at her with a wrinkled brow, a frown that said, I'll get these dirty rats.

"Whew, a stakeout. Sounds so sinister. I'm glad I don't have to go with you. Please, Tom, make sure you don't get hurt." She squeezed his hand protectively, shuddered a little.

He laughed reassuringly, patted her hand.

"Don't worry about me, babe, I can take care of myself. C'mon, let's drink up, take that look off your pretty face. Let's shower. I'll see you out front and follow you to your house."

He showered for the second time in one day. Another new record for a young Irish kid. He grinned as he soaped himself liberally. Scrubbed and toweled dry, he again sprayed Right Guard under each armpit and patted Aqua Velva on his cheeks and upper body. Tennis club, I love you! He sang one brief chorus of "When Did You Leave Heaven?", put on white duck pants, navy blue sports shirt, white cashmere sweater, inspected himself carefully in the locker room full-length mirror, threw a kiss at his image, and left the club to get his car. Bobbi waved to him from across the parking lot and pointed to her car.

* * *

He trailed her through the lovely, tree-lined streets of Bayside to the Cross Island Parkway. She signaled and turned abruptly at a narrow, paved road that climbed rather steeply for about one hundred and fifty feet and pulled up at the graveled driveway in front of her house. The house exceeded what he had imagined it to be. It was a white New England colonial, with a black shingled roof, large bay windows, sturdy square-cut columns on either side of the heavy green front door, and red brick chimney looming high over the second floor. There were small forests of high trees on either side, almost totally obscuring the neighboring homes. High green hedges and rows of flowering bushes grew abundantly along the front of the house, but the sloping, manicured, expansive lawn stretched out magnificently to give an unimpeded view of the water.

Tom slid out of his car and walked to the front door to join Bobbi, who was looking out at the water. He shook his head in wonderment. It was overwhelming, breathtaking. He took in the whole panorama, looking down from the crest of the hill to the endless expanse of Long Island Sound. There were all kinds of sailboats lazily gliding by, Sunfish, catamarans, some larger. In the distance they all seemed in miniature, the lowering sunlight shimmering in golden shards across their wind-stiffened sails, dancing about the blue green waters. He filled up emotionally, flooded with sharp nostalgia of his navy years, the scene evoking pleasant memories of incredible Pacific sunsets, all the good times, all the great guys. Bobbi looked at him, caught his pensive mood, put her arm around his waist, said quietly, "It is lovely, isn't it, Tom?"

"It's gorgeous, honey, just plain gorgeous. I guess you caught that look on my face. I love just looking at a water view like this. Somehow, it's soothing. Reminds me of the Pacific Ocean. I was crazy about sailing the ocean, loved the navy. When I look at the beauty of this and think of all the stink and squalor where I work, and yet it's part of good old New York City."

She squeezed his shoulders. "All right, sailor boy, enough reminiscence about your navy days. It's starting to get a bit chilly out here, let's go inside and have that drink I promised you."

He followed her into the house and in a fleeting glance could see that the inside was as beautiful and well appointed as the outside. She led him into the den. The four walls were filled with books snugly recessed in burnished, mahogany bookcases, gleaming parquet floor covered in various places by rich, figured throw rugs, oversized maroon leather club chairs, matching ottomans, and shiny mahogany end tables beside each chair, topped by brass, broad-based lamps. Tommy settled into the deep cushions of the club chair, put his feet up on the ottoman, yawned, and stretched out in luxury, like a contented cat. Man, my baby Bobbi didn't just leave Heaven, she lives there.

He couldn't resist a big grin as he heard her rattling around the kitchen, the noise the sweet sounds of fixing drinks. Kid, you came a long way from Sunnyside. Captain O'Connell should get a load of me now. I wonder what metaphor he would use to illustrate my present wealth?

She interrupted his reverie, appearing before him with a silver tray bearing a generous pitcher of martinis—silver bullets to thirsty cops—two crystal goblets, a small bowl of ice cubes, and a platter of canapes. She put the tray on a cocktail table in the center of the den and said, "I think this is a dry martini night, the perfect drink to celebrate our first day together. Does this suggestion meet with your approval, Tommy, dear, or am I too bold?"

He looked up at her, his face creased into a big smile, nodded his head vigorously. Looked her over once again. Christ, babe, and the way you look meets my approval. Knitted, royal blue long-sleeved sweater clinging close to those super tits, gray flannel skirt, no stockings, thank God, to hide those long, deeply tanned legs, no shoes—must have kicked them off in the kitchen.

She poured the martinis into the goblets, looked up. "If you notice, love, I dropped a few ice cubes in your drink to soften it up. I want you to be alert on your stakeout tonight," she laughed.

He grinned and reached for his drink, not saying a word,

kept looking at her. He didn't feel like talking, everything was too perfect to break the mood. She pushed his feet off the ottoman, tipped his glass good luck, pushed the ottoman aside, and sat on the floor cross-legged, directly in front of him as he lazed back in the vast comfort of the club chair.

"Here's the best of luck, Tom. I hope you'll always be safe and I hope I'll see a lot of you."

"Good luck to you, Bobbi. Thanks for the drink and thanks for having me to your home." He took a good swallow of his martini. Dry, cold, crisp. The blood coursed through his veins after the first long pull. She put her face up and he leaned over and kissed her lightly on the lips. A nice kiss. He sat back in the chair, took an easy sip of his drink, couldn't take his eyes off her.

"Take that big grin off your face," she chided him, smiling. "You look like the cat who swallowed the canary. Oops, I'll change that. The cool cat who swallowed the extra dry martini."

He burst into laughter. "It's just that I feel so good, Bobbi, and I never have a martini with a pretty lady without thinking of the old martini joke."

She laughed. "Oh, c'mon, Tommy, not the old joke about the second martini?"

"Exactly," he said, looking down at her, getting hot.

She looked up at him, took a long swallow of her drink, now a big grin on her face. "Well, let's at least wait until we get to the second martini, right now I'm floating on air."

He straightened up in the chair, his cock had shot up so suddenly it strained against his tight-fitting white ducks. He rested his left arm across his lap to conceal it and fought off the instant flush from his face that betrayed the surge of passion. Cool off, dummy, don't rush a good thing. Easy does it. The next half hour is going to be a crucial one. Here at my feet sits the bronze goddess of all time and she wears a very horny look. She turned her head for an instant and he stole a covert glance at his wristwatch. Holy Christ, ten minutes to seven. Less than four hours to go before I have to leave for work. He silently cursed the Job he loved.

Bobbi got to her feet, walked to the corner of the den and

put a Frank Sinatra record on the stereo. Mother of God, another miracle, the first song Frank is singing is "When Did You Leave Heaven?" She returned, drink in hand, and again sat at his feet.

"You know, Bobbi now I'm convinced that you're a gypsy mind reader. You just played my favorite song and nobody sings it like Frank Sinatra." He raised his eyes toward the ceiling, lifted his glass high. "Oh, to be overlooking Long Island Sound with a beautiful lady at my feet, sipping a super martini, listening to Frank Sinatra. Sweetheart, neither of us ever left Heaven, we're both there, right now."

She laughed. "You are funny, Tommy." She finished her drink, rose to her feet again.

"Excuse me for a minute, dear, I'm going to fix a fire in the living room. It'll take the chill out of the air. Don't you dare leave, I'll be right back."

She had the martini pitcher in her hand, almost brimming again, refilled, iced and freshened.

"Come on, lazybones, let's go into the living room and have another martini. Follow me."

She led him into the living room. Even a poor kid from Sunnyside could appreciate that it was done in exquisite taste. The heavy logs in the fireplace were burning brightly, filling the air with the sharp, crackling sounds of a fresh fire. There were identical long green sofas, opposite each other, about six feet from the fireplace, with matching cocktail tables in a Chinese motif in front of each of them. The entire room was covered in expensive-looking, light green broadloom. He was especially intrigued by a fairly long white shag rug laid between the cocktail tables, a few feet in front of the fire. Oh, baby, can this be our nuptial bed? He sat primly on one sofa, she on the other, both sipping their martinis, staring into the fire, fascinated by the beauty of the blue white flames. Tom inwardly chuckled. Christ, just like a Cary Grant, Ingrid Bergman movie.

"It does take the chill away, doesn't it, Tom?" Watching him nod soberly, she continued, "Oh, I forgot, I'm a terrible hostess. Here, have something to eat. The quiche is great."

He took a couple of canapes, ate them slowly.

She stood up again, seemed nervous. Shall I make my move

now? "Here, let me freshen your drink. God, I've started on my third already."

She spooned a few ice cubes into his outstretched goblet and filled it almost to the brim. She turned to put the martini pitcher on the cocktail table and he stole another quick glance at his wristwatch. Half past seven. He drank about half his martini in one long gulp. I better make my move soon or else get my off-duty gun out of the glove compartment of my car out front and kill myself.

He stood up, voice right, hoarse. "Bobbi, you look beautiful sitting there. I could love you to death."

She stood up, moved in front of the fire, her back to him, then turned. "Why don't you try, Tommy?"

He put his glass on the cocktail table, walked slowly towards her and crushed her in his arms. Her lips were as warm and eager as he anticipated and his cock grew as hard and more eager than he anticipated. Her tongue was inside his mouth, flickering in and out, then suddenly locked inside it—probing, searching. After an electric minute or two of kissing he stepped back, she moaned softly, raised her arms and he pulled her sweater over her head. He reached in back and unsnapped her brassiere. He kissed her deeply again, broke away, lowered his head and kissed her delicious nipples.

She broke away from him with a low animal-like cry and slipped out of her skirt and underpants. She stood before him stark naked, the bright light from the fireplace accentuating the contrasting soft white skin of her breasts and pubic area against the deep brown of the rest of her gorgeous body. It was Tom's turn to moan. He turned away and almost ripped off his sweater, shirt, pants, and socks, throwing them on the sofa.

He turned to her, held her close, kissed her fiercely, and put his finger into her vagina. He found her clitoris quickly and manipulated it gently. A moment later she shuddered violently and cried out as she reached orgasm. Still standing, she remained in his arms, head against his breast, Tom happy for her sudden come, hard as a rock in anticipation of the lovemaking that lay ahead. Now he was certain that he would make good, long love to her now that the initial frenzy had subsided a bit. She lowered her head and flicked her tongue against the nipple of his left breast—slowly, then faster and faster until he began to groan, his knees beginning to get weak.

He sank down to the shag rug, soft as a bed of roses. She was on top of him, lowered her head and ran her tongue across his stomach, his navel, and then in one quick gulp took his cock into her mouth. She adjusted, took a position between his knees and slowly, expertly, began to suck him.

He lay, head back, on the shag rug, eyes closed, and knew, definitely knew, that he had finally reached Paradise.

He was flying to the moon, on a magic carpet, his head slowly coming off his shoulders. He didn't feel her body turn, just felt his cock getting larger and steamier as she held it in her mouth. Suddenly her body was on top of his, her legs spread open, the sweet-sour smell of her vagina in his nose, her pubic hair around his mouth. What the hell is this? He pushed her off him roughly. She looked up in surprise.

"Oh, Tom, I'm sorry, I didn't warn you. I got so excited—I want you to do it to me while I'm doing you."

"No, no, baby, not tonight." He caught her body in his arms, turned her over, mounted her and in a wild couple of minutes of savage thrashing they came together with simultaneous cries of ecstasy.

Their passion spent, breathing almost normally again, snug in each other's arms, they were warm and serene in front of the blazing fire. He finally calmed down and broke the silence.

"Bobbi, love, that was really something. I felt like I was shot to the moon."

"Oh, Tom, it was so good, I loved it, too. Ooh, you were so big, I thought for a minute my insides were being ripped out."

He smiled proudly. Now here's a girl who knows how to make a guy feel good.

"I grew it all for you, babe, every foot of it."

They both roared laughing. He put his hand over her mouth, spoke to her very low, very conspiratorially. "By the way, what the hell were you trying to do before when you swung your legs around, smother me?" He began to laugh again, she pushed his hand from her mouth and howled. At last, after almost choking from laughing so hard, she turned, held his head in her hands and kissed him sweetly on the lips.

"You silly boy. I only wanted you to do it to me while I was doing it to you. You know, don't be so naive, sixty-nine—or whatever the French call it, *soixante-neuf*."

He roared laughing again. "Christ, I thought you were trying to suffocate me for a minute. My eyes were closed, I was on cloud nine, seventh heaven, when suddenly this big mound of pussy was in my face. Jesus, love, what a terrible way to die, smothered to death by a blond pussy."

His laughter was infectious; they both could hardly stop. Finally, Bobbi said, "Tom, thirty-two years old, c'mon, don't tell me you never did that, never tried sixty-nine."

"I swear, Bobbi, I never did. But I promise you that if I ever do, you'll be first on my list." He laughed again.

"What are you laughing at now, Tom?"

He composed himself, but had all he could do to keep from breaking up. "Well, honey, the guys I hang out with are mostly cops and we kid around, rib each other a lot. As you can imagine, sex is often the main topic of conversation. Sure I know what you mean about sixty-nine and I honestly never tried it. I guess it's a macho thing about cops. You know, like playing that game destroys the old macho image.

"Still, it comes up occasionally, and the cops have a very funny story about it. Want to hear it?"

"Love to. Go ahead."

He laughed again, warm, happy, and rejoicing in the sweet smell of her lovely body in his arms.

"Hold it." She disengaged herself. "I'll be right back. Let's have another martini." She took the pitcher off the cocktail table, dropped a few ice cubes in each goblet and poured fresh martinis. They sat up, backs to the sofa, tipped glasses, kissed each other lightly, and took deep swallows of the martinis.

"Now, go ahead, sweet, tell me your big macho cop, sixty-nine story."

"Okay, hon, I hope you think it's funny. Anyway, you have to understand that pretty near all station houses have what they call cop buffs. The buff is usually a frustrated cop type, usually a little slow in the brain department, but invariably the precinct cops love the guy. He runs errands for the cops, makes sandwiches for the inside guys, you know, things like that. Anyway, as the story goes, this cop buff, Angelo, was the pride of the Eighteenth Precinct on the West Side. He was a super Italian guy and all the cops loved him.

"Angelo had been around the Eighteenth for about twenty-five years and the cops decided to give him a testimonial party. They all chipped in, threw a bash for Angelo, and gave him an almost exact replica of a police shield as a gift. Angelo was overwhelmed. The party broke up about six o'clock on a summer night and Angelo, who lived in the Eighties off Columbus Avenue, started walking home uptown on the park side of Central Park West. He was half-bombed and held his new shield in his pants pocket, held it like it was pure gold.

"He got to about Seventy-sixth Street and Central Park West when he turned just in time to see a car jump a red light. He leaped out on the street, shield held high, and flagged the car down. It was a new convertible, top down, and a very pretty girl driving. Angelo hollered at the frightened girl.

"'What's the idea of passing a red light like that? You tryin' to kill somebody or hit somebody else's car? Whatssa matta with you? Are you crazy, or something?'

"'Oh, officer, I'm in an awful hurry, I'm terrible sorry.'

"'Sorry, heh, well, you'll be sorrier when I give you a ticket.'

"'Oh, please, officer, please, don't give me a ticket. If I get one more ticket, I'll lose my license for a year. Please get in the car, let's talk it over.'

"Angelo proceeds to get into the car, yelling at her, telling her no matter what, she's going to get a ticket. The girl starts the car, Angelo beside her, and pulls off Central Park West into Seventy-ninth Street and parks in a secluded glen in the park. She turns to Angelo, pleading with him, drops her blouse off her left shoulder and out pops a beautiful tit.

"'Please, officer, don't give me a ticket, just kiss me on the nipple of my breast.'

"Angelo nuzzles her breast—he's still half-bombed from the party—and says, 'You can't bribe me like that, lady, I'm giving you a ticket anyway.'

"She then drops her blouse off her right shoulder, another beautiful tit pops out.

"'Please, officer, kiss my other breast. I swear to you, I can't stand another ticket.'

"Angelo kisses her right tit nice and easy, comes up for air and says, 'Lady, no way, you get a ticket, I won't be bribed.'

"With that, the girl lays her head back, stretches out and raises her skirt above her hips. No panties on. She spreads her legs and says, 'Please, officer, please, no ticket, just kiss this.'

"Angelo takes one look at her pussy, opens the car door, leaps out, and says, 'Sorry, lady, I can't, I'm not a real cop.'"

Bobbi burst into a fit of laughter and Tom howled along with her. Gasping, she wiped the laughter tears from her eyes, put her arms around him, kissed him, and said, "Tommy, that's a very funny story, really funny. I nearly died laughing." She kissed him again, deeply, grabbed him close, slid down on the shag rug with him, kissed him fiercely, tongue probing his mouth, then his neck, then the nipples on his breasts until he was rock hard again. She turned, got on top of him, mounted him and rode him, head back in ecstasy, uttering little animal-like cries, until they both reached another orgasm.

They lay in each other's arms for a few minutes, exhausted, not saying a word, two supremely happy lovers. At last she disentangled herself, kissed him on the ear, whispered to him, "Sleep for a while, love, I'll fix you something to eat." She reached down, slipped a light blanket over him, kissed his ear again, whispered into it, "Someday soon, I'll make you a real cop."

She shook him gently. He stirred, opened his eyes, sat up, the blanket slipping down to his waist. She leaned down and kissed him. The kiss was a long one. He stretched his left hand over her head and looked at his wristwatch. Ten fifteen—*tempus fugit*—and Brother Aloysius said I'd never learn Latin. Better get rolling, don't want to miss the stakeout. Christ, she's beginning to breathe heavy again—there goes the tongue. He pulled away from her mouth, kissed her eyes, pushed her away with a quick caress, rubbed his eyes, now fully awake. He stood up, modestly keeping the blanket around his waist.

"I love you, Bobbi, but as they say along old Broadway, the show is closing." He laughed. "I have to get going, seriously."

"I hate to see you leave, Tom, but I know you have to go on duty. So, as long as you're talking Broadway, let's get the show on the road. Your clothes are there on the sofa, the bathroom is over there, I've made a tuna fish and tomato sandwich for you and I have water on for tea. Okay?"

He dressed quickly, crossed to the bathroom, filled the sink with cold water and plunged his face in a few times. He found a toothbrush on a rack over the sink and brushed his teeth. He smiled as he rinsed his mouth. I hope it's hers, I'd hate to get a communicable disease from someone else.

Dressed and washed, he went into the kitchen. She was sitting at the kitchen table, looking beautiful in a pink robe, sandwich and a cup of tea opposite her. He kissed her lightly and finished his sandwich and tea hurriedly. She walked him to the front door.

He drove slowly down the hilly road and soon slid into the heavy traffic on the Cross Island Parkway towards New York. In seven or eight minutes he peeled off onto the connecting Grand Central Parkway towards the Triborough Bridge. His thoughts were full of the preceding hours of the day, full of Bobbi, visions of her flashing through his mind, her sweet smell still in his nostrils. How goddam lucky can a guy get? He remembered back to the first day when he saw her in the club lounge. Cool, blond, bronzed—and what was that word? I got it. Unattainable.

He thought about Justine, remembering with a pang that he never called her all day. His thoughts again reverted to the past four or five hours with Bobbi. How lovely she looked in the glow of the blue white flames of the fireplace. Incredible, the large, white, firm tits, white belly and ass—against the deep tan of the rest of her lovely body. What a turn on! And the intense, inventive way she made love. He thought again of Justine. He shook his head to think that he had laid her the same way for eight years.

He pulled up close to the station house and parked his car.

My stakeout tonight is driving the radio car with old Charley Malloy as my partner. Good old Charley, fat as a house, waiting out the Job another six months until he reaches the mandatory retirement age of sixty-three. Sticking it out so he can retire on three-quarters pay. Meanwhile, I have to listen to his endless, nightly tirade. After a couple of stops at one or the other of the sector bars and Charley has belted down a couple of paper containers of rye and soda, he starts blasting the shit out of President Roosevelt. The first time out with Charley, the first time he heard him rave and rant about Roosevelt, he said, "What are you so mad at F.D.R. for, Charley, for getting us into World War Two?"

"Naw, for Christ sake, Tom, that had nothing to do with it. We had to go to war."

"Then, why? He's been dead for years. I thought he was a great president."

"Great, my ass. I hate him 'cause he repealed Prohibition just before I got into plainclothes. The fucking borough of Manhattan in plainclothes—what a rabbi I had—and he goes and repeals the Volstead Act. Makes bars and grills legal. No more speakeasies, no more sneaky booze stills. Can you believe that for lousy luck. That F.D.R. sonofabitch cost me a fortune. I would've owned a big house on Long Island by now—outright. I still got a mortgage on the little house my Mae and me raised our kids in. Repeal, just when I got my shot. Plainclothes in the borough for two years and I made shit. Just began to make a few bucks, then comes Seabury, and I get flopped. Fuck Roosevelt, fuck them all. Six more months I get out on three quarters, sell the house on the Island and move to Delray Beach."

Oh, please, Charley, not tonight, no Roosevelt, please. Tonight I fell in love again. And don't bring up Delray Beach, wherever the hell in Florida that place is. Go to sleep early, while I drive, ever on the lookout for crime. Don't snore too loud, don't fart too much, just sleep, Charley boy, just sleep.

He took off his street clothes, removed his uniform from his locker and dressed slowly. Everything in place, gunbelt checked, he went downstairs to the main floor to wait for the night sergeant's roll call. It was still a bit early; some late-tour guys were beginning to arrive and none of the four to twelve shift guys had yet begun to drift in. He went over to the clerical man, Leo Dolan, and talked about the Yankees' chances of winning the pennant. Paulie, the station-house cop buff, came in with a big aluminum tray bearing containers of coffee and bags of doughnuts. Tom took a container of coffee, a doughnut, and thanked Paulie. Good old Paulie—tall, painfully thin—but always smiling, bowing, anxious to please. He smiled at Paulie. I wonder if Paulie was ever a real cop.

Roll call over, alarms duly entered into memo books, Tom assumed the driver's side of the radio car. After a couple of minutes of grunting and groaning Charley Malloy finally wheezed, patted his pot belly—and it sounded like a sack of cement landed when he put his two hundred and forty pounds of lard and fat ass next to him.

"You better lose some weight, Charley, or you'll never make it with any of those young broads in bikinis down in Delray Beach."

"Fuck all those young broads in bikinis."

"That's exactly the idea, Charley, baby."

He started the car, eased off into the light traffic, and took off for whatever lay ahead until eight in the morning. He barely suppressed a grin at roll call. Very easy, light crime sector tonight. Everybody was taking good care of Charley. He may be a cranky bastard, but he'd been a great cop and everyone loved him. He mused, cast a sidelong glance at fat Charley—it was great how they all looked after the old warhorses. He cruised slowly through the streets, still noisy and brightly lit. Real quiet sector for the most part. Ninety-sixth Street north to 106th Street, Third Avenue West to Fifth Avenue East. Pretty good neighborhood. In fact, still a little ritzy along Park, Madison, and Fifth Avenues. Some great old apartment houses still standing—stunning pieces of architecture. In sharp contrast to the starkness of the mundane, square, high-rise apartment houses jumping up a short distance away in the Seventies and Sixties. They looked as if they were all designed by the same guy who designed the Washington Monument.

The first hour was very quiet, not even one call for their car.

About one thirty Tom stopped the car outside Joe Tobin's bar and went in and returned with two large containers of rye and soda for Charley and a tall Coca-Cola for himself. Three large, extra-dry martinis before the tour started was enough booze for him. He was still on a nice high, whether it was the aftermath of the martinis or the great loving he wasn't sure, but a wonderful feeling enveloped him. The radio barked out incessantly, turned low, the staccato voices of the dispatchers tonelessly filling the night.

Charley had knocked off his first container, was working on his second. He took a huge swallow, belched a few times, farted loudly a couple of times. Tommy opened his window wide. Charley swallowed another slug of the rye and soda, cursed Franklin D. Roosevelt in several ways, hoped he roasted in Hell, laid his head back and went to sleep.

Thank God, as he listened to Charley snore. He couldn't shake Bobbi out of his mind. The streets were almost empty as he cruised slowly along the avenues and up and down the quiet side streets. Three o'clock. Still quiet, not a call. Christ, how can I remember Justine when all I'm thinking about is Bobbi, the fireplace, the shag rug.

He drove slowly along East Ninety-seventh Street, between Park and Madison Avenues. Nice and dreamy. Suddenly a guy appeared under the street light about twenty feet in front of the car and frantically flagged him down. He had just passed the middle of the block. He waved his hand to the guy, who looked terrified. "What's up, pal, you look all excited?" Nice and cool. By now he was used to this behavior, guy frantic, probably has a flat or can't start his car, or lost his house key.

"Jesus Christ, officer, am I glad to see you. There's two guys sticking up a crap game down the block."

Tommy bolted out of the car. Charley slept peacefully.

"Calm down. Take it nice and easy, pal, show me where the stick-up is."

The guy pointed up the block. "The big apartment house on the right hand corner of Madison. You see the sign up there on the side, 'Garage,' they're in there."

"Okay, slow down, pal, slow down. How the hell do you know it's a stick-up?"

"Officer, I swear, I was in the game. I took time out to take a piss behind one of the parked cars. The two heist guys never saw me. They just went in and hollered, 'Hands up, mother-fuckers.' Boffo, just like that. They were talking when they passed me. They're two spics."

"How the fuck do you know they're two spics?"

"For Christ sake, they were talking spic, I listened to enough of that shit to know it. One guy has a light blue lumber jacket on and he's wearing one of those headbands. The other guy has like a yellow, kind of light-colored lumber jacket on. Jesus Christ, watch your ass, officer, they both had long guns in their hands."

"What's your name?"

"Tony."

"Okay, Tony, get on the sidewalk. Stand in front of the garage and wait there for a minute. I'll pull the car up in front of the entrance."

He gave Tony a push. He could see the guy was scared shitless. He got into the radio car, drove up in front of the huge garage door and parked next to the curb. Charley was still sound asleep. Unbelievable. Fuck him, he'd be useless any-way. Two stick-up guys, my cup of tea, could be the big collar I'm looking for, my route to plainclothes. Fuck calling for as-sistance, I'll nail these two spics dead bank.

He shook Charley awake. He woke up spluttering, dazed. "Wake up, for Christ sake, Charley, there may be trouble in this garage. If I'm not out in five minutes call in a signal thirty-two. You got that?"

"Signal thirty-two! What the hell is up?"

"Just take it easy, Charley. Monitor the calls, do as I say. Five minutes, signal thirty-two, got it. It may be a bunch of shit. Okay?"

"Okay, Tommy, boy. Watch your ass, kid."

Tony was still shaking, trying to make himself invisible in the shadows at the far corner of the garage door. Tommy was tense, but cool, senses on red alert. "Okay, pal, give me the layout, quick."

"You see the left part of the overhead door. That's a panel that swings in and out. It's there for the parkers who come in late at night. They have keys for the inside to unlock the overhead door. The panel lets them in. Got it? Now, once you go in, there's a slope you go down—thirty, forty feet—then turn right. You'll see parked cars. About ten feet you turn left you'll see rows of parked cars on either side. Way down the end on the right hand side you'll see a big delivery truck parked. There's a big light hanging from the ceiling right past the truck. The crap table and game are right there, hid by the truck. Okay?"

"Sounds good, very good. How many guys are playing in the game?"

"Thirty or forty!"

"You want to stick around in case I might need you?"

"Fuck that, officer, that's what you get paid for. So long, good luck, I'm gettin' the hell out of here." He turned and ran west towards Central Park like a scared rabbit.

Tommy pushed the door panel Tony had indicated. It swung in and he slipped inside the garage. Nice and easy, just like the guy said. A sloping cement driveway about fifty feet long with a brick wall at the end lay ahead. Tommy unholstered his .38 Smith and Wesson, his trusty piece. He took the slope, gun in hand, quiet as a predator tiger on the Indian plain. Thank God for crepe-soled shoes.

He flattened against the wall on his right at the opening, got to one knee, and seeing only parked cars, turned right. He moved quick as a cat burglar to the main floor. Tony was right. Rows of cars on either side, very dim overhead lights. He ran, crouched low, up about thirty feet and took cover behind a red Cadillac. He surveyed the scene from behind the hood. Again, Tony was right. There was the big truck at the far end. A heavy extension cord hung from the ceiling, throwing off a bright glare against the back and the right walls. He heard low voices, couldn't make out what they were saying. Then he heard a high-pitched voice, rapid Spanish, then a muted cry, a cry of pain. He moved up another few cars, took a low stance behind the hood of another Cadillac, a blue one. He smiled grimly, this is a real Cadillac garage. The gun felt good in his hand. He was glad he made the pistol range two weeks ago. Shot real good. You better shoot good tonight, pricko. Maybe these two spics will give up without a fight. Time to make my move, stop bullshitting. He took six bullets from his gun belt, put them into his right pants pocket. He opened his uniform blouse at the collar, unbuttoned it down. Here goes!

He let two shots go into the ceiling. In the close quarters of the garage it sounded like artillery practice on his old destroyer. Vroom, vroom. Ear piercing!

"The cops are here, you got it. You two spic cocksuckers come out with your hands up. Hands up, you hear. Come out."

The echo of the shots faded. Again, dead silence. Then a stream of slightly hysterical-sounding Spanish.

He crouched behind a front fender of the Cadillac, but had clear vision. I think they're talking it over, maybe giving up.

Boom, boom, crash. A couple of shots exploded against the windshield and side door of the car. The clatter of the exploding glass, the sharp ping against the door, the explosive shots— the noise was deafening. He ducked low, burrowed deep into his Cadillac foxhole. Give up, shit, these two spics are trying to take my head off. Maybe I should have called for help. Too late, now. He peeked from the fender, the left side, way down low and saw two pair of feet running from the cover of the big truck across the other side of the garage. The enemy were now about forty feet diagonally away from him, presumably behind another Cadillac. When he saw them run he didn't shoot, there was a chance they might be some of the crapshooters trying to escape with their lives. He tried them again. "Throw out your guns, *amigos*, you're surrounded."

"Fuck you, cop!" Then a lot of screaming in Spanish. Sounded like curses. That's my two boys. Boom, boom, two more shots ripped into the windshield. Pataboom, two more shots, one hit the right front tire, boom, it exploded like a cannon shot.

Jesus Christ, if I ever survive this I won't have to listen to Vinny's Korean front-line bullshit anymore. He ducked around to the rear of the Cadillac. He caught a quick look at a face peering over a hood. The guy with the headband. He ripped off two shots. They exploded off the windshield, glass shattered in the air. He heard a scream of pain. I hope I nailed you, you spic cocksucker.

Four quick shots rang out in return.

He grimaced, shrank way down again, nodded his head positively. Now I got you where I want you, you two rotten spic bastards. It all came back—the one lesson he and every young cop never forgot—the gunfight drill from the pistol instructor in rookie school. Remember one thing, you guys, ninety-nine out of a hundred would-be tough guys or heist guys that carry handguns use pistols holding six bullets in the chamber. Six-shooters, like the old Western movies.

Automatics are too tricky, too complicated, for them to handle. Only in the movies and on TV do they use .357 magnums and all that shit. Most of these guys carry guns to inspire fear, and unless they were trained in the service, they couldn't hit an elephant in the ass at twenty feet. If they tried handling an automatic they'd most likely shoot their cocks off instead of their target. Now listen closely, if you're ever in a gunfight and have good cover, try to count the number of shots fired at you. Most of these stupid bastards are junked up to bolster their courage and never dream of carrying extra ammunition. Count the shots off if you can, count accurately, and watch your ass.

He grinned ruefully. I wish I was in rookie school right this minute. Watch your ass, the time worn catchword of the Job. The Irish cops kidded the Italian cops—whattcha ya assa, Dominick, whattcha ya assa, Giuseppe. They all kidded the black cops like Chauncey and Big Ben—watch yo mother ass, brother. Enough of this shit, never mind my ass, I've got two bad spics trying to cleave my head off or shoot my heart out.

He got his head straight, figured what to do. Subconsciously he had counted the shots. He was sure he was right. Ten shots. Two left. He arose from his stooped position, peeked out from the rear of the blue Cadillac. He reached and got three more bullets out of his pants pocket, placed them on the rear panel above the car trunk, crouched and ripped three shots at the windshield of the car they hid behind. Boom, vr-r-room, ping-ng-ng, crash—World War Three just started. The reaction was just what he wanted—two quick shots peeling off in return. Wang-ng-ng, ping-ng-ng, boom. They crashed into the steel exterior of the Cadillac as he knelt behind it, grateful for its shelter. Thank you, General Motors! The thunderous echoes of the pistol shots reverberated sharply off the garage ceiling and walls, then subsided into a faint whine.

Dead silence. He almost felt their presence, though he knew that they were forty feet across from him. A sudden burst of Spanish in low tones floated over to him. It sounded like they were arguing. Oh, baby, this is it. Say your fucking prayers, don't waste time arguing, my *amigos*. You're going, you two cocksuckers. You'll never shoot at another cop. The war is over, you ran out of ammo, but boys, the enemy takes no prisoners. You did your best to kill me, now I'm fucking killing you.

"Cop, cop, I geev up."

"Throw out your guns, *pronto*."

A pistol sailed through the air and skittered across the cement floor with a harsh clatter. Headband, light blue lumber jacket suddenly appeared in the sparse overhead light. Young face, dark hair to shoulders, slim, pretty tall—stepped out, hands held high, yelled, *"Yo bencido, yo bencido, yo bencido!"*

Tommy sighted him carefully, left hand steadying his right and calmly fired two shots into his upper chest. The force of the first shot staggered Headband back and the second shot flipped him off his feet and his head made a thumping sound as the back of it hit a front fender of one of the parked cars.

A shrill, heart-stopping, shattering scream of agony filled the air as the echo of the gun shots died down.

"Angel, Angel! Fucking cop, you kill Angel. He *bencido*!" The yellow lumberjacket guy flashed out and threw himself on Headband's body. He threw his head back and screamed. His last scream.

Tommy had him sighted all the way, left hand steadying his gun hand, no more emotion than he felt on the pistol range in Central Park. He shot Yellow Lumber Jacket right between the eyes. He flipped over like a sack of potatoes, falling sideways, away from his beloved Headband. Some loud shouting came from in back of the truck—the crapshooters must have all shit themselves by now.

Gun in hand, Tommy walked over to the two dead heist guys. They lay in pools of syrupy, red blood. He kicked each body, nothing. Yeah, they were dead, all right. He felt high, a bit unreal, remote—but no remorse. Glad he killed them.

The shouting continued. "Shut up, back there, and every one stay right where they are or they get what these two fucks out here got. You straight? Shut the hell up and stay put!"

He again turned his attention to the two bodies. Dead as mackerels! Good shooting, Tommy boy. He looked down at Headband, now Angel, lying on his right side, left denim pants pocket facing him. Big bulge in front side pocket. Tommy reached in, removed the bulge. He took a quick look, rifled through it, a load of C-notes on the outside. A big bankroll. Better be on the safe side, the game might be on the payroll. He clipped a sheaf of C-notes off the roll, put it in his right pants pocket, put the big part of it in his left pants pocket and stepped back.

"Okay, whoever's the boss of the game, come on out. Don't try to bullshit me, now, I want the real boss. I got two dead stick-up guys out here and I want no more fucking around."

A hoarse voice answered. Under control, calm. "Take it easy, officer, I'm coming out. For Christ sake, don't shoot, I'm only running the game."

A dark, medium-sized guy stepped out, started walking towards Tommy. Blue sweater, gray fedora hat. He came closer. Jesus, it's Steve Maselli, the guy who gave me my first five bucks. And plenty of fins after that. A nice guy.

"Hey, Stevie, how are you?" He stretched out his hand. "It's okay, I'm Tommy Sloane, remember?"

"Holy Christ, Tom, am I glad to see you." He shook Tommy's hand enthusiastically, like a long lost brother. "What a night! It sounded like more shots fired than when I landed in Normandy. I see you nailed the two spic cocksuckers, huh. Good, that's two less. Nice going, Tommy. Look, I got a guy hurt back there, my stickman, Johnny Blue. That headband fuck hit him with his piece across the forehead to show how tough he was. The kid's bleeding pretty bad, let's see if we can do something for him. And by the way, they robbed me of the bankroll, can I get it off them?" Indicating the two dead bodies, shaking his head in disgust.

"No, here it is, it fell out of the headband guy's pocket," he lied easily, reaching in his left-hand pocket and handing the big part of the bankroll to Steve.

"Gee, thanks, Tom. I'll take good care of you later."

"Don't worry about it, Stevie, but listen, what the hell are you doing here with a crap game? I thought you only ran card games."

"You're right, Tom. I'm just helping out. This is Fat Georgie's game. He's also my boss. The game belongs on a Hundred and Fourth Street and First Avenue, but the division guys had a beef on it and we had to move until the heat's off. Everybody's okay, you know it. They rung me in to oversee things because I know everybody in the neighborhood. Tom, I'd appreciate it real good if you don't pinch me."

"Sure, Steve, I'll take care of you, but I'm afraid we have to pinch the game and the players. I'll make sure we spring you, don't worry about it."

He heard some shouts coming from the front of the garage. "You all right, Sloane. You okay, Tommy?"

He pushed Steve towards the truck, whispered to him, "Get back to the crap game guys. Get going."

Loud voice. "I'm okay, come on down, everything's clear. Killed two guys sticking up a crap game here."

Four uniformed cops ran towards Tommy, guns in hand. All radio car guys—Ray McCann, his partner Frankie Lopez, Charley Wilson, his partner, big Chauncey Williams.

McCann whistled when he spotted the two dead bodies, grotesquely sprawled in spreading pools of deep red blood. He spoke first. "Jeez, Tom, great shooting. You got them both."

Frankie Lopez shook his head, said, "You got two of my own kind, but the Puerto Ricans up here will give you a medal. The guy with the headband is Angel Rivera, the leader of the San Juan Savages, a big youth gang. The worst bunch of cut-throat kids in the city, and he was the boss. They shake the shit out of all the poor greenhorns who come here and rob whoever they feel like. He's been locked up a half dozen times." Frankie walked over and kicked the dead ass of Angel Rivera.

"Too bad it wasn't my luck to nail you, you cocksucker, you got what you deserved."

Charley Wilson—built like an ox, strong, tough bastard, over twenty years in the Job—spoke up, authoritatively. "Beautiful piece of work, Tommy. Listen, guys, there's gonna be a lot of shit about this. Two guys killed. Let's get rolling. Nobody touch anything until the top brass and the detectives come. Chauncey—go out to the car, get on the air and tell them what we got. We'll need an ambulance and a couple of patrol wagons for the crapshooters. Where's the game, Tom?"

Indicating the big truck, he said, "Behind there, Charley. By the way, it's Fat Georgie's game and Steve the Wop's back there. See if we can get him out, and some kid who got whacked across the forehead with a gun by Angel, our departed tough guy. He's bleeding pretty bad."

"Okay, the ambulance guys will take care of him. Okay, Chauncey, got it straight? Make sure someone rousts the captain and the detective squad commander, Lieutenant King. Okay?"

Chauncey—tall, black as ebony, nice guy, wide-eyed at the gory scene, only a couple of years in the Job—would follow Charley Wilson to hell and back again. He ran to the front of the garage and disappeared at the turn.

"What the hell took so long for old Malloy to send out the signal thirty-two, Tommy?"

He anticipated the question, braced himself with a dead straight face. Honest Thomas all the way. He lied glibly, easily, without conscience.

"I never dreamed I'd walk into this. I was parked up the block for a few minutes. I saw a couple of guys walk through the garage door. You know, the swinging panel outside. I couldn't believe my eyes. I figured maybe a couple of car strippers looking to boost a battery or some tires. Charley was asleep. Sound, you know how he sleeps. Anyway, I wake him up, and tell him to give me five minutes before he called a signal thirty-two. I didn't want a big megillah over some petty shit. I just walked around the bend to the main floor when they came out from behind the truck where the crap game they just heisted was. They saw me, dashed behind a car and fired a few shots at me. I rolled along the floor behind a car and took cover. That's about it. I worked my way up behind cars and shot it out with them. No choice."

Ray spoke up. "Christ, you are lucky, Tom. Here's one

gun—" pointing to a pistol partially hidden by the yellow lumberjacket guy's body. "Where's the other gun?"

They looked around. Tommy spotted it just underneath a car behind him. It must have slid under there when Angel threw it out. He fished it out with his foot and poked it in front of the dead bodies.

Charley took over. "Looks like two thirty-eights. This is getting to be some fucking precinct. Everybody up here wears a thirty-two or a thirty-eight, like their goddam underwear. Fellers, nobody touch a thing until the detectives get here, okay?"

"Charley, how about you and I go back and look at the crap game guys. They must be dying back there. Even if it's Fat Georgie's game we'll have to take it, but see if we can let Steve the Wop, you know, Steve Maselli, out. Let's go, the brass will be here any minute."

Tommy and Charley walked to the back of truck. To their complete surprise, the assembled crapshooters applauded vigorously, shouting words of praise—big grins of relief obvious on all their faces. Never were crapshooters, the most addicted of all compulsive gamblers, so glad to see two cops. Tommy felt like Mickey Mantle must have after hitting a bases-loaded home run. He grinned. I wonder if I should tip my uniform hat?

Tommy finally spotted Steve Maselli at the far end of the table, holding a couple of blood soaked handkerchiefs to a young, nice-looking guy's forehead. The poor kid's face was dead white, his ashen pallor accentuated by the brilliant light cast off from the huge overhead lamp hanging from the ceiling above the crap table. Must be Johnny Blue.

Tommy walked over to Steve and Johnny.

"Take it easy, kid, there's an ambulance on its way. Be here in a few minutes." He patted Johnny lightly on the back, felt a wave of compassion for him—Johnny Blue looked up at him, gratefully, mumbled a thank you. Tom whispered into Steve's ear, "When the big brass comes, you walk up to one of the guys like you want to piss, or faint, or whatever, one of them will take you up front and you take off through the door. They all know you, okay. Got it?"

Steve nodded his head, gripped Tom's arm—nice going, kid.

Charley spoke up. "All right, listen, all you guys. I hate to tell you this, but you're all going to have to take a gambling disorderly conduct pinch. You all are also witnesses to any future grand jury investigation. The two guys who stuck you up are lying dead out there and plenty of shit's going to hit the fan. So everybody, stay loose, piss against the walls, and the detectives and patrol wagons will be here shortly. I'm sorry, but there's nothing else we can do."

Cries of approval. We understand, officer. Crapshooters are universally peaceful guys. They only dream of making eighteen passes, breaking the biggest joints in Las Vegas or Monte Carlo. As long as no one got their balls shot off they were tickled to death to take a petty gambling pinch. They were outraged by the actions of the two stick-up spics. Sure, okay, take the money, but why whack a nice kid like Johnny Blue across the head with a pistol. For no reason. Sickening. Fuck those two pricks, the world is better off.

Tommy and Charley left their new-found cop fans and went back to the main scene. Big Chauncey was back. He assured Charley that he had followed his instructions to the letter, sent out all the necessary information over the air. Charley Malloy was still outside and had already sent a few alarms over the air. About five minutes passed before the first two detectives from the precinct squad arrived. A few minutes later Captain O'Connell and the precinct detective commander, Jimmy King, came almost running into the garage.

The two squad detectives hustled about the scene quickly but meticulously. They put gloves on, put the two handguns into heavy paper bags, noted the extensive damage the bullets did to the parked cars, searched for spent cartridges, and cautioned the crapshooters to remain as they were and to have proper identification ready. They were gathering every bit of evidence pertinent to the shootout. Tom watched them with admiration, impressed with their diligence and skill. Maybe I'll be one of you soon.

The captain sent the four radio car cops out to resume patrol, then talked to Lieutenant King in a very low voice off to the side. Tommy stood mutely about fifteen feet away. A few minutes later the patrol wagons and an ambulance arrived.

The attendants put the bodies on stretchers and hauled them out front. He asked them to hold up for a minute, thinking of Johnny Blue in the back. He walked back and the two detectives were writing down the crapshooters' names and addresses. He caught one of their eyes, nodded his head towards Steve in the rear. The detective winked. Okay. He went to the rear and helped Johnny Blue up out of a chair they had sat him in, winked at Steve the Wop to assist him. They half-walked, half-carried Johnny Blue out of the garage and boosted him into the back of the ambulance as one of the attendants plastered a large piece of gauze to his wound. Once Johnny was safely inside, the detective slammed the back doors shut. He then gave Steve a push—get going.

He walked back into the garage. The captain and lieutenant were still talking very quietly. Three more detectives entered the scene. Homicide squad guys. Strong faces, hard-looking guys. They talked to the captain and lieutenant for a few minutes, then walked over to Tommy and each of them shook his hand. Nice work, kid. Beautiful. Whacked them both out? Gorgeous. I told you, Mickey, the young cops coming up are as tough as the old-timers, and they got more brains. Where? In their ass! A big laugh all around. The other two squad detectives came from the rear and they all shook hands like old homecoming week. They all began searching the cars and garage floor for spent cartridges and noting further damage. Tommy grinned silently, patted his right pants pocket where the sheaf of hundred dollar bills rested, comfortably ensconced. Didn't have time to count it. Had to be a healthy score. Twelve, fifteen hundred. I hope these bulls aren't searching for money. He could barely suppress a big grin.

He remained on the side, respectfully waiting for the captain's signal to join them. Quietly, observing everything, determined not to speak unless spoken to. The patrol wagon guys led the crapshooters out, aided by two of the detectives. You would think they were going on a gambling junket to Vegas instead of the smelly confines of the station-house jail cells. They waved to Tommy as they passed, shouting their approval. By now, they knew his name. Atta boy, Tom. You're some cop, Tom. Remind me not to shoot it out with you, Tom—all words of praise. His face broke into a big smile. He waved his hand high, like a newly crowned middleweight champ. Enjoy your bus ride, fellows, enjoy your excellent accommodations waiting in those shithouse cells at the Hotel Twenty-third Precinct.

Crapshooters, bodies, radio car cops gone, the captain finally motioned to Tom to join them.

The captain spoke first. "Sloane, you did a great piece of work and by the shape of those two bodies they just took out I see that you handled it in your usual genteel manner. Suppose you tell me and Lieutenant King exactly what happened."

Tommy thanked him and told him substantially the same story he told the radio car cops who arrived first on the scene. He embellished his story here and there, but kept it practically the same. He stressed how he entered the garage merely thinking it might be some petty thief car strippers, guys who would look to clip a few batteries or other car parts. He emphasized that he instructed his partner, Charley Malloy, to call a signal thirty-two only if he didn't come back to the radio car in five minutes or so. Didn't want to make a big thing out of what I honestly thought was nothing, cap, and I figured, let old Charley take it easy. You understand.

They both listened intently. Nodded their heads frequently as he described the harrowing experience. Lieutenant King spoke up. "It must have been a bitch, Sloane. By the way, there weren't any bullets left in their guns when we retrieved them. Did you know that?"

Tommy feigned a look of absolute astonishment. "No shit, lieutenant, that was sure lucky for me. All I know is that they kept firing shots as they broke for the front of the garage, but like I just told you, I had sneaked forward behind another car. I'd laid dead quiet for a couple of minutes and they must have thought they shot me. Anyway, just like I said, they came out shooting and I nailed them. Thank God."

The captain took over. "It was a great job, Sloane, great. Where the hell did you learn to shoot so good?"

"I was a gunnery instructor in the navy, captain, and we had a pistol range on the base. I loved to shoot and practiced every chance I got. Then, as you can tell from my records, I never miss my shooting day at the arsenal range in Central Park."

"Super." The captain turned towards the sound of footsteps. More people arriving. "Okay, brace up, here comes Inspector McGeary."

Inspector McGeary came up to them with an entourage of four men, all obvious cops. He shook hands with the captain and lieutenant, remained oblivious to Tommy's presence. He was a good-looking, husky man, with dark hair, probably in his mid-fifties. He had a nice smile and the ruddy complexion of a guy who's been known to have a few cocktails. He wore an expensive looking tan cashmere coat over a navy blue suit, high collar white shirt, maroon silk tie. The first time he ever saw an inspector out of uniform. He was quite impressed. That's the way I'll dress when I become an inspector.

The laughs and conversation among the bosses ended. Inspector McGeary motioned to Tom to join them. He reached out, shook his hand. Surprisingly hard, rough handshake.

"The captain explained the incident as it happened, Sloane, and you are to be congratulated. A fine piece of police work. Furthermore, the lieutenant here tells me that one of the men you killed, this Angel Rivera, was a real bad apple up here. I understand we've had him in several times. Well, the world won't miss either of these two hoodlums."

"Now, Sloane, there are quite a few reporters and photographers outside clamoring to get in here to get your picture and to interview you. You just smile and say I did my job, what the public pays me for. You understand, don't you? I don't want you to elaborate on anything publicly. As a matter of fact, say as little as possible even to your wife and friends. We have to submit a full report. Two men shot to death, very young men. Even though they got what they deserved, we still have to satisfy the civil liberty people and the do-gooders who scream every time a cop kills someone. Never mind that they tried to kill a cop, threw twelve shots at you, we still have to file full reports and go through lots of red tape. Now, I'm going to call in the reporters. The camera guys will take your picture, the news guys will ask you a lot of questions. Just answer as I instructed and be very polite. Okay, Sloane. And by the way, once again, good work. I'm recommending you for the Combat Cross and the Medal of Honor. You earned your pay tonight."

Tommy gulped, got a lump in his throat. Tears momentarily rushed to his eyes. For the first time all night he was seized with emotion. He was afraid to speak, mumbled a faint thank you, shook the inspector's outstretched hand.

The reporters and photographers stormed down the center of the garage, notebooks and cameras at the ready. He regained his composure instantly. Christ, Bobbi, baby. I'm supposed to be on a stakeout. His uniform blouse was unbuttoned, white cashmere sweater underneath. His uniform hat was pushed on the back of his head. The press guys converged on the inspector, captain and lieutenant. He took off his hat, wiped his brow like the heat in the garage and the excitement was getting to him. He slipped out of his uniform blouse, put his hat and blouse on a nearby parked car. He brushed his hair with his hands. Hope I look okay. The inspector pointed to him and suddenly flash bulbs were flashing in his face, guys were shouting at him to look into the camera, other guys were hurling a barrage of questions at him.

He stood tall, head high, hands hanging loose, gun prominent on his hip, sober face—the way you're supposed to look when you just faced death. He wanted to look in tomorrow's newspapers like the original Stakeout Kid. Oh Bobbi, my love, I'll really be your hero now.

It was six o'clock in the morning when everything finally calmed down. The captain rode back to the precinct with him and Charley in the radio car. Fortunately, it turned out that Charley had picked up the captain and lieutenant and had been kept busy all night loading the crap game guys into the patrol wagons, assisting the ambulance attendants, and placating the press people. He was happy as a young rookie with all the activity and that made Tommy feel good all over. He had bullshitted him from the outset, but rationalized, what the hell good would he have been anyway.

The captain took him into his office. He felt bone tired, exhausted, could have stretched right out on the cot in the captain's office. The captain took a bottle of Cutty Sark out of his desk, walked over to a small refrigerator, put ice-cubes in two tall glasses. "Soda or water, Tommy?"

"On the rocks, Cap, please. A little water on the side."

They tipped glasses. The first long swallow of Scotch tasted as good as the cure all waters of Our Lady of Lourdes Shrine. Warm, sweet, blood flowing strong again, recuperated, and finally-healed.

He sat back, "Jesus, Cap, thanks a lot. Like the guy says on TV, I needed that."

The captain laughed, "You deserved a drink, Tom. Tell me, any qualms, any remorse, any guilt feelings about killing those two guys tonight."

He took another long pull on the Cutty Sark, finished it. He proferred the glass towards the captain, "Do you mind, Cap, I could use another."

The captain finished his drink, arose and came back with two fresh ones. Again, they tipped glasses. Tommy took another long belt, wiped his mouth, looked the captain right in the eye.

"To tell you the God's honest truth, Captain, I haven't a qualm in my entire body. I'm glad, proud, that I shot those two cocksuckers. They did their best to kill me and I did my best to kill them. I won, the ball game's over. Cap, you know me by now, that's it."

The captain smiled, "Good, Tom, I'm glad you feel that way. The top brass have come up with a program to have a psychiatrist counsel some of the guys who killed in the line of duty and experience trauma as a result. Do you think you might need a psychiatric session? Gets you a day off."

Tommy laughed, "Shit, Captain, I've been told I needed a psychiatrist a hundred times since I've been a young kid. But seriously, no good, not over killing those two punks tonight."

The captain laughed, "Good. Okay, come on, finish your drink, you must be dead tired. I'll get one of the radio cars to drive you home."

"No thanks, Cap, I have my own car outside."

"Fine, okay. I understand you're due to work two more late tours, then have the weekend off. Forget them, you're officially off now until Monday morning. It's possible you might have to

114

go downtown and answer some questions, but I'll see if I can delay it. Here, sign the bottom of the page and go out and dictate to Leo Dolan exactly what you told me about the shooting. Don't elaborate. I'll rewrite it in proper English and get it typed up over your signature. All right, anything else?"

Proper English. Okay, Captain, but not too many metaphors or similes, please.

"Yes, Captain, could I use your phone to call my wife?"

The captain got up, pushed the phone towards him, "Go ahead, take your time. I'll go out and get Leo ready for you." He paused at the door, "By the way, Tom, that was pretty slick the way you got rid of Steve Maselli."

Tommy laughed, dialed his home phone. It rang four times. A sleepy, muffled voice, "Hello, hello, who's this?"

"Justine, it's me, Tommy. I'm sorry I woke you up."

Big yawn, more awake now, "That's okay, Tom. I'm looking at the alarm clock. I have to get up in half an hour anyway. What's up? Are you all right? Why didn't you call me last night before you went to work?"

Because I was screwing the most beautiful woman in the world.

"Sorry, babe, but I got called in on an emergency. It's a long story. I'll tell you when I get home." He thought of Bobbi and the fireplace. "I had a little trouble tonight. No, I'm okay, don't get excited. Just take the morning off, tell them at the office you'll be in at lunchtime. Look, do as I say. I don't want to elaborate on the phone. I'll be home in less than an hour. Of course, are you serious? Sure I love you. Relax, I'm on my way."

He went upstairs to the locker room to change clothes and use the toilet. For the first time all night he finally had a chance to count the money that he skimmed off the top of the crap game bankroll. Thirteen hundred dollars! Was thirteen an unlucky number? He grinned. He wished it was thirteen times thirteen. What a life—less than fourteen hours had passed. He had made love to a gorgeous woman a couple of times, he had killed two despicable pricks, he had a couple of great Scotches with the captain, and now he was going home thirteen hundred dollars richer. Yes, it was a wonderful world.

Everyone shook his hand as he left the station house making him feel like some kind of hero. Driving towards the Triborough Bridge and home, his thoughts were full of what lay ahead. Money was the game! He mentally calculated that he had to get a further reward from Steve Maselli for his retrieval of the main bankroll, for turning him loose, and by his timely arrival on the scene thwarting the robbery of the crapshooters' individual bankrolls. He grinned, remembering their smiling faces as they were being led off to jail. No wonder the standing ovation!

As he approached the entrance to the bridge off the F.D.R. Drive, despite his weariness, he again reviewed the events of the shooting match. Who was to dispute his mysterious entry upon the scene? Certainly, the tipster, Tony, would never say a word. With his knowledge of the layout he had to be one of Fat Georgie's men. So much for that. The four cops first on the scene, the captain, Lieutenant King, and even Inspector McGeary accepted his version as absolute. The end of that worry. And like he told the captain he felt no remorse, no emotion whatsoever. Another big grin. He patted the fresh hundreds in his left pants pocket. Was elation an emotion? And surely there was at least another thousand coming from Fat Georgie for valor under fire. Another grin. To Fat Georgie, valor under fire meant upholding a contract at all costs. Horatio at the bridge! Horatio at the garage! Christ, I'm getting tired.

He reached the ramp leading to the vast expanse and imposing supporting towers of the Triborough Bridge, another connecting link from the quiet suburbs of Queens to the constant action and sparkle of Manhattan Island. He usually flashed his police shield and passed free through an extreme right hand lane, but saw some youngster selling the early morning *Daily News* in front of the pay tolls. He decided to buy a paper.

"Get yer paper here, please! Late *Daily News*, sir."

He was a young, obviously Puerto Rican kid about fourteen, shivering in the early autumn chill, wrapped in a threadbare sweater, denim pants, and baseball cap. Now here's a good kid, hustling his ass selling papers this early in the morning, not out robbing some poor fucking drunks like those young gang pricks.

There were a couple of cars ahead of him, none behind. He rolled down the car window next to him all the way. Fished two quarters out of his pocket, took the *Daily News* from the kid and waved to him to keep the change. Big tip, the paper cost only a nickel. The Puerto Rican kid's face broke into a big smile, showing nice white teeth gleaming in his brown, handsome face.

"Oh, *gracias*, senor."

"You Puerto Rican, kid?"

"*Si*, sir, I mean, yessir."

Tommy gave him a big smile. A big brother smile. "Tell me kid, what does *yo bencido* mean?"

The kid put his free hand to his head.

"You say '*yo a bencido*', sir. Means I surrender."

Tommy smiled, waved thanks to the kid and paid his toll. *Yo bencido*, I surrender. Shit you surrender! No more bullets left to shoot my head or my cock off and you surrender. Like we were playing war games when we were young kids with make believe rifles. Well, *amigos*, you said your last *bencido*. He pushed them from his mind, let his thoughts stray once again to Bobbi. I *bencido* to you, my love. He drove along happily, started to whistle "I Surrender Dear." Christ, Russ Columbo was a great singer. Almost as good as Frank.

Off the bridge he weaved through the early morning traffic. The soot from the smoky chimneys of the Long Island City factories was already fouling the morning air. He emerged from the ancient overhead railway streets of Astoria to the promised land of Sunnyside and Woodside. He parked his car in a spot he found on the street not very far from his apartment house. He looked at his watch as he emerged from his car. Twenty-five after eight. He still wore the same outfit he had on when he left the house just before noon yesterday morning. It seemed like last week.

He entered the courtyard of his apartment complex and saw

Justine standing there talking with three other women. She ran to him as he approached, almost screaming, "Tommy, Tommy, are you all right?" and threw her arms around him, kissing him all over his face and hugging him savagely—tears streaming down her cheeks.

"Sure, sure, babe, I'm fine, not a scratch." He kissed away her tears, hugged her back, calmed her. How the hell did she know about the shootout already? Probably some guy from the precinct called.

She broke away, smiled through her tears, clung to his arm, finally stopped sobbing.

"Tommy, your picture was all over the TV this morning. Oh, Tom, all the shots fired at you and the two men you killed." She wailed again, "Oh, it was horrible. I thought you'd never get home."

He finally quieted her down and walked with her to join the three other women, who evidently lived in the same complex. They greeted him with awe, as if he were Sergeant York or Audie Murphy.

The oldest of the women, a tired-looking, gray-haired lady, hugged him, looked directly into his eyes. "We need more good cops like you, Tom, with what's coming into New York. I pray to God every night for cops like you to protect my own." She hugged him again and kissed his cheek.

Tears rushed to his eyes as she held him. Once again a wave of emotion hit him, the second time since the shootout. He hugged her back, recovered quickly. Christ, I'm getting to be a real soft touch. Better cut that shit out.

"Thank you, Mrs. Costello, thank you."

They said good-bye at last, Justine still teary-eyed and gripping his arm in a deathlock.

Once inside their flat Justine regained her composure and rattled on about what a hero the announcers on early morning radio and TV were making of him. How great he looked in the white cashmere sweater she bought for him last Christmas in Bloomingdale's.

He grinned to himself. My stakeout sweater.

She fixed him a sumptuous breakfast of sausages, eggs, coffee, and toast—as only she could fix it. She sat across from him, gazing at him in adoration, waiting on him hand and foot while he ate ravenously. He remembered why he was so hungry, only one tuna fish and tomato sandwich in almost twenty-four hours. She fired questions at him while he continued to eat what he referred to as one of his pre-electric chair meals. He related the story substantially as it happened, leaving out the thirteen hundred he had snatched. He lied to her just as easily as he had lied to the captain. She never said a word, just put her hand to her mouth. As he ended, tears again rolled down her cheeks.

The sordid tale and breakfast finished, he pleaded exhaustion and excused himself to shower, change into pajamas, and go to bed. Not to mention hiding the thirteen hundred in the folds of a shirt in his bureau drawer. He wasn't in bed two minutes when Justine, stark naked and heavily perfumed, slid right next to him and before he could plead emotional drain or psychiatric depletion she was all over him. Her tongue was voracious, snaking inside his mouth, flickering across his chest, his nipples, back up inside his ears, panting like she did in their honeymoon days. His cock shot up, he grabbed her, turned her on her back and probably had the best lovemaking he'd had with her in a couple of years. When he finally came, he lay back almost as dead as the recent Angel Rivera, the Puerto Rican gunman, the slowest gun in the Caribbean.

He never opened his eyes until seven o'clock in the evening. He looked around, glad he was home, happy in the familiar surroundings. The last rays of the bleak fall sunlight were filtering through the softly swaying curtains of the open window of his bedroom. He was wide awake, as usual. The way the average cop wakes up whether from a radio car nap, a sneaked hour or two in a friendly coop, or at home next to his wife's ass. He was completely refreshed and lay back contemplatively and rehashed the events of the previous day.

Could all those wonderful things really have happened since I left the house about noon yesterday? He once again dwelt on beautiful Bobbi, the crackling fire, the white shag rug, the martinis—and the great loving. He thought of a word to describe her super tits. Conical! Should be magical! Her murderous bronzed body, the splashes of white in all the vital places. I wonder if by now she's heard or read of my whacking out those two guys last night? From Justine he now knew the pictures of him were in the white cashmere sweater. Good thinking after all the stakeout undercover horseshit I handed her. And the thirteen hundred lying over there snugly in my bureau drawer.

Beautiful, I'll take her out real nice Saturday night. Maybe dancing in New York. His face darkened. What will I do with Justine? Only for a minute. She'll probably be bowling, if not, I'll give her some bullshit story. I really shouldn't do this, she was so great this morning. She's a great lady and I really enjoyed that lay this morning. But new horizons are beckoning— I read that somewhere—perhaps even plainclothes as a result of last night. I liked the way Inspector McGeary looked me over. And the medals. What a horseshit world! Everyone for himself, and you first, Thomas.

Certainly new horizons are beckoning with Bobbi. He grinned, stretched lazily, maybe even new positions. I wonder if I should really be remorseful about killing two guys. Maybe I should put the act on—like I'm really shook, really sorry. Fuck them!

He got out of bed, went into the bathroom, relieved himself, plunged his face repeatedly in a sinkful of cold water and brushed his teeth.

"I'm up, Justine. Make me a Scotch on the rocks."

Justine never did go into work that afternoon. She maintained her vigil while he slept and answered in a low voice the many telephone calls he received, reassuring everyone that he was exhausted but otherwise in good shape. She handed him a list of the phone calls along with the brimming Scotch on the rocks. Several were from various guys he knew from the Job, but the most notable ones were from Grandma, his sister Rosemary, Vinny Ciano, and Mrs. Schuyler of the *Daily News*, who called twice. He just nodded his head at the latter—has to be some girl reporter seeking an interview—meanwhile complimenting Bobbi on her discretion.

He decided to call only Rosemary and Vinny. His sister first and Vince, who had left two numbers, one at home and one that had a familiar ring, second. He put Bobbi on hold until tomorrow, content to have a few drinks, and dinner at home with Justine.

It had been one of the most pleasant nights they spent together in years. Three nice Scotches on the rocks, beef stroganoff on a bed of brown rice for dinner, a couple of Remy Martin brandies after dinner, and another wild lovemaking session with Justine. When they finished making love she held on to him as if he were Rhett Butler about to leave the plantation. Sated at last, she finally started her soft, exhausted snore. He disentangled himself, sleepy but not quite ready to cork off. He contemplated his present and future life.

The first item on the agenda. Why does everyone expect me to be so shook up? Do I really have a conscience? The answer, truthfully—no! Oh, I guess I'm good in some ways, pretty square with my partners if they're square with me, but overall the only person whose welfare I'm interested in is Tommy Sloane. And to an extent, Justine, of course. But how can you remain not cynical in a world like this? The world is undoubtedly full of shit. Everyone is on the take, and all I hope is that I get my shot at plainclothes and my chance to live the good life. Yet, all they worry about is a cop who gets paid shit making an occasional buck from some meaningless horseshit. Big deal—bookies, number guys, crap or card games. What about everything else a cop has to face? Okay, the other night I had the drop on those two guys, had them almost at my mercy because they were two stupid fucks. But how about the next time out, maybe I'll be the one to get my ass shot off.

He patted Justine's firm ass. He almost laughed out loud—watch your ass, Justine. His thoughts turned to his new love girl, Bobbi, the Mrs. Schuyler of the *Daily News*. Lady reporter. I'll have to renew my strength tomorrow with my pal, Vincenzo, eat some pasta fazoole, veal parmesan, with plenty of red wine. Gee, I have to make sure I call her in the morning as soon as I wake up. His brain began to whirl—plainclothes, Inspector McGeary, Captain O'Connell, their faces smiling, shaking his hand, patting him on the back. He fell sound asleep.

Justine left a note on the kitchen table.

Sweetheart,

Off to work. You were sleeping so peacefully I didn't have the heart to wake you. I know you're having dinner with Vinny tonight and I'm with my company bowling group. Don't stay out too late, see you about midnight—

I love you—your Justine.

He couldn't believe it, he had slept until ten o'clock. He took a long shower, had just toweled himself dry, when he heard the bedroom phone ring. "Hello, Tom?"

He recognized her voice immediately.

"Yes, it is, Mrs. Schuyler, but I'm sorry, no more interviews today, I've been besieged by the press."

She roared laughing. "Oh, Tommy, I was so concerned. I was going crazy figuring a way to get in touch with you, to see if you were all right. I knew it was your wife on the phone, so I just pretended I was a reporter from the *News*. Oh, baby, I was so shook up. I was sitting having my morning coffee and all of a sudden your face flashed on the TV screen and the story of the shooting. I nearly fainted. Are you alone? Can you talk?"

"Yes, Bobbi, I'm home all alone."

"You got the two guys for whom you were on stakeout, right, Tom?"

Already a lady cop!

"I got them, honey, killed both of them. Their stick-up days are over."

"Oh, Tommy, it must have been awful."

He could almost feel her shuddering, quivering, on the other end of the line. The catch in her voice excited him. Christ, I'm beginning to get hot all over again, I feel like running out to Bayside. I must be going crazy. Cool it, pal, the captain is surely due to call today. Stay put, Thomas.

"Well, it was a little hairy for a while, sweetheart, but I only had one shot that almost hit me."

Her voice rose. "Almost hit you. My God. Where?"

He smiled, not where you're thinking, dear.

"I was wearing a lumber jacket on the stakeout," he lied inventively, "and one bullet tore through the top of my left sleeve, near my shoulder."

"Oh, my God, Tom, a foot over and it would have hit your heart. You'd have been killed. Oh, my God, how terrible."

Just the reaction he expected.

"Relax, babe, I'm all right. Fine. And don't repeat that to anyone, it's all very confidential. You can never let the underworld know a cop nearly got knocked off."

"Of course, Tom, I understand. I'll never repeat it. Oh, darling. I'm so glad you didn't get hurt. You know, seriously, I had a premonition, bad vibes about you when you left. Then when I turned the TV on to get the early news and saw you, I nearly died."

"Didn't I tell you that you were really a gypsy mind reader and missed your true calling."

She laughed, now gaily, no longer apprehensive.

"When I see you I'll wear a long skirt and a sequined headband. I'll be a real gypsy for you."

"Swell, but no headbands. Headbands remind me of somebody in my past." Mostly the recently departed Angel Rivera.

"Anything you say, love. Are we on for tomorrow?"

"Absolutely, unless something completely unforeseen comes up. Did you make up a game?"

"Yes, a good match. Are we going out later?"

"Sure thing. Dance, dance, dance. Okay?"

"Super, Tom. One o'clock at the club."

"Fine. One thing, Bobbi, I don't think I can stay all night."

Disappointed voice, depressed. "Why not?"

"I'm supposed to be on tap for further interrogation. You know, just in case," he lied glibly. "After all, babe, I did kill two guys and you know all the civil liberties crap something like that entails."

Mollified, subdued, once more aware that she was speaking to an authentic hero.

"All right, love, I understand. Tommy, I can't wait to see you."

"Good-bye, love."

He took a taxicab across the Queensboro Bridge and arrived at Mike Manuche's restaurant at Second Avenue and Forty-seventh Street, shortly before five-thirty. He had taken particular pains to dress carefully. Light gray three-piece suit, white button-down shirt and dark blue knitted tie. Waiting for Vinny at the bar, which was heavily bedecked with pictures of famous figures of the sporting world hanging between and above the light brown wooden panels interposed among the large back bar mirrors, he ordered a Cutty Sark on the rocks. As he raised the glass to his lips he caught a full front view of himself in the mirror. He decided unequivocally that he looked great. The bar was just beginning to fill up with well-dressed guys and sophisticated-looking, elegantly dressed women when Vince arrived.

He spotted Tom at the far end of the bar, hurried to him, gave him a big hug and a kiss on the cheek.

Tommy feigned a swaying of the lower body, as if he were about to faint. "Oh, Vince, you Italians are so emotional. I really didn't know you cared so much."

Vinny laughed, gave him another bear hug, stepped back and looked him over minutely.

"I swear, you Irish bastard, you never looked better in your life. You sure came a long way from pushing the old wheelbar-row. Where'd you get the tan? Christ, you look more like a wop than I do."

Tommy clutched his heart. "Please, don't say that."

They both laughed, delighted to see each other.

"I joined a tennis club out in Bayside. Very fancy, real nice. I'm playing a lot, as much as I can. I love the game. And how about you? You keeping in shape?"

"Pretty fair, Tom, I feel good. I swim on the arm at the Hotel Biltmore pool a couple of times a week, then take a sauna bath. I also have a friend who belongs to the N.Y.A.C. and he arranges a guest card whenever I want, so I get a good workout there every couple of weeks. I love the place. Now that I'm a confirmed New Yorker I'd really love to become a member someday."

"You like living in the city, Vince?"

"Tommy, I swear to God, I love it. My wife, Connie, loves it. My new son, Anthony, loves it. That reminds me. When are you and Justine coming over to see the baby?"

They touched glasses good luck, sizing each other up. Friends for over four years now, best friends. Both dressed beautifully, the image of two young professional or career men. A long way out of the overalls and cement shoes. Proud of each other.

Tommy told Vince the story in a low voice. He didn't embellish it, didn't bullshit him, told him the exact truth. How he left old Charley Malloy in the radio car when he got the tip because he figured Charley would be useless anyway. He told him that he honestly thought the two spics would give up without a fight once he threw a couple of shots in the ceiling and told them they were surrounded. How surprised he was when they elected to shoot it out. Then how he counted the number of bullets fired, just like rookie school. Then, their surrender when they ran out of ammunition. And then, how he whacked them both out.

Vinny listened intently throughout his narrative, occasionally nodding his head affirmatively. When he finished, Vin waved to the bartender, ordered two more Scotches on the rocks. He waited for the bartender to serve them, reached for his glass, motioned Tom to reach for his, and actually clanked his glass against Tom's.

"Beautiful, beautiful, Tommy. That's what we all gotta do. Whack those heist bastards out, that's the name of the game. But Jesus Christ, Tom, did you realize what a chance you took? Honestly, I love you, but it was an idiotic thing to do. Now, all kidding aside. Forget dumb wop or dumb mick, wasn't it a crazy move?"

"Now that it's over I agree completely, Vince. I guess I'm overanxious. I'm so determined to make the one big collar to get me out of uniform and into plainclothes I swear I'd almost take any kind of a chance. I admit it was stupid. But like I said,

I thought sure they'd give up when I threw up a couple of shots. They must have been on some kind of junk to make them so brave."

Vinny knew now that he had opened himself up to real department danger but was at least glad that Tommy understood it.

"Now for some good news. Fat Georgie is a very good friend of my father-in-law, Charlie. He evidently raved to Charlie about you. The timing couldn't be better. There's one or two openings coming up in the Borough West Squad. Charlie has a lot of things going on the West Side. Legit things. He's been a good friend of the deputy chief's for almost thirty years, since the chief was a young cop. Tom, if we can pull this off you'll be the happiest guy on the Job. Next to the two five-borough squads—the chief's office and the P.C.'s squad—the Borough West is the sweetest touch in the city. What do you think?"

"I think it's terrific, Vince, but what about you? Why aren't you trying for this job with guys like Charlie punching for you?"

"For one simple reason, Tom, and you're the first cop to know. I'm quitting the Job, submitting my resignation as of the first of the year."

Tommy's face registered his shock. "You're kidding me, Vin, cut it out."

"I swear to God, Tom, I'm leaving, my mind is made up. I'm just gonna stick around for the Christmas money. I couldn't care less about that except I don't want to leave my regular radio car partner, Joey Morrison, with a new guy to worry about trusting around holiday time."

"But why? Why are you leaving the Job? I thought you loved it. I can't believe it." Tommy really didn't expect an answer.

Vince shook his head in amazement as he intently listened to Tommy. This Irish bastard is the luckiest guy in the world to escape with the bullshit story he handed the bosses. He couldn't resist a smile as he studied Tommy's face. What a convincing liar—walk into a world class shootout without calling first for a backup and come out an all time hero. That's my Tommy boy. He put his arm around him and said, "Now for some good news, etc. etc. . . ."

"Look, forget it, for lots of reasons. We'll talk about it over dinner. I've made a reservation at Frankie and Johnnie's on West Forty-fifth Street. After we eat we'll go around to see my father-in-law, Charlie, who wants to talk to you. I'll explain everything over dinner."

Vinny received a big welcome from Johnny Phillips, the owner of Frankie and Johnnie's, one of the better steakhouses in New York, the city of great steakhouses. It was an unexpectedly well-done, intimate restaurant on the second floor of a non-descript building on the corner of Eighth Avenue. The decor was theatrical, with paintings, prints, and blowups of ads for hit shows—past and present—adorning the walls. Tommy looked it over, approved, a nice place. Johnny Phillips seated them at a corner table for two overlooking the hustle, bustle, scheming, conniving street of Eighth Avenue.

They ordered two Cutty Sarks on the rocks. Tommy leaned over to Vince, low voice. "Looks pretty expensive here, and this isn't in the Seventeenth so you're not on the cuff. What's the score?"

"Don't worry about a thing, Irish. Charlie has already called Johnny and the tab is on him."

"Great! But I wasn't worrying, I have a couple of hundred in my pocket."

"A couple of hundred? You mean to say things are that good in the Twenty-third?"

"I didn't tell you the *pièce de résistance*." He then related to Vince about grabbing the crap game bankroll out of the dead stick-up guy's pocket, skimming off thirteen hundred for himself, and giving the bulk of the money back to Steve Maselli.

"Beautiful—" Vinny's favorite adjective—"beautiful. I tell you, for an Irishman you're getting smarter every time I see you. You'll make some helluva plainclothesman. And it was good thinking to give the bankroll back to the crap game boss. You'll be a trusted guy from here on."

"It won't get back to your father-in-law, will it, Vince, about the thirteen hundred?"

"For Christ sake, of course not. We're like brothers, Tom,

and I would've done the same goddam thing. You saved them over fifteen grand from what I heard. They're tickled pink."

"Fifteen grand? How'd you know that?"

"Charlie was visiting Connie and the kid when I came home from work yesterday. He had already seen your name in the paper and your picture on TV. He must have already called uptown and got the lowdown. Naturally, he knew what great friends you and I are. He figures that I was anxious as hell about you and he reassured me that everything was fine. He wants to talk to you. Okay?"

"Sure. I'd love to see Charlie again."

They ordered salad, steak, and hashed brown potatoes. The meal was delicious. Finished, Vince ordered coffee and two Remy Martins. Tommy savored the pungent aroma of the fine brandy, patted his contented stomach, and realized that he was on his first step in learning how the really rich live. He knew he'd get there someday.

"Okay, walio, you've had the floor all night. Let's get to the main point. Why are you leaving the Job?"

"It's very simple, Tommy. As you know, my wife, Connie, is their only child. To say they love her, little Anthony, and me is the understatement of the year. Maria, my mother-in-law, I think I told you before, has cancer. Had both breasts removed. Anyway, they have a place in Boca Raton, Florida, where they want to live most of the year. By the way, Tom, she's a wonderful woman, like a mother to me. Charlie wants me to run his business. All strictly legit. Oh, of course, there's some shit attached I'm not so crazy about. You know, a go-go girl dance place, a taxi dance hall, a couple of fag joints. But he has a few real strong places, a beautiful Italian restaurant right near here, a busy commuter bar in Penn Station, and a really wild young people's dance place. You know, like rock-and-roll shit. It's called the Candy Mint Lounge. You won't believe your eyes when you see it. Charlie wants to give me five hundred a week on the books and five hundred off the books. And that's just for starters. How about that? Now, wouldn't you give that a shot if it was offered to you?"

"Jesus, Vin, it sounds terrific."

"Now I'll fill you in further. He's got a bad feeling about my being on the Job. It's not that he's ashamed of my being a cop. He loves the idea, introduces me to all his buddies. But he feels that there's another explosion coming. We've become very close and he doesn't want me to take a chance and maybe get jammed up. He did a bit in Elmira when he was a kid and he hates jail with a passion. He's sixty-seven, everybody in the mob loves him, so he just wants to go to Florida, play a little golf, and hope and pray her cancer was caught in time. Now, you get the picture. You go into the Borough West where most of our business is and make sure you take care of your blood brother Vinny or I'll kick the shit out of you. Okay, come on, let's go see Papa Charlie."

He signed Charlie's name to the check, generous tip and all, they both shook hands with Johnny Phillips on the way out and walked down Eighth Avenue one block to West Forty-fourth Street. They turned east past Seventh Avenue and Broadway, finally stopping at Villa Pompei. Vinny nodded his head and winked, the indication that this was Charlie's fine Italian restaurant. They entered, Tommy looked the place over, glanced at his watch—ten minutes past nine. H'mm, for a restaurant in the theatrical district long after curtain time it was doing a helluva business.

Vinny led Tommy to the rear where Charlie was seated with two other guys. One, by his tremendous girth, had to be Fat Georgie. Charlie leaped up at the sight of Vinny approaching and embraced him as if he had just returned from the wartime rigors of Anzio Beach. He also embraced Tom, though not as fervently. Introductions were made all around. Fat Georgie gave Tom a crushing handshake that almost made him wince.

They both ordered Remy, while Charlie, Fat Georgie, and a guy named Patsy, who was probably Fat Georgie's bodyguard, drank red wine. The initial amenities over, Charlie spoke.

"Tommy, the other night you handled yourself like a pro. I don't mean just killing those two sonofabitches, but how good you were to Steve Maselli and how you had enough sense to snatch the bankroll off the dead spic and give it to Steve before the bulls got there. To me, and Georgie here, who's been my friend for over thirty years, you showed a lot of class. George, I know you want to say something to Tom."

In a surprisingly even, well-modulated voice, Fat Georgie said, "I think Charlie just about summed it up. You have the thanks of myself and my men. I've heard nice things about you, Tommy. It was also a very decent thing you did to make sure young Johnny Blue was taken to the hospital in the ambulance. By the way, Tom, they had to put twenty stitches in the poor kid's head where that bastard hit him with the gun."

He reached into his inside coat pocket and came up with a long white envelope.

"Here's a little token of my appreciation, Tom, and that goes for the rest of my guys. This is all yours, strictly yours. Everyone else involved got taken care of. You understand, right, Tom?"

Tom slipped the envelope, which felt nice and thick, into his inside coat pocket. It caused the jacket of his new suit to bulge a little, but he said a secret prayer that the same kind of action would always cause his coat to bulge a little. "Thanks a lot, George, you really didn't have to do that," he said modestly. "You guys uptown are more than nice to the precinct guys and we all like you."

"Good, I'm glad to hear it, Tom. All you guys in the house, plus the bulls, know how we do business. Only gambling houses, numbers, games—and a couple of after-hour clubs. No broads, no junk, no schmeck of any sort, and that's no bull-shit."

With that manifesto, Fat Georgie arose from the table, Patsy also dutifully arose, both shook Tommy's hand, kissed Vinny and Charlie and left.

As they were walking towards the front door of the restaurant Tommy put on a troubled face, like a pouting child. Vinny looked at him quizzically.

"What's up? Why the long face?"

"Aw, gee, why didn't I get a kiss good-bye?"

That broke up Vinny and Charlie.

The laughter subsided, Charlie again got serious, leaned across the table, face close to Tom and said, "Tommy, I assume by now that Vinny has told you about his quitting the Job and managing my affairs. I guess you can see by now that I love Vinny as if he were the son I never had. He's good to Connie, he's given me a grandson, and knowing how close you two are, I think you'll agree he's a helluva kid."

Tom, feeling the Scotches and the brandy, made a doubtful face, shrugged his shoulders. Another big laugh.

"You should be an actor instead of a cop. Anyway, here's the story. There's an opening coming up in the Borough West squad in a couple of weeks. One of the men is being made sergeant in the next set of appointments off the sergeant's list. Should be no longer than a couple of weeks. I had Vince scheduled for the vacancy, but the more I thought about it the more I hated the idea. Let's face it, Tom, plainclothes is no bed of roses. I've been around New York a long time. I've seen more cops get into trouble over run-of-the-mill shit, minor stuff, than I could ever believe. Some headline-hungry young D.A.—or the press themselves—love the publicity they get out of nailing a cop. I've seen some good cop friends of mine go to jail and to be honest it broke my heart. I don't wish going to jail on anybody. If it ever happened to Vinny I think I'd go crazy. We talked it over, he's going to resign and stay with me. He'll run my operations, all legit. He'll make plenty of money and when I die, he, Connie, and their kids will have everything anyway.

"Now here's where you come in. The deputy chief of the Borough West squad, Eddie Moclair, is a personal friend of mine from way back, since he was a young cop. He originally had the contract for Vince, but now, especially after the publicity you got killing those two spics, you're a natural to be his replacement. You get it, Tom. So far, so good."

So far, so good! The best news of my entire life. He nodded.

"All right, that's about it. We'll get the ball rolling next Monday and you should get the word in a week or so. Okay, enough talk. Let's have one more drink and get home to our wives where we belong."

They said good-bye to Charlie amidst plenty of hugging and kissing. Tommy's feet were hardly touching the sidewalk as they wended their way towards the East Side. His head was in the clouds and his feet were dancing on air. Vinny was talking a mile a minute as he usually did with half a load on. Tom was nodding yes, interjecting an occasional "That's right, you're right, Vince. One hundred percent right. No question about it, Vin," but meanwhile his brain was whirling with one word—plainclothes. Better yet, plainclothes in the Borough West. The Borough West, four sweet divisions in the really swinging part of New York City.

They turned into East Forty-sixth Street, then into Park Avenue, and continued uptown. The city was ablaze under the clear, starry skies and the lights emanating from the tall office buildings and gracious hotels that lined both sides of lovely Park Avenue, the most beautiful street in old New York.

They reached the fifties and Vinny asked Tom if he'd like a nightcap. Tommy, now cold sober in spite of all the drinks, his brain pulsating a mile a minute as he meditated upon his recent good fortune, readily agreed. A good idea. He was anxious to confide in Vince about his new love affair, his passionate infatuation with Bobbi, how he couldn't seem to get her out of his mind. He was reluctant to bring it out earlier, waiting for what he perceived to be the correct time. He knew that Vince was a staunch family guy from the old school, doubted that he had ever cheated on Connie since he met her.

They walked over one block to Lexington Avenue and stopped at a small bar. Vinny ordered two Cutty Sarks on the rocks, positively the last drink of the night. Solemn promise. They tipped glasses good luck as always and Vinny continued talking. Half-listening, Tommy meanwhile was trying to determine exactly how to bring up the delicate subject of Bobbi Schuyler. Vinny finally came to a pause.

"Let's get off the topic of the Job for a minute, Vin, I've got a problem I'd like to discuss with you. It's kind of personal and you're the only one I can confide in."

"What'd you do, kill somebody else?"

"No, worse than that. I think I'm falling in love with another woman."

"Another woman? Are you serious? When did all this happen?"

He proceeded to relate the impasse he had reached with Justine. Life with her was beginning to bore him, particularly the night after night listening to her bowling bullshit. How he had become fascinated with Bobbi at the tennis club. How strikingly beautiful she was, and, without going into the intimate details, what a wonderful lover she was. Since he'd been with her he just couldn't get her out of his mind.

"She live out there?"

"A mansion, practically, overlooking Long Island Sound."

"She married?"

"Twice, but now she's a widow."

Incredulously—"A widow?" He motioned to the bartender. "We better have another drink."

The drinks came, they tipped again, silently took long pulls on the fresh Scotches.

"You say, a widow, right. How old?"

"Thirty-six."

"Well, like all broads she's probably chopping off a few. Giving her the best of it she's nine, ten years older than you, right?"

"Whatever, she looks terrific."

"And you don't feel the same about Justine any more?"

"Vince, that's the strange thing. I still feel tender towards her, she's a good wife. But like I said, she's slowly boring me to death."

"You want my advice?" Sounding like the Pope.

"What the hell am I telling you all this for?"

"Okay, take it easy. Tom, all I can say is that you live with a woman a few years—she's bound to bore you occasionally. Especially if you don't have kids together to occupy half your life. Me, I'm content with Connie. I'm crazier about her now than the first day I met her, and I nearly dropped dead at the sight of her that day. She's so much better educated than me, she's widened my interests a thousand percent. She's a great wife and the best lover I've ever had. What the hell more can a guy want?

"But understand, Tom, Connie's a big city girl. Justine is a small town girl. Bowling, TV, and all that stuff you complain about are big things to her. You asked my advice, for Christ sake don't do anything rash. Have a fling with this chick, Bobbi, get it out of your system. Roll with the punches with Justine, Tom, she's a good kid. You got a good wife, remember that."

With these sage words of wisdom they finished their drinks, paid their tab, and left the bar. They walked further uptown and parted company with bear hugs at Fifty-ninth Street and Second Avenue, where Tommy caught a cab across the Queensboro Bridge and home. On the way he removed the white envelope Fat Georgie gave him from his inside coat pocket and to his delight found a thousand-dollar wrapper around a crisp sheaf of twenty-dollar bills. Another wonderful night!

He had just placed the fresh thousand between the folds of another shirt in his bureau drawer and settled into bed when Justine arrived home. She undressed, finished her ablutions in the bathroom quickly and snuggled up next to him, clinging to his back. He pretended that he was in a deep sleep, only rousing himself briefly to pat her hand. He murmured what he hoped was an exhausted "How are you, hon?" and breathed very deeply. No way, babe, not tonight. I'm saving all my strength for tomorrow. He quickly fell asleep. He dreamed that he and Bobbi were playing Pancho Gonzales and Maureen Connolly for the national mixed doubles title on center court at Forest Hills.

He again woke up late, almost ten o'clock. He heard Justine bustling about the kitchen, fixing breakfast. He washed up and appeared in the kitchen dressed in white slacks, shirt, and sweater. He was hungry, ready for another of Justine's usual great Saturday morning breakfasts. She described in minute detail the previous night's bowling, he nodding brightly between mouthfuls of sausages and eggs as she carried on as if describing the women's Olympic Games. He never mentioned the prospect of going into plainclothes to her, merely saying that they had a wonderful dinner, great night, and Vince was very funny and particularly asked to be remembered to her. While he ate and listened to her prattling on, he was silently scheming what kind of excuse he was going to make about tonight. Traditionally, on the rare Saturday nights that he was off work, they always went out together—at least to a movie or for a few drinks and dinner in one of the good neighborhood restaurants along Queens Boulevard.

"Tom, you look like you're dressed for playing tennis today, and I saw your garment bag on the living room sofa. What's up?"

"That's right, hon. I'm due out there at the club in a couple of hours."

"What time will you be home?"

"Gee, I forgot to tell you the reason for the garment bag. I might have to work tonight. Like I told you, the captain called me yesterday and spoke to me for a long time."

Her face fell, at least a foot. Sharply—"You said he called, but what has that got to do with tonight?"

He assumed an exasperated pose, got up from the kitchen table shaking his head in despair. He threw his hands in the air and said, "I don't know what the hell they expect from me in this Job. I think they're trying to drive me crazy." His voice almost breaking.

Suddenly alarmed, fear in her voice, she arose, walked to him and put her arms around him, consolingly. "Oh, Tom, what is it? Don't get so upset. Please, calm down, sweetheart."

He turned to her, looked into her face with pleading eyes. "The captain said they got a tip that there was another guy involved in the stick-up. He was outside in the getaway car. The squad detectives think they know where his hangout is, where we can pick him up. They want me to be in on the arrest, think maybe it'll help me make the detective bureau or plainclothes. You know, hon, I hate to leave you, but orders are orders, especially in the Job."

For a spur of the moment alibi, Tom, you get the All American Liar's Award.

Relieved voice, smiling again—"Oh, Tom, of course I understand. You had me worried for a minute, all the tension, all you've been through. I know how hard you've worked and how you risked your life to get ahead in the Job. You go ahead and do whatever you have to do. I'll go to church tonight with the girls I bowl with and play cards afterwards. Don't worry about me, dear, I'll be fine."

Pain now excised from his face, rueful grin—"Swell, Justine. I'm so glad you have something to keep you busy."

As long as she's in this mood I might as well make plans for many a future night in front of the fireplace!

"You see, Justine, there's a whole gang of stick-up guys up there and by luck it seems that the two guys I shot were apparently the gang leaders. The inspector, McGeary, and Captain O'Connell are determined to wipe them all out. For some reason they want me to work along on the case. Could be plenty of hours, might mean plenty of late nights, but if I make plainclothes it will be all worth it."

The words came out of his mouth so easily that *he* almost believed them.

She hugged him, kissed his mouth. "Tom, like I said, do what you have to do. Just don't get hurt, I love you too much."

He received a very friendly welcome at the tennis club from Pedro, the Cuban locker room man, all the way to most of the members he met. Good work the other night, Tom—good boy, Tom—nice going, Tom—plenty of handshakes. He opened his locker and on top of his tennis sneakers lay a large gift box, labeled Saks Fifth Avenue. A white envelope was entwined among the red ribbons. He opened the envelope. "To my stakeout hero—love, your gypsy mind reader."

He couldn't resist a grin as he opened the package and was overwhelmed by what he saw inside. An obviously expensive, gorgeous, white cable-stitched tennis sweater with the traditional navy blue and red v-neck. He had always wanted a sweater like this, but thought they were sort of ostentatious. Particularly when he watched some of the members strolling around the club inevitably clad in one of them. Astute as always, he noted that it was usually the worst players parading around in the fancy sweaters. But now he held his new prize in hand, nuzzled the soft, fleecy wool, and renewed his vow of love for Bobbi.

She didn't see him approach, but as she turned toward him, she looked so beautiful his knees momentarily got weak. She just looked into his eyes and shook her head. Her look said enough. He wore his new sweater across his back with the sleeves tied around the front of his neck, just like he saw Billy Talbert, Rod Laver, and his idol, Pancho Gonzales, wear their sweaters on TV. He winked at Bobbi, pointed to the sweater, mouthed a thank you, puffed a kiss.

They took their positions on the court and began the usual warm-up volley for seven or eight minutes. Their opponents were Bea Blaine and her sweetheart, Harold Furash, a couple in their early forties, but both excellent players. Bea, short, firm, and shapely, was reputed to be an ex-nightclub dancer and she still retained her old chorus girl agility. Harold was a college basketball referee, a little slow but a good player. Some of the guys at the club kidded him and referred to him as half-court Harold, because he never tired himself running up and down the basketball court, making the infraction calls from midcourt with what he termed unerring judgment.

They played for the usual drinks afterward and lost the first set eight-six, but won the second set seven-five. The play was so intense and enjoyable that the four of them unanimously decided to call it quits after the second set. They had been playing without interruption for over two hours and were all beginning to tire. Tom was delighted by this decision as he knew that a long night stretched ahead of him. Harold and Tom each bought a round of drinks in the club lounge and he and Bobbi excused themselves. Tom explained that he had to go to work and Bobbi pleaded an early dinner date. As they walked towards the locker rooms Bobbi told Tom that she would wait outside for him.

He showered, toweled himself dry, sprayed deodorant liberally under each armpit and doused his cheeks and chest with Aqua Velva. He dressed carefully in the clothes that he packed in the garment bag. Dark gray flannel slacks, navy blue blazer, blue oxford button-down shirt, striped tie, and new French Shriner black loafers. He studied himself painstakingly in the locker room mirror and decided he looked every inch the image of a sharp Borough West squad plainclothesman.

Bobbi was patiently waiting in the parking lot, still in her tennis clothes, as he came outside. He pulled up behind her in the driveway about ten minutes later and stopped only momentarily to admire the scintillating waterfront view. He had more urgent business on his mind. She was just inside the living room when he reached her and came into his arms immediately. The next five minutes were a complete haze. Their lovemaking was almost frantic. Tom was naked, out of his clothes in ten seconds flat, Bobbi in five seconds flat. She was half-heartedly protesting that he should wait, at least let her shower, but the combination of her perfume and the animal acrid but sweet smell of her body after the strenuous tennis almost drove him crazy.

Finally, the world stopped spinning and the earth stopped moving as they lay spent in each others arms after what he positively identified in his mind as the best fuck of his entire life. He kissed her ear.

"Here we are again, babe, on the old shag rug."

She laughed, hugged him close, kissed him on the lips.

"Oh, Tommy, that was simply wonderful, maybe it is the rug. But, ooh, Tom, now I'm really sweating. I'm sorry. Let me up so I can shower."

He responded by kissing her mouth, the ring of perspiration on her neck, the beads of sweat between her breasts, and couldn't resist sucking the dark pink nipples of her fabulous tits.

"Tom, please, you're turning me on again. Let me up—Oh, I love you, sweetheart." She pushed him away, sat up, caressed his hair. "Put some clothes on, you wild man. I'll be back in a few minutes smelling like a rose and bearing ice-cold drinks."

She was standing. "What's your pleasure?"

He raised his head, peered at her through half-closed eyes, marveling at her perfect body. He laughed. "My pleasure? You really want to know?"

She laughed. "C'mon, silly. We're going dancing, remember? I'm dying to see if you dance as well as you play tennis and other things."

"What other things am I good at?"

"Don't be a smart ass. What do you want? A martini?"

"Martini? No good, too early. How about a nice Scotch on the rocks, water on the side. Okay, babe?"

"Super, love. I'll put a robe on, bring in the drinks, then I'll shower."

"Forget the shower for a while, for Christ sake. You smell great, relax. Bring out the drinks and we'll take it easy. It's not even five o'clock yet."

He got up from his beloved shag rug and put on his shorts, slacks, and shirt. He stretched out contentedly on one of the sofas. Unbelievable! I can't seem to get enough of her. What a body! And sweet as sugar, good tennis player, intelligent—boy, Tommy baby, have I got a girl for you. I'm not leaving her tonight under any circumstances. Give me Bobbi Schuyler or give me death! He broke into a grin. Christ, I have to call Justine later and tell her we're hot on the trail of the mythical getaway driver. Don't wait up for me, dear, it looks like a very late night. Sure does, here comes my baby with a bottle of Johnny Walker Black, a bowl of ice cubes, a pitcher of water, and two on the rocks glasses. I knew she never left Heaven!

After she made the two Scotches, she tipped his glass and settled on the sofa opposite him.

"Okay, my hero, tell me just what happened to you the other night. I was so frantic the next morning when I saw you on TV I was ready to die. I can't believe how you bounced back, how great you look. Tell me honestly, any repercussions, any remorse, any hangups?"

"Not a single one, babe. They were two very bad guys," he said modestly, lowering his eyes and sipping his drink. He then proceeded to again recite the wild garage shootout, explaining how he and his stakeout partner happened to separate, his partner tailing two of the gang and he the other two that led him to the garage. He lied easily, convincingly, with an innocent face. Between sips of his drink he matter-of-factly described, very low key, his heroics.

"They actually fired twelve shots at you." Her eyes registered horror.

"It seems like a hundred, but that's how many spent cartridges the homicide detectives found."

"And one pierced your lumber jacket at the shoulder, only missed your heart by a foot?"

Face now very grave, humbly—"I sure got lucky, I guess."

"Oh, Tom, thank God. Ooh, I get panic-stricken just thinking about it." She finished her drink, crossed to his sofa and kissed him. "Enough of this talk for the night or I'll go into a depression. Make yourself another drink, darling, while I go in and shower." She turned to leave, he grabbed her robe from the rear, lifted it and slapped her smartly on her lovely ass.

She jumped a little—"Oh, Tom, you're so fresh—" pulled away and turned towards him as she was leaving the living room. "Where are we going tonight?"

"How about New York, some fancy place?"

"Not really, Tom. Let's stay on the Island. I thought we might go to a great restaurant out near Oyster Bay. They have wonderful seafood and on weekends have a real good band for dancing. Okay with you?"

"Sounds fine. Go ahead, scrub up and look beautiful for me."

They left Bobbi's house about seven thirty and following her directions, drove her car to a picturesque waterfront restaurant. It was her recommendation, Captain Hook's, and it was a superb choice. The place was still almost half-empty and Tom slipped the maitre d' a fiver. He led them to an extreme corner table for two overlooking the Sound. In his usual cop fashion he noted the many features of the decor as he followed the maitre d' and was very pleased. Long Island nautical all the way. Life preservers, ships' bells, heavy coils of rope, mahogany sailing yacht replicas, blowups of pleasure craft pictures and all sorts of boating gear adorned the walls of the restaurant. The chandeliers lighting the room hung at scattered intervals, their bases consisting of spoked ships' steering wheels. Yessir, very nautical, pleasing to an old navy man.

The restaurant began to fill rapidly and they had just ordered their second drink when the band arrived. It consisted of four early middle-aged-looking men playing piano, bass fiddle, drums, trombone, and a much older-looking guy who played clarinet and trumpet. To Tom's delight, the first set they played was all Glen Miller, Hal Kemp, and Tommy Dorsey music; the type of music his sister Rosemary had taught him to dance to. From the enraptured look on Bobbi's face as she turned listening to the easy, muted trumpet leading the quintet through a series of sweet jazz hits of the late forties and early fifties, he knew that she loved the same sound as he did. She snapped her fingers rhythmically and stood up.

"All right, my hero. You've been hinting around what a great dancer you are, let's put you to the test."

"Okay, sweetie, you will shortly be in the arms of the Bishop Molloy Fred Astaire."

The dance floor was polished parquet, quite spacious, and as yet, not too crowded. She fit perfectly into his arms and danced as well as she played tennis. And—he grinned slyly—did other things. The band slipped into a bouncy rendition of "Tuxedo Junction" and the gray-haired trumpet player took the lid off and almost blew Captain Hook's bistro right out into the adjoining water. He dazzled her with a smooth, fast foxtrot blended into sporadic spurts of the Lindy Hop, throwing her out and weaving her underneath an extended arm, giving her plenty of whirls and curls as they finished up with a flourish just as the set ended. They both laughed happily in unison as they walked off the dance floor back to their table.

"You know something, you never cease to amaze me. You're just as good a dancer as you are a tennis player."

"Thank you. And how about, ah—and other things?"

She laughed, a lovely, light laugh, sipped her drink and shook her head with an amused gleam in her eye. "I don't want you to get too conceited, so I won't answer that wise guy question."

He smiled the benign smile the conqueror bestows on one of his captive subjects. He scrutinized her again as he took a long belt of his new tall Scotch and water. Beautiful, she owns the word. She wore a simple black and white polka dot dress that emphasized her curly, dark blond hair and deep tan. Substantial gold earrings, necklace, and bracelets on either arm. No wedding band to remind her of days gone by, just an ample diamond ring on the fourth finger of her left hand. Elegant. He felt proud, sitting opposite her. He said, "Before I start to tell you how great you dance, Rita Hayworth, which might take an hour, let's order dinner."

"Oh, you flatterer. But I love it. You're right, let's order. Will you allow me to suggest?"

"Suggest? Christ, Bobbi, not here, right at the table!"

She burst into laughter, cupped her hand over her mouth, leaned towards him. "Not again, you sex maniac. C'mon, I mean dinner. I suggest the seafood dinner—shrimp cocktail, clam chowder, and filet of sole. That sound fine with you?"

"Great. And a bottle of good white wine to go along with it."

She motioned to the waiter and gave their order. The dinner and wine were both excellent. They both ate with the ravenous appetites gained from a few hours of good tennis, good sex, and good Scotch whiskey. Finished dinner, they again danced to the melodious strains of "Dancing in the Dark," "Time on My Hands," and "Stardust." They glided about the dance floor cheek to cheek, Tom savoring the fragrance of her hair as he held her close. They walked back to their table as the set once again ended and he ordered two Remy Martin brandies and a pot of coffee.

Bobbi leaned across the table, face close to his. "Tom, I don't know how to say this, but I know the dinner check will be pretty expensive. Can I help? Forgive me if I'm wrong, but I know cops in New York aren't exactly overpaid."

He laughed. "No, babe, you're right. Grossly underpaid would be right. But I happen to be fortunate enough to have inherited an income from my father's estate to help me financially." He lied just as easily and glibly to Bobbi as he lied to Justine. A real pro.

"It's only a little over six hundred a month, but it sure helps."

"That's wonderful, Tom. Gee, dear, your father must have died young."

"Yes, he had one of those lingering diseases, but luckily he didn't last too long." He sure had a lingering disease, the same lingering disease a lot of the Irish have—booze. He smiled sadly. "He was a real great guy—" another monstrous lie.

She patted his hand consolingly, looked up with widened eyes as a couple approached their table.

"My God, look who's here! Jane and Harvey Thompson! What a surprise!"

He stood up, shook hands with Jane and Harvey, a couple whom he barely recognized from the tennis club, and invited them to sit down and have a drink.

The four of them engaged in small talk about the club, their tennis prowess, the excellent food and marvelous band here at Captain Hook's. Tom ordered two more Remy Martin brandies and two vodka and tonics for the Thompsons. The two girls arose and excused themselves to repair their makeup and whatever else girls do in the powder room.

Harvey longingly eyed the swinging, beautiful, retreating black polka-dot ass of Bobbi and said, "Great girl, isn't she, Tom?"

"Bobbi's a lot of fun, a real nice person." He felt an inquisition about to take place, parried the inquiry neatly.

Harvey leaned across the table in his best imitation of a C.I.A. agent, winked, and said in a low voice, "I hear she's a terrific piece of ass, Tommy."

He sat back thunderstruck, blinked, felt as if his head was about to explode. If he had an axe handy he would have chopped Harvey's ugly face in. He gripped the end of the table, made a strenuous effort to remain calm, not to put his fist right through this stupid bastard's big nose.

A trifle hoarse, but evenly, he said, "I wouldn't know, Harve, and if I did I wouldn't discuss it with anybody," looking straight into Harvey's bloodshot eyes. He was about to go on, but now shocked into complete sobriety himself, it dawned on him that good old Harvey was smashed out of his mind.

Harvey took a long swallow of his vodka and tonic. "Look, no hard feelings, Tom, but I'm not revealing any secrets. At least six or seven guys in the club fucked her." He laughed drunkenly. "Teddy Grant told us she almost screwed him to death one night on a white shag rug in front of the fireplace. The way he described it, the rug, the fireplace—Christ, I think I'd be willing to die that way. She's got some figure, some good-looking woman."

Tom sat back listening to his dreams being crushed with a half smile, but inwardly his mind was reeling as if he had been hit by a truck. What the hell am I going to do with this drunken, mouthy cocksucker? Challenge him to a duel? He was in his late forties, wore thick eyeglasses, had a prominent paunch, and by reputation was one of the worst tennis players in the club—if not in America. I'd love to backhand him right across his mush. But let's face it, what really is killing me deep down, the guy is probably repeating the truth. With a curt wave of his hand he finally cut short Harvey's fantasies about Bobbi.

A distinct edge to his voice—"Okay, Harve, I'm just a platonic friend of Bobbi's who so far has only played tennis with her. Maybe someday soon I'll get lucky and get a shot on the old shag rug, but until then, knock it off. I don't want to hear any more of your shit about her."

Harvey backed off immediately, his voice now blurred. "Gee, Tom, I hope I didn't upset you. Don't misunderstand me, I didn't mean anything wrong. I still think she's a great girl."

Didn't mean anything wrong, you drunken fink bastard, you only just caused my love life to shatter in a million pieces. What a stupid fuck I am, anyway. A real sucker. Know-it-all Tom, wise guy supreme. Falling in love with an older broad who's been around since I was a young kid. Well, so much for my new romance. When she returns I'll call Justine and tell her I'll be home early. That's right, Jus, we nailed the getaway driver. Tough kid, but we have him in custody at last. Sure, of course, I'll be home tonight.

The girls came back from the powder room, Jane and Harvey finished their drinks, excused themselves amidst the hugging and kissing clubmates indulge in when they meet or part, and Harvey, steadied by Jane, wobbled off into the moonlight.

"They're a real fun couple. Not very good players, but a million laughs at a party. Harvey's a stockbroker, very successful on Wall Street."

"Really." Very cold in spite of his vow not to betray his inner emotions. Harvey a successful stockbroker? The flannel-mouthed prick should write a gossip column, he'd be another Walter Winchell.

"There's the band playing again. Let's dance, love."

Tommy danced by rote. Gracefully, skillfully, but with no feeling, as if he were an automaton. She nestled in his arms, blissfully unaware of any schism, humming the dance tune, nice and high after all the Scotch, white wine, and Remy Martin brandy. The set over, they returned to the table.

As he held her chair he glanced at his wristwatch. Eleven thirty. He excused himself, saying that he must call his office.

"I thought you were off duty until Monday, dear—" a bit apprehensively.

"Not exactly, Bobbi. Remember I told you that I'd have to stay in touch tonight with my squad commander about the getaway driver." He lied so convincingly, had handed her so much horseshit, now recognizing that she was half-bombed, he figured she was sure to accept the mythical getaway driver bit as gospel. He was certain of one thing. Big-mouth Harvey had driven a spike into his heart and the love affair was over. He'd be goddamned if he was to be snickered at as the eighth— maybe ninth, tenth, and eleventh—man on the totem pole. Better break it off abruptly. Sever the love knot quickly.

He phoned Justine.

"Hello, oh, Tom, I'm so glad you called. I worried about you all day. Coming home?"

"In about an hour or so. I have a few details to clean up and I'll be on my way. Yep, we got him, everything turned out fine. You hear music? Oh, we have the radio in the squad room on and we're having a drink to celebrate. Sure, if you want to wait up for me, fine. See you later, honey."

He returned to the table wearing his number one worried look. He waved to the waiter for the check, turned to Bobbi and said, "Bad news, babe, I have to take you home and go right into New York and report to the squad room."

Tears of anguish clouded her eyes. "Oh, Tom, why? Do you have to leave me tonight? I want you so much."

Maybe you can call one of the army of troops you've been fucking, to take my place on the old shag rug.

Even voice, controlled. "That's the nature of the Job, sweetheart, you're always on call. It seems that they picked up a couple of more suspects in the stick-up mob and they need me there for the interrogation and the line-up."

They waited in the parking lot for the attendant to bring her car. A harsh light shone brilliantly above the restaurant entrance to illuminate fully the expansive parking area. They waited in total silence for the car. She seemed stricken by the sudden turn of events, not yet reconciled to his having to leave her. He looked sideways at her. Suddenly, somehow, she looked older. The heartless glare of the radiant overhead light sharply defined her profile, disclosing a few lines under her eyes and in her forehead. Perhaps they were caused by the long day—tennis, sex, dancing, all the drinking—but now her face looked almost haggard.

As usual, Vinny's right. No way she's thirty-six. You can bet she probably chopped a good four or five years off her age.

He was happy to get back to the congenial atmosphere of the Twenty-third Precinct Monday morning and looked forward to his radio car tour. All the guys kidded him about the shootout as he changed into his uniform in the locker room and the duty sergeant called out, "Wyatt Earp Sloane," when he reached his name during roll call. A big laugh all around the station house. The routine was the customary one—a few ambulance calls, traffic accidents, family fights, one D.O.A.— nothing out of the ordinary. He reflected upon Bobbi from time to time. He wondered whether he did the correct thing the morning after Harvey's heart-chilling revelations had aborted their flight to the moon.

He had risen early, careful not to awaken Justine, who slept late on her days off. He had made a light breakfast of juice, coffee, and toast and driven out to the tennis club. He arrived there shortly after eight and only Pedro the locker room man was on hand. He emptied his locker, cramming all his tennis clothes and rackets into the garment bag that he had left there the day before. He tenderly fingered the tennis sweater Bobbi had gifted him with, undecided whether to keep it or have Pedro arrange to place it back in her locker.

Too melodramatic, he determined, and stuffed it into the bulging garment bag. You made up your mind to cut the umbilical cord, so cut it. No more Bayside Tennis Club, no more

Bobbi Schuyler, and no more acting like a love-struck kid over a strange piece of ass. What a chump! After nine years of being faithful to Justine I meet one great-looking chick and almost go overboard. In fact, no more faithfulness. From now on the old navy adage will apply—love 'em and leave 'em.

Back at the precinct, he rationalized his behavior. He wasn't acting prudish, just couldn't handle the idea of a bunch of other guys constantly around who fucked the girl he was sweet on.

So what. He knew he'd miss Bobbi for a week or two, but he'd be goddamned if he would ever again lie in bed worrying about some girl. Get the money and you'll get all the beautiful girls you'll ever need. There's a million out there like Bobbi. He shrugged her memory off, smiled, a million girls—Christ, I can't fuck that many but I'll sure try my best when I hit the big time.

The days rolled by into Friday. He attended to the various situations that were part of a radio car cop's life in his usual efficient fashion, but he was mentally occupied with the summons to plainclothes duty that Vinny's father-in-law had assured him was certain. Shortly after one o'clock on Friday, just as he was about to give up the ghost until the following week, a call came over the air alerting him to report to Captain O'Connell when his tour finished.

The next few hours in the radio car were probably the longest of his life. He alternated between delicious fantasies of untold wealth, the high life, gorgeous women—and fits of depression that something would go wrong. He would get out of uniform, sure, but be sent to the Youth Squad a shithouse assignment that held little promise of a change in life style.

When the call came over the air he was riding with Jimmy Wynn, a young black kid, who had almost two years on the Job. A nice kid. Between chores they talked about the Yankees, the football Giants, and the Knicks' chances in the upcoming basketball season. All light talk, occasionally broken up by a run to the inevitable ambulance call or traffic accident. Nothing hysterical, a quiet Friday morning. The four to twelve and the midnight to eight shifts would get plenty of excitement. Friday starts the weekend early and the booze flowing. From five or six o'clock on, the good old Twenty-third was usually a bitch to work in.

Jimmy dutifully noted the captain's message in his memo book as it came over the air and poked Tommy, who smiled gleefully. But he noticed that he became very restrained, very pensive, the next half hour.

"You lose your voice, Tom? You haven't said a word in half an hour. You worried about seeing the captain?"

"No way, Jim, that's why I laughed. I think it has to be good news."

"It has to be after that shit you handled last week. I gotta tell you, Tom, you sure were cool the way you came down on those two guys. Super Tom, my main man." He laughed, punched Tommy's arm.

He stood at attention in front of Captain O'Connell, who was concentrating hard on some papers on his desk. The captain looked up, frowning. "Oh, Tommy, excuse me. Relax, take off your hat, unbutton your blouse, take it easy. I'll be through in a minute. Care for a drink?"

"I'd love one, Captain."

"Good. There's Scotch and some glasses in my closet over there in the corner. Get some ice cubes out of the refrigerator and make a couple on the rocks. I'll just finish this directive from the police commissioner's office."

He made the two drinks, placed one on an empty ash tray lying on the captain's desk and held his until the captain finished reading. The captain folded the paper, motioned him to sit down, and tipped his glass good luck.

"I have very good news for you, Tom. I received a call from Deputy Chief Moclair's office, the Borough West, this morning. You are ordered to report to Chief Moclair at ten o'clock Monday morning. The shoofly lieutenant, Frank Gerrity, is a personal friend of mine, a great guy. I called him personally to see what the order is all about and it seems they chose you to replace a man who's about to be promoted to sergeant. Congratulations, Tom, all the luck in the world." He reached out and shook his hand.

Even though he expected the good news, it still hit him as almost unreal. Thank God for Vinny, for his father-in-law, for the sergeants' list, for the spics who couldn't shoot straight. He gulped, took a healthy swallow of Scotch, found his voice.

"That's really good news, cap, thanks a million."

The captain stood up, drink in hand, gave him one of his penetrating looks. "I don't know who your rabbi is, Tom, but whoever he is, he's a heavyweight. The Borough West is one helluva good assignment." He sipped his drink thoughtfully, weighing his words carefully, and continued, "You've been a good cop here for me in the Twenty-third and I appreciate it. I'll certainly give you a high recommendation to Chief Moclair. Your actions, or your reactions I should say, last week in that garage stick-up were excellent. I spoke to Inspector McGeary and we agree that you should be nominated for the Combat Cross, one of the highest awards for valor in the department." He walked around his desk, stood close to Tom, voice lowered, as if reluctant to continue. "Now, Tom, one word of advice. You're going to be assigned to suppress vice and gambling. In plain English—whores, fag joints, bookmakers, number guys, and card and crap games. Not to mention after-hour clubs and bustout cabarets and gin mills. I could urge you to listen to me and my words of caution for the next hour, but it will probably go in one ear and out the other. I've been around this Job a long time and observed many a chesty cop. You come close to taking the cake. In many ways it's a good trait for a cop to have plenty of confidence, to bat the shit out of anyone who defies him. What I'm trying to say is—take it easy over there. You don't have to break any heads or shoot anybody unless by accident you run into a major crime being committed."

He took the bottle of Scotch and made himself another drink. He sipped it, trying to find the exact words to make his most important point. Finally—"And money, money's the big thing. You're sure to be exposed to it, to plenty of it. Be extremely careful, use your head, don't get into any jackpots. And my last and best bit of advice. Make sure you go to school, study, and become a boss. Use the brains the good Lord gave you." He reached out and tipped Tom's glass smartly.

"Once again, good luck, Tom, you're going to need it." He

didn't know that he just uttered one of the greatest prophecies since Nostradamus spoke.

Tom smiled, shook hands, thanked the captain politely, and left the office.

The late autumn weekend was drab, cold, and rainy—the gray chilled air a herald of the imminent onslaught of another bitter New York winter. He stayed at home and read almost the entire two days, taking time out only to watch his beloved New York Giants beat the Los Angeles Rams on television in a game played on the West Coast. Another good omen. He didn't miss the tennis club, the inviting arms of Bobbi, or even Justine as she chatted on, fixed his meals, and went off bowling. When his concentration strayed from his book, he would put it aside for a while, lay his head back, and fantasize about his upcoming interview with Chief Moclair Monday morning.

He arrived at Borough West headquarters, located on the top floor of the modern Eighteenth Precinct building on West Fifty-fourth Street, shortly before ten o'clock and was immediately ushered into Chief Moclair's private office on the extreme end of the top floor of the building. Chief Eddie Moclair was fifty-two years old and looked barely forty-five. Slim, wiry build. Thick, graying black hair, blue eyes, ruddy complexion, impeccably dressed in an expensive-looking blue pin-striped suit. At first glance he reminded Tom of pictures his father showed him of Dapper Jimmy Walker, the legendary former mayor of New York. A real movie star! These inspectors and chiefs must get picked for their good looks.

"How are you, Sloane?" Shaking hands with a firm hand grip.

"Fine, thank you, Chief—" returning with a strong grip.

"I guess by now you know why I sent for you, Tom. We have an opening in the squad and I intend to fill it with a young but experienced patrolman. We have an outstanding recommendation from your commander, Captain O'Connell, concerning your conduct and police work. I also wish to add my congratulations on the exceptional way you handled that situation in the garage uptown a short while back. Very good work."

"Thank you very much, Chief."

"I was also pleased that there were no repercussions from any of those civil liberty people who lately seem to want to run this Job—" he smiled—"without facing any of the hazards, of course. I understand they were two pretty bad kids whom the good Puerto Rican people up there will never miss. By the way, any psychological effects—trauma, nerves, sleeplessness?"

"Nothing at all, Chief—" humbly—"I was just doing my job and figured it was them or myself."

"Better them, Tom." He nodded vigorously.

I love the first name basis so soon. Tom, Tommy. Beautiful!

"All right, Tommy, let's get down to why I have you here. As of today, you're transferred to my command, the Borough West, comprising the first, third, fifth, and seventh divisions. I'm sure that your transfer will meet with approval downtown. You are now officially off until Wednesday when you report to the police academy for the normal two-week refresher course that is now a requirement for all newly appointed plainclothesmen. Check in with me early next week and I'll see that Lieutenant Burke, your immediate superior, gets to meet you and introduces you to some of the men you'll be working with. Once again, good luck, and it's a pleasure to have you with us."

He reached out and shook Tommy's hand.

"Thank you, Chief, you won't regret it."

End of interview, beginning of the most interesting and enriching phase of Tommy Sloane's young life.

He left the Eighteenth Precinct office and decided to walk over to the East Side where Justine worked to give her the good news and treat her to a celebration lunch. It was a cold, windy morning but he strode elatedly across the city, heedless of the weather, with the jaunty air of a guy on his way to a lawyer's office to claim a hefty inheritance from a distant uncle whom he barely remembered. He stopped at a drugstore to call Justine and made their luncheon date at the Press Box, a well-known restaurant in the Grand Central area convenient to her.

When he reached the vicinity he looked at his watch, realized that he had about an hour to kill before meeting Justine, and decided to drop into the men's bar of the Hotel Biltmore to sample one of their famous Beefeater martinis. It was not yet noon, but the elongated bar was already almost filled to capacity and over half the tables in the dining room were occupied. He ordered his extra dry Beefeater Gibson and as he sipped, he casually surveyed the room in his usual sharp-eyed cop fashion.

All well-dressed guys either selling something or buying something, the guys doing the selling picking up the drinks and luncheon tabs. He smiled in amusement. The same scene was taking place at this hour in a hundred other restaurants in midtown Manhattan. He took a long sip of his icy drink, its warmth now spreading through his loins, his spirits high, full of love for his beloved city. Yessir, the city that was soon to be his domain. His ever-vigilant roving cop's eye continued to appraise the comfortable scene and was attracted by a stocky, middle-aged guy with the pushed-in face of an ex-prize fighter. The guy was evidently a well-known habitué of the room. He stopped at brief intervals at various tables, occasionally making a notation on a pad he carried in his side pocket and every so often exchanging sums of money with the table occupants.

Tom didn't want to be too obvious so once he got a fix on the guy he studied his actions from the large back bar mirrors. The guy was acting like he had a license. He was at the bar only ten feet from Tom when he peeled off money from a healthy-looking bankroll and gave it to a well-dressed guy whom he stopped to talk to. He evidently said something funny because a big laugh ensued as he passed the money. Ah ha, a comedian as well as a bookmaker.

He finished his martini, ordered another. By now the room was filling up, the bar was jammed and the fun-loving bookie made his rounds of pad notations and money exchanges at an accelerated rate. As he slowly sipped his second drink he observed the bookie leave the bar and head for the adjacent hotel lobby. Tom left his change of ten dollars on the bar next to his half-finished drink and casually walked out to the lobby. Sure enough he spotted him in one of the string of lobby phone booths, pad in hand, in all likelihood calling in a string of wagers to his main office. He proceeded to the men's room and returned to the bar. Either this clown has to be on the pad or he's the ballsiest outlaw in town. He had a dinner date later in the week with Vince and made a mental note to check out whether this guy was okay or not. If he wasn't, he was sure to be at least a five-hundred touch. He finished his super martini, tipped the bartender generously, and left to join Justine in an all-time high mood.

The plainclothes refresher course was conducted at the new police academy, a really impressive building located on East Twentieth Street, off Third Avenue, a mile below midtown Manhattan. It was his first visit to the new academy and he was extremely impressed by the grandeur of the interior and the accoutrements—gymnasium, library, swimming pool, large, airy classrooms, lecture halls—all of which were in sharp contrast to the meager surroundings of his rookie school days. Like every young veteran or seasoned veteran cop before him he had one thought as he looked around—these new rookies sure have it made.

The classes were administered in an informal manner by a graying, good-looking Italian lieutenant named John Cassese. There were only nine other men besides himself, all of whom conducted themselves in an extremely guarded fashion. They all trod lightly, very circumspect, as if they were sure there was a stool pigeon planted in their midst who would report to Internal Affairs any hints that their route to plainclothes duty was prompted by greed. They were simply here to rid the city of the evil elements fostered by illegal vice and gambling. None evinced a sign or a word to indicate that this new plum would lead to a better life ahead for themselves and their families. Or perhaps, God forbid, if not handled correctly, a much worse life.

The first couple of days were spent in endless, repetitious discussions of the penal statutes embracing the various crimes they were empowered to suppress. They were taught the proper means of surveillance necessary to effect bookmaking arrests as well as number guys, crap and card games. Cassese dwelt at great length on the problem of after-hour clubs and illicit bars and cabarets. He taught the proper procedures to raid and close these unsanctioned premises. He delved deeply into prostitution, defining the differences between common streetwalkers and high-price call girls, painfully delineating the evidence necessary to bring them before a court.

He lectured forcefully on the pimps and madams who controlled most whores. Sourly and vindictively against the hated pimps, somewhat wistfully, almost forgivingly on the ways of the high-class madams. Tom barely hid a grin as he caught the softened tone of voice as John Cassese expostulated on some famous New York madams. Good old Lieutenant Cassese probably had his hot Italian blood rinsed out plenty in a high-class whorehouse when he was a young plainclothesman.

Tom Sloane's school days finished for the weekend and he went uptown to meet Vince for dinner at Gian Marino restaurant on Lexington Avenue off East Fifty-eighth Street. It was a warm, intimate restaurant, the great Italian food a treat for them. It was Tom's choice because he loved the place and beforehand had warned Vince that it was his turn to pick up the check. They met at the bar shortly after five o'clock, arriving within minutes of each other. They hugged briefly, glad to shed their overcoats and escape the biting winds swirling about the gray city. Vito, the bartender, never asked, just put two rocks glasses in front of them and filled them with Cutty Sark.

They tipped glasses good luck, each taking a good belt out of his drink. Vinny wiped his mouth, poked Tom in the ribs, raised his eyes to the ceiling and said, "God, Scotch is the best thing you invented since you made Italians."

Tom laughed. "You know something, walio, after what you and Charlie did for me I almost agree with you. Except the first best thing God made was the Irish, then the wops."

Vinny laughed again. "C'mon, if the Irish were invented first they would've drank all the Scotch before the Italians got there. Okay, stop the bullshit. Let's have the good news, Borough West man. What's happening?"

"You won't believe it, Vinny. I'm back in rookie school being taught by a handsome Italian lieutenant how to make a good collar. For an Italian, I have to admit he seems like a helluva nice guy."

"What's his name?"

"Cassese. John Cassese. Know him?"

"Not offhand. But what the hell, if he seems like a nice guy just go along with the act, the whole process will be over in a couple of weeks. What else is new? What are your plans?"

"Well, I guess when I report there officially I'll be assigned a partner and take it from there. By the way, I had a drink at the men's bar in the Biltmore the other day and watched a guy booking there who had the balls of a lion. Do you precinct guys know anyone who's connected there?"

"The Biltmore? Even around Vanderbilt Avenue and the neighborhood I don't know of any okay guys."

"How about you and me snatching him next week? He looks like an easy touch."

"No good, Tom, I've already made it clear that I'm resigning from the Job and I'm not taking any chances from here on. Besides, Charlie would raise hell with me if I got into a jam now."

"Okay, but will you quietly check this guy out for me?"

"I'll let you know next week. He'll still be there, they think they're all invulnerable."

They had another drink and Gian, the good-looking, curly-haired middle-aged owner, personally escorted them to a rear table in the back room where they usually sat. They ordered baked clams, veal marsala, tortellini—along with a bottle of the best chilled Chianti.

They exchanged some small talk through the meal about home, their wives, interspersed with the inevitable gossip about the Job. Vinny pushed his empty plate aside, wiped his mouth with his napkin, patted his stomach and said, "Delicious, really delicious. This is the life, pal, the life we were meant for." He raised his glass of wine, tipped Tom's glass, looked him straight in the eye. "May it always be this way, Tommy, baby."

Tommy just looked at him, almost overwhelmed by emotion, could actually have hugged him. At that precise moment he felt that he never loved anyone as much. He just nodded and smiled, afraid that his voice would break if he spoke.

"Let's get to the real McCoy. Are you aware of what you're going up against in your new detail?"

"I assume I'm aware. Catching gamblers, whores, and fags should be a lot easier than the shit you run into in a radio car."

"I agree with you completely. But what I'm really talking about is the money you'll be making and how you're going to handle it."

"First let me get my hooks on some real cash and I'm sure I'll know what to do with it."

"You know, I love you, but you're still thick as shit. What I'm trying to say is have you figured out a way to hide it? You can't buy real estate or invest it in the stock market because the commissioner of investigations or the Internal Revenue Service will string you up by your balls if they ever catch you. Here's what you do. First thing, you rent a bank vault under an assumed name or a phony company. Nothing illegal about it, just keep it quiet so Internal Affairs doesn't get wind of it. I'll take care of that through Charlie, a small bank on West Forty-eighth Street, good friends of his. No questions asked, we'll give you the bank guy's name, he'll take care of it, okay?"

"That sounds terrific, Vince. As a matter of fact, I have about three grand stashed among my shirts in my bedroom dresser. I'd like to put that away for openers."

"No problem. I'll arrange it and you can do everything as soon as you finish school and start working days."

"Swell. Now I forgive you for kidding me about Bobbi. You really had my ass."

Vinny stretched across the table, mussed Tom's hair affectionately, laughed. "You'll meet a million nice broads in Manhattan West. Buy them a drink, give them a bang if they want one, but don't fall in love. You have a nice wife, hang onto her."

"You sound like Cardinal Spellman, or the male Dear Abby."

"Both personal friends of mine." Vinny laughed. "By the way, have you the faintest idea of the cash you're about to make? You know, what the whole touch could be?"

"I would guess it's pretty healthy. How can you miss? Greenwich Village, Garment Center, up and down Broadway, half of

Harlem—beautiful. I almost get a hard-on just thinking about it."

"Save those hard-ons, you'll need all you can get of them someday. Seriously, I'd say conservatively you should grab about ten big ones a month."

Tommy whistled very low. Hesitantly, he said, "Ten thousand bananas?"

"Easy, for Christ sake."

"How'd you come up with that figure, that kind of dough? How good is your information?"

"My father-in-law Charlie gave me a pretty good rundown on what you should expect. If there's one guy outside the Job who knows what's going on inside the Job it's Charlie. He's very interested in you and he wants you to enjoy a long and rich career in the Borough West. Or as the high-class in-the-know guys call it, Manhattan West."

"Charlie's a real sweetheart. There's one thing for sure, Vinny, whatever I can do to help him, and you, when you leave the Job goes without saying. The sky's the limit, understand."

"We know that, Tommy. C'mon, drink the rest of your wine. On the way out we'll have to have a brandy with Gian at the bar or he'll have a heart attack. One more thing, I'll call you at home about the guy at the Biltmore. Thanks for the great dinner. About time you picked up a check."

"Up yours, walio. If what you say is true about all that moolah I'm going to make, we'll eat like kings the rest of our lives."

The next week at the police academy was spent repeating the same old routines and procedures drilled into the class by the patient and ever cheerful Lieutenant John Cassese. Tom steered clear of his fellow classmates, not once stopping in any of the nearby bars for a drink. He went directly home every night after school, arriving well before Justine. The nights she went bowling, he ate dinner in a small neighborhood restaurant, caught a movie locally and still was home ahead of her. Surprisingly, she asked very few questions about his new role and he didn't volunteer too much. His philosophy was simple: what she didn't know would never bother her. When she did occasionally question him about the vagaries of plainclothes work he just intimated rather secretively that it involved everything from counterespionage to the most baffling homicide cases. In anticipation of a future question or two regarding a sudden influx of money, he lied glibly that he would be receiving a hefty raise in salary as a reward for his promotion. Like all good wives, she was delighted at this news and began to make plans to replace furniture, refurbish the apartment, buy new clothes, and do all the things women throughout the years habitually do when the home financial situation improves.

Thursday afternoon late. One more day of school. Lieutenant Cassese loosened his tie, casually sat on top of his desk at the front of the classroom. His dark, handsome face broke into a big grin. Here it comes, the Fireside Chat.

"Well, men, we're coming to the end of the road. I hope I taught you as well as possible to prepare yourselves in some degree for plainclothes work. At least, as much as I could from textbooks and the Code of Criminal Procedure. But by now all you young guys know it's a tough life for a cop out there on the street. All ten of you guys have spent anywhere from two to eight years in uniform. You all know the kind of shit coming into New York. They're coming by boat, plane, and bus. It's getting tougher to be a cop every day that passes.

"Don't try to become an instant hero when you hit the squads you're assigned to. You'll make plenty of good collars and hopefully a lot besides vice and gambling arrests. Remember one thing, be proud of that badge you wear. New York cops are the best cops in the whole fucking world. There'll be plenty of temptation out there, every hour of the day. Be careful, watch your ass. I'm not about to lecture on any payola shit as that isn't my concern. My role was to try my best to teach you the elementary guidelines to make proper vice and gambling arrests. How to book a prisoner, how to draw an arrest complaint, and so on. You will, in all likelihood, be assigned to work with an experienced partner. Go slow and listen to him.

"Don't do anything on your own until you've been around a few months. I don't mean not taking prompt action if you run into a stick-up, mugging, or other violent crimes that demand instant response. I'm referring to vice and gambling. Just remember, we're never going to stop it, we just try to control it, to keep it from getting out of hand. We want to keep New York City as clean as we possibly can. And now boys, the last and most important message. Be here in this classroom tomorrow at nine o'clock sharp. You are to be addressed by one of the bosses in Internal Affairs. You all know what Internal Affairs is—the office empowered to root out graft and corruption in the Job.

"Again, I repeat, I haven't mentioned one word to you about money, bribes, temptation—anything of that nature. You will be delivered your sermon tomorrow morning. Be prepared for it. Go to bed early. It's going to be your last school day, but a very important one. Lay off the booze tonight. Come in here tomorrow with a clear head because you're going to get plenty of advice and a long lecture on the evils and pitfalls that plainclothesmen are exposed to. I'm sure you'll hear countless stories about cops on the take whose careers were ruined and some poor cops who eventually went to jail. You'll hear about cops who fell in love with call girls and left their families. I could go on because I've heard it fifty times, but you'll hear it from the feedbox tomorrow.

"I guess that's it. Good-bye and good luck, men. I enjoyed working with you. Come on up here—I'd like to shake hands with you and I sincerely hope that in some small way I helped you become a better cop."

Tommy was fifth in line and as he waited, he studied the handsome lieutenant's face. Thick, graying hair, dark skin without a blemish or a wrinkle, nice teeth, and the confident air of a successful stock broker. Oh, my Don Ameche lieutenant, I wonder how good plainclothes was to you through the years. I hope you have a swollen bank vault somewhere under an assumed name. A real nice guy, though, a real nice guy indeed, Tommy thought, as he thanked him and shook his hand.

He left the police academy thinking about tomorrow's lecture. Please God, not one of those ascetic, Irish horseshit artists who probably never left a desk, never made an arrest, didn't know shit from shinola about the Job. From the corner he

159

turned and looked back at the academy. No matter what, next week I'll be off to the races.

He took Lieutenant Cassese's advice, passed up his couple of predinner cocktails and went to bed early with a book. He arrived at the police academy about quarter of nine and went directly to his usual classroom. He engaged in some inconsequential conversation with a couple of the guys while one and all waited patiently for the apocalyptic sermon. An air of concern prevailed, a detectable pall of anxiety, as if the embryo vice cops awaited the Sermon on the Mount.

About nine fifteen the cherubic, young Irish inspector in command of the police academy ushered in a swarthy, middle-aged man of medium height and stocky build with a bull neck and tough-looking face. He had to be one of two things—a guinea hit man or a boss cop—and logic favored the latter.

The academy commander was very brief.

"Gentlemen, this is Inspector Arthur Del Vecchio, the chief of the Internal Affairs Division. Next week you men will be joining various plainclothes squads throughout the city and at the request of the police commissioner my good friend Inspector Del Vecchio has been requested to speak to you concerning some of the evils facing you in the enforcement of the vice and gambling laws." He turned, shook hands with Del Vecchio and said, "See you later, Arthur, perhaps we can have lunch in my office."

See you for lunch. Christ, three hours away. This is going to be one long pain in the ass. Tommy studied Del Vecchio closely as he walked to the classroom door with the commander. So this is the famous Arthur Del Vecchio—better known in the Job as Attila the Wop. His fierce reputation was legendary in the Job. Cut your balls off quicker than a Colombian coke dealer. To the relief of all cops, the word was that he wasn't as tough and mean as he used to be.

Tom reflected, as Del Vecchio cleared his throat and gathered some notes before him, I guess if he got too tough there would be nobody left to contain the really bad guys. And what's all this with the Italians being the paragons of virtue all of a sudden? Could it be all the Popes being Italian for so many generations? First Lieutenant Cassese, now Inspector Del Vecchio. What the hell happened to our original leaders? The souls of integrity, the honest Irish bosses. He covered his mouth to contain a big grin. His thoughts were back to his growing up among the Irish—Big Paddy, Grandma, Aunt Mamie.

In his early upbringing and street-smart learning, the Irish were always evaluated as first in matters of honesty. Italians were a distant second and Jews were dead last. Blacks and Hispanics weren't even rated and the lesser minorities were considered too dumb to steal. He almost laughed out loud. Of course, the Irish were the evaluators. Christ, when you remember what you heard from the old Irish when you were a kid you could almost die laughing.

Attila spoke. Deep, resonant voice. Surprisingly good diction—for an Italian, he'd have to tell Vinny later. He spoke evenly, seldom raising his voice, only allowing traces of venom enter into it when he discussed the inevitable graft and corruption faced by the men in the Job. He outlined at great length the men who had fallen by the wayside, the men who had gone to jail for grave malfeasance. He emotionally urged the ten men who were listening raptly to his every word to resist all temptation, to turn in anyone who offered a bribe or any fellow cop guilty of accepting a bribe.

As he droned on Tommy wondered what air raid shelter Del Vecchio lived in. Had to be on the remote outskirts of Long Island, safely insulated from what the hell was going on every day in New York City. He shook his head. Can this guy be for real? He stole a covert glance at his fellow classmates, who seemed in awe of the evangelistic exhortations of the Italian Billy Graham. He knew in his heart, as they surely did, that everyone present was on some sort of contract and chafing at the bit to get their hooks on some ready cash.

This too shall pass, dear God, and Attila the Wop finally came to a halt about eleven o'clock. At peace with himself, convinced that he had purified the minds of the ten young cops in his mesmerized audience, he closed with the ringing words, the last admonishment—stay clean, boys, and be proud to be one of New York's Finest. He shook everyone's hand and wished them all good luck. God knows, they were all going to need it.

Del Vecchio gone, Tom shook hands with all the guys, vaguely promising to get together real soon. That was it. Next Monday he would report to Borough West. He left the police academy and went out into the very balmy, sunny December day, a harbinger of bright days ahead. He looked at his watch. Almost eleven thirty, not too bad, plenty of time to accomplish a couple of missions on his agenda in the Grand Central area.

He had a date with Justine for lunch at one o'clock and he had a date with an old club fighter turned bookmaker a bit earlier at the men's bar of the Hotel Biltmore. The only difference was Justine was expecting him and the old battler was definitely not expecting him. Vinny had checked in with him by phone the night before, and assured him that the guy was strictly an outlaw, as discreet inquiry resulted in no one knowing of a bookmaker in the vicinity.

He rode the Lexington Avenue subway uptown to Grand Central. As he walked through the cavernous railroad station he plotted his strategy. He was well aware that the action was on the east side of Fifth Avenue, the dividing line. The East Side belonged to the Borough East squad, alien territory, but he felt that if he encountered a beef he could plead ignorance. But he was secretly confident there would be no beef, the score would be like taking candy from a baby. He grinned, I'll only take a piece of him, won't hurt him, just clip him for five hundred or so. I'll just practice what I learned all week, good experience for the future. Besides, this guy is really brazen the way he's working without an okay, a real threat to the security of all good plainclothesmen.

He entered the men's bar just before noon and the scene was an almost exact replica of his previous visit. He didn't check his overcoat, which safely hid the bulging gun on his hip, just loosened the front buttons and stood at the center of the long bar and ordered his favorite Beefeater Gibson martini on the rocks. The first long, icy swallow was luscious, removing the acrid dryness from his mouth that Attila the Wop's tenacious, bullshit lecture had cemented there. He enjoyed another, easier swallow, grinned. Old Attila should get a load of my act today.

The flat-nosed bookie came into the bar right on schedule. Tom turned his back to him and observed him through the back bar mirrors as he nursed his martini. The same scenario—the small pad, pencil notations, surreptitious exchange of money—a textbook example of handsome John Cassese's brilliant teaching. And now, my good lieutenant, I shall put your short but splendid education to the acid test. After about twenty minutes of making his rounds among the tables and at the bar the bookie exited toward the hotel lobby. Tom waited a minute, left his unfinished drink and change of ten dollars on the bar and followed his quarry out to the lobby.

He spotted him almost instantly in one of the line of telephone booths against the wall of a narrow part of the lobby. His luck was good, all the adjoining booths were vacant. He looked through the glass door of the phone booth and saw a small pile of white memo pad slips on the shelf next to the coin telephone into which the bookie was chattering away. He took his police shield out of his pants pocket, pushed the double-paneled door in with his foot and grabbed the white slips off the tiny shelf. The bookie gave a sharp cry of surprise, tried to jump up but the phone booth door, and Tommy's leg pinned him against the wall of the booth.

"What the hell are you doing, you crazy sonofabitch? Are you nuts?"

Tommy flashed his police shield right in front of the bookie's startled eyes. "It's not what I'm doing, pricko, it's what you're doing. You are under arrest for bookmaking. To be precise, for violating section nine-eight-six of the Code of Criminal Procedure. Just get your fat ass out of that phone booth and keep your mouth shut or I'll shove this shield down your fucking mouth."

"Take it easy, young fellow. Christ, I didn't make you for a cop. C'mon, please, let's go out to the front of the hotel nice and easy and maybe we can talk this over."

"Okay, pal, nice and easy. You walk ahead, I'll be right behind you. Sit down on one of those big sofas in the lobby and I'll sit next to you and take your pedigree."

The bookie did exactly as instructed. Tom, following him, carefully assessed his prey. *Nice, brown, expensive-looking suit, typical wise guy white on white shirt, silk tie, cordovan shoes—all the signs of an affluent member of the gambling establishment. Somewhere along the line he has to be half-ass connected. I wonder how much of a shake he can stand.*

The bookie sat heavily on one of the large sofas and Tom sat right next to him, like an old friend. He saw the beads of sweat on his forehead, the deep anxiety on his face. The bookie spoke first, in a low voice. "Where are you from?"

Harsh voice. "What the hell do you mean, where am I from? I'm from downtown, the gambling squad. All right, give me your right name and your correct address." He pulled out a notebook and pen from his inside suit coat pocket.

"Look, officer, my name is Frank Maloney. I used to fight around New York years ago, maybe you remember me?"

"Sorry, Frankie, you were before my time, I don't remember you. You'll have to go, nothing I can do to help you."

"Christ almighty, I can't stand another pinch. Honest to God, I'm okay with the division and soon I intend to be okay with everybody. I'm just building this here thing up pretty good. Gimme a break, please. What's your name?"

"Tommy. Look, if you're okay up here I'd hate to make the pinch inside the Hotel Biltmore. Could sure cause a lot of bad shit."

Panic-stricken voice. "Oh, Jesus, the manager is a good friend of mine, lets me get away with murder. Don't make it in the hotel, please."

"Okay then, Frankie, I'll put the pinch on the corner of East Forty-fourth Street and Vanderbilt Avenue. Cost you five hundred."

Just short of hysteria. "Five hundred! Christ, for five hundred you should let me go altogether. Please, Tommy, gimme a break."

He looked at the sweating bookie with ice-cold eyes, without an ounce of compassion. He weighed two possibilities in his mind. I could probably get a thousand, but I can leave him smiling by only grabbing five hundred.

Softer, kinder voice. "Okay, Frankie, you're one of my own kind and I must admit I'm always partial to ex-fighters. Tell you what. Go into the men's room over there, count out five hundred and come back and shake hands with me. Just make sure that the cash is in your hand and I'll put the slips in your coat pocket. Even exchange. No bullshit, get going. I got a load of your bankroll at the men's bar so I know you're carrying pretty good. Get going."

"Gee, thanks a lot, Tommy. I'll be right back."

He returned in a few minutes, pressed Tom's hand with the lovely, familiar, crunchy feel of newly minted money and all was well once again at the Hotel Biltmore.

"Tom, you forgot. Can I have my slips back?"

Magnanimously—"Sure, Frankie, here they are."

"Thanks a lot, Tom. By the way, what's your last name?"

"I'll let you know when I come back in a couple of weeks to put you on for downtown. Okay?"

"Fine, Tom, but give me at least another month, will you please. And please, keep me under your hat until I'm ready to go on. Stop by and see me for Christmas."

"Absolutely, Frankie, whatever you say. Now wait here in the lobby until I finish my drink and get my change. See you in a few weeks."

"Thanks again, Tom, I really appreciate it."

He went back to the bar, finished his martini, left the bartender a nice tip and waved good-bye to Frankie as he walked through the hotel lobby to the street. His face broke into a satisfied grin as he walked over to Lexington Avenue to meet Justine outside her building and take her for lunch at her favorite Chinese restaurant, the Gold Coin. Lieutenant John Cassese would have been proud of the expertise I showed on my first arrest—excuse me, handsome John, my first shakedown.

He almost laughed out loud. Attila the Wop Del Vecchio would have strung me up by the balls if he ever knew what I did after one of his famous two-hour anticorruption lectures. Those nice five hundred corrupt dollars in my left pants pocket feel awful nice, Attila, my honest headhunting enemy. The next martini I will shortly have in the Gold Coin will be raised on high in tribute to your words of wisdom.

Tommy passed the weekend in a slightly nervous state in anticipation of what lay ahead on Monday morning. The overcast skies and brisk, chill winds of early December had descended upon the city and he stayed at home secure in the quiet and warmth of his apartment. He watched a little TV, read sporadically, but mostly engaged in his favorite pastime, contemplating his future. He ruefully accepted the fact that a Florida vacation was out of the question this coming winter. He would miss it, of course, but plainclothes life heralded the glamorous aura of cozy cocktail lounges and intimate restaurants, as opposed to the bone-chilling days and nights of walking deserted snowbound streets or riding in drafty, cheerless radio cars.

He made himself a tall Scotch and water and thought upon his conversation the previous week during dinner with Vinny. Was Vinny's information correct? Was Manhattan West going to be that strong? Ten grand a month? He sipped his drink and laid his head back and his feet up on the new leather Barcalounger Justine had just bought as a recent addition to the apartment. Ten grand, Christ, I hope it's twenty grand, I can handle it. He smiled, if the racket is as easy as shaking down that chump in the Biltmore the other day, what's it going to be like when I'm a legitimate Borough man?

He was wide awake in bed early Sunday night trying to concentrate on a James Bond book. It was difficult as his mind constantly strayed from the political intrigue and perils of James and the omnipotent M to the coming joys of Greenwich Village, Madison Square Garden, the Latin Quarter, and countless areas, arenas, and night clubs soon to be under his jurisdiction. Justine was in the living room watching her favorite TV program, "The Ed Sullivan Show." Once again, his attention enmeshed in the hazardous duties of the intrepid

Bond, plainclothes temporarily but resolutely banished from his mind, he was almost unaware of Justine opening the bedroom door and going directly into the bathroom.

He was suddenly torn from an impending assassination attempt on the life of his favorite cop by an insidious Middle East thug when Justine jumped on top of him, deliciously naked. Ian Fleming flew from his hands, which were soon occupied squeezing her nipples and fingering her clitoris as she kissed him voraciously. He had just reached a nice, rosy hard-on a chapter ago when James made mad love to a delectable Oriental, so Justine's unexpected abandon was a welcome surprise. He turned her roughly on her back and she wrapped her legs around his waist like a vise and they made love frantically. They both came almost immediately but he stayed hard inside her and pumped away for another ten minutes. Justine almost went wild underneath him before he came again, almost exploding as she clung fiercely to him.

They finally fell away from each other. The heavy breathing, finally subsided. He laughed quietly. "Piece, great piece, at last."

She laughed. "Well, my favorite undercover detective, I was beginning to think you were tired of me. You haven't made love to me in over a week so I was determined to get you tonight."

She kissed him tenderly on the lips, a nice, easy kiss. "It was so good, Tom, it was wonderful. Was it good for you?"

Just as good as James Bond's slant-eyed, Oriental dish, sweetheart, whom I just mentally laid fifteen pages ago. His response was just as tender. He put his arm under her head, pulled her face to him and kissed her head. "It was terrific, babe, the best ever."

"Oh, Tommy, dear, you always say that, like we're never going to make love again. But I'm so happy you still love me, still make love to me so good."

He yawned, stretched lazily, reached out and snapped his bedside lamp off. He kissed her again, lightly. Christ, it really was good. "Of course, I love you, babe."

Maybe I do, who knows. He again thought of Bobbi, compared her to Justine, gave the nod to Justine. Not as fancy maybe, not as many tricks, but at least she's all mine. He yawned again. All his apprehension about tomorrow was gone. He felt drained, awfully tired, but great. Nothing like a good fuck to dispel your fears, to make you sleep the sleep of the just. He smiled. The corrupt just. The Justine just!

"Goodnight, sweetheart."

No answer, a faint snore, she was already sound asleep. He turned her gently, cuddled up to her back, put his hand on her small, firm ass. He smelled the faint perfume on the nape of her neck, her hair. I guess in a lot of ways I still love her. He smiled again. All day long he had been jumpy, nerves on fire, sure he'd never sleep. Now completely tranquil, he sighed contentedly, exhaustedly, fell sound asleep. He had a rare, dreamless night and never moved until the alarm clock shrilled at seven the next morning.

He shaved, showered, and dressed carefully in his best gray suit, white button-down shirt and dark blue tie. The full-length mirror on his bedroom closet door convinced him that he looked just as sharp as the plainclothesmen he used to see in criminal court. He had coffee and juice with his recent Oriental sweetheart, Justine, donned his new camelhair overcoat and went off to meet his fate.

He took the E train on nearby Queens Boulevard to Fiftieth Street and Eighth Avenue and walked up seamy Eighth Avenue to the Eighteenth Precinct, home of the Borough West. Home of all his years of dreams and aspirations of future wealth. It was shortly before nine o'clock and the only cop in the third floor squad room was the clerical man, Jack O'Keefe, who introduced himself. He gave Tom a cup of coffee from an electric percolator plugged into the wall socket above a table at the far end of the spacious squad room.

There were six plain office desks, all covered with telephones and steel wire trays filled with papers. A dozen heavy-duty chairs were scattered about the room. Rows of file cabinets lined the walls. Tommy sipped his coffee and wondered vaguely if James Bond and M's office looked anything like Borough West.

His new friend, O'Keefe, pointed to a closed door in the far corner of the room and said, "Chief Moclair is in there in conference with Lieutenant Burke. Those two and myself always are the first to arrive. We come in pretty early, about eight o'clock. The rest of the guys come and go more or less as they please. They make sure to stay in contact by telephone so that we know what court they have a case in or where we can reach them if we need them. One super thing around here, Tom, nobody breaks your balls. The chief's a great guy. Just make your collars, watch your ass, and you'll never be bothered. I understand you're replacing Eddie Scanlon, who just made sergeant, another great guy. I think you should know you're the first new man in the squad in almost two years."

Tommy whistled. "They've all been together two years?"

O'Keefe laughed. "Almost five years. Three years in the fifteenth division in Queens before Chief Moclair got promoted. He took eight of the men, all the squad called for, over here when he was transferred. He's a very loyal man."

"It's easy to see that. I only met him once and he couldn't have been nicer to me."

"The best. You'll meet him again as soon as Lieutenant Burke comes out. Both of them want to say hello to you."

Just then the lieutenant came through the door. Well dressed, slim, brown hair, glasses, middle forties, could be taken at first glance for a successful doctor. He walked directly over to Tom and shook hands. Very friendly.

"I'm Lieutenant Burke, Tom, lots of good luck to you. I know you're going to do a good job for us. For the first couple of months take it nice and easy, nobody expects any miracles around here. Try to be sure to make good collars, ones that stand up in court, and keep your nose clean. Also, watch your ass, you've got some bad neighborhoods to oversee, really bad.

"Most of the men will be in shortly and I'll introduce you as they arrive. You're replacing a helluva cop in Eddie Scanlon, but from your own record as a cop we're all sure that you have the knowhow and the balls for the job. I'm teaming you up with his old partner, Billy Driscoll, a real nice young fellow not much older than you. Stick with Billy, let him guide you for a while, and in a few months I expect to see you become one of my top men."

Two cops who came through the squad room were distinct opposites. One was tall, blond, blue-eyed, with an angular build and an innocent face. The other guy was obviously Italian, looked like he just finished playing the mob boss on a TV cop show. Dark-skinned, heavy-set, thick eyebrows, bushy hair, quite a bit older than the blond guy.

The lieutenant said, "Come here, you two, I want you to meet the new member of our squad, Tommy Sloane."

They walked over, the blond guy smiling and the dark guy scowling, almost ferociously.

"Tom, this is Pete Petersen and this is Joe Marchetti."

They shook hands. Pete, nice and firm. Marchetti, limp, like he just picked up dog shit. Tommy smiled his best smile, voiced his pleasure at meeting them. It never fails, the handwriting on the squad room wall. This guy Marchetti is one of those hard-nosed wops who's sure as Christ going to break my chops. Fuck him, let him try.

Three other guys straggled in and the lieutenant introduced Tommy to each of them as they arrived. He tried to place each name in his memory bank. Buster Smith, Larry Cuccia, Lenny Beck. They all seemed very friendly, shook hands vigorously, wished him well. The five of them sat around at various desks kidding and laughing, occasionally using the telephones. It was a very relaxed atmosphere, like the cocktail lounge at one of the better private clubs. Only the booze was missing.

The lieutenant called to Tom, who was sitting alone pretending to read the *Daily News* but slyly sizing up the byplay. He took him to the inner sanctum, Chief Moclair's office, and the chief gave him the same welcome wagon speech he had received two weeks previously. The sermon at last over, he shook Tom's hand, again wished him luck and he exited from the office, leaving the lieutenant inside again with the chief.

He knew in his heart that they were discussing him, felt he made a good impression. As he resumed reading the newspaper he thought about the lieutenant and the chief. Not a mention of the word *money*. Not one admonition of exposure to temptation, avoiding graft, none of that bullshit whatsoever. Be a good cop. Make good collars that stand up in court. Make sure you're prompt when we need you—like the game was actually on the level. The usual old army game. In case of a stink the generals know nothing. Why not? If I were a boss I would do the same thing.

After about a half hour of waiting a tall, good-looking, curly-haired guy wearing dark glasses came in the room to shouts of applause and laughter. It all seemed very affectionate.

Lenny Beck, a stocky Jew with a nice smile, brought him over to Tom.

"Meet Jerry Dillon, Tom, the craziest fucking Irishman in New York and that takes in a lot of territory."

Tom laughed, shook hands, noted the firm grip, expensive clothes, and great grin in that order.

"How are you Jerry, Tommy Sloane. Pleased to meet you."

"Glad to meet you, Tommy Sloane. Thank God, another Irishman. I was deathly afraid they were going to replace Scanlon with another Jew, Swede, or worse than death—another guinea."

A chorus of good-natured laughter, mixed with boos.

Tom said, "Irish all the way, Jerry."

More boos.

Jerry pulled a chair over and sat next to him. Later in life Tom often reflected that he was the one guy who broke the ice for him the first uncomfortable morning in the squad room. He was Lenny's partner and the only bachelor in the Borough West. A very funny guy, whose purpose in life appeared to be to fuck every available model, show girl, secretary, or stewardess in New York City. Tom was finally feeling at ease when one of the phones rang—Pete Petersen answered it and waved that it was for him.

"Hi, Tom, Billy Driscoll. I'm awfully sorry I'm not there to meet you on your first day, but I've been stuck with some asshole case down here in criminal court since nine o'clock."

"Billy, please, don't worry about it. The guys here have been very nice to me. As a matter of fact, Jerry Dillon was just describing some new sex positions to me."

Billy laughed. "That crazy bastard. There's one thing for sure, he'll never die of old age. He'll drink and fuck himself to death. Listen, how about meeting me for lunch about twelve thirty. I'll be out of here shortly and I'll scoot uptown quick as I can."

"Perfect, where?"

"How're you dressed?"

"My best suit."

"Good. I'll meet you in Dinty Moore's on West Forty-sixth Street. Know where it is?"

"Sure. See you at twelve thirty."

"Great. I'm looking forward to working with you, Tom. See you soon."

The men gradually left in pairs, all stopping to shake hands again with Tom, except Joe Marchetti, who merely grunted a good-bye. Jerry and Lenny stayed with Tom until just before twelve and heartened him with big handshakes and funny words of absurd advice, which took some of the sting out of Marchetti's coldness.

Shortly after twelve he left the squad room, turned towards Broadway and walked down to West Forty-sixth Street and Dinty Moore's restaurant. The noontime crowds, the theater marquees, the lavish restaurants, the whole panorama captivated him. He smiled. He didn't realize that as he walked, he was unconsciously humming the old Jimmy Walker song his father had taught him as a kid.

"In Old New York, in Old New York!"

What a wonderful song! And what a great mayor Jimmy Walker must have been. My kind of guy—loved clothes, broads, and money, not one of those mouthy, squeaky-voiced, breast-beating pricks like Fiorello LaGuardia. Or one of those would-be honest horseshit artists like Bill O'Dwyer. Jimmy Walker made no bones about it. He rejoiced in the good life and everybody loved him. Christ, would I love to be mayor. I'd be just like Jimmy Walker!

His dreams of political glory came to a halt at West Forty-sixth Street and he turned down the block to Moore's restaurant. If ever there was an elegant, traditional Irish chop house it was Dinty Moore's. Gleaming mahogany bar to the left as you entered, beveled glass back bar mirrors, glistening maroon-topped bar stools and rows of expansive, immaculate dinner tables. Snowy tablecloths and equally snowy, folded, neatly inverted napkins covered the tables, which were surrounded by heavy dark wooden and maroon leather chairs. The waiters and bartenders were spotless in maroon jackets, white shirts, black bow ties and trousers.

Moore's was just beginning to fill for lunch but the bar was already fairly crowded. Tom ordered a Cutty Sark on the rocks and furtively scanned the bar for someone who might be Billy Driscoll. No sign. About five minutes later he got a slap on the back, turned, and a heavy, sandy-haired, obviously Irish guy said, "Tommy Sloane, as I live and breathe."

Tom laughed. "Billy, how are you? How'd you recognize me? I'm going off my rocker here trying to pick you out."

"Don't you know I'm a real great undercover cop? How could I miss? I saw your picture all over the papers and on TV about a month ago. Besides, who could miss your Irish kisser?"

They laughed together. A nice guy. Christ, what a relief! Billy ordered a bottle of beer and another Cutty Sark for Tom. He looked Billy over as they chatted. This guy really likes to drink. Must of had a nice build, but now his belly bulged a little over his pants. He had a few whiskey lines around his nose and under his eyes even though he's only a few years older than I. Well, that's what living in the fast lane sometimes does and baby, from now on I'm living right next to him.

They had another drink at the bar, Billy switching from beer to Scotch. A few minutes later he motioned to the maitre d' and was led in very friendly fashion to a table in the rear of the restaurant. They chatted together like two old business pals over another drink and Billy suggested the corned beef and cabbage for lunch. He laughed. "You can't eat in Moore's for the first time and not order corned beef and cabbage or old man Moore would never allow you in here again." It was superb.

All during lunch Tommy was on the end of his chair waiting for Billy to drop some clue about what sort of money to expect. They laughed, joked, exchanged views about the New York Yankees, the football Giants, broads, books they just read—but the vital subject of money was never raised. He didn't want to appear overanxious or too hungry so he bit his tongue and let his destiny lie dormant. Sooner or later, dear Lord, one of these Manhattan West sonofabitches has to bring up my favorite subject—money.

Billy called for the check, just glanced at the bottom line and whipped off a fifty-dollar bill from a generous bankroll. He tipped the waiter generously and folded a five-dollar bill and slipped it surreptitiously to the maitre d' on the way out.

They both involuntarily shivered a little in the bitter New York air as they stood outside Moore's.

Billy said, "Christ, it's getting cold, especially after leaving a nice, warm, fancy saloon. But duty calls, we've got a collar to make or else we could've stayed in Moore's another couple of hours."

Tommy, excitedly—"A collar? Sounds terrif, Billy. Whereabouts?"

"Uptown, West Ninety-sixth Street off Columbus Avenue. A bookmaker I have some information on. Should be a piece of cake."

"Great. Well, we can take the Broadway IRT up to West Ninety-sixth Street and we'll be almost right there."

Billy looked at Tommy in sheer disbelief, a mixture of amusement and disdain. "The IRT? For Christ sake, Tom, you're a real *in* guy in the Job now, a Manhattan West man. You don't take the fucking subway or bus as long as you're in this office. You either use your own car, one of the unmarked cruiser cars assigned to us, or a taxicab. Here comes a taxi, let's go."

Tommy couldn't resist a grin as he settled back in the taxi on the way uptown.

"You know something, Billy, you and I are going to get along real good. You're my kind of guy. Where were you born and raised?"

"Born and raised. Only the real Irish use that expression." He laughed. "Brooklyn, where else?"

"What part?"

"Bay Ridge. Still live out there with my wife and two kids. Where are you from?"

"Queens. Around Sunnyside and Woodside. Still live there with my wife. No kids. Where'd you go to school?"

"My old man was an ex-plainclothesman. He sent me to Brooklyn Prep with the Jesuits. Where'd you go to school?"

"Bishop Molloy, with the Christian Brothers."

"Well, as you can easily see, we are two honest Irish Catholic policemen keeping the city clean." Billy roared laughing. The good Scotch whiskey was loosening him up.

Tommy laughed along, still maintaining his cool about money, keeping the conversation going about school and how strict the Jesuits and the Brothers were. They emerged from the taxi at the corner of West Ninety-fifth Street and Columbus Avenue, Billy brushing aside Tommy's attempt to pay.

They waited on the corner as the taxi took off and in less than a minute were joined by a skinny, dying-looking guy who Tom judged to be about fifty years old. He was bundled up in a stocking cap and heavy mackinaw, but his face was pinched and beet red from the cold. He had obviously been waiting in the vicinity for Billy to show up, meanwhile freezing his balls off.

"Gee, Billy," he whined, "you're almost an hour late. I hope we don't blow this guy, he knocks off pretty early."

"Go fuck yourself, Sonny. We got here as fast as we could. Say hello to Tommy, my new partner."

Subdued, a limp handshake. "Hiya, Tom."

"Hiya, Sonny."

"Okay, Sonny, let's get started. Where's this guy you got for me operating and what's his name?"

The stool pigeon gave a detailed account of the bookmaker, the premises where he operated, the hiding place for his work—all the action to the most minute detail.

Tom shook his head, marveled at his accuracy.

Billy reached into his pants pocket and peeled a hundred-dollar bill off his roll and handed it to Sonny.

"Aw, Billy, can't you make it two hundred? You know, Christmas is coming."

"Up your ass, Sonny, it's only Monday and we need another collar this week. See if you can set up something good for the end of the week and I'll take good care of you. You got that straight?" Hard voice, very authoritative.

"Sure, Billy, you can bet I will. I'll call you Wednesday. I think I have a real beauty for you guys, a number controller. Okay, good luck. So long, Tom, nice to meet you."

"So long, Sonny." Tommy watched him as he shambled off. So this is how the world of plainclothes works. He looked inquisitively at Billy, waiting for some explanation.

It didn't take long. Billy caught the questioning stare.

"C'mon, let's get going, I'll explain as we walk. Here's the whole setup. You and I have three stool pigeons, this guy Sonny you just met, a guy in the Village and another in midtown. They are all doormen in big apartment houses, and doormen are all horse players. They also place bets for tenants of the apartment houses who are horse players. So it follows, they usually know every bookmaker within a radius of five miles. They also know all the whorehouses in the neighborhood from their fellow doormen. Sonny's a doorman in a fancy apartment on Riverside Drive. Knows the neighborhood like he owns it.

"So you see, Tom, our three stool pigeons set the collars up for us. Like shooting sitting ducks. Now you got the picture."

Tommy just nodded his head. They continued to walk towards the day's prey, turning left on West Ninety-sixth Street towards Amsterdam Avenue. Tommy still felt that Billy was being a little cagy with him, not about to reveal the whole plot, just the edges of the scenario.

West Ninety-sixth Street was a wide cross-town two-way traffic thoroughfare lined with stores of all varieties on both sides of the street. They stopped in the middle of the block and Billy pointed to a store almost directly across the street.

"See that over there, Tom, Millie's Novelty Shop. My ass, that's a front for a new bookmaker in town called John the Syrian. And now, Tommy boy, we are going to stick one up John's Syrian ass. He was a small-time runner around the neighborhood for a big outfit downtown and recently decided to branch out in business for himself—" Billy laughed— "without even applying for a license."

They crossed the street, entered the store, and swiftly hurried past a startled middle-aged fat woman who stood behind a long glass counter containing a smattering of Millie's novelties. They pulled aside a ceiling-to-floor flowered curtain and found themselves inside the horse room. John the Syrian sat behind a desk, busily writing down the bets of three guys gathered around him. A scratch sheet, a white pad, and a pile of slips and money were in front of him.

Billy motioned to Tommy to stand at the curtains as he waited for John, the outlaw Syrian, to finish obliging his customers. The hopeful optimists, at last sated, their dreams of huge pari-mutuel payoffs spinning in their heads, they walked towards Tommy. To their utter astonishment, he smiled at them as he raised his hand with his shield held high. Billy, too, just smiled at John, the stricken Syrian, who buried his head in his hands at the sight of Billy's shield in his outstretched hand. Billy scooped the slips, scratch sheet, and money off the desk and took John off into the far corner of the room.

Tommy calmed the now frantic horse players, soothing their fears of imminent arrest, waiting for a further signal from Billy. Tommy couldn't help but grin as he looked across the room. After about five minutes of spirited conversation with John, Billy called to Tommy to allow the horse players to leave. They laughed in relief, shook hands fervently with Tom in gratitude, and scurried out like frightened deer. Billy, the money and the betting slips now ensconced in a bulging white envelope, sat at the desk with John like a young doctor counseling a thoroughly dejected patient who just learned he had cancer.

Billy called him over and said, "Tommy, I want you to meet John Magaganian, better known to sports fans and horse players in the neighborhood as John the Syrian."

Billy continued, "Tom, John here doesn't seem to be a bad guy. From what he says he used to work for some friends of mine. I hope he's telling the truth about knowing the guys he mentioned or he better take the next plane to the Middle East. He tells me that he's okay with the division and planned to put us on soon, but we've heard that bullshit a hundred times. Anyway, we're going to book him, but we'll make the collar on West Ninety-fifth Street and Columbus Avenue so we won't jeopardize his sister Millie's store. Okay with you?"

Magnanimously—"Anything you say, Billy."

John, the crestfallen Syrian, was safely booked in the Twentieth Precinct, sweating it out for the bail bondsman to get him released. They took a taxi back to midtown. It was by now about five o'clock in the afternoon and almost dark, so Billy suggested that they stop for a drink at the St. Moritz Hotel on Central Park South. Plenty of lovely single girls, plenty of action. Big wink. Nice, happy grin.

Tom, eyes widened by the spectacular events of the day, was almost overawed by Billy's casual attitude as he made the arrest. Christ, and what a welcome he received in the precinct. All the bosses practically kissed his ass. The sergeant at the switchboard even called the bondsman's number for John the Syrian. At that moment, he would have gone to Outer Mongolia to have a drink with Billy in hopes that a few shooters would loosen him up and give out the complete rundown on Manhattan West according to the gospel of Vinny Ciano.

It was just past five when they arrived at the hotel and checked their coats in the checkroom just outside the bar. The circular, elegant bar was almost filled. True to Billy's promise, it was crowded with attractive, apparently unescorted women. But beautiful girls or sex was the furthest thing from Tommy's mind. Underneath his smiling, cool exterior his mind was churning. When in the name of God is this smiling Irish prick ever going to confide in me?

They ordered drinks and Billy laughed over the arrest of John, how shook he was when they grabbed him. But as he talked and joked he looked over the assemblage of women with a roving, well-practiced eye. He finished his drink and said, "C'mon, Tom, drink up, have another. We'll have a couple more then go somewhere and eat about seven thirty, okay?"

"Whatever you say, Billy, you're the boss."

He clapped Tom on the back and laughed. "Not your boss, Tommy, your partner. You'll be just as hip a cop as me in nothing flat. It's all strictly a facade, a bullshit racket. The only reason for our existence is to stop New York from becoming another Las Vegas or Monte Carlo. Everyone at the top knows you can't stop people from gambling. You just try to keep it under control. The same thing goes for street whores, call girls, fag joints, crap and card games, and after-hour joints. We're here to keep them from becoming too bold, too blatant. Unfortunately, you give some of these pricks an inch, they take fifty yards. You get the picture, Tom?"

Here it comes, he's finally beginning to level with me. "Sure, Billy, where the hell do you think I've been the past three years, in the priesthood? I've been in East Harlem, pal, where you get educated pretty quick."

"No offense intended, Tom, that's for sure. Of course you're educated, know the score. Oh, by the way," he reached into his pants pocket, pulled out a roll of bills, peeled off two one-hundred-dollar bills and handed them to Tommy.

He explained the largesse. "I nailed John for five hundred to make the collar away from the store and to give him his work back so the players don't make any foul claims once they hear about the pinch. I kept enough shit to convict him if I have to. I gave Sonny a hundred for setting up the pinch and I had a few other expenses around the station house. For now, you take this and whatever I get from the case I will take all expenses out and then we'll split. All right with you?"

"Thanks a million, Billy. Look, I don't quite know how to put this, but at least give me some idea of what to expect every week, or every month, or whenever. I'd also like to know the guys and the joints who are okay in case I come across them. If you're not around and I run into something, what the hell am I supposed to do?"

"You mean a gambling situation? A bookmaker, number guy, crap game—something like that?"

"Exactly, for Christ sake! I know whores and stick-up guys and muggers aren't on the payroll."

Billy laughed uncertainly, weighed his words for a minute.

"Look, Tom, I'll be working with you every collar that you make. Just take it nice and easy and in a few months everything will be laid on the table, right in the open. Please, take my word for it. In the meantime I promise you'll do very good with me. Again, please, Tom, just believe in me."

"Billy, I don't want to embarrass you. I only met you today and I already feel I know you for years. I also like the way you handle yourself. Real easy, real cool. None of that tough guy cop shit locking up a harmless bookmaker. But for Christ sake,

Billy, you guys have had five years of the good life. My fucking tongue's hanging out down to my belly button waiting to grab some real cash. Now does that explain my feelings? Is that a straight answer?"

Billy slowly sipped his drink as Tommy railed away. He no longer looked around the bar for a friendly eye from a pretty girl. Incipient trouble from the new recruit loomed on the horizon. His brow creased in perplexity. He obviously had a lot to say, but he wasn't sure how to say it. He motioned to the bartender for another round, gaining time, collecting his thoughts. He tipped Tommy's glass with the fresh drink.

"Good luck, Tom, we'll always need plenty of that in the Job. Okay, somewhat to the point, hopefully some kind of answer. You met Joe Marchetti today, am I correct?

"Now take it easy, kid. All the guys call him Joe the Boss. Half-kidding, half on the square. He goes back a long way with the chief. He's a lot older than most of the guys, has over twenty-five years on the Job. Like I said, he's very close with the top brass and handles their end nice and smooth. We had a meeting last week and it was obvious he was pissed because the word was out that you were replacing Eddie Scanlon. He had been touting some friend of his for the opening and couldn't believe you edged him out. He claims that he doesn't want you to know too much for a few months. He wants to make sure you're a hundred percent before you get the complete breakdown.

"There was plenty of disagreement, particularly from me, as I was the guy picked to break you in. However, he more or less insinuated that these were orders from the top, so we sort of let it go at that."

He punched Tom's arm, tipped his glass good luck again. "C'mon, smile, Irish, let's go to Broadway Joe's, have a big steak, and then visit a few night clubs where the guys who run them are great friends of ours. You want to get laid tonight?"

Get laid! That's the last thing on my mind. I'm dying to know how rich I'm going to get, what the hell I can expect from my end. He shook his head as he looked at Billy. Joe the Boss, eh, another fucking cross to bear, another jinx.

"No, Billy, thanks anyway, not tonight. I'd rather we just

talked and have you school me a little and introduce me to a few of the right people. Okay with you?"

"Fine, Tommy, let's get out of here."

He woke up with a slight hangover, looked at his wristwatch, ten o'clock. Justine must have gone off to work very quietly. He got out of bed, went to the bathroom, relieved himself, brushed his teeth, and took a couple of aspirins. He went into the kitchen, fetched a can of beer from the fridge and sat back on his new Barcalounger. He sipped his soothing beer and reviewed his first day in Manhattan West. He grinned, not too bad. There's one thing for sure, I'm not about to attempt to keep up with Billy Driscoll in the drinking department. He's a real pro with the booze. But a nice guy. No matter what place they hit everyone seemed to love him. He smiled again as he thought about his first day as a plainclothesman.

John the Syrian, the first bookmaking collar, was a real rocking chair. In fact, the Borough West, excuse me, Manhattan West, looked like one big rocking chair. Billy and himself, the redoubtable new team, were expected to make a quota of about fifteen collars a month between the two of them. Christ, with all the vice and gambling going on around the West Side of Manhattan they could make fifteen collars a week in a breeze.

The setup was perfect. Three stool pigeons on the payroll to program the gambling pinches. All varieties of whores, pimps, and homos to snatch any time they felt like making one. He frowned, cursed out loud. One fly in the ointment, Joe the Boss. There's bound to be a major confrontation with that guinea bastard. What a crock of horseshit! Doesn't want me to know too much, like I was a young rookie. I paid my dues in the street and in the radio car, goddam it.

He smiled again. Not supposed to know too much. In one day Billy gives me the whole arrest procedure, a couple of hundred for my pocket, and introduces me to about fifty wise guys the same night. Joe the Boss. I'll face that hard-on when I get to it, no use worrying.

He stretched, yawned, another day ahead on the Job. Better

shower and get dressed. Billy was in criminal court drawing up the arrest complaint against John the Syrian. Christ, I wonder what shape he's in. Beautiful chick he wound up with. Good luck to him. I was glad to grab a taxi to home and bed. Lunch at one today in Greenwich Village, wants me to meet the top Italian honchos. You'll be the death of me, Billy boy, but I'm going to love the way I die.

Billy looked like death warmed over when Tommy met him for lunch in a fancy Italian restaurant in Greenwich Village. He had a tall Scotch and soda in front of him at the bar and greeted Tom with a weary smile and a limp handshake.

"I think I'm going crazy, kid. The girl, Lucille, I wound up with is a hat-check girl in a place on the East Side. I've known her for a couple of years. She's a real sweetheart, but some night she's going to fuck me to death."

He shook his head, smiled tiredly, slapped Tommy on the back. "But what a way to go, right, Tommy baby."

Tommy laughed dutifully. Please, Billy, don't tell me any love stories today, get down to the real nitty-gritty, tell me money stories.

"Anyhow, you look in pretty good shape, Billy," he lied, "but I'm glad I left you when I did, I was exhausted. I have to work myself gradually into this night life routine of yours. By the way, where did you manage the different suit, clean shirt, and new tie?"

"I keep a couple of suits and half dozen shirts, sets of underwear, and ties at Lucille's. I do the same thing with a couple of other chicks around town. It makes life easier when you're working late, having a few drinks and don't feel like going home. Listen, Tom, you'll fall into it sooner or later. From now on, pal, you're going to taste the good life. Just make sure that you make the most of it, you only go around once."

Tommy laughed. "But like the wise men say, if you do it right, once is enough. Seriously, Billy, how does all this staying out all night go down with your wife? Doesn't she beef?"

"You can't be serious," Billy laughed. "Christ, Tom, I'm always working on a big case. Top secret, of course. Besides, I bought her a beautiful home on Shore Road in Bay Ridge. I also send my two kids to an expensive private school, and give her everything she wants. She even has a cleaning woman two days a week."

"How do you explain all that on a couple of hundred a week in case they ever catch up to you?"

"Easy, Tommy boy, she has a rich mother. All plainclothesmen have rich in-laws, goes with the Job. Okay, enough of that horseshit, here comes Frankie and Sally now."

Two well-dressed, middle-aged, nice-looking guys came up to them at the bar and Billy introduced Tom as his new partner. Everyone shook hands enthusiastically. Within the next hour another ten or twelve Italian guys dropped into the bar and had a drink with Tom and Billy. The latter group were obviously all underlings of Frankie and Sally, but all seemed very friendly with Billy, as if he were a blood relative instead of an Irish cop.

Tommy noted that all these dark-skinned, sharp-looking guys were dressed almost identically in blue or dark gray suits, white shirts, and dark ties. He acknowledged each introduction with a firm handshake and a ready grin, meanwhile incongruously being reminded of the old Communion joke the Irish guys used on the Italian guys at Bishop Molloy High School.

"Hey, Tommy, when are the two times Italians receive Communion?"

"When they're eight years old and when they go to the electric chair."

Always a big laugh. He couldn't resist another grin. These guys all seemed like nice guys, though, very polite—as long as you stayed on the right side of them. The booze flowed, there were plenty of laughs and high good humor, when finally the indoctrination of Tommy Sloane into the hierarchy of the Greenwich Village wise guy set was accomplished. As they filed out of the restaurant expressing their good wishes he realized that no one had a bite of lunch, whiskey the sole sustenance. The high life begins early on cold December days.

Frankie was last to leave and when he shook hands Tom felt the gorgeous sensation of something green being pressed into his hand.

He looked Tommy dead in the eye and said, "I heard all about you from Fat Georgie. It was nothing but nice things. We're all glad to have you around. Be good, have a nice Christmas."

"Thanks a lot, Frank. I'm sure I'll get along with you guys the same way you get along with Billy." He slipped the money from his hand into his pants pocket.

Billy standing a few feet from him, winked broadly at him and Frankie hugged him and whispered into his ear, "Tom, Billy's a great kid, but see if you can get him to take it easy on the sauce. Jesus, don't ever try to go drink for drink with him or you'll soon be dead."

Tommy turned away from Billy and walked Frank to the restaurant door.

He said in a low voice, "I'll do my best, Frank. Rest assured, I feel the same way about the sauce as you do. Okay, once in a while, but every day, forget about it."

Another brief hug, Frankie left and Tommy returned to the bar to rejoin Billy.

"Well, Billy, what do you think, did I get the stamp of approval?"

"You sure did, Tom, and if you reach into your pants pocket you'll find five hundred dollars Frankie laid on you as a gesture of friendship."

Tom reached into his right pants pocket and pulled out five neatly folded hundred dollar bills. He whistled and laughed gleefully.

"You don't miss a trick, Billy. Now this is what I call a beautiful gesture of friendship. C'mon, we'll split it."

"No way, Tommy, that five hundred is all yours. Frankie asked me if it was okay to stake you. Like I told you last night, just hang in there, I'll make sure that you're all right."

"Thanks, Billy, you're a real sweetheart. Well, what do you say, enough booze? How about having some lunch?"

"Good idea, but let's get out of here. Christ, it seems like I've been drinking Scotch since I woke up this morning. Let's go uptown to Gallagher's Steak House for lunch. My stomach is growling, I feel like eating a big filet mignon."

"Terrific, let's go."

The rest of the day and balance of the week were spent in similar fashion, drinking and eating in the best restaurants and night clubs. Tommy was well aware that he was being show-cased to the higher class wise guys around the West Side, but he couldn't care less. He was becoming almost pathological at Billy's continued reticence about the monthly cut. He lay awake night after night, especially if he cooled the booze during the day, twisting and turning in bed, wondering if the first of the month would bring in the ten or eleven grand Vinny led him to expect. But he bit his tongue, determined not to get disturbed with Billy, to play the waiting game. Still, the malevolent face of Joe the Boss Marchetti chilled his thoughts just as the bitter cold of December chilled his body.

Another week rolled by, broken up by a few visits to the squad office, and most notably, a meeting with each of their other two stool pigeons, Harry in Greenwich Village and Manny in midtown Manhattan. In contrast to the rheumy-looking, shambling Sonny of Riverside Drive, both of these two operatives were slick, small-time gambler types, who knew the city as well as the smartest cops. Harry was a stocky, middle-aged Irishman, with the crafty blue eyes, heavy brogue, and obsequious manner of an I.R.A. informer. Manny was a tall slim Jew in his late twenties. He wore tortoise shell–rimmed glasses and had a scholarly air about him that suggested any number of vocations except his real one, a luxury hotel doorman. They had a drink with each of them, Billy gave them each a hundred dollars for Christmas, and both individually swore an oath of allegiance to the new kid in town, Tommy Sloane.

They only made one collar all week, the numbers man that Sonny had earlier promised he had on tap for them. He wasn't a controller, only a runner. He was an affable, young Spanish guy who took the pinch in stride like a veteran practitioner. He was so unflappable it was almost as if he expected it. After they booked him they decided to call it a day and do some Christmas shopping. Tommy left Billy with the promise to meet him the next morning in criminal court to run through the routine of drawing a complaint and arraigning a prisoner.

Free of Billy early in the afternoon, he decided to call Justine and take her to her favorite store and to dinner. He took a taxi to the Biltmore Hotel, deciding to revisit his old pal, the bookmaking pugilist, Frankie Maloney. What the hell, might as well pick up the expenses for tonight; he did tell me to stop by for Christmas. He called Justine from the lobby and arranged to meet her at four thirty in the Gold Coin. She was thrilled, laughingly complaining that she hardly saw him any more. What suit was he wearing so she would recognize him? He hung up with a smile. She's really right, I've had very little time with her the past couple of weeks. He smiled again, tonight he'd make it up to her.

The Biltmore men's bar was wall-to-wall martini drinkers. He edged into a space and ordered a Beefeater extra dry Gibson. A couple of these, he thought, as he had the first cool, delicious sip, and I might whip Justine right back home and into the sack. Halfway through his drink he spotted the bookie through the back bar mirrors. He turned and caught his attention by a subtle wave of his hand. The exfighter looked stunned for a moment, like he'd caught a right hand he was supposed to dodge, but recognition brought a big smile to his face. He joined Tom at the bar and they shook hands like two long lost friends, the handshake making Tommy richer by a hundred dollars.

"Thanks, Frankie, everything okay?"

"Great, Tommy, couldn't be better. By the way, what downtown squad are you in?"

"I was just transferred to Manhattan West a few weeks ago," he lied, "but the good news for you is that they're going to consolidate the two borough squads into one and I'm going to be one of the main guys. You know I'll take good care of you, Frankie, as I found out since that you're a nice guy and were a helluva fighter in your day," he elaborately lied further.

Frankie beamed happily. "Gee, that's good news, kid, I really appreciate it. Stay in touch, Tom, I gotta get back to work."

"So long, Frank, good luck and Merry Christmas." He watched the retreating figure of the bookie and couldn't resist a grin as he ordered another Gibson.

Justine was just coming up to the Gold Coin when he arrived. She threw her arms around him and kissed him hard on the lips. In spite of the cold and swirling winds his cock shot up instantly as he squeezed her tight. Christ, I haven't been laid in two weeks and she feels gorgeous.

"Hi, honey, what do you think? Shall we go straight home or go shopping?"

She laughed. "Neither, wise guy, I know what you have in mind. We'll get to that later. First we go inside and have a drink so I can get to know my husband again. Then we'll have something to eat and go to Bloomingdale's. I've got a hundred things I have to buy for Christmas."

They were seated and Tommy switched to Scotch and water, Justine ordering her usual white wine.

"You look tired, Tommy. How's the new assignment going?"

"I love it, Justine, but this undercover work really wears you out!" he lied, smiling at her wearily, a worn-out foe of crime.

He looked her over closely, loved her sharp features, brown eyes, and white teeth underneath a tight-fitting fur hat. I'll give her my Christmas present now. He hadn't bothered to put any money between the shirts in his bureau drawer this morning, so he mentally calculated how much he carried. Had to be five or six hundred, plus the hundred from the Biltmore men's bar bookie.

"Justine, you know how I hate to shop and how much you love to shop. Suppose I just give you money for Christmas, okay?"

"Gee, Tom, that will be great."

He took the money out of his left pants pocket, and counted out five hundred dollars with his hands below the table. He put the rest of the money back into his pocket and with a big grin reached across the table and handed Justine the money.

"Merry Christmas, sweetheart."

She was astonished at the bulk of the money, but not too numbed to count it carefully below the table. "My God, Tommy, you just gave me five hundred dollars. Where did you get it? I can't believe it."

If you only knew, my love. But he stuck to the old cop credo, tell your wife nothing, what she doesn't know will never hurt her.

"That was my reward money for the shootout in the garage," he lied, smiling, rejoicing in the delight registering on her face.

"Oh, Tommy, this is wonderful. What a great Christmas this will be. Can I spend it all?"

"Of course, love, that's why I gave it to you. We won't have too many money worries any more, dear, I get a big raise with this new job and a generous expense account," he lied further, with the calm assurance of a family lawyer ticking off the good-ies contained in a hefty will to the only heir.

Tears rushed to Justine's eyes, she covered his hand, squeezed it tightly.

"Tommy, I love you so much. You're such a wonderful guy."

He smiled modestly. "Enough, babe. Behind every good guy is a great woman. C'mon, let's have one more drink and then something to eat. After that, you can buy out Bloomingdale's."

The rest of the night was one of the better ones in Tommy's life. They laughed, bought outrageous presents, taxied home, and made terrific love for a couple of hours.

Justine woke him up with a kiss on the lips. She was dressed for work and ready to go. She looked so good he grabbed her close, but she pushed him away, explaining that she was already late and that he had to get up for court. Christ, I almost forgot, I have to meet Billy in criminal court. I better take it easy on the booze myself and stop worrying about the other guys.

He had the breakfast Justine laid out for him, showered, and dressed carefully for his first appearance in criminal court since he was last there in his wrinkled uniform, tired and needing a shave. Today he would mix it up with the equally well-dressed, sharp, fellow plainclothesmen, the same guys he watched in awe a few months ago. Billy was in court when he arrived and intro-duced him to about ten plainclothesmen from various parts of the city. They all seemed to possess a quiet air of self-confidence, as if to the manor born. All beautifully tailored, big smiles in some cases revealing expensive, gleaming, capped teeth. They laughed and joked easily among themselves, with the cama-raderie of junior business executives at an exclusive country club. He kept a smile on his face, shook hands firmly as he acknowledged each introduction, enjoying the boisterous scene.

The only unhappy guys around this court were the prisoners waiting to be arraigned. For a brief moment he was caught in déjà vu, brought back to the cocktail lounge at the Bayside Tennis Club, felt a stabbing pang at the memory of Bobbi Schuyler. He abruptly dismissed it from his mind. What a life! After only two weeks he was already beginning to feel a sense of elitism engendered by plainclothes. Everyone appeared to look up to you—bosses in the Job, wise guys, fellow cops, court officers, restaurant and night-club owners—an unbounded array who all seemed sincere. And the money, while still very important, was already beginning to feel like cigar store coupons. No matter what you spent one day, the next day you woke up there was still plenty out there to be made. He broke into a grin involuntarily as he watched Billy's moves. Eyes a little bloodshot, face puffy, but still in command of himself as he shook hands with new arrivals and accepted the subtle adulation due a Manhattan West man.

After the complaint was drawn, Tommy properly instructed, Reuben Gomez, number runner, finally arraigned, they walked from the courthouse in the freezing air up a couple of blocks to the comforting warmth of Peggy Doyle's Courthouse Saloon. A good half hour before noon, the bar was already jammed with a uniquely diverse crowd of plainclothesmen, detectives, lawyers, bondsmen, and lower- and top-echelon wise guys. Christmas was but a week away and a festive, holiday spirit prevailed in the smoky air of Peggy's Place, as all the real *in* guys called it.

They found a spot at the bar after Billy shook hands and introduced Tommy to what seemed like fifty guys. The bartender set up a tall Cutty Sark and water for Billy without even asking and looked expectantly to Tom for his order. Holy Christ, not another day of drinking, he silently prayed, but in self-defense ordered a Bloody Mary, tall, lots of ice.

"There are more contracts made in here than are signed in Hollywood," Billy laughed, as he took a long swallow of his drink. "Peggy's a nice girl, comes from Ireland. Her old man's some kind of horse trainer," he smiled, indicating the general mass with a wave, "that's why you see so many guys look like bookmakers in here. All this horsey shit decorating the place seems to attract the wise guys and their lawyers."

Tommy looked around as he sipped his drink. "I like Peggy's Place, Billy. It's colorful, to say the least. So tell me, what's the reason we stopped here? You know something, I'm just beginning to get inside your devious Irish psyche. You almost never do anything or go anywhere without some sort of plot in mind. Am I right, Billy boy?"

Billy laughed, finished his drink in one long belt. He winked broadly, the Scotch flowing through his veins, at peace with the world.

"Whew, that was what I needed! Okay, wise ass, you're getting smarter by the day and I'm sure you'll turn into a great plainclothesman. Here's the scoop. In a few minutes we have a meet with our old pal, the numbers runner Reuben Gomez's boss. He's some new heavyweight spic named Carlo. Used to be the number racket was controlled by the Irish. Then came the wops and the niggers. Now the spics are coming along real strong. The way they're rolling into New York every day in another couple of years all cops will have to learn Spanish just to communicate."

"*Sí, señor,*" Tommy grinned showing off his Twenty-third Precinct Spanish, "and here comes your *macho caballero* right now," indicating a tall, slim Puerto Rican approaching them. He was accompanied by a pudgy, bald, well-dressed lawyer.

"Very good, Thomas, you may have to translate, but I hope my friend Abe Pearlstein, his lawyer, will conduct the proceedings in English."

They shook hands all around and adjourned to a table in the back room of the restaurant. They ordered fresh drinks and Tommy looked over Carlo, dressed to slay on sight any available *señorita*, right to the big diamond in the lobe of his left ear. He was in sharp contrast to his fat, affable lawyer. After some initial haggling, the outline of a protection contract for Carlo's army began to take shape. Carlo confessed to having twenty or so runners and had a grandiose notion of branching out further. He and Abe pleaded with Billy for a temporary armistice that would lead to a peace treaty to be ratified at the next squad meeting of Manhattan West.

Billy, with a Churchchillian air, assured Carlo that so long as he was a good friend of Abe Pearlstein's, a veteran and trusted criminal lawyer, he would put it on the squad agenda. After another round of drinks he pledged that a negotiated peace with Carlo's troops would be in effect by the first of the new year. The amount to be paid was tossed around, the proper identification to be carried by the runners in case an accidental bust was agreed on, and they repaired back to the bar for another drink to cement their new found alliance. Harmony again reigned in the new Caribbean!

Tommy nursed his second Bloody Mary very slowly through all the dickering. He watched with sly amusement and a great deal of respect how smoothly Billy handled all the arrangements. A genuine pro, he concluded. He marveled at Billy, who drank steadily as he counseled Carlo, and calmed him when he tended to become hysterical and hurl a barrage of indecipheral Spanish at them. They finished the sit-down with an emotional embrace from the aspiring Spanish numbers king and a thousand-dollar retainer for time spent.

The two of them alone at last, Tommy said, "You know something, Billy, when you get transferred out of Manhattan West, God forbid, they might have a place for you in the United States diplomatic corps."

Billy grinned. "You just have to use the old cold cream, Tom. Pat them on the ass, take their money, and send them on their way. You take the numbers game away from the Puerto Ricans, their beloved *bolita*, you break their hearts. For Christ sake, I'd rather see these kids running numbers than becoming stick-up guys. As you can see, it's all a lot of shit, anyway. We might as well grab the dough while we can, because sooner or later it has to become legitimate. Okay, enough, don't let me get started on that again."

Billy turned away from Tom, then back to him, and said, "Here's five hundred for your end of the conference. C'mon, one more drink and we'll go uptown and have lunch in Dinty Moore's. From now on until after Christmas we declare a moratorium on all collars, a short amnesty on all vice. It depresses me to lock up anyone around Christmas time. From here on we go Christmas shopping."

"Please don't mention Christmas shopping, Billy. I hate that worse than bowling and my wife loves to do both. God, I went through all that torture last night at Bloomingdale's."

"My use of the words Christmas shopping is entirely different from your idea of Christmas shopping, Tommy baby. You and I are about to visit all our cousins, the next few days, plus a lot of fringe type night clubs and bars we let get away with murder all year. We'll be very busy and a lot richer at the end of the week. C'mon, let's get out of Peggy's Place before Attila Del Vecchio, chief of Internal Affairs, shows up and raids the joint."

Tommy laughed. "Christ, what a haul he'd make today, a real Christmas basket."

"But he knows enough not to bother lovely Peggy, she knows all the judges and they all love her."

The next week was surrealistic. Tommy lost count of the gambler cousins he met and the sleazy go-go girl joints, gay bars and after-hour clubs they visited. The money rolled in from all angles and the shirts in the bureau drawer became fuller with each new insert of green. He did his best to control his drinking, not even attempting to keep up with Billy, but each morning he awoke tired and hung over. Under the shower each morning he vowed that he would go on the wagon that very day.

But each day brought a new twist. One day it was the squad Christmas party in the upstairs private room of Gallagher's Steak House. The next day a private party of all the downtown and borough squads in the downstairs banquet room at Toots Shor's. It was getting so that as he set off to meet Billy he wondered if the afternoon was to be capped by a private party in the Rainbow Room.

One thing buoyed him, the guys in the squad treated him well, accepted him as an equal. The only depressing note was the grim, sour face of Joe the Boss, who still greeted him as if he were a pariah. He shrugged his frigid attitude off, figuring his present lot in life was a vast improvement over all the bullshit that he had to contend with in the Twenty-third Precinct at this time last year.

A couple of days before Christmas he realized with a sharp pang that he hadn't seen or even called Vinny in weeks. He reached Connie by phone and made a date for him and Justine to take them to dinner at the Copacabana on Christmas Eve. We'll have a real celebration, Connie love, Frank Sinatra is appearing.

The Copa, as it was unanimously called by all the in guys and legitimate steady patrons, was the top night-club restaurant in

New York City. One of the most loved features were the Copa Girls. Eight gorgeous, long-legged beauties, internationally famous for their stunning looks and disciplined dance routines. The background music was also excellent and the top entertainers in the country headlined the show. Lena Horne, Jimmy Durante, Tony Bennett, Peggy Lee—and countless other stars of the cabaret world. But the star of stars was Frank Sinatra and Tommy deliberately chose the Copa to meet Connie and Vinny because like all Italians, and nearly every other race, they were crazy about him. Tommy had prevailed on Billy to make a phone call to one of the bosses and arrange a really good table. No problem, said Billy.

Tommy and Justine had just checked their coats and were in the lobby when Vinny and Connie arrived. They exchanged embraces as if they hadn't seen each other for years instead of merely weeks. It was still too early in the evening to go downstairs to the main dining room so they decided to have a drink at the bar in the cocktail lounge. The girls paired off immediately, prattling away, and Vince and Tom tipped glasses and squeezed each other's arms affectionately.

"I thought you forgot about me now that you're in the big time, you Irish prick. Did Ma Bell go on a holiday? Do you realize that I'm on terminal leave from the Job and somewhere on the West Side every day?"

"Now don't start, please, for Christ sake. I knew in my heart when I made the date with Connie that you were going to scream at me." He put his hand on Vinny's shoulder, contritely. "Please forgive me, Vince. Each day is so goddam full, so completely wacky, I fall in bed each night like a dead man."

Vinny tried to keep a straight face, tapped Tommy's jaw, couldn't resist a grin. "Okay, it's Christmas time, and you're taking Connie and me to see Frank, so I accept your apology. But no more of that absentee shit, you understand. I miss you."

Tommy felt immensely better, grinned. "I was really hoping Frank would be at the Paramount Theater where you used to sneak in and see him when you were a kid. One thing for sure, it would be a helluva lot cheaper."

"Paramount Theater, my ass. My father-in-law, Charlie, is a good friend of Frank's. He took us to see Frank a few times."

"Every walio in America is a personal friend of Sinatra's, according to them. He's half-Irish anyway, you know that?"

Vinny looked startled, took the bait. "Are you serious, you dopey Irish bastard?"

"Of course I am. Where did he get the blue eyes? No Italians have blue eyes, they all have brown eyes. I'm telling you, his mother or his grandmother was Irish. I swear, I read it somewhere—" keeping up the rib with a straight face.

"I'm surprised you're so ignorant, honestly. A lot of Italians from the north of Italy have blue eyes."

"Gee, maybe you're right, that's from way back when Ireland conquered Italy." Tommy couldn't control himself any longer and burst out laughing.

Vinny laughed sheepishly. "I really can't believe you the way you can argue with a straight face. You had my goat for a minute. Anyway, enough about Sinatra. Seriously, your face looks a little puffy, like you've been drinking a lot. Am I correct?"

"That's the understatement of the year."

"What about going to the gym? They sure as hell don't serve booze in the gym."

"You're absolutely right, Vin, I haven't worked out in over a month. But you have to understand, this job is like one continuous merry-go-round. Everything you do seems to revolve around drinking. You're in and out of restaurants and bars all day and night. Besides, where the hell are you supposed to meet these guys you have to deal with, in a goddam diner or Greek coffeepot?"

"I know, I know, Tom, you're right. But you have to learn early in the game to take it nice and easy. By the way, your new partner, Billy Driscoll? A nice guy?"

"Super, Vince. A real sweetheart. The only trouble is, he's got a wooden leg that all the booze flows through. I swear to God, the guy has at least fifteen or twenty drinks a day and hardly even changes his expression."

"I heard through the grapevine that he drinks pretty good. For Christ sake, Tom, don't try to keep up with him. Back off a little, fake it out. Have a glass of wine, a beer, something easy."

"I try, honestly, but it's murder in the first degree. Plainclothes is like one big party, you always seem to be on the town."

"How's the cash flow?"

"Unbelievable! Like having a season pass to Fort Knox. In less than a month I've made almost five G's. But something's bothering me a lot, something I have to talk over with you. Let's have one more drink and we'll go downstairs to our table. Okay?" His face had suddenly assumed a troubled, harsh look in the shimmering light of the cocktail lounge.

Vinny scrutinized him closely, not missing the new look. "Sure, Tommy, anything you say."

The bartender set them up a fresh drink. They could easily see that the girls were too busy talking to notice their desire for privacy, so they tipped glasses good luck, and in a low voice, Vinny said, "All right, I've seen that look on your Irish face before. There's trouble in Paradise, right?"

"Not exactly trouble, just yet. But I sense it coming, feel it in my bones."

"Okay, let's have it. Get it off your chest now before you spoil my Frank Sinatra night worrying about you. Besides, confession is good for the soul."

Tommy smiled, banishing the grim look, and said, "Nothing in the world is going to spoil our night, Vince. Anyway, here goes. You ever hear of a Manhattan West guy named Joe Marchetti? They call him Joe the Boss?"

"Sure, I met him with Charlie a few times. A real asskisser. He impressed me as being purely full of shit. Charlie told me later that he's been on the teat for years, always up the top of the bosses' ass."

"You got him dead right. But somehow, he seems like the squad leader among the men. He treats me like I'm shit, barely acknowledges my existence. It seems he had a friend of his in mind for the opening in the squad and he's miffed because I got the job instead. I've got this deep-down feeling that he's going to screw me somehow and I'm not sure how to handle it."

"Tom, take my advice, listen to me. You don't take any shit from anybody. Don't let this bum try to get the upper hand on you because you're new to the squad. You've got plenty of weight behind you with Charlie in your corner, so if he tries any funny business on you like denying you a proper cut of the action, go right for the jugular. You got that straight?"

"Good, pal, that's all I needed to know, that I have a little strength. Now I feel relieved. Okay, drink up, it's almost eight o'clock, time for our reservation downstairs."

Joe Lopez, the maitre d', led them to a choice front row table in the raised section of the restaurant. It was directly in front of the dance floor where the show took place. Vinny winked and nodded his approval as Tommy thanked Lopez with a handshake containing a twenty-dollar bill. The four of them were studying the dinner menus trying to decide what to order when Tommy put his aside and said, "Suppose I order for everybody, okay?"

"Go ahead, Tommy boy, you're picking up the tab."

He motioned the waiter to his side and said, very expansively, "Four shrimp cocktails and two Châteaubriands, medium rare, with Béarnaise sauce. And two bottles of Moët & Chandon champagne with plenty of chill on them."

The waiter jotted down their order. Vinny again nodded his head, smiled approvingly. "Moët & Chandon, eh, Irish. You sure came a long way from Georgie O'Neil's place."

Tommy laughed happily. "Nothing but the best from here on, Vinny baby. What could be sweeter on Christmas Eve than two bums like us drinking French champagne with the two best-looking girls in New York. And then, Frank Sinatra for dessert."

Everyone joined in the gay laughter.

The dinner was delicious, the wine superb. They toasted each other with every refill. Sated with the fine food, glowing with the great wine, they settled back as the room darkened to a roll of the drums and the gorgeous Copa Girls scampered out to open the show to wild applause from the packed house. Their dazzling routines over, the stand-up comic having milked the crowd for a hundred laughs, Frank Sinatra came onstage with a cup and saucer in his hand singing, "They've Got an Awful Lot of Coffee in Brazil."

The Copa rocked from side to side when he finished the pop tune and quieted immediately as he raised his hands and greeted the assemblage graciously. He then sang for almost an hour—sweet love songs and sad love songs—to a hushed audience and plenty of glistening eyes. Tommy stole a glance at

Vinny's face, didn't miss the rapture in his eyes as he clutched Connie's hand. He swore later that he wasn't sure who Vinny loved more, Frank Sinatra or Connie.

The show finally ended with a standing ovation for Frank and a peppy routine by the Copa Girls. The lights about the room spurted on and the four of them snapped back to reality. They shook their heads, smiled almost shyly at each other, still enthralled by all the lovely songs. Tommy waved to the waiter and ordered more champagne.

"C'mon, tell the truth. Is this the life we were meant for or isn't it?"

Connie laughed. "Oh, Tommy, I can't thank you enough. What a great night! Frank was never better, right, Vinny?"

"Every time I see him or hear him he seems to get better, sweetheart. Tom, what a great idea to take us to see Sinatra. A real treat."

Justine said, "I honestly still can't believe I saw Frank Sinatra in person. Oh, Tommy, it was absolutely wonderful." She leaned over and kissed him on the lips.

Tommy flushed with pride at the compliments, glorying in his role as host. The fresh bottles of champagne arrived. He waved away the waiter's attempt to pour the wine, took over the chore himself. He raised his glass, they all touched it and each others. He sat straight up in his chair and said, "Tonight, on Christmas Eve, I'm with everyone I love. Let's make a toast to being together on future Christmas Eves as long as it's possible." He grinned and winked broadly. "Drinking champagne, of course."

With suddenly sober faces, they raised their glasses, drank their wine, and kissed each other.

Vinny said, "Hey, let's not get too serious. Let's have another toast that Tommy always picks up the check for the French champagne."

A big laugh all around.

They finally left the Copa about one o'clock in the morning after a couple of nightcaps in the bar which Vinny insisted on buying. After much hugging and kissing outside the night club they went home in separate taxis. Justine clung fervently to

Tommy in the taxi, whispering in his ear that she could barely wait until they reached their apartment. True to her word, he had just finished brushing his teeth when she pulled him out of the bathroom and onto their bed. The songs of Sinatra, the delectable wine, the memorable evening, infused a passionate session of lovemaking that Tommy was sure would cause him to shrink at least a foot.

Fortunately, he woke up intact the next morning to the sounds of Justine quietly singing in the kitchen and the rattle of dishes as she prepared breakfast. He lay in bed waiting for his head to clear and strained to listen to her surprisingly good voice. He smiled. She was singing "Say It Isn't So." She's some great kid and I guess I really love her. Another thing, a really good thing, she's not a female district attorney. Never questions me about money, about how late I stay out. I have to admit her eyes widen once in a while, but what the hell, you can't blame her for that. He grinned, from rags to riches in one easy month.

They spent Christmas Day at his sister Rosemary's new house with all the relatives bouncing in and out, including his beloved Grandma McElroy. Grandma now lived with his Uncle Tom, his mother's brother. Tom looked at her in adoration, pained to see how she was aging. He smiled. Maybe older, but just as bright and firm as ever. As usual, she was the center of attention and justly received the fanciest and most expensive presents. He basked in the gay conviviality, happy to spend the momentous day in the company of his loved ones. He sat next to Grandma for hours, explaining at great length the intricacies of his new undercover assignment. She questioned him sharply about the potential of graft and the dangers associated with "dirty money," her expression. He laughed and lied as glibly as ever, sidestepping all questions of any involvement he might be exposed to in gambling and vice. He loved her dearly, forever grateful for having raised him after his mother died. He knew that she felt strongly about the illicit money his father made, was sure it ruined her daughter's marriage. But drink in hand, happy as a clam, he looked her dead in the eye and lied cheerfully and convincingly.

Christmas Day and Christmas week soon gave way to the joys of New Year's Eve and the exciting portents of the new year ahead. Tom and Justine danced New Year's Eve night away at a local Queens night club with her bowling pals and their husbands. He drank steadily, laughed, and carried on as if without a care in the world. But the image of Joe the Boss gnawed at his brain and heart throughout the gaiety as it had all during the festive week. He had only appeared twice at the squad office during the holiday week, but it was back to business as usual after the new year rolled in and the specter of impending trouble loomed ahead in the person of Joe Marchetti.

There was the usual joking and casual bantering taking place in the squad room when all hands finally reported for duty after the hectic holiday season. Most of the wisecracks were directed at Jerry Dillon, the perennial bachelor, large dark glasses hopefully hiding an apparent monumental hangover. He seemed too worn out to lash back at his tormentors, only managing an occasional curse punctuated by an obscene gesture.

Billy shook Tom's hand warmly, embraced him, and wished him all good luck in the year ahead. Tom looked him over carefully, decided Billy had indeed had a harrowing week. His eyes were very bloodshot and his face puffy and bloated from the whiskey, but his manner was cool and charming as always. Tommy, slightly shaky himself, silently hoped the days ahead would be quiet.

They went into high gear immediately. Their three intrepid stool pigeons turned up two outlaw bookmakers, a number runner, and a high-stake multitabled card game. The collars, the court appearances, the peace agreements following their arrests quickly consumed the week until Friday. Billy, somewhat mysteriously, told Tommy to take Friday off, explaining that he had some personal business to attend to. He was grateful for the weekend off, escaping the freezing weather by staying nice and cozy at home reading and watching TV.

Justine did her usual bowling routine on Saturday night, but cooked up a storm for him. He ate like a condemned man and with firm resolve stayed free of the booze for three days. He once again promised himself to return to working out in the gym and to give the booze a rest. Well, he grinned, at least a slight rest. It's a tough world out there.

Billy called him Sunday night to arrange a date for lunch at Dinty Moore's the next day. He slept late, took a long shower, and as he dressed in front of the full-length bedroom mirror he complimented himself on how well he looked after being absolutely dry for three days. Billy was already at the bar when he arrived, the usual tall Cutty Sark and water in front of him. Tommy shook hands, looked into the visibly troubled face of his partner, changed his mind in midair from a Coca-Cola to a duplicate Cutty Sark and water.

"You look terrific, Tom. Have a real good rest over the weekend?"

"Thanks, Billy, I feel great. I didn't do a thing but eat, read, watch a little TV and sleep. Didn't touch one drink the whole three days."

"Christ, I wish I could say the same, Tom. Anyway, here's good luck." He tipped Tommy's glass.

Tommy took a pull on his Scotch. Ooh, that first Scotch tastes so good. He took another long swallow. Mother's milk!

"You look like something's bothering you, Billy, like the doomsday posters. Everything okay?"

"To be honest, Tom, I'm very tired. Too much goddam partying. I'm really going to try to take it easy on the booze this coming year. At least I promised my wife that I would. But, you're right, I do have something on my mind. Let's drink up and get a table and have lunch; it concerns you."

Well, at last. Here it comes. The bad news I've been anticipating for over a week.

They were seated at a table in the back room and ordered a fresh drink. Billy leaned close to Tom.

"Put your hand under the table, Tommy, I have an envelope for you."

He did as instructed and Billy passed a bulky envelope to him. He surreptitiously slipped it into his inside jacket pocket.

"What's this all about, Billy?"

"That's your cut for the month, Tommy."

"How much is there?"

"Fifteen hundred!"

Tommy's face flushed, his eyes clouded, and in a harsh voice he said, "You reach under the table, Billy, and when I return the envelope, stick it up your ass."

"Jesus Christ, Tom, please don't get excited. I swear, this isn't my idea. I've been awake half the night worrying about how you would handle this. To be honest, I don't blame you one bit for being pissed off. But please, at least keep the money. Let me explain how it happened."

"Billy, don't misunderstand me, I'm not sore at you. I realize this cheap shit doesn't come from you, you're too nice a guy. It's Joe the Boss who called the shot, am I right?"

"Absolutely, Tom, you're dead right. I argued with him at the squad meeting and so did most of the other guys, but he was adamant about it. He insisted that you have to wait six months before you get a full cut. I tried explaining how difficult it was to have a partner who was being shortchanged, but he refused to listen."

Tommy shot up halfway out of his chair, eyes bulging with rage, straining to keep his voice low.

"Six months!" he said incredulously. "Why that rotten, low-life, guinea fuck."

"Please, take it easy, Tom. Christ, a couple of tables of people are staring at you. Look, here's how he palmed it off. He gave us all the same horseshit about that's how the bosses wanted it. You know, the old army game. Wait until you are completely trusted, until everyone establishes faith in you."

"Do you go along with that? How do you like my performance so far?"

"Of course I don't agree with him and so far I love the way you handle yourself. I argued with him for over an hour. To be honest, so did most of the other guys. But as usual—and for years—Joe the Boss won the argument."

Tommy relaxed, took a long belt of his Scotch. He sat back, vaguely satisfied with Billy's answer. He remembered Vinny's words at the Copa. They came back with great clarity. Marchetti was an asshole. Don't knuckle under to him. You've got plenty of weight with Charlie in your corner. Okay, Joe the Boss, you fucking disgrace to the wops. I'll catch up to you later. He knew Billy was telling the truth, knew that he was as disturbed as he was. But he had to take action immediately, grab the bull by the horns.

Billy hid his embarrassment behind the luncheon menu, which he pretended to study. Tom sat back in his chair, slowly finishing his drink.

"Feel like ordering some lunch, Tom. I haven't had a morsel of food since I woke up this morning. Had one cup of coffee and dashed out of the house." He looked at Tommy's face, knew he was smoldering, murderous. Let's do anything to change the subject of money.

"Do you mind if we wait a few minutes, Billy? Order another drink, please."

Tommy weighed what he had to say next very carefully. He didn't want to offend Billy, he wasn't exactly displeased with him, but he was extremely disappointed that he didn't take a firmer stand in his behalf. Who the fuck did this Joe the Boss character think he was—Jesus Christ?

The fresh drinks arrived. They tipped glasses, and Tommy said, "Billy, I'm going to ask you a very tough question. Please tell me the truth, don't give me any runaround. How much was the monthly cut? How much did I get screwed out of?"

Billy looked at Tommy's distressed face, felt miserable, wished he was somewhere in Outer Mongolia. Anywhere but opposite his new partner in Dinty Moore's. And Jesus, he is my partner and the makings of a good one. He sipped his drink. Suppose one of these days we run into a real tough situation. Not the fun and games horseshit with gamblers and whores. The real McCoy—a stick-up, a bank robbery. Christ, a cop's life often depended upon his partner's actions. He decided to tell him the one hundred percent truth. Nice and easy, toying with his Scotch, "Eleven thousand, five hundred, Tommy!"

"So I got beat out of ten thousand? Just like that, right?"

"What the hell can I say, Tom? Of course you're right. Marchetti took out the bosses' cut as usual and each guy got a little over a thousand extra as his end. Tom, I'm perfectly willing, in fact, I want to give you my extra bit to show how I feel. Suppose I do that?"

"I appreciate that, Billy, but no good. I'll handle this my own way. There's one thing you can go to sleep on, I'm striking while the iron is hot. I want to confront this guy Marchetti today. Today, you get it? Not tomorrow or the day after."

Billy's face assumed deeper worry. Hesitantly, reluctantly, he said, "Today? Why today? Jesus, Tommy, wait until you cool off a little. You're liable to do or say something you'll be sorry for."

Tommy leaned across the table, his face inches from Billy's. So close he could smell his stale whiskey breath. "Listen, Billy, I don't give one good fuck what I say to this guy. Furthermore, I don't intend to remain a Manhattan West man for six months working for peanuts while this prick decides my fate. Who elected him to decide how much I should get? I want mine now! Today, you got that straight? And if I don't get it I declare war."

The ultimatum off his chest, he felt immense relief. He took a long swallow of Scotch. He put his glass down, feeling calmer at last, and said, "Okay, Billy, let's get something to eat. Then we'll go search out Joe the Boss."

Billy put his head back, rolled his eyes up to the ceiling as if in mock prayer. "Please God, spare me having to break in any more new partners the rest of my life in the Job."

Tommy laughed, the tension lifted.

"Be honest, Billy, am I a bad partner?"

"Outside of being thick as shit like all the Irish, I think you're a terrific partner. But what the hell, Tom, I have to admit you're right this time. Now, let's eat. I'm pretty sure I know where Marchetti hangs out almost every Monday. If we're lucky we'll nail him there later."

"Where?"

"In a pretty snazzy bowling alley on University Place in upper Greenwich Village. He bowls in some league there a couple of afternoons a week. Thinks he's pretty good the way he talks about it."

Tommy laughed out loud—incredulously. "Bowl? You're kidding, he bowls? For Christ sake, I should have known."

Both in a more congenial mood, they finished lunch and took a taxi downtown to the University Bowling Lanes. The sparkling interior was much more plush than the local Queens bowling alleys to which he occasionally was forced to accompany Justine. There was a spacious balcony containing a long bar and about fifteen tables overlooking the bowling area. The restaurant expanse was softly lit, fully manned and equipped, and appeared in excellent taste. Tom surveyed the bowlers from his raised perch, trying to locate Marchetti, and was faintly surprised to see such a good crowd taking up all of the twelve highly polished lanes.

Sure enough, there was Joe the Boss, clad in bowling shoes and traditional silk bowling shirt, surrounded by a bunch of similarly dressed cohorts laughing it up on lanes three and four. Tommy shook his head as he observed him. The life of the bowling group. He smiled in spite of his inner hatred. Maybe I'll speak to Joe and arrange a home match with Justine's Holy Rollers. Billy nodded to him and they went to the bar and ordered their usual tall Cutty Sark and waters.

"So this is where the despotic piece of shit hangs out, Billy?"

"Only on Mondays and Wednesdays. He bowls with a group of mostly Italian business guys from around the Village."

"What happens if something serious comes up and he has to make a collar on one of those days?"

"God forbid! With Joe the Boss, bowling takes precedence over everything."

The drinks came. They tipped glasses good luck. Tommy knocked his off in two long belts, motioned to the bartender to set up two more. He again tipped Billy's glass, took a long swallow.

"Wait here, I'm off to see my Neopolitan nemesis."

Billy smiled, winked, indicating his acquiescence. He was nice and rosy from the good lunch and the fine Scotch whiskey, no longer apprehensive. He sipped his drink as Tommy left, amused, anxious to see how his new partner would manage the confrontation. After all these years he was sick and tired of Marchetti's dictatorial ways, his word inevitably being accepted as law. This kid will take him down a peg. Go get him, Tommy.

Tommy walked deliberately behind a couple of rows of spectator chairs and stepped down the narrow aisle between bowling lanes four and five, just out of Marchetti's immediate field of vision. He felt a sharp revulsion at the scene unfolding a few feet away from him. Marchetti must have just bowled a strike because his silken clad pals were enthusiastically patting him on the back and pumping his hand. Christ, like he was Joe DiMaggio after hitting a bases-loaded home run.

Marchetti, a happy grin creasing his swarthy, movie villain features, prepared to take a seat to await his next turn at the line when he spotted Tommy on the edge of his group. He walked directly to him, the big grin erased, his eyes wary, cold.

"What the hell are you doing here, Sloane? I didn't know you bowled. Where's Billy Driscoll?"

"Billy's at the bar, Joe. You're right, I don't bowl and have no intention of ever bowling. I'm here to see you, period."

"What's on your mind that can't wait a day or two?"

"What's on my mind that can't wait an hour is that you fucked me, Marchetti, fucked me without even a kiss and we resolve it today, you understand, today." Voice rising, face flushed.

Marchetti looked around nervously, turned back to Tommy, attempting bravado. "Now just a minute, kid, no one talks to me like that. What the hell do you mean, saying I fucked you?"

"You know goddam well what I mean and don't give me any of that kid shit. When do you finish your bowling bit?"

"In about half an hour."

"I'll be waiting at the bar for you." Tommy turned abruptly and walked back to the bar and rejoined Billy.

"Well, come on, how did it go, my shy, retiring Irish partner?"

Tommy grinned, relieved to sit back, enjoy his drink.

"I know for sure, Billy, that I'm the last guy he wanted to see or ever expected to see in the University Bowling Lanes."

"How'd he seem to take it? A little shook up?"

"He's real shook up. He probably won't be able to hit a bull in the ass when he bowls his next turn. At first, he tried to come on strong like he always does, gave me that kid shit. But I can tell, I'm sure I have him on the run. I told him I'd wait for him here until he finishes bowling. Look, Billy, seriously, if you feel uncomfortable and want to avoid being mixed up in our argument, take a walk. I promise you, I won't feel bad if you leave. It's my personal beef, not yours."

"No good, Tom, no way. I'm staying right here while you two have it out. I told you that I argued like hell on your behalf at the squad meeting and I want you to be convinced I was on your side all the way."

Tommy gripped his arm, affectionately mussed his hair. "Thanks, Billy, you're a real sweetheart."

They ordered another drink, sat quietly, watched the various bowling groups. A tremendous spectator sport. Tommy grinned. He watched Joe's team closely and was pleased to see that none of his pals jumped with joy after he bowled, indicating that Marchetti had more on his mind than strikes and spares.

Joe the Boss joined them at the bar after the match ended. His bowling group departed amid a thousand hugs and handshakes. His face was set, grim, as he approached them. His greeting to Billy was cut, abrupt. In a hoarse voice—"What's this all about, Billy, bringing this young punk here where I bowl?"

Tommy stepped away from the bar and hit Marchetti with a stinging backhand slap across the face. Joe the Boss almost went to his knees from the force of the blow. He reeled back and Tommy straightened him up by clutching the collar of his silk bowling shirt. Eyes glazed, blood dripping from his nose, Marchetti was totally stunned.

"You call me a punk once more and I'll kick the living shit out of you right here, you no-good cocksucker. Just say it again, just once."

Billy startled, paralyzed for a moment, jumped between them and pulled Tommy away. The bartender gasped, got dead white, looked as if he was about to have a heart attack.

"For Christ sake, Tommy, are you crazy? C'mon, take it easy, please." He pushed him a few feet down the bar.

Marchetti collected himself. A little shaky, felt his nose, looked at his blood on his fingers.

"Get out of the way, Billy, I'll kill this kid."

"For Christ sake, Joe, relax. He's twenty years younger than you and ten times stronger. Get hold of yourself. You were wrong, Joe. You've got no goddam right calling him a punk. You deserved a smack in the face. Now calm down, both of you. Joe, go into the men's room, wash up and change. I'm sure you have another shirt to replace your bowling shirt."

Marchetti retreated to the men's room off the bar, muttering invectives as he went. Tommy stood silently at the bar, drink in hand, but still agitated and visibly trying to control his rage.

"Tom, that was completely uncalled for, especially in a public place like this. There's no worse scene in the world for civilians to see than two cops going at it. You can bet your ass everyone who saw this little fiasco will be repeating it at least ten times the next few days."

"I'm sorry, Billy. I know that I probably shouldn't have smacked him, but from the first day I laid eyes on that prick, the lousy way he treated me, well, I hate that sonofabitch. Then to think he had the nerve to call me a punk. That was the last fucking straw. Nobody calls me a punk and gets away with it."

"Tommy, I guess in some ways you were absolutely right. But you have to admit, it's one helluva way to start negotiations for a full cut."

"Billy, you're my partner, you get this straight. And what I'm going to say goes for everyone else in the squad. I either get my full cut or I don't want a fucking dime. I go my own way, piss on everybody."

He said it with such intensity, Billy was momentarily floored, nonplussed. He sipped his drink, spoke very carefully.

"What do you mean by that remark?"

"I'd prefer to wait until the idol of the Italian bowling world comes out of the men's room and the three of us talk it over."

Billy mollified, couldn't resist a grin. This guy is a real pisser. "Here comes the fallen idol now and thank God he has a clean shirt on."

The three of them sat down at a rear table off the far corner of the bar. Marchetti, nursing a slightly swollen nose and an injured air, refused a drink while Billy and Tommy ordered a fresh one from the lone waitress in attendance.

The drinks came and the two partners tipped their glasses without speaking, wishing each other good luck with their eyes.

Marchetti opened the conversation almost as if he were

about to cry, in a choked, querulous voice. "You know, Sloane, you got some goddam nerve hitting me like that. What the hell's wrong with you? You some kind of a nut, or something?"

"I'm far from crazy, Marchetti, no kind of nut. As long as we're sitting here, let's understand each other. You hated me from the start because I got into the squad instead of your hand-picked pal. Well, that's too goddam bad. Shame on you. From the opening gun you treated me like shit. Yeah, just like a piece of shit from the day you laid eyes on me. Today, you meet me in a bowling alley, haven't the slightest clue why I want to see you, except maybe a guilty conscience, and you call me a punk. The next time you call me a punk, I'm going to beat the living shit out of you, no more backhands. Now, you got that straight?"

Marchetti stirred in his chair, face red beneath his bushy eyebrows, unsure whether to remain seated or get up. Tommy raised his hand, he sat back. Tommy took the envelope containing his supposed cut that Billy had given him at Dinty Moore's and threw it on the table.

"Now the first thing you can do is shove this fifteen hundred dollars up the top of your ass. I want my full cut and I want it tomorrow at the latest. Understand one thing, Marchetti, I don't bullshit. I want another ten thousand by tomorrow afternoon and my full share from here on. Either I get it, or I'm going to raise so much hell in Manhattan West you'll wish I was dead."

"What is this, a threat? Maybe you'll be dead sooner than you think."

Tommy leaned across the table, grabbed Marchetti by the collar of his new, clean shirt and said, "If I ever even suspect you have the balls to try it, I'll kill you first, you no-good cocksucker."

Billy grabbed Tommy's arm. "Jesus, will you two please take it easy. People are watching us, for Christ sake."

They all sat back, Marchetti looked frightened. His voice quavered. "Billy, will you explain what this is all about? Why is this kid talking so whacky? I thought we treated his case fair and square at the meeting. You know the rules about new guys."

Billy leaned close to Marchetti and in a very low but strident tone, said, "Joe, I warned you at the meeting that depriving Tom of a full cut would cause nothing but trouble. I wasn't alone, so did most of the other guys. As far as the rule about new guys, since when did we ever have a new guy? Tom's the first new guy we've had in two years. You know goddam well this was strictly a Joe-the-Boss new rule. What the hell is the difference whether we give him fifteen hundred dollars or fifteen thousand dollars? If he's a plant or a stool pigeon he already knows enough to put everyone in jail, especially me. C'mon, let's have some peace. Kiss and make up, for Christ sake. For the love of God give Tommy his proper cut and that will end all this bullshit none of us needs."

Tommy listened intently to Billy's every word, meanwhile studying Marchetti's face to determine his reaction. The stronger Billy's words, the more he noticed Marchetti's face sagging, the look of defeat replacing the former arrogance.

Billy's speech over, Tommy spoke up. Not argumentatively; he was almost conciliatory. His mind was whirling, but one thought predominated. Get the money, baby, get the money, that's the main item on the agenda.

"Listen, Joe, I'm sorry I lost my head and hit you, but you're just as responsible as I am for what you called me. Where I was born and raised nobody calls anybody a punk and gets away with it. Another thing you might as well get straight, I'm no goddam young rookie out of the academy. I've got almost three years in the Job, in one of the toughest precincts in the city. I've made over a hundred arrests. I shot and killed two guys. I've been stabbed and took my share of whacks on the head. Last but not least, I've been on all kinds of payrolls both on foot patrol and in radio cars. I didn't get picked for Manhattan West by accident, common sense should have made you know that. And as long as we're on the subject, if you really want to know who my rabbi is, it's Charlie Mattuci. If you're in as solid with the bosses as you claim you are, go ahead and check that out. Now I don't know if I'm going to be there six months or six years. All I know is that for as long as I last I want whatever is coming to me one hundred percent. I wasn't lucky enough to have your run, or the other guys' run, in plainclothes. By this time, you guys should be nice and fat. I'm on the balls of my ass."

He paused, calculated the effect he was having on both Joe and

Billy, resumed. "I want the same cut as everyone else. I also want the same responsibility for picking up payrolls and everything else the Job entails. That's my story, the way I feel. There's no other way, else I go out on my own and get it myself. Okay, Joe, it's up to you, you call the shots. When can I have your answer?"

Marchetti looked directly into Tommy's face, the hate embedded in his eyes. But the tremor in his voice betrayed his fear. The bravado was gone, it was an old man's voice.

"That was a helluva speech. You not only hit me in the face without warning, now you're threatening the whole squad. What are you trying to say, that you'll blow the whistle on us?"

Tommy's face grew ice cold again. He shook his head.

"You know, Joe, a remark like that deserves another smack in the face. Look, let's stop all the horseshit. I don't want to be a friend of yours nohow, I just want an answer. Do I get my full cut or not?"

Marchetti looked across the table at Billy, nodded his head towards the bar. Billy got the message. He rose to his feet, put his hand on Tommy's shoulder and said, "Stay here for a few minutes, Joe wants to talk to me privately."

Tommy nodded his assent, stayed seated at the table while the two of them went to the bar about fifty feet away. He never looked up, just sipped his drink nice and easy. He felt confident, knew in his heart his bluff would work. What the hell, if it didn't and Joe the Boss had the tremendous clout with the top brass that he pretended to have, well, good-bye Manhattan West and hello Central Park.

Marchetti ordered a beer, Billy the usual Cutty Sark and tall water. They were silent as they waited for their drinks. Billy studied Joe's face. He was getting old. His swarthy skin had deep seams, his eyes were watery, his hair and bushy eyebrows steel gray. Billy knew that he had over twenty-five years in the Job. Had to be in his fifties. Must have at least a million. Been on the real, big teat for untold years. Doesn't go for spit, good home guy, no broads. Someone said he hasn't got the first dollar he made, he bought a wallet with it. Has two kids, one a lawyer in New Jersey, another a teaching nun in some Catholic school in Westchester. Might need one's counsel and the other's prayers before he finishes up in the Job.

The drinks came, they tipped glasses, Joe spoke up. "What the hell goes with this kid, Billy, can you tell me? He sure is one wise guy sonofabitch. I'd like to put a hole in the young fuck for hitting me in the face like he did. Wait until I see Charlie Mattuci and tell him what happened. I betcha this young prick hardly even knows Charlie."

"Look, Joe, don't bet on it, because I happen to know that he's very close to Charlie. He's Charlie's son-in-law's best friend. You know, the good-looking guy, the ex-cop, Vinny Ciano."

Surprised voice. "Oh, really, how about that?"

"Okay, now listen to me, Joe. We've been together a long time. I've always gone along with what you say because I respected your age and your years in the Job. It goes back to what I kept repeating at the meeting last week, and most of the guys agreed with me. Sloane is entitled to a full cut. He's here, in Manhattan West, whether you approve of it or not. It's like being married, for Christ sake. You know the old line, for better or for worse. Why don't we stop all this bullshit and give him the ten grand he's got coming and we'll straighten it out during the month. Please, Joe, do it for my sake. I'm the guy who has to work with Sloane every day, remember that."

"Maybe you're right, Billy. I guess you're the one we put on the spot, having to work alongside him. But deep down I don't trust this kid. Jesus, his eyes flash when money is mentioned. I checked him out a little, asked a few friends of mine who worked with him in the Twenty-third to give me an opinion. They said he has plenty of balls, but he's a real cold-blooded, money-hungry fuck."

"Joe, be honest, what's wrong with loving money? Doesn't that apply to all of us, to ninety-nine and nine tenths of the people on earth? Truthfully, in the short time we've been together, I've found Sloane to be a real nice guy. Furthermore, he's bright, a real smart cookie, and like you said, plenty of balls."

"A real smart cookie, eh. Maybe that's what I don't like about him. Too fucking smart for his own good, from what I hear. Okay, you tell him that he'll have his full cut by Wednesday. It'll be about nine grand 'cause everyone will have to kick in whatever extra they got. I'll give it to you to give to him and I'll alert the other guys. What happened today dies here, okay? I'll just pass the word that I had reason to change my mind, that it was embarrassing to you. We'll just let it go at that. Okay?"

He finished his beer, extended his hand.

"I'm leaving now, Billy, I don't want to even say good-bye to that Irish prick. I only wish I was twenty years younger. Right now, I feel very old and very, very humiliated. Just remember, I'm going on record. I don't trust this hungry bastard."

"C'mon, Joe, cheer up. You were dead wrong. You never call a young cop a punk, you're insulting his manhood. Okay, time will heal everything. You go and I'll go back to the table. Don't worry about your beauty, your nose is only swollen a little and you never were a threat to Rudolph Valentino even on a good day."

Marchetti finally smiled, punched Billy's arm, patted his head. "You're a good kid, Billy." He left.

Billy walked back to the table and rejoined Tommy, who had sat with his back to them all during their conversation at the bar. He sat on the edge of his chair, eagerly awaiting the verdict from Billy.

Billy purposely kept him in suspense, motioned for the waitress to bring another drink. The drinks came, he tipped glasses with Tommy. A big grin on his face.

"Okay, Tommy, my boy, you just won the war."

A wide smile of exultation lit up Tommy's face. His first reaction was unspoken but deep-seated gratitude to Vinny for his advice and everything else he had done. What a nice dinner I'm going to buy you and Connie, walio. He clanked glasses exuberantly with Billy, secretly offering up a toast to Vince. His face assumed a sober expression.

"I really appreciate what you did for me, Billy, and I'll never forget it. I'm sorry I blew my top and smacked Marchetti, but all the hate I held inside me for that bastard exploded when he called me a punk. But what the hell, there's one thing for sure, he and I could never be friends in any shape or form."

"I wouldn't worry about it, Tom, things like this blow over. You know the old saying, time heals everything. Besides, to be dead honest, Joe was absolutely wrong all the way. Well, I guess we've had enough excitement for one day. Suppose we drink up, get my car, and take a ride to my house in Brooklyn and

I'll square you up. I've got plenty of cash stashed around the house to take care of you. By the way, Joe the Boss, always the sharp pencil man, decreed that you got nine grand coming, not ten. We all have to kick back enough to make up your correct share. He's a real beauty, right, Tom?"

Tommy shook his head. "I met hard-headed guys before in my life, but this guy wins the prize. Billy, seriously, it isn't necessary to square me up today, I can wait a few days."

"No good, Tom, we'll do it today, get it over with. Besides, I've been telling my wife Betty all about you and she's anxious to meet you. My two kids will also be home from school and you can say hello to them. I'm half-dead, anyway. Do it today, we'll all be happier. You go home with a bundle of cash and I'll get to have dinner with my family and a good night's sleep for a change."

They took a taxi back uptown and picked up Billy's car in a garage a few doors down from Dinty Moore's. Tommy was inwardly overjoyed at the way things had gone, but all during the drive to Brooklyn he concealed his elation and kept up a composed, easy conversation with Billy concerning the endless policeman's topic, the Job. They roared laughing, recalling different hilarious incidents, laid out their plans and schemes for future action, and in surprisingly short order pulled into the driveway alongside Billy's house.

It was a handsome, dark red, two-story brick house high above a raised lawn on beautiful Shore Road in the Bay Ridge neighborhood of Brooklyn. It overlooked the Narrows, a marvelous, blue gray expanse of water lying in the heart of New York Bay; a confluence of water formed by the joining of the Hudson and East Rivers. The giant magnificent span of the Verrazano Bridge loomed high in the sky almost directly overhead, connecting Brooklyn with Staten Island. Tommy thrilled to the awe-inspiring vista, deeply moved as always by the sheer beauty of an endless waterfront view. He vowed that someday soon he would own a home on the water.

Billy's wife, Betty, answered the doorbell's ring. She kissed him affectionately, her candidate for husband of the year. She shook Tommy's hand in greeting, enthusiastically remarking how terribly pleased she was to meet her husband's new partner. Betty was tall and slim, with blue eyes and long brown hair. Her tanned face was split by a wide grin, revealing slightly protruding, very white teeth behind a generous mouth. Tommy decided that she was almost as pretty as Billy had bragged, taking in with practiced eye her nice figure encased in a tweed skirt and cashmere sweater, set off by a string of expensive-looking pearls. A true and honest plainclothesman's spouse, right out of the local paper's society page. She spoke almost breathlessly, how terribly busy she'd been all day, how terribly sorry that the house was such a mess. Tommy, as he looked around, thought it was spotless.

Betty bustled about, taking their coats, making them comfortable. She made drinks from behind a living room bar that was set up in the corner of the large and tastefully furnished room. She served them, sherry for her, Cutty Sark and water for the boys. She raised her glass in welcome to Tom, threw a kiss at Billy, and fetched the two children from the downstairs playroom. Billy Junior, aged nine, was blond and very courteous, as was his sister Jane, aged six. They both hugged and kissed their father, Junior shook hands firmly with Tommy, and little Jane kissed him.

The wholesome family scene made Tom feel great, but he felt a momentary pang about his own childless marriage in the presence of the two fine-looking, well-mannered kids. He once again made a silent vow to discuss children with Justine, to find out once and for all what the hell caused their apparent infertility. The two kids were sent downstairs to play and Betty in short order informed Tommy that she was a graduate of Mt. Saint Vincent's College in Westchester County and how terribly anxious she was for Billy to resume his aborted college career and get his degree. Tommy nodded vigorously and affirmatively as she talked about her college, her hospital volunteer work, her kids, her house, and her husband. After the second drink he concluded that Betty was a complete bore, a social climber, and if she used the word terribly once again, he was going to scream.

Mercifully, all good things come to an end, and when Betty finally came to a halt for a few seconds, Billy winked at Tom and said, "Make us another drink, please, darling, and I'll show Tommy around the house."

"Fine, dear, but I'm terribly afraid it's a bit upset, the cleaning girl hasn't been here in a few days."

"Don't worry about it, honey, I'm sure Tom won't mind."

Drinks in hand, they went upstairs, where Billy led the way to the master bedroom. He sat down on the edge of an enormous king-sized bed and motioned to Tom to sit in a lounge chair a few feet away in the corner of the room.

"She sure can talk, right, Tommy?"

Tommy smiled. "She was probably nervous meeting a big celebrity like me, Billy. But she's very nice, a very good-looking woman."

"Thanks, Tom. She's really a good skate, too. Tries to put on the dog a little too much, but she's a good wife and a good mother. Her old man was a plainclothes lieutenant for years. Got a brother a doctor. I guess Daddy did pretty good. Educated his kids the best and takes it nice and easy down in Florida. Betty takes good care of me and doesn't ask too many questions. What more could a guy want? Especially in the racket we're in. Jesus, Tom, a woman should be canonized for putting up with the likes of us."

Tommy laughed. "Canonized and immortalized, Billy."

Billy laughed, arose from the bed and closed the bedroom door. He walked across the room, opened the door of a large closet, reached up and took a hat box off the overhead. He laid the hat box on the bed, removed a layer of silk handkerchiefs, and came up with a manila envelope. He put the envelope on the bed and took out a pile of hundred dollar bills wrapped in thousand dollar units. He pushed nine units towards Tommy, motioned to him and said, "Count those if you want, Tom, but I'm sure I'm correct. There should be nine thousand there."

Tommy arose from his chair, sat on the edge of the bed next to Billy and almost lovingly fingered the piles of hundreds. Nine units, nine thousand dollars! His eyes glistened, he was almost afraid to speak, decided to make a joke. "You're in the wrong racket, Billy, the way you handle money you should become a bank teller."

Billy laughed. "Jesus Christ. Some case, me a bank teller. I'd have my hand in the till the first week surrounded by all that cash and probably wind up in jail the second week. No wonder some of those poor, underpaid bastards embezzle the banks they work for. What a temptation! No thanks, I'll stick to being an honest cop."

Tommy laughed, but couldn't take his eyes away from the money. He scooped it up reverently and said, "That's the game, Billy, an honest cop. Okay, pal, I assume this is all mine?"

He turned, looked up at Billy, who had a strange expression on his face. Unsure, puzzled.

Once again—"Well, is it mine?"

"Oh, sure. You bet, it's all yours, Tom. Listen, you have one envelope I gave you at lunch. Will this fit into that or shall I get you another?"

"No, just give me a couple of rubber bands to wrap around this gorgeous nine grand. I'm sure that'll do the trick."

Billy slipped a couple of rubber bands off the bedroom door-knob and handed them to Tommy. He proceeded to wrap the money expertly into two bundles and slip them into his jacket pocket.

They relaxed, sat opposite each other. Billy on the edge of the bed, Tommy back on the lounge chair. They reached to the floor for their drinks and raised their glasses. "Once again, Billy, I'll never forget this. Never, not as long as I'm alive."

"You got it, Tom, it's yours, it was coming to you. But in all honesty I do have something I'd like to say to you, or else I'd feel remiss. Look, I don't want you to take this too personally, I don't want to hurt your feelings. We're partners, we'll see a lot of action together, and I honestly like you. But, Christ, Tommy, you seem obsessed by money, like it's a fixation. Every conversation we've had you invariably turn it towards money, like it's the only thing that matters with you."

Tommy sipped his drink, weighed his answer carefully. "Oh, I wouldn't exactly say that, Billy. I'm sure I have other values. Remember one thing, you and the other guys in the squad, actually most plainclothes guys, are so used to money it's like cigar store coupons to them. There's exceptions to the rule, of course, like my old pal, Marchetti. Now me, Tommy Sloane, I have yet to get a taste of real money, of a real good shot. I look at you and your family here in this beautiful home and I want someday to have one just like it. I can't wait to afford a house with a waterfront view. I had an affair with a girl a while back who had the same kind of house off the water. When I thought about it after we broke up I wasn't sure what I missed most, her or her house." He smiled at the memory of Bobbi, continued.

"I want that nice house, a new car and all the other things that go with money. You already have them, Billy, you take it all for granted. If I seem a little too money hungry, okay, you're right. But remember one thing, Billy, in spite of all the sanctimonious horseshit they preach in church and in school, I've come to the conclusion, and you've agreed with me, that most of the whole fucking world is money hungry. That goes for judges, politicians, business tycoons, presidents, pimps, evangelists, cardinals, and into the night. So that's the way I stand, Billy, money hungry, just like the rest of the people in this world of ours."

He rose from the lounge chair, put his hand out to Billy and said, "Don't worry about me, pal, I'll be the best partner you ever had."

Billy grinned. "Okay, Tom, let's go downstairs and have that drink with Betty now that you're an Irish millionaire."

They finished their drinks and said good-bye effusively, promising to have dinner with him and Justine within the next couple of weeks. Billy insisted that Tom drive his car back to Queens, pointing out that neither one had court the next day and Tom could pick him up any time in the morning.

"You're sure you can find your way out of Brooklyn, the borough of kings?"

Tom laughed. "I'm no dope. I marked off the Brooklyn-Queens Expressway on the way here and that leads me a couple of blocks from home."

He caught the Belt Parkway a few blocks from Billy's house and soon was on the Brooklyn-Queens Expressway. His heart was singing as he drove along and he couldn't resist an occasional touch of the large bundle of cash in his coat pocket. Well, you finally got into the big time, Tommy baby. He wondered if he should confide in Justine a bit. Decided against it. Stash the money in the shirt drawer of his beloved chest of drawers and tomorrow right into the safe deposit vault. But I will take her out to dinner. Some real fancy place a little further out on Long Island. A sudden thought hit him. Shit, I hope she's not bowling tonight!

It was shortly after seven o'clock when he arrived home. Justine was in the kitchen, heard him slam the door and walked out to the living room, greeting him with a big kiss.

"H'mm, you smell good, must of arrested a whole barroom today."

He laughed. "Just a few Scotches to celebrate a big case I just busted," he lied easily. "Come on, off with the apron, I'm taking you someplace nice for dinner."

"Oh, Tommy, that's great, I really didn't feel like cooking tonight. Relax in your favorite chair and I'll make you a drink. Then I'll freshen up to go out. Okay?"

He sat back on his lounge chair, tall Scotch and water in hand, happy as a clam. The bulge in his jacket pocket made him feel like John D. Rockefeller. How sweet it is! Over ten grand in one easy day. He thought about Joe the Boss, knew that he made a mortal enemy. He dismissed him, fuck him. He thought about Vince. We both came a long way from the work shoes, pal. I love you.

Justine ready, he drove her in Billy's car to Captain Hook's on Long Island, the scene of his shattered romance with Bobbi. Justine loved it, and over dinner and more drinks he promised her everything just short of the moon. She loved it—all through the night.

Book Two

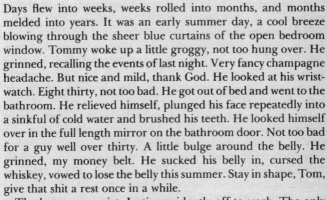

Days flew into weeks, weeks rolled into months, and months melded into years. It was an early summer day, a cool breeze blowing through the sheer blue curtains of the open bedroom window. Tommy woke up a little groggy, not too hung over. He grinned, recalling the events of last night. Very fancy champagne headache. But nice and mild, thank God. He looked at his wrist-watch. Eight thirty, not too bad. He got out of bed and went to the bathroom. He relieved himself, plunged his face repeatedly into a sinkful of cold water and brushed his teeth. He looked himself over in the full length mirror on the bathroom door. Not too bad for a guy well over thirty. A little bulge around the belly. He grinned, my money belt. He sucked his belly in, cursed the whiskey, vowed to lose the belly this summer. Stay in shape, Tom, give that shit a rest once in a while.

The house was quiet, Justine evidently off to work. The only sound he heard was the gentle purring of the downstairs air-conditioners he asked her to start when she left the house. He spread the curtains and looked out the window, just as he did every morning. As always, the view thrilled him. His own view, his dream come true. He broke into a big, satisfied grin as he scanned the sailboats gliding smoothly along the serene blue green waters of Little Neck Bay.

About a year ago they had bought their dream house in

Whitestone, one of the more elegant neighborhoods of Queens, bordering on Little Neck Bay. His fantasy of owning a waterfront home was realized at last. Justine was amazed that they could afford to buy a home of such magnificence for thirty thousand dollars. She really would have dropped dead had she known that he had paid another thirty grand for the house under the table. He smiled. Another coup of Vinny Ciano's, who had heard of an older wise guy who wanted to unload the house and move to Florida.

The deal was quickly arranged. He put the house in Justine's name, showing a carefully saved five thousand from their bank, a phony ten-thousand-dollar loan from his brother-in-law Billy, and received a nice low-rate mortgage for fifteen thousand. He grinned again, pleased in retrospect about his business acumen. Marvelous what a great deal maker you become after ten years as a Manhattan West man.

He backed away from the window, stretched lazily, scratched his head, undecided what to do with himself. He didn't feel like getting dressed, dismissed the idea of going to the office. It was Friday, a day he and his new young partner, Frank Donahue, usually took it nice and easy. Besides, they were well ahead of their quota of collars for the month. He drew on a pair of shorts, grabbed a white terrycloth robe off a closet hook and went downstairs.

He went into the large, spotless kitchen with the intention of making some breakfast, changed his mind in midair. He took a tray of ice cubes out of the fridge. Fuck coffee, this was a Bloody Mary morning. He went into the spacious, tastefully furnished living room to the ebony, modern bar standing in the far corner of the room. He plucked a round, stemmed glass off the back bar, shook some ice cubes from the tray into the glass and reached into the lower side compartment behind the bar for a bottle of Smirnoff vodka and a bottle of Bloody Mary mix. No tennis today, this is a Bloody Mary morning. He grinned, and at one this afternoon a luncheon date at the Plaza with a beautiful girl I was out with last night.

He settled comfortably in his beloved Barcalounger, sipped his Bloody Mary and gazed out the windows beyond the outside terrace to the bay. Now what in the name of Christ could beat this wonderful world? He whispered her name as he thought of her. Constance. *My friends all call me Connie. I shall call you Constance, my countess.* Constance Ward. What a nice name.

It all started very casual, but all minor miracles seem to happen that way. He was standing at the bar in Gallagher's Steak House having a drink with a bookmaker friend, Bernie Wolf. One of Bernie's gambling clients, the head of a big advertising agency, he found out later, spotted Bernie at the bar on his way out after lunch. Bernie invited him for a drink and he called to a girl waiting a few feet away to join them. He introduced her as Constance, his top copywriter, a very bright young lady. They were here planning a new campaign over lunch.

Tommy and Constance looked into each other's eyes as they shook hands and the world rocked a little. Tall, dark, cropped hair, blue eyes, white silk dress accentuating nice tanned skin. Generous mouth, big, white teeth. Tommy took a long sip of his Bloody Mary, savoring the memory. It was all too simple. Bernie and the advertising honcho bullshitted off to the side for a couple of minutes, deep into some gambling talk. Tommy waved to the bartender, Scotch for him. For you, dear? White wine, please.

Low voice—"You married, engaged, anything?"

A low laugh—"Nothing of the kind. I just broke up with a guy. I'm not ready for marriage. I want a career for myself. How about you?"

Face suddenly sad. "Unfortunately yes, at the moment. But unhappily. Making plans for a divorce," he lied through his teeth. Very low voice—"Where can I call you?"

"Call me at the office in about an hour. Gaines and Townsend, Twelve-twenty Sixth Avenue. Ask for me, Constance Ward. Don't forget, now." Another nice laugh.

Bernie and the big advertising guy rejoined them at the bar and they shook hands all around. Tommy and Bernie finished their drinks and the business they had met to discuss and Tom left Gallagher's a few minutes later. He looked at his wristwatch, ten minutes to three. He walked up Seventh Avenue to Central Park South and the New York Athletic Club. He had a guest card there through a bookmaker friend who was an old and respected member. He kept a change of clothes in his friend's locker and it had been a long day for him. He decided to take a good swim, steam bath, and massage so that he would be nice and fresh for what promised to be a lovely evening. But first the phone call.

"Hello, Gaines and Townsend."

"Constance Ward, please."

"One minute, please."

"Connie Ward, here."

"Constance, Thomas Sloane here. The same Thomas who fell in love with you less than an hour ago."

She laughed again. What a nice, refined laugh. Thank God, not one of those squeaky, high-pitched laughs.

"You sure do come on strong, Tommy Sloane. Who writes your material? Where are you calling from?"

"The New York A.C. I figured I'd take a good swim, steam bath, and get all perfumed up so I'd be nice and fresh when I meet you for a drink later."

"You're fresh enough already." Another nice laugh.

"But when you get to know me you'll find a really humble man. Okay, enough. How about we meet at Rose's restaurant, right down the street from your office?"

"That sounds great, Tommy. Five thirty okay?"

"Super. See you then."

He did ten laps in the pool, steamed out, had a great massage, changed into fresh underwear and a clean shirt and left the club attendants with generous tips all around. They arrived at Rose's almost simultaneously and kissed each other lightly, their first intimacy, but a flush of pleasure caused each of them to break out in a big smile.

It had been a perfect night, he mused, as he sipped his Bloody Mary. He had sat at a table in the back room with her and ordered a bottle of Moët & Chandon champagne. The subject of careers soon came up and she was startled to find that he was a New York detective. He lied easily, not bothering to explain that he was a plainclothes vice cop, deciding for the moment that detective sounded much more glamorous. Some of her more pointed questions he fended artfully, as usual with various women, surrounding himself with the aura and mystique of the fearless New York law man. As the night went on he could tell she was getting more and more fascinated as he shrugged off the incredible dangers of his daily forays against the archcriminals that everyone knew lurked in every nook and cranny of New York. From Rose's they went to Twenty-One and on to dine and dance at the Rainbow Room. They sipped their champagne through the sparkling evening, filling each other in on their backgrounds, their aspirations, and slowly edging towards love.

He couldn't resist a broad grin as he took a deep pull on his Bloody Mary. How chaste he was! If Constance only knew that he had had the wildest doubleheader fuck of all time the night before with the insatiable Eve Andersen, the Blond Bombshell, the Swedish Queen of the Latin Quarter show girls. He just held Connie's hand at the table, like a prep school kid on his first real date. He did hold her real close when they danced and kissed her deeply on the lips when he dropped her off at her Upper East Side apartment. The good times lay ahead.

He debated for about half a second, arose from the lounge chair and fixed himself another tall Bloody Mary. Just like a disciple of yoga loves to sit cross-legged on a mat, head contemplating his navel while he meditates, Tom loved to stretch out in his favorite chair, sip his drink and contemplate his past and future. This was one of those mornings and his mind was filled with more than Constance; it was a kaleidoscope of the events in his life over the last ten years.

He truly loved the world of plainclothes, had really found his niche. He was smart enough to know that it couldn't last forever, but while it did he savored every day. There were a few hateful aspects of the Job. He despised having to arrest whores, especially high-class call girls; he always felt guilty afterwards. It was an unwritten rule not to take money from prostitutes, but most plainclothes guys—and plenty of high-ranking law-making guys—were friendly with a few well-known madams. Except at an occasional party—usually given in a hotel suite by a big gambler—he seldom made love to a call girl, though some of them were beautiful. For him, getting laid was never a problem. There were enough models, show girls, stewardesses, divorcees, and career girls around to more than satisfy his healthy libido. Another big grin, another sip of his Bloody Mary—and there was always Justine, ever willing and ready.

All you needed was to dress nicely, look good, have a great line of shit, and most of all, plenty of money. Even after piling up a safe deposit box full of money, he still loved to make it. Some guys actually got blasé about money, satisfied with their monthly cut, delighted to live way higher than they ever dared hope. Not me, baby, I'll get up in the middle of the night to make a good score.

He drove a BMW sports car, registered in his sister Rosemary's name. Justine drove a two-year-old Ford registered in her name. Like all clever plainclothesmen, he quickly learned the lessons of subterfuge.

The age-old credo that the fallen ones had never adhered to—never display too much sudden affluence. He bought his clothes off the rack in Rogers Peet. Nice, conservative, nothing flashy. With his trim build, tanned good looks, and easy manner he appeared more like a young executive than a plainclothes vice cop. But then, so did most of the other plainclothes cops in the city, except the horse's asses who went around in ludicrous disguises to arrest a poor numbers runner or a bookmaker. What a lot of shit those guys were.

Making the quota of collars was as easy as his next sip of his Bloody Mary. He still retained two of the original three stool pigeons he had inherited from Billy Driscoll, Sonny from Columbus Avenue having died from cirrhosis of the liver. But fortune smiled one night and he added his star of stars, a young black guy named Willie Baker. Willie was a miracle man, the best stoolie in New York. Christ, what a cop he'd have made. He grabbed Willie one day while working uptown. He thought he had a numbers runner, but to his amazement found ten nickel bags of heroin on him. Locking up a felony, possession of drugs, was a pain in the ass. Fingerprinting, mugging, night court, grand jury—too much procedure. He let Willie off the hook with the solemn promise that Willie would supply him with all the outlaw gambling joints, number stores, and bookmakers uptown. A better pact was never made and they both prospered.

He only worked when he felt like making a score or to get on the board to make the arrest quota, fifteen collars a month for the team. Like falling off a log. He grinned. The stool pigeons brought back the sad memory of Billy Driscoll. What a nice guy! He took a long swallow of his Bloody Mary, shuddering at the recollection of those three long days almost a year ago.

Billy lost what for a lot of cops is their toughest battle. The battle of the bottle. He had been drinking progressively more as they worked alongside each other month after month. Tom used to marvel at his capacity, a definitive iron man with the booze. He continued to work his few days a week, made his collars, kept his court dates, led the good life and screwed the best-looking broads. He still loved to make a great score—of which there were plenty—and always conducted himself in the cool way that Tommy remembered affectionately from their first day together.

But just like death and taxes, booze inevitably has to catch up to you. The tell-tale signs of the alcoholic began to become more pronounced; the veins around his nose more noticeable, the florid, bloated face, and the slightest slurring in his speech as the evening wore on.

The calamitous night it started was a night Tommy would never forget. They had a long but good day—a couple of good collars and one good score. They started drinking about five o'clock and parted about ten o'clock. Tommy tired, a little bombed, decided to call it a night and go home. He left Billy at the bar drinking with a brand new girlfriend.

They had an important lunch date the next day with a prominent wise guy and Billy never showed. Unusual, very strange. Not a phone call, nothing. Tom covered for him, explaining that he probably was tied up in court, but deep down he knew that Billy was free and he was worried and puzzled as he was always so reliable. The day passed without a word from him and Tommy's worry increased. The second day his wife Betty called. Where's Billy? Good question! He lied easily and allayed her fears, explaining that they were working on a big hush-hush case. The third day he began to get frantic. The lieutenant and the guys in the squad were asking sly questions about him. He lied with his stage actor's sad face—Billy's mother was very ill in Rockaway and Billy was staying at her house maintaining the vigil.

The only one he confided in was Jack O'Keefe, the clerical man, who was always on day duty. He loved Billy as much as Tommy and promised to let him know the minute he received the slightest indication of his whereabouts. He called Jack every half hour and at five o'clock the third day he got the bad news. Billy was in the girl's apartment, the same girl he had left him with three nights before. She had called Jack O'Keefe, left a phone number, and he relayed it to Tommy. He called and she gave him her address and apartment number. She implored him to hurry over. Fortunately, it was only a short distance from where he was, just off Central Park West in the seventies.

Tommy sipped his Bloody Mary, shook his head sadly as he recalled the regrettable scene. The girl, Bernice, turned out to be one helluva kid. Like a lot of great-looking New York girls she was a part-time actress, full-time waitress. She was also really crazy about Billy. When he arrived, Billy was sitting in a chair in the living room, dressed only in his underwear. A half bottle of Scotch was on the end table next to him and he held a full drink in his hand. Tommy quickly surveyed the scene and to his horror saw Billy's snub-nosed detective special pistol on the table partly obscured by the bottle of Scotch.

He walked over to Billy, shook hands nice and easy, shielded him from the table with his body and with his left hand slipped the pistol into his coat pocket. Easy does it, baby.

"Having quite a party for yourself, heh, Billy."

Billy looked up at him, his face a tableau of sadness, and began to cry. Quietly, tears just rolling down his cheeks, then almost hysterically, deep sobs convulsively wracking his body. Tommy put his arms around him, held him tight, crooning to him, consoling him, patting his head gently. The sobs finally subsided. Loud voice, almost shouting.

"I'm no fucking good, Tom, no fucking good to my family, no fucking good to anybody. Christ, I want to die, want to kill myself. I even put the goddam gun in my mouth and didn't have the balls to pull the trigger. But I'll do it, I swear to God I will, Tommy."

Jesus Christ, what a day! What did F.D.R. say? Yep, a day of infamy. He sipped his Bloody Mary, shuddered at the memory. He finally persuaded Billy to get dressed, gave Bernice a big kiss and a couple of hundred, and took Billy in a taxicab straight to Roosevelt Hospital. He identified himself as a cop to the emergency room personnel and received a private audience with the intern on duty. With a straight face he gave the young doctor a bullshit story of how Billy's nonexistent brother was killed in a car crash the previous week and as a result he'd gone on this horrendous drunk.

He removed all Billy's money and jewelry except for about twenty dollars as they prepared to admit him to the detoxification ward. Billy finally sedated, he left the hospital and went to see the very worried Lieutenant Burke. He explained the situation as briefly as possible, leaving out the almost fatal gun incident. The lieutenant shook his hand warmly, saying that he and the chief would never forget his good thinking and prompt action. Temporarily relieved, his spirits again darkened as he slid into his car parked outside headquarters to take the long drive to Brooklyn and break the sad news to the almost hysterical, frantic Betty Driscoll.

He smiled as he sat back and took another long pull on his Bloody Mary. Thank the good Lord it all had a happy ending, just like the movies. After five days at Roosevelt Hospital, he and Betty drove Billy up to New Canaan, Connecticut and placed him in a famous sanatorium for alcoholics.

The chief covered up beautifully for Billy, citing the stress of the Job as the cause of a severe nervous breakdown. Tommy grinned. Stress! This kind of stress I could live with the rest of my life. He drained his Bloody Mary, looked again at his watch. Plenty of time. Briefly debated having another Bloody Mary. Why not? A wonderful lady and a wonderful day lay ahead of him. He again grinned as he arose to mix his drink. Take it nice and easy, Tommy baby, watch your ass.

He returned to his favorite chair, fresh Bloody Mary in hand. He shook his head, sipped his drink, contemplated booze, the Irish weakness—the gradual decimation of the original Manhattan West Squad. Billy Driscoll, finally nursed back to health and sanity after six very expensive weeks in the exclusive sanatorium for alcoholics. Tom heard from him periodically; he was now a successful realtor in south Florida and with a great disability pension through the efforts of Chief Moclair. Good old stress!

But how much more fortunate in life Billy Driscoll had emerged than poor Jerry Dillon. Good old Jerry! The smartest, nicest, best-looking cop in the squad. The swordsman of Broadway, the best-fucked cop in the annals of police history.

Tommy winced, almost felt a physical pain as he remembered how Jerry died. A few months after Billy's problem was resolved, handsome Jerry Dillon was found dead in an airline stewardess's apartment on the West Side. The beautiful stewardess had left him in an exhausted sleep while she went off on an overseas flight for a few days. Poor Jerry evidently died in his sleep. Heart attack? What else? How much Scotch can you drink, how many cigarettes can you smoke, how many girls can you fuck?

The fatal day she returned the horrified stewardess found poor Jerry stone dead. The real tough part was that poor Jerry, always immaculate about his person, had evidently been dead a few days and was beginning to stink worse than a three-day-old Bowery derelict D.O.A. One good thing, the radio car cops who responded were terrific guys. They found about two thousand in his pants, which were hanging over a bedroom chair. The radio car cops called the squad office, reached Lieutenant Burke, and gave him all Jerry's possessions. The bankroll, expensive wristwatch, and of course, the perennial plainclothesman's diamond pinky ring.

He still found it hard to believe Jerry was dead. What a great guy! Always with a ready wisecrack and a big smile. Strangely, it turned out that Jerry had only one living relative, an old Irish aunt who had raised him since he was a young boy. The lieutenant gave Aunt Nellie everything they found, including the keys to Jerry's fashionable apartment off Central Park West. They all silently prayed Aunt Nellie found his loot.

Tommy sipped his Bloody Mary thoughtfully, smiled ruefully, mind straying to the Irish booze jokes. Ironically, he mused, how close to home they hit. Ah, dear Lord, you gave the Irish all the attributes—wit, charm, good looks—then you killed it all, you invented whiskey. How true! Then the other one, a real pisser.

Pat goes to Mike's wake, greets the wife, Nora, tearfully. "What happened to Mike, Nora, for the love of God?"

"Oh, Pat, poor Mike was drinking something awful for the last six months. Afternoons, then in the morning, finally the last few weeks he got the jaundice and kept drinking until here he is, in his coffin."

"For God's sake, Nora, why didn't you enroll him in A.A.?"

Raised eyebrows. "Oh, Pat, for Christ sake, he was never that bad."

Again he smiled, sipped his Bloody Mary. Typical Irish? He hoped not, not quite, anyway. He laid his head back, the soothing vodka easing the bad memories, erasing the pain. The Irish were still the greatest and there was some consolation in an article he had recently read. The French led the league in alcoholism, with the Russians neck and neck with the Swedes and Icelandics in a photo finish for second. He grinned again. Truthfully, what was really the worse fate? To join Alcoholics Anonymous and spend the rest of your unsmiling life with a grim face and an unbending manner, devoid of the joys of a couple of crisp martinis to break the ice while you softened up a beautiful chick at cocktail hour. And then what the hell were you supposed to do when you went into Jim Costello's, Jimmy Weston's, or P.J. Clarke's? Hiya Tommy—hey, Tommy baby— what'll you have, Tommy boy? Jesus Christ, if I ever ordered a 7-Up or a Coca-Cola everyone would drop dead.

Yessir, New York was Saloon City. No doubt about it. Where the hell else were you going to meet a pal, a girl, or a wise guy? In a candy store? A Greek coffeepot? Tom smiled, no, I guess I'll keep my membership up in Alcoholics Positively. But thinking back to Billy and Jerry he silently vowed to be more temperate. A daily vow. He grinned again—and I won't succumb to the inevitable danger of stress. What a lot of bullshit that was. This kind of stressful life I could gladly put up with until they lowered me into the grave. His mood suddenly turned melancholy. Yes, the good old Manhattan West had lost some good men during his tenure. Billy, Jerry, and just recently Lenny Beck, the good-natured Jew, retired from the Job to open his own steakhouse on Long Island.

He sipped his drink again, face clouding over. There's one

hateful sonofabitch I guess will never leave, Joe the Boss. Though on the surface they maintained a cool but polite relationship, they still never spoke to each other outside the office except when absolutely necessary. He's one bastard they'll have to carry out of the Job. And he positively won't die unless God lets him take his money with him. Don't let him up *There* until you get your square cut, God.

Fuck Joe Marchetti! He drained his Bloody Mary, debated briefly about mixing another, reluctantly decided against it. Stay nice and sober today, Tommy boy, nice and even. A wonderful day and a wonderful lady loomed just ahead in the wonderful city of New York. Soon my beautiful countess, my comely Constance, soon you'll be in my arms. Take it nice and easy today, Irish, watch your ass.

He went back upstairs, took a long shower and shaved. He patted a generous portion of his favorite aftershave over his cheeks, his neck, his breasts, smiled—never can tell—across his abdomen and over his groin area. He dressed carefully, dark summer-weight trousers, white shirt, black knit tie and linen, lemon-colored sport jacket. The color scheme enhanced his deeply tanned face. Even so, he returned for reassurance to the full-length mirror on his closet door at least five times to convince himself that he was truly gorgeous.

How can my sweet Constance ever resist me today? He smiled into the mirror. I hope not, dear God, or it's going to be an awfully lonely night in the suite I have arranged in the St. Moritz Hotel. Gratis, of course, through the courtesy of the management, always ready to oblige a Borough West man. He looked at his watch, just past eleven o'clock. Christ, he was itchy this morning, even my balls are tingling. Has to be the love itch, the longing for Constance itch.

He went downstairs into the kitchen, put a kettle of water on the electric stove for instant coffee. His stomach rumbled, growled, reminded him that he was hungry. No breakfast, can't live on Bloody Marys alone. He split an English muffin and put it into the toaster. The muffin toasted, he spread some grape jelly over it, ate hungrily, sipped the coffee. Delicious! He hesitated, shrugged a little, went back to the bar and took a bottle of Remy Martin brandy from the side cabinet. He added a real good shot to his coffee. Perfect. He drank the coffee slowly, sniffing the sweet aroma of the brandy, reveled in the sweet, tangy taste. He suddenly thought of Justine. Should he leave her a note? Good idea, never know what lay ahead the next couple of days.

> *Sweetheart,*
> *I have to go underground. Supersecret, very heavy assignment. I won't be home for a couple of days. I will try to call you at least by tomorrow night. Good luck in your big bowling match tonight.*
>
> > *All my love,*
> > *Tommy*

He put the note under a water glass on the kitchen counter.

He backed his car out of the driveway adjoining the house and headed for the Grand Central Parkway, the arterial link to the Queens Midtown Tunnel and midtown Manhattan. The smooth hum of the BMW's motor, the wide comfortable bucket seats and the rich gray leather interior of the imported German car gave Tommy a luxurious sense of well-being. He switched on the car radio; the first sound he heard was Frank Sinatra singing, "When Did You Leave Heaven?"

He hummed along with Sinatra, loved the song. Was this a mere coincidence or not? The same great song he associated with the only two women who had really struck his fancy since he first fell in love with Justine. He lightly tapped the steering wheel with his knuckles for good luck. I hope and pray that Constance has had a helluva lot less lovers than Bobbi Schuyler.

He still retained all of his radio car driving skills as he maneuvered through the already heavy start of summer weekend traffic and exited from the tunnel at East Thirty-seventh Street and Third Avenue. He planned on leaving his car in a garage on East Fifty-fifth Street, off Eighth Avenue. It was owned by a man who was very friendly to the guys in the squad.

The cross-town traffic was heavy as he wove across town towards Eighth Avenue and his mind wandered back to the Job as he drove slowly from light to light. His brow unconsciously wrinkled and his face darkened as he recalled the events and the rumors that sprung up the last few weeks on the Job. No question about a lot of ugly gossip being tossed around about another corruption probe about to surface concerning the Job.

Jesus Christ, when are they going to quit these goddam bullshit investigations? What the hell did they ever prove, except to lower the respect the cop on the street received. When they're all over, a few poor cops go to jail, a few more get busted from the Job, a few of the top brass resign, and the same old shit goes on that always went on. New York was a unique city, in a class by itself, and the New York cops did a tremendous job. The fucking politicians and judges ought to investigate themselves. Who else made the stupid laws preventing gambling and getting laid? Who else made the murderous laws protecting the worst kind of criminals? Christ, now we have the Miranda decision—read a guy his rights before you can arrest him. He laughed. I'd kick him in the balls just before I'd read him his rights. Christ, if I ever read a bookmaker or a numbers guy his rights he would think I was either crazy or a faggot cop.

He finally reached Eighth Avenue and headed slowly uptown, his mind still churning, enraged about the two pricks in the Job that were raising all the stink. One shithead cop, crying to everyone who would listen to him because he wasn't made a detective, and the other a young sergeant who went to Harvard or some snooty college, who wanted to be appointed instant police commissioner. What the hell was this sergeant doing on the Job if he went to Harvard? Why wasn't he down on Wall Street where he could expose the really big corruption? Worst of all, the new mayor, another Ivy League type, an airhead who knew as much about inner city politics and intrigue as my asshole.

He stopped for a light at West Fifty-second Street. The car radio was blasting out Dixieland jazz. He put back his head and sang out, "Oh Lordy, lordy, bring back Jimmy Walker." He grinned, looked down the block to his right where Gallagher's Steak House stood, the love temple where his new romance blossomed. He resolved to banish from his mind all of his impending fears. He would never be deprived of his present ecstatic state of life. The dream life. The money life. What a life!

He turned into West Fifty-fifth Street and was greeted enthusiastically by Chico, one of the Puerto Rican garage attendants. He slapped Chico on the back like an old pal, slipped him a five-dollar bill, and told him to stow the car in a dark corner as he was on a big case and might not be back for a few days. He looked at his wristwatch. Ten minutes to one—perfect timing. He walked cross-town to Sixth Avenue and turned left up to West Fifty-ninth Street and right to Fifth Avenue and the Plaza Hotel. He went directly to the Oak Room, as usual filled with celebrities, power, and beauty, all stage set in mellow oak, brass, and a general feeling of grand prosperity.

He surveyed the scene with the quick, well-trained cop's eye. No Constance as yet. He politely edged himself into a space towards the center of the crowded noontime bar and ordered a tall Smirnoff vodka and tonic. He held a good vantage point of the entrance from the hotel lobby to the Oak Room as he set a vigil for his tardy love. He smiled in satisfaction as he sipped his delicious, tall icy drink—a constant vigil. No—a Constance vigil. His eyes strayed around the vast room occasionally, as always marveling at the texture of the oak-paneled walls, the glistening long mahogany bar, the muted lighting, the sheer smell of success created by the aura of well-dressed women and sartorially splendid men.

He sipped his drink. Tom, my man, you sensed it all the time. It had to happen this way. You were ordained to live the good life. Swept away in the reverie of present and future wealth, eyes approving his reflection in the back bar mirror, he felt a soft tap on his shoulder, the sudden scent of fragrant perfume. He turned, a trifle startled.

"You were expecting someone, am I correct, Thomas?" She laughed, the nice soft laugh.

"Constance! Gee, I'm sorry, I was dreaming. How are you, sweetheart? You look beautiful."

"No kiss?"

He moved closer, barely had to lean over, she was as tall as he was. He kissed her nice and easy on the lips. Christ, she smelled good. He felt the familiar tingling. There it goes, my cock shooting up like a skyrocket.

He created a little space for her at the bar. The guy on his left took one piercing look and hurriedly offered his bar chair. Thank you, thank you very much. Nice guy, but hands off, I caught the look. But who wouldn't look? Constance wore an off-white linen suit over a tan, ruffled blouse. But the show stopper was the hat. A light brown fedora that magically set off her blue eyes, white teeth, tanned skin, and a face that belonged on a magazine cover rather than writing advertising copy for the inside pages.

"What's your pleasure, love?"

She looked Tommy up and down, gripped his arm, seemed to like what she saw.

"Is this going to be a long day?"

"As far as I'm concerned, a long month."

She laughed. "The good news is, Tom, that I'm through at the office for the weekend. I worked all sorts of hours this week on a new campaign and my boss gave me the afternoon off as a reward. He's really a wonderful man. And with the way they're finally recognizing that women have talent he's promised to make me a v.p. pretty soon. He personally thinks I'm some sort of genius, but to be honest it's mostly because I'm surrounded by a bunch of idiots who automatically got hired because they have polite degrees from Ivy League colleges."

Tommy laughed. "You still haven't ordered your drink, genius."

"Well, let me see. It looks like to my advanced brain that you're having a nice, tall, very cold vodka and tonic. I'll kiss you again, right here at the bar in the Oak Room if you order one for me."

"Promise?"

"Promise!"

Tommy waved to the bartender. "Bartender, please, ten tall vodka and tonics."

After two drinks they sat down to lunch in the far corner of the Oak Room, assisted by a very obliging captain who was spurred to almost ostentatious hospitality by a ten-dollar bill Tommy slipped into his willing hand.

Tommy, with a winked hurray from Constance, ordered a

bottle of Chardonnay to go along with the delicious lunch. They were both starved, ate their cold lobster salad hungrily, slowly sipped the luscious wine. And they talked and talked between bites and sips.

"Let me ask you something, hon, with your snide remarks about Ivy League schools a while back, where did you go to school?"

"I graduated from Middlebury College in Vermont and took my masters in journalism at Columbia. We lived at the Parc Vendome on the West Side. But sweetheart, commuting up there was a real survival course. I would have made a good police woman after a solid year of traveling back and forth by subway to Columbia."

He laughed. "You look like a pretty hard case. Pretty, anyway. Just think about it, maybe we would have become partners. Oh, babe, would I love to have you next to me in a radio car."

She laughed. "Ooh, that sounds wonderful, Tom. And you, where did you go to school?"

He lied gracefully. "I graduated from prep school on Long Island and was all set for college when I was called to go off to the Korean War. When I came home, after all I was through, I just lost interest in going back to school.

"Well, Constance, now that we officially know each other, where would you like to go from here?"

"Anywhere you say, but no gunplay. Okay?"

He grinned, paid the check, tipped the waiter generously and said, "Well, to be honest, I do have to go see the general manager of the St. Moritz Hotel, just down the block on the Park. How about that?"

"Sounds lovely, let's go."

It was a gorgeous New York early summer day, with a faint, fragrant breeze emanating from the verdant corners of Central Park. It cooled them as they walked, Constance clinging to his arm, Tommy pleasantly aware of the envious glances tossed his way by oncoming guys of all shapes and ages. Yes, indeed, Constance is my comely countess.

They entered the hotel lobby and Tom seated Constance while he excused himself and went into the executive offices on the main floor. He announced himself and was swiftly ushered into Ken Denby, the general manager's office. Denby was a tall, slim, blond man in his middle forties. A great friend of Tommy Sloane's. There is a regular occurrence in New York that makes the police a very necessary adjunct to the large hotels. Out-of-towners come in on business, big shots in their own bailiwicks, and after too many drinks wind up with a hooker. New York street-smart guys know that there are good hookers and bad hookers. The good ones are usually well-recommended call girls, the bad ones the bar girls and the street hookers. The bad ones make love really well, put the out-of-town big shot in a great mood, then surreptitiously drop a little dope in his drink. The big shot wakes up a few hours later with the most torturous hangover of all time and minus his money, gun, jewelry, and credit cards. Tommy had first helped Denby a couple of years back and it was accomplished without a trace or murmur of publicity. Kenny told Tommy the story of how one of his prominent guests had been ripped off and he prowled the neighborhood and grabbed a pimp off West Fifty-seventh Street and Sixth Avenue, who was fingered by a hooker he had once befriended.

He took him off the corner about midnight, led him to a dark spot off West Fifty-sixth Street and kicked the living shit out of him. Just before the pimp was convinced he was about to die, with Tommy's pistol at his head, he was warned that if the gun, credit cards, and jewelry were not returned by the next night every whore and pimp in the area better leave for Canada. Fuck the money, let her keep that. In response to that gentle persuasion, all articles were promptly returned at the appointed time the next night. Frontier justice! New York justice at its best.

That bit of heroic valor formed a deep bond of friendship between Ken Denby and Tommy Sloane. He was amazed and overjoyed at Tommy's feats, sometimes dismayed when Tom explained his simple tactics. Don't worry about it, Kenny, a good beating is what they need once in a while. That's their headache, part of the pimp game.

"How are you, Thomas, everything okay?"

"Fine, thank you, Kenny. I hope the hotel isn't too full, that I'm not inconveniencing you?"

"Of course not, Tom, always room for you. In fact, I have reserved a nice suite for you. Here are the keys, so you won't have to go to the front desk. I'll send up some wine and hors d'oeuvres later. Sound all right with you?"

"Great, Ken. Make it Chardonnay, please. Come on out and meet my new girl."

"A new one? You replaced the blond Amazon? I thought she was outstanding."

Tommy laughed. "This is real class, brand-new, and I already am halfway in love with her."

"Not again?"

"This time for real."

They walked out to the lobby and Tommy introduced Kenny to Constance. She was so gracious and charming his eyes almost fell out when she stood up and shook hands with him. They chatted briefly, Ken asked them into the bar for a drink, had one with them and excused himself to return to his office. He shook hands good-bye and when Constance turned towards Tom, Kenny turned, rolled his eyes towards Heaven, gave Tom a broad wink and walked away with his right thumb high in the air.

I assume she meets with your approval, Kenneth. I couldn't agree more, pal.

"He seems like a really nice man, Tom. A good friend of yours."

"A real good friend, babe, a really nice guy."

As they talked and sipped their wine at the bar he was scheming exactly how he was going to approach the subject of going upstairs to the suite. He didn't want to appear too impulsive, too brusque, come on too strong. He laughed, smiled, squeezed her hand affectionately, toyed with his drink—all the while figuring the right time to make his move.

Unconsciously, she gave him his opening.

"How come you and Kenny, a big shot hotel manager, became such friends?" she asked, almost as if Tom had planned the question.

He sipped his wine thoughtfully, weighed his answer carefully. This lie has to be the coup de grace. The all-time winner.

"We became good friends a couple of years ago. It seems that the hotel hired a guy as a bell-hop around that time. He was good-looking, young, hard worker, polite—everyone liked him. But he had presented a false identity. Everything from phony social security card, new alias, you name it. He was also one of the best young burglars that ever came out of Chicago. Did a stretch at Joliet, Illinois. For weeks on end there were all sorts of valuables missing from guest rooms. A piece of good jewelry, a couple of hundred in cash, American Express cards. Things like that. Not every day, but nearly every day. These capers were driving Kenny and the security guys in the hotel crazy. Anyway, I was assigned to the case in an undercover role and not to bore you with further details, I busted the guy within a week."

Constance's eyes positively glowed.

"Oh, Tom, that's an incredible story. Marvelous. Come on, don't be mean. Please, tell me more. How did you finally get him?"

Oh, Constance, my love, you too are a lady district attorney. Please God, are they all the same? Even the earthbound goddesses?

"Okay, Ms. Frank Hogan, mistress of our eminent district attorney."

Constance burst out laughing so hard, heads turned towards her. She covered her mouth, gasped, "Go on, you crazy nut."

He smiled, his brain whirling, I better make up a good ending. It hit him—I got it.

"Anyway, I posed as a maintenance man, worked a few days sizing up the personnel, and decided it had to be a bell-hop. They were the guys who always knew when people were entering their rooms or leaving them. And they could always spot a guy down the hall leaving his room. I lifted the prints of a few bell-hops off luggage they had handled and sent them downtown to the forensic laboratory. The fourth set turned out to be our man, Edgar Barnes, alias Patrick Stanley, keymaker and burglar *par excellence*.

"We got a warrant, searched his apartment and found more room keys than they have out in the lobby at the front desk. Edgar, pardon me, Patrick, is now doing five to ten years at that well-known winter resort upstate called Attica."

Constance was overawed to be in the presence of such a formidable foe of crime.

Time to make my move. The setting is perfect, the scenario is written. Cool voice.

"Listen, love, that's one of the reasons I'm here today. Kenny called the office and requested me to be on tap here today as they're having a problem with a waiter who is apparently doing a number on some rooms. They are waiting to catch him in the act and want me here to make the arrest. Ken arranged a place in the hotel for me to stay. How about we leave the bar and go upstairs and have a drink? You can be sure Kenny always has the best for me when he needs me."

Constance's eyes narrowed mischievously for a moment, then she broke into a big smile. What a smile! The sensuous lips parting, the big white teeth, the blue eyes lighting up. In a very low voice, she said, "You wouldn't dare try to take advantage of me up there, would you, love?"

Tommy laughed, touched her face gently.

"Not unless you wanted me to, sweetheart. It would sure spice up the stakeout detail."

"We shall soon see, Thomas, my humble undercover man, we shall soon see. Come, let's go upstairs."

Tommy, calm exterior, heart palpitating wildly, waited for the elevator, gently holding Constance's hand.

The suite was magnificent. Wide picture windows overlooking Central Park. The panoramic view of the early summer lush, green foliage, almost like a dense, virginal forest only marred by the tiny strips of roadway and the cars scooting along as if in miniature. The surrounding skyscrapers and the exquisite architecture of the elegant apartment houses along upper Fifth Avenue was breathtaking.

Constance stood facing the picture windows, looking out, absorbing the beauty of the scene. She shook her head in disbelief, turned to Tommy and said, "What a lovely setting, sweetheart, for our first lovemaking."

He just looked at her, speechless, patted her shoulder. Her face seemed so gentle. She removed her hat, shook out her dark, cropped hair, turned away and sat back in a nearby lounge chair and closed her eyes.

She looked so beautiful, his knees got weak. Easy does it,

Tommy boy, don't rush. Oh, God, I solemnly give you permission to take me after three days of Constance.

He turned and walked to a table set at the far corner of the living room. Surprise!

"Hey, great. Look, hon, Kenny has a couple of bottles of wine over here on the ice. What a nice guy! Chardonnay! Beautiful! How about I fix you a glass?"

"That would be perfect, Tom."

He removed his tie and jacket, hung them in the bedroom closet. Super, king-size bed. I love you, Kenny. Oop, the gun. He slipped it into his jacket.

He uncorked the wine, poured two glasses and brought them over to where Constance sat. He handed her one. They tipped glasses, sipped the wine. He kissed her nice and easy, sat at her feet.

She looked down at him and broke into a grin.

"Tell me the truth. Are you sure you're here on police business? If not, you and your general manager pal are the two greatest co-conspirators of all time. Everything seems so perfect, so planned. I can't believe I'm here. I'll bet you any money a waiter will shortly knock on the door and bring in a tray of hors d'oeuvres."

She's a smart ass all right. His face reddened.

"They're already here. On the table, behind the wine."

She howled, laughing. Her laughter was so infectious he lay his head back on the carpeting at her feet and howled along with her.

Their laughter finally subsided, tears running down their cheeks. She extended her hand, "Come on, lazybones, get up here and kiss me. I refuse to lie on the floor with you. I have a new designer suit on that I just bought in Henri Bendel's."

He jumped up, pulled her roughly out of the chair and kissed her. No nice easy kiss this time. A burst-of-stars hard-on shot up during their first deep kiss. She opened her mouth wide and their tongues clashed hungrily. Constance moaned, Tommy moaned. They were both naked on the king-size bed about a minute later. He kissed her eyes, her mouth, and reveled in her long-legged, tanned, round-assed, firm-titted body. They kissed each other almost frantically, her hands squeezing his biceps hard, her legs spread, high in the air.

"Ooh, Tom, you're so strong. Ooh, Tom, easy, easy. Ooh, you're so large."

He couldn't resist a smile as he entered her slowly. She was very tight and her oohs and aahs about the size of his penis made him feel like Superman. But the sheer ecstasy of Constance, the sweet smell of her body, her anguished cries had him ejaculating like a madman long before he wanted to come. But evidently not too premature for she was as passionate as he was. She pulled him to her convulsively and pressed his face against her hard breasts.

Almost purring, very softly—"Oh, Tommy, Tommy, that was so good."

A minute or two passed in her arms. He sat up, turned, looked at her again, kissed her gently on the lips. Jesus Christ, she was beautiful. The bright shiny afternoon sun streaming through the bedroom windows only enhanced the beauty of her tanned skin, blue gray eyes, shiny cropped hair, parted mouth, and gleaming white teeth. He kissed her gently again.

"You know something, you're not a bad-looking kid."

She laughed, pulled him back down close to her and in a muffled voice said, "Well, you're not too good-looking, thank God. But you are strong-looking and that's the kind of guy I like."

They both laughed and kissed easily.

"Well, suppose you put on panties and a brassiere and I'll put on my shorts. We'll put our feet up outside, enjoy the view, and drink a little wine. How about that?"

"Gorgeous!"

They pushed two of the lounge chairs together facing the captivating vista of Central Park and uptown New York. They sipped their wine, held hands, and talked. They discovered that both sets of their parents were dead. She a lone orphan, he with his only sister, Rosemary. Constance described how her parents had died within months of each other, a couple of years back. Her parents had married late, her mother had had her at age thirty-eight. Her father was a banker, died suddenly of a heart attack, her mother six months later of a broken heart. She was left a nice inheritance, bought her own co-op where he dropped her off last night and had a fairly nice monthly income from their estate.

Tommy told his tale with slight embellishment, of course.

Grandma McElroy, who practically raised him, had died almost two years ago. He lied easily about his small inheritance, a little over six hundred a month plus a beautiful home on Little Neck Bay in Whitestone.

Still, the lady D.A. prodded. What about your wife? Please, it's too painful to talk about now. Let's forget that subject for a while. He squeezed her hand gently. She turned, smiled gently, blew him a kiss to alleviate his apparent marital stress. He arose, poured some more wine. They tipped glasses again. She turned. "You must be a really brave guy, Tom. The Korean War, gunfights, catching thieves, being stabbed, all that violence." He gave her his number one stalwart grin. All in a day's work. That's life, babe.

They were back in the bedroom an hour later. This time he was more gentle, slower, time to show off his time-honored, long-acquired expertise. Constance nearly went crazy before he finally came. She lay back away from him, panting.

"Oh my God, Tommy, you almost killed me. I never knew making love could ever be as good as that. Oh, dear Lord, I love you so much."

He cradled her head in his left arm, pulled her close and kissed her eyes softly. He felt an almost overwhelming tenderness towards her. Christ, all I was doing was plotting to merely fuck her. She was so goddam gorgeous. Now I can't hold her close enough, can't bear the thought of leaving her arms.

He shook his head and smiled. Maybe my ultimate fate is being resolved, or at least getting even with me. He usually went through his devious machinations; with false shyness and much more false sincerity, he bullshitted his target for the day or night, got laid, and couldn't wait to leave. There were a few exceptions, but after two or three encounters they fell into the same category. But Constance—so beautiful, so bright, so innocent in bed, so completely lovable. Oh, dear God, what have you wrought?

She opened her eyes, put up her face, leaned over and kissed him.

"How could I possibly fall in love with a man I only know a little over one full day?"

"The Irish charm, babe, the Irish wit."

"The Irish conceit, you mean. Oh, Tommy, it's more. I'm

racking my brain searching for the right word for you. I've got it! You're charismatic. You know the word?"

"Sure, same thing I said before—charm, wit."

She untangled herself from his arm, sat up in bed.

"You're almost right. It means more or less like an aura that surrounds a person, like a religious aura."

"Me, religious. Forget about it."

"Oh, silly, I don't mean religion in that context, in the organized sense. I mean sort of mystical, like you can do almost anything you wish to accomplish."

"Sweetheart, I just accomplished my greatest feat this afternoon. I made love twice to the most beautiful girl in New York and she had ten orgasms."

She fell back on the bed laughing, turned, punched his arm and said, "Oh, you liar, I did not have ten orgasms."

"How many?"

She roared laughing, almost choked, and said, "I think about nine," and laid her head back and howled. Tommy almost fell out of the bed laughing.

She finally got her voice back.

"I have another confession to make, Tom."

"Go ahead."

"You are the first guy for whom I ever carried my diaphragm along on a date. I swear, honestly."

"Good. I wondered about that." A little jealous note crept into his voice. A bit sharply, he added, "Okay, as long as we're having true-confession time, just who did I replace that you needed a diaphragm for?"

"Oh, Tom, for heaven's sake. I'm twenty-six years old. Every girl in New York City has a diaphragm by age twenty-one or else she has a hole in her head."

"That wasn't my question." Cranky voice.

"Hmm, once a cop always a cop. Are you going to kick the living shit out of me—as you so nicely put it—and make me confess my love life?"

He laughed, his rancor eased. "Talk, talk, you rotten bitch or you're dead."

She laughed again, reached over, put her arms around him and kissed him hard on the lips.

Tommy shuddered, responded by clutching Constance almost desperately. He felt weak, emotionally overwhelmed. Good Christ, I can't get enough of her. They lay together, almost as one. Tommy Sloane knew that he was one hundred percent head over heels in love.

He put his arm under her head, her sweet-smelling hair against the side of his face. In a minute she was sound asleep. She snored very softly. His eyes began to droop. He kissed her eyes again, brushed her lips, released his arm from under her head. He turned and felt her clinging to his shoulders as he fell asleep.

While Tommy Sloane was slowly and inescapably falling in love and immensely enjoying the body, mind, and spirit of Constance Ward, turmoil reigned in other areas of New York.

On fashionable West End Avenue on New York's upper West Side, Chief Edward Moclair lay restlessly in bed trying to induce sleep. He lay back, hands behind his head, careful not to disturb his wife, who was quietly snoring beside him. He had a date to play golf the next morning at Winged Foot Golf Club in Westchester County. The date was for ten o'clock on the first tee and he had the alarm clock on the night table next to him set for eight so that he would be in plenty of time. He muttered a silent curse as he glanced sideways at the illuminated dial clock. One thirty. He'd play like a shit tomorrow. He wanted to be fresh and strong. He loved to play golf, especially at Winged Foot, one of the world's great courses.

His mind kept reverting to the conversation he had late that afternoon at the Twenty-One Club with an old friend of his, George Cohen. George was a top executive of a department store chain. Through his long career in the Job, from cop to deputy chief, Ed Moclair had done numerous favors for George. A strong bond of friendship also developed.

George, whose chain of stores advertised widely in the *New York Times,* had lunched earlier in the day as a guest of the paper's top brass in the executive dining room in the New York Times building. Over lunch, the subject of large-scale police corruption surfaced. They spoke of how the seamy tale was unfolded to some of their people by two honest cops. One a regular cop, the other a sergeant. They spoke of how a top investigative reporter team had been assigned to check out the allegations and also to do a series on corruption.

George Cohen was dismayed as he listened to the conversation. He finally entered into it and tried to dissuade them from disgracing even a small segment of the Finest. He knew how valuable cops had been to his organization through the years. He pointed out the havoc of the recent riots in Harlem, the constant influx of the various minority groups, the inroads and barriers placed on law enforcement by liberal groups. He staunchly maintained that public support of the police was almost mandatory. Certainly we don't need another horseshit corruption investigation over gambling payoffs or other petty victimless crimes. Police need public confidence. Vice versa.

No, no, George. If we feel that there is corruption among our police, it is our duty to report it. And so George argued to no avail, ate his lunch, and thanked the *Times* executives politely. He walked to a corner phone booth and called his old pal, Chief Ed Moclair. He asked could he meet him for a drink.

They sat at a corner table in Twenty-One. George filled Moclair in on every aspect of the abortive luncheon conversation as Moclair toyed with his drink and listened quietly.

George named the two informant policemen mentioned during lunch, verifying rumors and gossip that had already reached the chief's ears. He shook his head as he listened. Those two no good scumbags! Rats! Finks!

That was all that was on his mind as he fought to sleep. He breathed in deeply. He was very tired, a long day. A shitty day! Better call my trusted lieutenant Jack Burke in the morning before I leave for golf. Have him over for dinner, a couple of drinks, talk things over. Eyes beginning to close. Things are getting too close, too serious. He finally fell asleep.

Tommy and Constance arrived at the Villa Pompei on West Forty-fourth Street, East of Seventh Avenue, in a jubilant mood. Tom had planned on a meeting with Vinny. It was just getting dark, New York was aglow in a splendid rosy red sunset in the West. They went directly to the bar and ordered two tall Smirnoff vodka and tonics. Vinny was nowhere in sight but Tommy knew that he was somewhere on the premises. Probably in the kitchen, he conjectured, as he had called earlier from the movie theater and received a very threatening "You better show up, you Irish bastard, or you're dead."

They were both in high spirits after seeing the two Lina Wertmuller films. Fortunately, the depressing movie was the first part of the double feature, the comic one was the second. They both laughed so hard at most parts of the second movie they left the Cinema Village smiling and chuckling as they recounted to each other the various hilarious antics of Marcello Mastroianni.

They were just finishing their initial drink when Tommy looked up and saw Vince almost right next to him. He wore a light tan suit, high-collared white shirt and a dark brown, polka-dot tie. This dago sonofabitch looks more like a movie star every day. I'm going to pay for a plastic surgeon to operate on his nose. Then I'll manage him, make him a household name.

He put out his right hand, but feigned a boxing pose, chin tucked behind his left shoulder, left fist clenched against his side. Vinny laughed, shook his outstretched hand, hugged him, and said, "You're right, protect yourself, I should smack you right in your dumb Irish kisser. Two weeks gone by. No phone calls, no stopping for a drink, and please, don't give me that working on a big case shit."

Tommy laughed. "You're so discreet, so well-mannered. Vince, you really amaze me."

Connie was laughing, anxious to meet Vinny, whom Tommy had been raving about to her off and on since they first met. Tommy introduced them. They shook hands, then Vinny leaned over and kissed her cheek. He was visibly impressed and said, "A lovely name, Constance. My wife's name is a variation, Concetta, and I love the name. You're just as beautiful as she is. May I call you Connie?"

"Everyone does but Tommy. Sure, Vince, and thank you for the nice things you said."

"Be careful, Constance, he's an Italian heartbreaker. Wait, I really mean ball-breaker."

They all roared laughing.

Vinny put his arms around her shoulder and said, "What the hell is a great-looking girl like you doing with a mick cop like this guy?"

She laughed happily, proud to be between two strong, great-looking guys. She didn't miss the eyes of the other women at the bar sizing her up.

"I guess it's part deep affinity with the Irish, part mutual attraction. I am half-Irish, Vincent."

"I hope the other half is Italian, the half where you got all your good looks."

"Sorry, *signore,* the other half is Romanian."

"Romanian! You're the image of an Irish countess. You're kidding me."

"No, really. Mother emigrated here from Constanza on the Black Sea just before World War Two. She was a concert pianist there. Never played a concert hall here, only for her family and friends' pleasure. She was a wonderful person. God, how I miss her."

Tommy interposed, "You never told me that, Constance."

"You never asked. In your pure chauvinistic way you just assumed I was pure Irish. Besides, I hate to talk about my mother. Look, I'm getting teary-eyed already, thinking how much I loved her." Her eyes were wet, her voice shook a little.

"Oh, Connie, I'm sorry. Please forgive me. Eddie, let's have a fresh drink over here. The same for this handsome couple and a Cutty Sark on the rocks for me."

The drinks arrived and a festive mood was quickly re-established. Vinny personally seated them at a rear table after they finished their second drink. Constance surveyed the decor of the restaurant as they waited to be served and said, "This is really a nice place, Tom. I've been here before for lunch, never for dinner, and I always enjoyed it. Does Vincent really own it? He seems so young-looking. And you were young cops together. It's hard to believe. You're both too damned smooth to be cops. You should be stock promoters, or confidence men."

Tommy laughed. "Thank you for the compliment. Yes, dear, Vinny does own the place and a lot of other places around town. He married Connie, the daughter of a big Italian contractor, who was an only child. His father-in-law turned a bunch of properties over to Vinny and he's been very successful."

Not too bad a lie, Charlie Mattuci was in many ways a contractor. Who knows how many contracts Charlie had handled in his life?

The waiter arrived and Tom ordered for both of them at Connie's behest. Tortellini with clam sauce, veal marsala and a bottle of Chianti. Vinny visited with them from time to time, but he was kept busy in and out of the kitchen and table hopping around the dining room talking to groups of customers.

The restaurant began to empty out as it drew close to midnight. They were having espresso and Vinny at last joined them and ordered an espresso for himself and a round of Remy Martin brandy for the table. They told him how much they enjoyed dinner. Constance, ecstatic about the place, leaned over and kissed Vinny's cheek with a murmured thank you.

"That was nice, Connie. You're going to enjoy it even more, Irish. I picked up your check because the beautiful girl you brought in added so much class to the joint."

They all laughed, Constance blushing.

"Oh, Vinny, are you another one of those heartbreakers like this guy?" She ruffled Tommy's hair.

"Absolutely no basis for comparison, Con. Italians are much better lovers than the Irish."

She laughed. "In which case I'd now be officially dead." Another big laugh. Constance excused herself to go to the powder room.

"Well, *compagno mio,* what do you think?"

"Extraordinary, Tom. Lovely, charming. Seems to have it all."

"She's also very bright. Has her master's degree in journalism. Columbia. She has a big job in advertising. Gaines and Townsend, one of the biggies."

"Great. You can tell she's smart. Does this mean that you're in love again?"

"Don't be a wise bastard. No, I'm not sure about love, but I'm crazy about her."

"Look, Tommy, don't do anything foolish. Have your fling with her. I don't blame you, she's one terrific chick. Then, get her out of your system. Listen, forget the love-bird shit for a while. Like all girls she'll be in the ladies room a half hour, so let's talk about something more serious. What are all these rumors going around about another cop investigation about to pop up? Soon, I hear. And I heard from a reliable source that one of the squealers is a wop cop. *Dio mio*, a disgrace to his own race, my race."

"I've been hearing some gossip about it, Vince, but nothing substantial. Everything seems normal at Manhattan West. Business as usual. No warnings from the bosses. No speeches, nothing."

"Well, Tom, Charlie called me from Florida the other day and he casually mentioned that trouble was brewing, to warn you to watch your ass. That's why I called you a couple of times, why I was so pissed off when I didn't hear from you."

"I'm sorry, Vin, really I am. I meant to catch you at the Candy Mint Lounge last Thursday afternoon. I was in Gallagher's with Bernie Wolf when I met Constance with one of his clients. The world stopped. Lights out for a couple of days after that."

"Okay, Tom, let's get serious before Connie returns to the table. This mayor we have is a complete shithead. He gives into every demand the minority races make, three quarters of whom are on home relief. The police commissioner he picked is from out of town, for Christ sake. Can you believe it? A nice enough guy, but what the fuck does he know about New York City? The city needs a guy born and raised in New York. A guy who came up in the ranks of the Job in New York to become police commissioner. Am I right?"

"Of course you're right. Common sense dictates that."

"Now our handsome mayor wants a civilian review board so that every time you kick a would-be tough guy in the ass you are liable to be brought up on charges. And how about Washington, D.C.? Every politician and his crony are getting rich down there and our shit-kicking president fills the Supreme Court with liberals as he poses as a friend of the minorities. What a bunch of assholes, sitting in their ivory tower. They hand down decisions like Miranda, suppression of evidence decisions that make it almost impossible for cops and detectives to convict the worst sort of scum. They outlaw capital punishment, costing the taxpayers zillions to keep a lot of the world's worst shit that indiscriminately kill little kids, old ladies, any poor soul they feel like belting out. Everything to protect the criminal. Fuck society.

"I wish they would do a few tours in Harlem, San Juan Hill, the South Bronx or the lower East Side of Manhattan. They would drop dead of fright."

Tommy shook his head sadly. "The whole world is going nuts, Vince. All the goddam drugs, half the young kids carrying guns, the punks locked up for a serious crime who either get dismissed or a slap on the wrist sentence on a reduced charge. Cops are getting so that they don't give a shit any more."

"You're telling me. But one thing, Tom, nobody gets away with a thing in my joints. I've got bouncers and the first time a guy gets out of line he gets thrown the hell out. If he starts to get tough, wants to fight, we kick the shit out of him. And that's the way it used to be with the police. Everyone respected a cop. Then, the same horseshit liberal politicians, judges, and district attorneys, who are in most ways responsible for the increase in crime, want to crucify a cop who takes a deuce or a fin from a gambler. Meanwhile, they discredit the entire Job. What a world!"

"What's the solution, Vince?"

"Tom, confidentially, in another couple of years I'm selling out. All the joints. Charlie speaks to me a couple of times a week and we've discussed it very thoroughly. He misses me, Connie and the kids. Wants me to move to the East Coast of Florida and open up a real good restaurant there. I love the idea."

Tommy's face assumed a look of mock horror.

"You would leave me? Go to Florida and leave your best pal on earth?"

Vinny laughed. "It might break my Italian heart but I sure would. Seriously, I have something very important to say to you."

"Go ahead."

"Tom, promise me that when the shit starts to hit the fan, you'll immediately resign from the Job and take it on the lam. You must be up to your ass in cash after almost ten years in Manhattan West. Irish, take the money and run. Don't take any chances of winding up in fucking jail."

"Jail. Jesus Christ, don't mention that word. Listen, I know your heart is in the right place and you're giving me good advice. But what the hell would I do if I ever left the Job?"

"Look, Tom, we've both discussed it many times and we agree. Neither of us are religious, we only have one life. Live it to the hilt. We don't believe in any of that hereafter horseshit. I honestly love you like a brother, Tom. Promise me, the first sign of the roof about to cave in, you'll get the hell out of the Job."

"I promise, Vince, that if I see the roof falling in, when the head hunters start to hunt in earnest—well, then I'll take the fence. I'll get the hell out of New York, maybe out to San Diego, California. I love it out there."

He gripped Tom's arm. "Good boy, Tommy. Okay, enough said, here comes your Constance. She's almost as good-looking as my Connie."

"I'd say, about a tie."

She returned to the table smiling, a little blush added to her cheekbones, looking more lovely than ever.

"Well, I hope you didn't cut me up too much while I was gone. Why the faces? You two look more like two guys who just got caught robbing a bank."

"I told you she was smart, didn't I, Vince?"

Vinny laughed. "You're right, Tom, she would make a good lady cop. Okay, let's drink up. One more for the road, then I'll drop you two off at the Saint Moritz and go home to my Connie. My car's outside."

"Someday I'd love to meet her and the kids, Vinny. Tommy raved about her and said that the kids were beautiful."

"Why not? They take after their old man." Vinny laughed, evading making a date, thinking about Justine.

Tom said, "Except luckily, the two kids didn't inherit their old man's nose, thank God."

Another big laugh. Another Remy Martin. Lots of hugs and kisses when Vinny let them out at the entrance to the St. Moritz. He exacted a dead promise from Tom. A phone call or a visit at least every other day.

Back in the hotel suite.

"Gee, Tommy, what a nice guy."

"I told you, Constance. He's the greatest. My best friend in the world."

"There's something else there, Tommy. He loves you as much as you love him. His eyes lit up when he first saw you."

"That's because he's a closet Italian fag." Tommy laughed.

"Some fag. Just looking at him, I'd hate to be on his list, his wrong side."

"You're not kidding, hon, he's one tough sonofabitch."

"Oh, babe, I'm dead tired. Let's go to bed."

"No nightcap?"

"No sir, to bed, my love. I'll have my nightcap right there, if you don't mind."

They both laughed. They shared a great intimacy by now, felt very casual about each other. Constance washed her face, brushed her teeth, emerged from the bathroom stark naked. He whistled as she passed him, slapped her hard on the ass. She jumped, gave a little cry of pain and he fled into the bathroom.

Washed up, teeth brushed, he got into bed next to her. She snapped the light out on the night table next to her and cuddled close to him. She had parted the bedroom window drapes and a silvery stream of moonlight bathed the room, casting a bluish glow over her irresistible body. He kissed her. Her tongue searched for his, she reached for his cock. It was rock hard.

"Oh, my, Saint Peter. You really have a gorgeous peter."

"It's all yours, baby."

They made love for what seemed like forever to Constance. She moaned, came, clutched him tight, came again, almost screamed a couple of times. Oh, Tommy, Tommy. I love you so. Finally, he couldn't contain himself any longer. They came together convulsively—moaning, shuddering.

They lay quietly in each others arms. At last completely sated. The heavy breathing had finally stopped. He kissed her eyes, held her close, her head in his arm.

"Will it always be this good, Tommy?"

"Well, when you get more experienced, sweetheart, I'm sure it will get better for me."

"You dirty rat." She laughed, purred contentedly, snuggled her head to his chest, and fell sound asleep.

He kissed her fragrant hair, reviewed the last two days with her. Incredible. He never enjoyed a woman so much. Very funny, exceptionally bright, beautiful, and I can't seem to stop making love to her. Christ, my cock won't stay down. Another few days with her and I'll wind up in the paraplegic ward in Roosevelt Hospital. He grinned, what a way to go!

Jesus, I hope Justine doesn't challenge me when I get home tomorrow.

He disentangled his arm from underneath her head, kissed her hair again. He turned over on his side and felt her burrowing under him, her arms clinging tightly to his shoulders. A long day, he mused. A long fucking day. His thoughts reverted to his conversation with Vinny when Constance left the table. His brow creased in anger. Fuck it, he wasn't going to get upset by the rumors of the two stool pigeons who were responsible for the upcoming probe. Maybe I should take a walk, get the hell out of the Job. I've got over three hundred thousand in the safe deposit box. Three hundred big ones. Christ, I haven't even counted it in three or four months. Just drop in the money and leave the bank. And I guess I could get close to a hundred thousand for the house the way we fixed it up.

But then what the hell would I do? Open a saloon like a lot of other cops. Shit, I drink enough now. I would probably wind up like Billy Driscoll, or worse. Poor Jerry Dillon. Maybe become a private eye. He turned, looked at Constance, snoring gently. Knocked dead, out like a light. He grinned, knocked fucking dead.

A private eye, not a bad idea. Go away, far away with Constance. What about Justine? Jesus Christ, yeah, what about Justine? He fell sound asleep.

Deputy Chief Inspector Edward Moclair sat at ease in a wide comfortable leather club chair in the spare bedroom of his apartment that his wife had converted into a den. It was a luxurious room in the lovely high-ceilinged apartment; built in the prosperous 1920s and still in mint condition. Sturdy mahogany book shelves lined the walls on opposite sides of the den. Heavy leather ottomans were scattered around the room, a long sofa covered with a rich fabric was opposite the club chairs, in front of which was a round, dark-stained oak cocktail table. Several lush paintings adorned the walls along with several bits of gold-framed memorabilia attesting to the chief's bravery both in the United States Navy and the Job.

Tall Scotch and water in hand, he settled back happily in his beloved club chair. He had had a great day at Winged Foot. Played good golf in spite of being tired. Ninety-six. Not bad for the west course at Winged Foot, a real tough track. He sipped his drink, waiting for his best friend, Lieutenant Jack Burke, to finish making his drink from the ebony portable bar in the far corner of the room. Jack returned and sat in the matching club chair opposite the chief.

They reached over and tipped glasses good luck. They engaged in some small talk for a few minutes. The chief described his game to Jack, the ups and downs, and how his host, Joe Savoca, was so hospitable and generous to him. Jack Burke finally spoke. "Sounds like you had a wonderful day, Chief, and I'm pleased you played so well. Any time you break a hundred on the west course you're playing great. Did you win any money?"

"Twenty dollars. But God knows what Savoca beat big Don Scott for. He had a grin from ear to ear when we finished. They have all kinds of weird bets—double, double press, all that sort of shit. You need a computer to figure it all out."

"But you won twenty bucks. Great. By the way, Chief, the weather's beautiful now. When are we going to play together?"

"Real soon, Jack, we'll play Wheatley Hills on Long Island, a fine course. Inspector O'Connell is a member and he's invited me at least ten times."

"That sounds real good, Chief. Okay, boss, you didn't get me in here from Bayside to talk golf. Come on, what's on your mind?"

The chief sipped his drink, weighed his thoughts gingerly. Jack Burke was ten years younger than he. He studied him for a moment as Jack took a long swallow of his drink. He loved Jack as if he were his younger brother. Jack had worked for him as a young detective when he was a squad lieutenant supervisor in a busy Queens precinct. A good man. As he rose through the ranks he kept in touch with Jack, had an occasional drink with him. And when he was made a full inspector and placed in command of the fifteenth division, he tapped Jack, now a lieutenant, to boss the squad of plainclothesmen.

"You guessed right, as usual, Jack. I sure as hell didn't bring you here to West End Avenue to talk about my golf. I had a couple of drinks yesterday with my old pal, Georgie Cohen. You must remember him. Anyway, to make it brief, George attended an executive luncheon at the New York Times building yesterday.

"During the course of lunch the subject of the Job came up. It seems that the top guys at the *New York Times* have given the green light to launch an investigation concerning allegations of corruption. They're being fed most of their ammunition by those two rat bastards who are causing all the stink in the Job. If only we had a real police commissioner, instead of this no-balls out-of-towner, he would transfer these two bums to Staten Island or the asshole end of Queens and warn them that if they kept up this shit, he would break them. Yessir, Jack, kick their goddam asses out of the Job."

"Chief, you're dead right. I can't believe what these two guys are getting away with. What the hell are they trying to prove? And the mayor. Jesus Christ, he should no more be mayor of New York than the sainted Mother Cabrini. He hasn't the slightest idea of what's going on in this town. It's murder! I'm getting disgusted, too, Chief. What do you propose?"

"Jack, you're not only my trusted lieutenant, you're my best friend. You've been dead square with me from the first day. We had a great run together. Almost fifteen wonderful years. Jack, I think it's time to call it a day.

"Let's discuss it logically. We both have accumulated plenty of money. We'll both receive nice pensions. I'll be goddamned if I'm going to stick around and let some bullshit politician or some snot-nosed special prosecutor decide my fate. No witch-hunting grand juries for me. I was a young detective lieutenant in Queens during the Harry Gross investigation in Brooklyn and my heart bled for some of the top brass they tortured during that one.

"Jack, I always took a silent oath that it would never happen to me. I was appointed to the Job in nineteen thirty-five. I enlisted in the navy the day after Pearl Harbor. Two years later I was made an ensign and came out a lieutenant junior grade. I commanded a landing craft through five invasions including the worst, Iwo Jima and Guadalcanal. I have the Navy Cross and a Purple Heart, hit in the arm at Iwo Jima.

"Through my years as a cop, detective and up through the ranks to deputy chief, I've made seventeen major felony arrests. Homicide, armed robbery, rape—you name it. I've received five major decorations in the Job for valor. But all of that is in the past. If they got one crack at me they would crucify me if they could.

"Jack, now, let's get down to the nitty-gritty. We both know we grabbed our share of cash. All of which we considered legitimate. Only gambling money. No drugs, prostitution, none of that garbage. If what we did is a sin, too goddam bad. I'll answer to my Maker if I ever meet Him."

He took a long drink of his Scotch and water, resumed.

"So, Jack, I've definitely made up my mind to put in for retirement. Unfortunately, or perhaps fortunately the way the world is going, the wife and I have no children. As you know, because you and your wife stayed there, a few years ago I bought a condominium in West Palm Beach, Florida. It's right next to a golf course and there are a dozen more in the area.

"I asked you here today, Jack, so that I could brief you on my immediate plans. What the hell, Jack, I might as well put it right out on the table. I'm betting we're due for a major scandal to explode in the Job. The real top brass, the guys who outrank me, are vying against one another to curry the police commissioner's favor. Most of these shitheads, including the P.C., couldn't tell their ass from a hole in the ground. By and large they're book men. They don't know a goddam thing about what's happening out there on the street."

"Chief, I couldn't agree more. Your hunch is right and I think you know me well enough that if I felt differently I would disagree."

He got up slowly, took the chief's glass and walked over to the small bar in the corner of the room. He returned with two tall Ballantine Scotch and waters. He handed one to the chief, tipped his glass good luck and eased back on the soft leather cushions of the club chair.

"Okay, you're the boss. You go first. What do we do?"

"Good enough, Jack. Exactly as I predicted you would react.

All right, here we go. I'm putting in for my vacation to start a week from Monday. Altogether, with time coming to me, I have between five and six weeks owed for vacation. My wife and I are flying to Florida. I intend to empty out one of my safe deposit boxes and transfer the cash to a safe deposit box in Florida." He sipped his drink, laughed.

"Christ, I hope the plane doesn't crash. If they ever found all that cash on my dead body they'd probably indict me up in Heaven. That is, if I ever get there."

They both laughed, sipped their drinks.

The chief continued, "My young nephew, Jimmy, is a lawyer in Boca Raton. He arranged everything for me my last trip down there. I already have a checking account and a safe deposit box in a bank down there. Perfect. No problem about a bank. About a week after I'm in Florida I intend to fly back on an early morning plane, take a taxicab to New York, empty out my second safe deposit box and catch a late afternoon plane back. That will be it. As the French say, the *dénouement*.

"When my vacation time ends in Florida, I'll submit my resignation from the Job. I'll plead as a reason my wife's ill health or some kind of horseshit like that. I have about two months terminal leave due me with full pay, so I should be officially finished with the Job by the middle of September. I don't anticipate any investigation to get under way officially for nine months to a year. The minute I receive the first alarm I'm off to Ireland for the duration.

"Thank God for the Irish, especially their brilliant lawmakers. No reciprocal witness laws, no extradition treaties for anything short of murder. What a great race! We'll visit County Cork where my parents came from, then we'll visit County Mayo where my wife's parents came from. I then plan to rent a cottage on Dingle Bay, in County Kerry. I understand it's a really beautiful setting, with some fine golf courses to make it more enticing. I'll play golf as often as I wish, read to my heart's content, visit the local pubs, do all the things I always wanted to do. Most of all, I'd really like to recapture some of my Irish heritage, drink in the atmosphere of the Old Sod. How does that sound for a pretty well-thought-out game plan, Jack?"

Jack Burke, chuckled, shook his head, took a good belt of his drink and said, "Chief, I always admired you for your brains, your clear thinking in tough situations and your reluctance to make too quick judgments. Now don't get me wrong. You, above all people, know I'm not the type of guy who'll kiss anyone's ass, to butter anyone up. But somehow you always seem to have the knack of anticipating things and then to come up with the correct solution. Jesus Christ, they should have made you the police commissioner, a man who really understands what a cop has to face every day and the things that make New York tick. But you and a few other capable bosses were passed over because you were real street cops. They put in some egghead with two or three college degrees who knows shit about what's going on. Well, forget about all that, Chief, you're absolutely right, our days are numbered."

The chief nodded grimly. "You have the floor Jack, my boy, keep going, get to the game plan."

"Okay, Chief. To get back to where we were, your game plan is fantastic. It's just like one of those fairy tales we read when we were little kids in school. Only now the fairy tale is going to come true. A beautiful condominium in sunny Florida, a year in lovely Ireland. Lots of golf, good books, occasional good whiskey, and best of all, no more goddam headaches.

"You've been shot at over ten times in your life between the navy and the Job. It's a miracle you were only wounded once. By all odds you should have been killed years ago. Fortunately you survived. Best of all you survived in good health, with all your marbles and with plenty of cash. Chief, I hope and pray you'll have a helluva good old age."

"Thank you, Jack. Go on, the nitty-gritty, let's hear it."

"Now the way I look at it, Chief, you go and do what you have to do until all this crap blows over. I'll do pretty much the same. But you must promise me that we'll never lose each other, never lose our friendship. When things return to normal we'll visit each other as frequently as possible? Promise, Chief?"

The chief leaned over with outstretched hand and gripped Jack Burke's right hand very hard. His eyes were moist, "A promise, Jack, a dead promise."

They tipped glasses again, sipped their drinks, and Jack continued, "Okay, Chief, you old Yankee and football Giants rooter, here's my game plan. To regress for a minute, I knew goddam well from the concerned look on your face the past week or two that something deep was troubling you. I mentioned it to Helen, saying that sooner or later you'd confide in me. Anyway, she and I went out to the Hamptons last weekend to stay with some friends and one night we lay awake in bed and discussed our future plans for when the bubble burst.

"My oldest, the boy, John, as you know is a pre-med junior at the University of California at Berkeley. He wants to continue his medical studies in California when he graduates. He loves it out there. There are several wonderful schools—Stanford, Cal-Davis—a few other great ones. His marks so far are excellent. He should be accepted out there and would love to practice in California eventually.

"My daughter, Anne, graduates next week from Mary Louis Academy out in Queens and she's near the top of her class. She's already been accepted at several good colleges including the University of Southern California. Helen and I have decided to enroll her at U.S.C. and move out there when I retire. We'll move somewhere between Los Angeles and San Francisco to be accessible to both kids. Best of all, we both love the idea of living in California."

Jack Burke threw his head back and laughed gleefully. "Chief, I have to tell you my secret. I'm way ahead of you. Helen and I went out to Berkeley a few months ago for Parents Weekend. Beforehand, I spoke to John and had him get a safe deposit box in the same bank where he maintains a checking account for his college expenses. When we flew out we had about two hundred thousand that I emptied out of one of my boxes and when I got there I stashed it in John's safe deposit box." He laughed. "Christ, Chief, don't bring up the subject of plane crashes." He went on, "Now I intend to send Helen out first with part of the rest of my cash and I'll follow her with the balance. I'll spread that cash around in a couple of safe deposit boxes out there in a way no one will ever trace it.

"The minute you resign, or retire is the better word. When it becomes effective in a month or so, then I'll submit my letter of retirement. I also have a couple of months accumulated leave with full pay. I'll arrange to sell my house in Bayside and rent or buy a house in California. We'll be near both of our kids. As you know, I have my degree in political science from St. John's University. Whenever we had a couple of drinks together I must have told you a hundred times how I always wanted to be a lawyer. But like a million other horny soldiers I married Helen when I was home on leave from the army during the war. That ended my dreams of a law career for a while and eventually I wound up in the Job. It wasn't too bad a trade, right, Chief?"

They both roared laughing.

"Anyway, to end my plan, I might go back to college and get my master's degree in criminal justice. Then I would like to teach in some college in California. I've got a nice pension to get by on, sneak a little cash out of the box once in a while so that we can live in our accustomed good style and let the chips fall where they may. Sound okay, Chief?"

"Great plan! Wonderful, Jack. The only disturbing feature is that we'll be separated for a year or two. But all this horseshit investigation malarkey will eventually die just as the other circuses."

A voice called from the kitchen, "Edward, dinner will be ready in fifteen minutes."

"Thank you, love. Jack, make another drink, please. I have a couple of more questions before we have dinner. I'd like to know what you intend to do about the men who work for us."

Jack nodded thoughtfully, arose from his chair. He went to the small bar and made two generous Ballantine Scotch and waters. He handed one to the chief and they tipped glasses ritually.

"First, Chief, let's have your opinions, your ideas. Right here we'll let it all hang out. What we say will always remain between just us."

"Good. All right, first the two shoofly lieutenants, Frank Gerrity and Paddy Quinn. Then the plainclothesmen directly under your command, plus the clerical man, Jack O'Keefe, a wonderful kid. I honestly worry about all of them. They did their work, were very loyal to us, and never gave us too much concern. We lost a couple of good men to the booze in Billy Driscoll and Jerry Dillon, but considering the pitfalls along the bright lights of Broadway, the temptation out there, I'd consider we were very lucky."

"Extremely lucky, Chief. A bunch of good men. Okay, I'll start from the top, see if you agree. The two shooflies, Gerrity and Quinn, both have more than enough time in to retire. They're both pretty healthy, had a good run, and I know they're both anxious to leave the Job. Now the men. Joe Marchetti. He has as much time in the Job as you, Chief, and probably twice as much cash. He might be cheap but he's trustworthy. He's the only one who ever handled our cash and it was always given to me. You never entered the picture. All anyone can ever do is guess about you getting any money and you can trust me with your life. I'm sure Joe will retire the day you do."

Jack took a long swallow of his drink, smacked his lips, smiled. "The nectar of the gods, Chief. Okay, down the list. Next comes our next Italian hero, Larry Cuccia. Complete opposite of Marchetti. Quiet, unassuming, never says much. But a real good cop, made plenty of good arrests. Larry came in the Job with me so I know he's got his time in and will retire. He also loves to play golf and loves Florida.

"Next we have the Swede, Pete Petersen, Joe Marchetti's partner. He has his time in. After putting up with Marchetti for nine years he'll be glad to retire. Next comes Buster Smith, now that Jerry Dillon's dead, the best-dressed cop in the Job. Buster also has his time in. He's divorced and free and easy. He can settle down wherever he pleases. He'll never go back to wearing a uniform. The monotony of dressing in the same blue suit almost every day would kill him. He's a sure bet to retire."

The chief laughed. "Good. How about the next four, the younger guys?"

"Well, Chief, the next in line is Tommy Sloane. He's a helluva cop but a strange guy. He doesn't mix much with the other men. Sort of a Lone Ranger type guy. He does his work, makes some real good collars. I know that he and Marchetti hate each other. Something from way back when he just joined the squad. But, personally, I have no squawk with Sloane at all. He's very respectful, does what you tell him. He was recommended to us pretty good, remember, your old pal, Charlie Mattuci?

"Anyway, Sloane's a nice enough kid, but I'm just a bit leery of him. Christ, every wise guy on the West Side knows him. He gets around like horseshit at the race track. That's what bothers me, the way his name keeps cropping up. It seems like whenever I meet a guy, a heavy contract that requires my presence, they invariably say—'oh, you're Tommy Sloane's boss.' It's weird, Chief, but I honestly can't find fault with the kid. We have to put him somewhere when you're replaced and the new chief brings his own squad in. Maybe not the detective bureau right away, but something decent."

"How about the warrant squad, Jack? The captain down there, Bob Keegan, is a good friend of mine."

"Perfect, Chief. Okay, the three young kids. What about them?"

"Well, there's young Frank Donahue, who replaced Billy Driscoll. I know that he's been going to law school a few nights a week, with my permission, of course. In my heart, I believe he'll quit the Job when you retire. He's very smart, anxious to become a lawyer, did pretty good with us the last year and a half, so he should be able to finish law school during the day sessions. Should make a good lawyer with the smarts he picked up in Manhattan West."

The chief laughed again, a contented laugh.

"Then there's the other two kids. Jimmy Doran, who replaced Jerry Dillon, and young Irwin Auslander, the Jewish James Bond, who replaced Lenny Beck. They both have about seven or eight years on the Job and will probably have to go back on patrol. Young Auslander is on the sergeant's list, should be made in a year or less, so he's okay. I think young Jimmy Doran would make a helluva detective. Bright kid, loves the Job. Let's see what we can do for him. Last of all, Jack O'Keefe, our terrific clerical man. A great kid. He has a few years to go before he can retire, Chief, we have to do something nice for Jack O'Keefe. He's been a special kind of guy for us all through the years. He received a small end every month and I'm sure the men personally took care of him once in a while, but he's got six kids, the oldest twelve, and I'm sure he could use a nice farewell present."

"Good idea, Jack. I'll be sure to place him somewhere if the new chief doesn't keep him. As for his gift, you tell Joe to prorate the money from the two of us and the other men. Give Jack O'Keefe twenty-five thousand dollars. He deserves every penny of it and I'm sure everyone will agree."

"Great, Chief. Very generous!"

A high-pitched call from the kitchen—"Dinner is served, sweetheart."

Little did Tommy Sloane know the honeymoon was coming to an end as he squeezed Constance's hand and roared laughing at Marcello Mastroianni. Not the quasi honeymoon he had embarked on only a day before with his comely Constance, but the irrevocable termination of his golden days as a Manhattan West man. The ominous warnings of Vince at the Villa Pompei when Constance left the table disturbed him, but only briefly. Too many people involved, too many big shots picking rich roses off the money tree to let two squealing rat bastards upset the apple cart.

He would have been shocked if he had ever been privy to the frank conversation of the chief and Lieutenant Jack Burke, making their plans both for their idyllic old age and the simultaneous fall of Tommy Sloane and company. But ignorance was bliss the next morning, as Constance woke up first and slipped quietly out of bed, careful not to disturb Tommy. She showered and dressed while Tommy still slept. She finally decided to awaken him, pushed his shoulders very gently. He sat up instantly, the ever-alert street cop. He collected himself, yawned, smiled at her and rubbed his eyes. She smiled back, leaned over and kissed him nice and easy on the lips.

"You are some sleepy head, my dear, it's almost ten o'clock. I thought for a while that you were dead you were sleeping so soundly. You were so knocked out you didn't even snore."

He laughed, squeezed her hand.

"If I died you would have been indicted for felony murder in the first degree. Fucking a poor, helpless, unarmed cop to death in a hotel suite. I can see your picture on the front page right now. BEAUTIFUL AD EXEC KILLS HERO COP IN HOTEL ORGY. And in the follow-up story on the inside pages—weapon found between statuesque beauty's thighs."

Constance laughed, pulled him out of bed and said, "Get up, you lazy bedroom hero. Out of bed. Come on, shower up, brush your teeth, and get dressed. When you finish, we'll order breakfast and then take a nice walk in Central Park. It's beautiful outside. I have to go home pretty early this afternoon and begin work on a new campaign we're starting at the agency on Monday. What are your plans?"

He turned at the bathroom door, anticipated that question beforehand, had his usual glib answer ready and waiting. Eyes downcast, very sincerely—"I'm afraid I have to put you in a taxi to get you home, hon. I'm scheduled for day duty this afternoon. I have to report to the squad office about two o'clock and see what they have in store for me. My car is parked in a garage near the office and if we're not too busy I'll probably go home early, about seven o'clock tonight. Anyway, I need a shave and a change of clothes."

Her voice tight, disappointed—"Oh, Tom, I was hoping you would come home with me and see my apartment. I thought it would be nice for you to read the Sunday papers while I did some work and then we'd have a couple of drinks and I would fix you a light supper."

"Gee, I'm sorry, sweetheart, that sounds so wonderful. But I honestly do have to report for work. Okay, love, excuse me now. Let me go to the john, buff up a little and get dressed. Order some sausages, eggs, juice, coffee, and whatever you like from room service. I'll be with you in about ten minutes."

He shut the bathroom door, shook his head and sighed. Why do I have to tell these goddam lies all the time? I better get home to Justine this afternoon or she'll have a shit hemorrhage. Worse yet, send out a thirteen-state alarm! And first chance I get I better make some excuse and get down to the lobby and call her. He soaped himself under the steamy shower. I got it! When room service comes, I'll grab the elevator down to the lobby to get the papers and call her from there. His mind eased, he sang under the shower.

He toweled off, brushed his teeth, looked himself over minutely in the mirror. Outside of needing a shave he concluded that he looked pretty damned good. He was exuberant. Hummed his shower song over again as he combed his hair.

God, Constance would drive anyone crazy. Oh, babe, how I hate to leave you.

He drove his BMW almost absent-mindedly towards White-stone and home after he dropped Constance off. He maneuvered mechanically, always the formidable radio car cop, through the light Sunday afternoon traffic. His mood was ecstatic. He felt happier than any time he could remember. His thoughts were filled with various images of Constance, all of her visual delights. Her blue eyes, toothy white smile, smooth tanned skin, unbelievable body. His mind danced, saturated with technicolor shots of her in every conceivable pose in or out of bed. Standing, sitting, naked, dressed. Her complete abandon making love, her wild almost guttural cries, followed by incredible tenderness afterwards. Jesus Christ, I'm really falling in love.

His thoughts strayed to their conversation as they walked through lush, fragrant Central Park earlier in the day. Constance mentioned that she received a week's vacation every ten weeks because of all the overtime she put into her job. One was coming up shortly. Tom, would it be great to go away together. His scheming mind searched for the proper trip as he wended his way to home and Justine. Suddenly his mind reverted to a meeting he had with a well-connected bookmaker a couple of months back. He had done him a heavy favor and the big shot staked him real good. He further mentioned the possibility of putting him on a junket to Las Vegas. That's it! Four days in Vegas!

The gambler had laughed when he made the offer. Bring your best girlfriend, kid, nobody brings their wife to Las Vegas. Tommy grinned, remembered the big shot laughing. You can say that again! Just give me the word, kid, and I'll arrange everything with my pal, Big Julie. Perfect. Vegas, here we come!

I'll have to call young Frank when I get home, meet him early tomorrow morning. Get our asses into high gear, step up our collars so that we have our quota in real early. I better get my story together real soon for Lieutenant Burke and Justine.

Leave Kennedy Airport Thursday afternoon and return Sunday night. Four glorious days! Christ, it should be a hanger to get away. He was so lost in his reverie of resplendent gambling casinos, long-legged show girls and flashy floor shows he almost overshot his home street and landed in Little Neck Bay.

Justine met him at the front door and kissed him hungrily in the mouth. She held him tight.

"Oh, Tommy, you really need a shave and you look so tired. Was it a tough couple of days, sweetheart?"

He held his arm around her waist, closed the door. "It was murder, hon, but I think we finally got this mob right where we want them. We should be able to move in on them early next week. God, I am tired. How about making me a tall vodka and tonic and maybe a sandwich?"

"Anything you say, love. You poor guy, the way the police department works you. You must be exhausted, trailing those crooks night and day."

He smiled tiredly, the dedicated cop smile.

"Ah, it wasn't too bad, hon. And it's tailing, not trailing. It will all be worth it when we pinch the whole rotten gang. They even have out-of-town members of the mob working with them in New York." He smiled inwardly. Might as well lay a little groundwork for the Vegas trip right now while she's all sympathy.

She returned from the kitchen in about five minutes with a large serving tray bearing his drink, a Coca-Cola for herself and a plate of tuna fish sandwiches. He sipped his drink and ate hungrily. Between bites and swallows he regaled Justine with his stirring exploits of the two previous nights he and young Frank Donahue spent tailing the mythical heist mob. He slyly interposed an occasional mention of a mysterious Mr. Big whose voice they taped on their hotel room telephone wire tap. Justine, he had to be from somewhere out West. He and Frank figured out afterwards from some additional calls they taped later that Mr. Big must reside in Phoenix, Arizona. As he readied his reasons for having to go out West real soon to pick up Mr. Big, he mentally calculated from his meager geographical knowledge that Phoenix had to be close enough to Las Vegas to establish his alibi.

He nodded slowly as she flooded him with questions, not hearing a word she said. His mind was on one thing, one city, Las Vegas. In spite of many solid invitations he had never been to Vegas. He seldom even gambled, except for a rare visit to the race track. Hell, gambling is a sucker's racket. Where else did all that cash come from that he and a lot of other cops were salting away in the cool interiors of bank vaults?

But what the hell, life is short. I used to love to shoot crap and play cards both as a kid and when I was in the navy. I'll take a little shot at the dice table, maybe play a little blackjack. He smiled inwardly. Blackjack was sure good to him in the navy. He sure clipped some of those rube farmer boys enough to live far beyond the sparse salary good old Uncle Sam paid him. But, dear Lord, forget about what happens to me when I gamble, just give me four days of Constance.

Justine finished her recital of her not-too-lovely weekend, filled with anecdotes of her bowling, card games, and church-going with her girlfriends. She urged him to tell her more about his criminal chase. She listened intently as he elaborated on his cops and robbers fabrication. She gripped his hand hard, leaned over and kissed him when he described his dangerous pursuit of the arch villains. He shrugged, smiled grimly, you never know when you might buy it, babe. If those two guys had a back-up cover it might just have been curtains for young Frank and me.

Justine shuddered, patted his cheek, hugged him fiercely. "C'mon, Tom, let's change the subject, it sounds too scary. Besides, nothing can happen to you. I went to Mass Saturday night and Sunday morning. I prayed, offered up my Holy Communion, that you would be safe, that God would look out for you."

He smiled, squeezed her hand tenderly. How sweet of you, dear. For a few minutes the other night with Constance I really thought my heart would stop. I needed your prayers, Justine, needed God's help. I'll need Him again soon, dear, and your prayers as well. In Las Vegas with Constance, the dice and blackjack tables. He yawned, put his hand to his mouth, and said, "Gee, I'm sorry, hon, excuse me. I just can't help it. I'm so exhausted, really sleepy. Suppose I go in and rest for a while, then take you out to dinner."

"Oh, Tommy, that would be great. Poor dear, you must be exhausted. I'll go in and turn down the bed and pull down the venetian blinds to darken the room." She left his side to get the bedroom ready for her beloved foe of crime, her sweetheart, drained dry by his ceaseless vigil.

He arose when she left, crossed the room to a bookcase set against the wall opposite him and picked out a volume of Norman Mailer's short stories to read while he awaited sleep. Might as well begin to get real intellectual to keep abreast of my brilliant Constance.

He had called Frank Donahue on the phone before he took Justine to dinner and they met as agreed at eight o'clock the next morning in a dingy coffeepot on the lower fringe of West Harlem. Willie Baker, his *café au lait* Harlem stool pigeon *par excellence*, arrived about ten minutes later. Tom and Frank shook hands with Willie, exchanged pleasantries, ordered his breakfast. Tom, sharp eyed as ever, immediately decided that Willie wasn't at his best physically. Hopefully, just a bad hangover. Jesus Christ, not back on the shit again, not the old needle he swore to Tommy he had given up for life. They munched their soggy doughnuts and sipped their hot coffee. Tommy observed how Willie's hands shook when he lifted the coffee cup to his lips, how he finally had to grasp it with both hands.

He gave Frank the raised eye, motioned with his head towards the phone booth in the rear of the restaurant and said, "Frank, suppose you go back and call the squad office. Tell Jack O'Keefe to tell the boss what we're up to. Explain to him that we should be busy for four or five hours, probably wind up in gambler's court this afternoon. We'll stay in touch. Okay?"

Frank nodded, arose quickly, Tommy's mere suggestion a monarchical command. He mused as he walked to the phone booth in the rear. He could never get too close to Tommy. Well, neither could anyone else. He very seldom went out socially with him except for an occasional drink and dinner together. Perhaps it was because of his own preoccupation with law school three nights a week, studying the other nights. No question, Tommy was a strange guy. But he had to admit he owed a lot to Tommy. Who else made sure that he got his proper share of the take right out of the starting gate? Further, Tom always split any score they made right down the middle, was always fair and square about money. And Christ, what a partner to luck out with. Tommy had a network of informants and ingenious stool pigeons that made their quota of collars for the month so simple the Job was one big picnic. He dialed the office number, felt the nice cool couple of hundred nestled in his left pants pocket, thought about the safe deposit box growing nice and green each month. Yessir, life with Tommy Sloane in the paradise called Manhattan West was one big bowl of cherries.

With Frank safely out of earshot, Tommy leaned across the table to Willie and in a low voice said, "What's the matter, Kid Chocolate? You're shaking and sweating like a scared rabbit. Out all night fucking some of that super uptown black pussy?"

Willie laughed, a little relieved, hadn't missed Tommy's grim look.

"You said it right, Tommy boy. I sure as hell didn't get much sleep last night. Man, I swear, she was sweet as brown sugar. But I swear, Tom, I feel all right, just a little tired. Look, here's the setup for today. I have two solid number runners for you guys. Both are dead outlaws. They belong to a new guy on the block. A dude up here from the West Indies. Thinks he's a real bad nigger. Says he's never gonna pay no law. He's called Big Teddy. We'll break his balls, won't we, Tom?"

Tommy smiled, nodded his head. As Willie spoke Tom studied him carefully, not too pleased with the way he looked, especially the way his hands shook. He decided to come right at Willie, straight to the point. Face suddenly grim, voice harsh—"Willie, you and I have been together a long time now and we've been a pretty good team, right?"

"That's right, Tommy."

"Okay. Then I don't want you to shit me, understand. I've been a good friend to you, Willie. I'm the same guy who got you off the junk a few years ago. The same guy who arranged to detoxify you. When you got straight you gave me a dead promise you'd never shoot up again. Now Willie, tell me the truth. Are you using the shit again?"

"Oh, no, Tommy, honest. I just drank a little too much whiskey the last two days. That's all, nothing else."

"You sure, Willie? Come clean, I'm your main man, remember me—what else you fucking around with?"

Willie dropped his eyes, looked about to weep.

"Well, Tom, this chick had a few rails of cocaine and I sniffed a few times. You know how it is, Tom, layin' up with a queen chick. You don't sniff some shit she offers you she right away thinks you're some kind of faggot."

"I knew goddam well something was wrong with you, Willie. You oughta know better, for Christ sake, a few sniffs is how it all starts. I'm warning you, Will, the next time you get hooked, you can forget about your old pal, Tommy Sloane. Then we are officially through, you get it."

"I swear, Tom, no more junk—" he laughed uncertainly, trying to lighten the charged air—"it's okay if I have a little Jack Daniels and some pussy, ain't it, Tommy?"

Tommy laughed. "The staff of life, Willie." Might as well get off his back, he's one helluva stoolie, makes the vice squad life a lot easier.

"Okay, Willie, I have your promise. That's good enough for me. Let's cut it right here, Frank is coming back to the table."

They made the two number-runner collars Willie had set up, plus a good score after they arraigned their hapless prey in gambler's court later in the day. The hitherto hard-nosed West Indian outlaw number controller was waiting outside the courtroom with a lawyer friend of Tom's, who introduced them. He was meek as a pussycat and handed over an envelope containing a thousand dollars as an introductory fee. Tom made a temporary armistice with the assurance of a permanent peace treaty as soon as the squad met.

Finished for the day, young Frank off to his Fordham Law School classes, he called Constance. They made a date to meet for a drink when she was through at her office. They met in a restaurant on Third Avenue in the Seventies called J.G. Melon.

He was sitting at the bar with the owner, Jack O'Neil, having a drink when she surprised him with a bear hug and kiss on the ear. He kissed her nicely on the lips and introduced her to Jack. She looked Tom over, shook her head at his get-up. He was dressed in what he called his Harlem outfit. Open sport shirt, khaki slacks, buckskin shoes, and a navy blue warm-up jacket. Eyeing him carefully she said, "Now don't tell me you worked today. You had to just finish playing softball dressed like this."

The drinks came, Jack excused himself, and they sat at the bar holding hands, facing each other, exuding the radiance of their new-found love.

She tipped his glass, grinned and said, "Gee, I'm getting just like you. I almost tipped my coffee cup to a girl I work with's cup this morning during coffee break. Oh, Tommy, I thought about you all day, could hardly concentrate on my new campaign. How about you? Catch any crooks in your construction worker's disguise?"

He lied easily. "No, sorry about that. We were on a plant up in Harlem. We're trying to nail a big hijacking ring up there. We have a pretty good line on them and should crack the case in a few days."

Her eyes widened as she looked almost worshipfully at her hero. She squeezed his hand.

"Whatever you do, Tommy, please don't get hurt."

"No need to, sweetheart, these guys are what we call *fences*, the guys who buy the stolen merchandise. We're just laying on them until a big load of swag is delivered. Then we step in and nine times out of ten the fence will give his mother up to avoid a long jail sentence. He'll lead us to the real tough guys, the hijackers themselves. We usually take them by surprise, without a struggle."

His story sounded so plausible he almost believed it himself. By the intent expression on Constance's face a helluva lot more interesting than describing pinching two poor, harmless numbers collectors.

"Okay, Tommy, enough cop talk, it makes me too nervous thinking about the risks you take. You said you wanted to talk to me about something important. Let's change to that subject. What's up?"

"Well, Con, yesterday when we took our walk through Central Park you mentioned about a vacation coming up. I also have some time coming to me. How about taking a trip together?"

"Oh, Tommy, that sounds wild. Where? When?"

"It's up to you, sweet, but I was thinking about the end of the month."

"Tommy, the timing is marvelous. I have to go to Detroit on Wednesday for about five days. The new campaign I'm working on involves next fall's new car styles for General Motors, one of our biggest accounts. The following week after I return will be perfect to go away."

Mock horror registered on his face.

"You're leaving me on Wednesday? For almost a week. I'll never survive without you for that long."

She laughed. "You're a born survivor, Tom, you'll manage to make it while I'm gone. All right, forget the jokes and stop acting for a few minutes. Just where do you intend to whisk me away to and deflower me for a week?"

"You promise not to scream when I tell you?"

"Promise!"

"Las Vegas!"

She had to stifle a cry with her hand held against her mouth. She took a long belt of her drink.

"You're not serious. You don't mean Las Vegas."

"The one and only Vegas, sweetheart, the mecca of the gambling world."

"Tommy, I can't wait to go. I've read so much about Las Vegas, always hoped I'd make it someday."

"The day is just around the corner. Okay, you're on, you agree."

"Super. But Tom, I really don't know a thing about gambling. The only card game I play is bridge."

"I'll teach you enough for you to get by at the blackjack table. Anyway we'll see all the shows, meet a lot of good friends of mine, and live the life we were both meant to live for four wonderful days."

"Four days? I thought a week."

"No, sweetie, that's all the time I can take. I have it arranged for us to leave J.F.K. Airport on a Thursday afternoon and we'll be home late the following Sunday night. Sound good?"

"Oh, I wish it was four months, but I'll take the four days."

"Great! We're all set, then. What about we have another drink and grab a cheeseburger here, they're out of this world."

"The drink is fine. Then we walk a few blocks to my apartment and I'll make you a cheeseburger."

"Anything else on the menu?"

"As soon as we lock the front door you can have my body as the first course."

"Do we have to have another drink?"

"On second thought, no. We'll have one after you make me safe for my trip to Detroit. Tommy, make it so good no man will appeal to me for a week."

"I'll make it so good it'll last a year, babe."

Tommy was at his best the next few days, the essence of the true racket-busting cop. He programmed his stool pigeons individually, urging them to come up with as many outlaws as possible, promising them each a healthy bonus in return. In short order he and young Frank Donahue made seven arrests between them by the end of the week. Their quota of collars in for the month, he worked relentlessly to make enough scores to ensure a sizable bankroll he felt necessary to afford the hedonistic joys of Las Vegas. When five thousand was safely tucked between the folds of one of his favorite shirts he mentally declared a temporary pause in his fight against all forms of vice.

While Constance was counseling the marketing czars of the automobile industry in Detroit, Tommy played the role of the dutiful husband to the hilt. He was home next to Justine in bed every night and made love to her twice, eliciting delirious moans of happiness and ecstatic avowals of her love for him. He capped his husband-of-the-year performance by taking her to dinner and a hit Broadway musical. But he never failed to casually mention how the squad was closing in on the hijacking mob. How it appeared practically imperative that he soon fly out west to Phoenix, Arizona, to pick up Mr. Big. He always assumed a grim face when he raised the subject of Mr. Big, muttering a sharp curse in her hearing about how time-consuming the Job was. One rotten pain in the ass but it had to be done. Justine would invariably pat his face and hug him in recognition of his intrepid dedication to duty.

On the surface all appeared well in the squad room of Manhattan West. Chief Moclair was off to Florida on his annual vacation, according to Jack O'Keefe, the clerical man. This caused a few raised eyebrows and some comments among the men. Funny he should go down to steamy Florida just as the weather in New York was getting quite warm. The blistering days of July loomed on the horizon less than two weeks away. He's the boss, it's his privilege.

Lieutenant Burke seemed more preoccupied than usual, his thoughts seeming at a distance as he occasionally briefed one pair of partners or the other. Tommy dismissed any implications of trouble in the lieutenant's distracted manner. He attributed his mood to his increasing duties of state during the chief's absence. He waited for the appropriate moment and took the lieutenant aside in the squad room late in the week. He explained how he and Donahue had attained their quota of collars for the month and asked his permission to go out of town the latter part of the following week. Just down to the Jersey shore, lieut. You know, a little sun, swimming, and tennis. Just bringing the wife and my sister and brother-in-law.

Sure, Tommy, sure. By all means, get away for a few days. You've been working hard and doing a great job with young Frank Donahue. He'll be one helluva lawyer when he gets his license after all he's learned with us. Right, Tommy? A big wink. Go right ahead, by all means. Tell Donahue to take a few days, too. You guys sure deserve it.

The arrangements for his dream trip went off smoothly. His big shot gambler friend went all out in making the accommodations. The original plan of going along on the regular junket plane with the hoi polloi gamblers was scrapped. No, sirree, not you, Tommy old pal. Not after the favors you've done me. Yessirree, the big favor kid and his best girl were flying out TWA in the first class cabin with a dozen selected high rollers. All guys who were financially capable of blowing a hundred grand or two without blinking an eye.

The only disquieting note that jarred his enthusiastic visions of his forthcoming magical trip was the alarming conversations that kept cropping up. They appeared to arise no matter where; the squad room, over a drink with the men, in gambler's court with the guys from the various plainclothes squads throughout the city. Even with a few wise guys he met for a drink or to discuss a contract.

The two rat bastards were yapping away, like a pair of wolves at a frightened baby deer. The frustrated would-be detective and the unofficial would-be police commissioner were blabbing their respective heads off to whomever would listen to their revelations of alleged corruption in the Job. The cops, bosses, and gamblers to a man hated these two guys.

The old-timers in the Job would get vitriolic in their condemnation. With red faces they would recall the old days of the tough police commissioners, who ruled with an iron hand. Men who took no shit from anyone. Except for the most extreme cases, the welfare of the cop came first. He had the toughest job in the world. The old-timers would laugh ironically in fond recollection. These two rat bastards would be shipped out to precincts so far on the outskirts of New York they would need a road map to get to work.

The out-of-town P.C. and the Ivy League mayor haven't the balls of a gnat. That was the almost unanimous consensus of the men in the Job. The newspapers are hinting of an impending probe. The specter of an investigative crime commission loomed over the Job, with the willing acquiescence of the mayor, anxious to keep his political skirts clean. The key word being hurled about was one that is connected with every ambitious headline-seeking politician throughout the world—graft.

Tommy just shrugged his shoulders at this ugly gossip, shook off his forebodings. Away with their prophecies of doom. He had reached his personal goal, his nirvana. Fuck them all. His mind was on one thing at present. No, two things. Las Vegas and Constance.

*   *   *

They met by prearrangement the following Thursday noon at J.F.K. Airport. Constance looked absolutely bewitching in a sky blue, short-sleeved dress, set off by a pearl necklace, tanned bare legs, and beige high-heeled shoes. She looked as if she had just stepped out of the centerfold of *Vogue* magazine. He stood rooted in the lobby of the TWA terminal drinking in her beauty as he watched her glancing around about twenty feet away while he was partially obscured by passersby. Her eyes lit up when she saw him approaching and she greeted him with a muted cry of joy and a fierce hug and kiss. All over the lobby heads turned to gaze at the handsome couple. So this was the lucky guy this striking girl was waiting for.

He broke away from her embrace, held her apart, kissed her once more and said, "Did you bring your tennis racket, sneakers, shorts, all that stuff?"

"God, Tommy, you really are romantic. Yes, copper, I brought everything you told me to bring. And wait, sweetheart, until you see your darling in her new bikini."

He laughed. "For Christ sake don't dare try it on now, there are enough guys already drooling over you in the airport."

She laughed. "Forget about other guys. I'm all yours, Thomas. For the next four days at any rate. Then I might fly up to Reno and give you up."

The plane departed about a half hour later. They held hands and discussed the events that had taken place during their enforced absence from each other. My God, ten days apart. Seemed more like ten years. Yes, things had progressed simply super in Detroit. Everyone pleased, loved our ideas for the fall debut. And how about you? Yes, dear, we caught the hijacking mob. He felt safe with the hijacking tale, had recited segments of it so often to Justine he was beginning to feel as if it really took place. An honest-to-God real arrest. Oh, how I lie!

Constance was absorbed, almost breathless, as in a calm, low voice he related his lurid, spurious experience. She gripped his arm hard as he embellished his lie, kissed his cheek, comforted by his nearness. Her lover, her hero, had survived another harrowing escapade in defense of society's natural prerogative to live in peace.

The lissome stewardess came by, greeted them with welcoming eyes and flashing smile synonymous with stewardesses everywhere. Something to drink? A bottle of Chardonnay, please.

They tipped glasses. Good luck, we'll need it all in Vegas. They sipped their wine. Delectable. He reached into his left coat pocket where he had cached three one-hundred-dollar bills before he left the house in Whitestone. He pressed them into Constance's hand. She looked at the money in her palm, her face registered dismay. She said, "Oh, Tommy, please, this isn't necessary. I have about a hundred dollars in cash and my checkbook. What more do I need?"

"Constance, my love, don't refuse, or you'll go down in the *Guinness Book of Records*. Especially, a real recent record, on a plane headed for Las Vegas. Take it, you'll soon find out you'll need it."

She put the money into her purse and said, "You're so generous, Tommy. Besides, who am I to defy history?"

He smiled contentedly. He couldn't remember ever being so happy. He squeezed her hand hard, felt like standing up in the middle of the first class cabin and singing a couple of stanzas of "When Did You Leave Heaven?" his all-time favorite ballad. Another big grin as he sipped his wine. Better not, all these long-faced high rollers I'm surrounded by will think I'm crazy. He recalled another of Constance's few failings. She didn't know how to play blackjack. He took a pack of playing cards from his other coat pocket and released the food tray concealed in the seat in front of Constance. He spread the playing cards on the tray, removed the jokers and shuffled the cards.

She looked at him inquisitively. "What's this maneuver all about, Alfred Scarne?"

"How the hell do you know about Scarne?"

"We've discussed how much I read. Simple. I read an article about him recently, very fascinating man."

"Terrific guy—but forget about becoming a female Alfred Scarne, just pay attention so you don't disgrace me. Unfortunately for you, they don't have any contract bridge gambling tables in Las Vegas. They play baccarat or chemin de fer, neither of which I understand. They also play poker and blackjack. You won't be playing any poker, so I'll teach you a little about blackjack, also called twenty-one. Are you at all familiar with blackjack?"

"Honestly, no, Tommy. I have heard a lot about the game, know the total twenty-one wins. Other than that, not an inkling."

"Well, knowing twenty-one wins is a start. Let's go."

For the next hour he explained the intricacies of blackjack to her. He showed her how to split pairs in the first two cards dealt down, how to double down, aces either one or eleven in your count. He passed on all the expertise he had gathered through his boyhood, the U.S. Navy, and his gambler friends of the present—he also cautioned her not to speak at the table. The blackjack dealer was His Holy Eminence. Silence was golden.

He played several hands with her and soon her natural intelligence took over and she began to get a grasp of the game. She was really into it, her eyes shining excitedly, when the stewardess broke the spell by serving dinner.

Constance looked at Tommy with adoration as a long limousine picked them up at McCarran Airport, the driver greeting them with a placard stenciled Sloane on his chest. They were whisked off, bag and baggage, to a sumptuous suite at the Dunes Hotel on the world-famous strip, the pride of Las Vegas, Nevada. They unpacked, hung their clothes in a walk-in closet in the bedroom and he rang room service and ordered a bottle of Smirnoff vodka, tonic, and ice cubes.

The waiter arrived with the order about five minutes later and they sat opposite each other with raised glasses in a toast to success at the gambling tables. Their flushed, happy faces exuded the joy they found in each other. Constance arose, kissed him softly on the lips and walked over to the huge picture window in the middle of the living room wall. She thrilled to the magnificent view of the sun drenched, jagged, low-slung brown mountain range in the distance.

"Oh, Tommy, dear, I keep talking about Heaven and you keep singing about it. All laughing and kidding aside, I think that right now we're finally there."

He got up from his chair and walked over to her and embraced her. His voice was husky, very emotional.

"C'mon love, into the bedroom. I want to go straight up to Heaven right inside you."

They made love tenderly at first. Then the tempo increased rapidly. Constance began to utter her faint animal cries and sob passionately as she came repeatedly. Tommy finally exploded inside her, shuddering convulsively, with a deathlock hold on her. The fever subsided, the cries dwindled into whimpers, they finally calmed down, arms around each other. She shook loose, dissolved the spell, came back to reality. A long *whooo* was her first sound.

"And so, Thomas Sloane, is that exactly what you had in mind when you said we would both get a big bang out of our Vegas trip?"

He laughed, kissed her eyes, and said, "I swear, hon, it was the furthest thing from my mind until I saw that great ass of yours outlined against your dress as you were taking in the view."

"Is that what it was? Next time I'll stand sideways."

He laughed again. "Then it'll be your great tits turning me on. Jesus, Con, will it always be like this? I can't get enough of you."

"Hopefully you'll become tired of me in another thirty or forty years. All right, Tommy, enough. Let's get dressed. We have another three days and three nights to make love. Right now, another drink and down to the casino and break the house. Is that the correct Las Vegas lingo?"

He laughed. "Break the house my Irish ass. We have some chance. Okay, here we go. Get up, use the bathroom first. I'll snooze for a little bit."

"Not too long, sleepy head. I'll be bathed and dressed in fifteen minutes."

He was already nodding off. He barely winked at her. Christ, she really knocks me dead. She shook him awake, hovering over him, looking gorgeous in a white linen pants suit. He showered, dressed and they sat and had one more drink together. No rush, the gambling casino was open twenty-four hours a day.

* * *

The next few days fulfilled their fondest dreams of what Las Vegas was all about. Tommy took it nice and easy, gambling cautiously at the crap table. The atmosphere was electric at the table. The players whooped and shouted in ecstasy, moaned and groaned in despair. He loved it. The first day, ahead a couple of hundred betting the no-come line, he took a break for a while.

He wandered over to the blackjack table where he had ensconced his gambling partner. He took a position about six feet in back of her and surreptitiously watched Constance playing. She was completely enraptured, winning with a triumphant smile, losing with a careless smile. Probably forced, he thought. But obviously in her glory, loving every minute of it. She heeded his warning not to speak, just holding up her outstretched palm to stick, scratching the green cloth with her fingertips to indicate another hit. He'd have to tell her later that she played blackjack as good as a five-hundred-dollar hooker. A seasoned veteran of a hundred Las Vegas gambling junkets.

When not in the casinos they were royally entertained at several of the larger hotels—the Sands, Riviera, Caesar's Palace. The word had been sent out West by the New York wise guys to take good care of Tommy Sloane and guest. His newly met friends in Vegas went all out. The best was none too good. They were shown to the finest tables at all the top shows. Along the way they were introduced to Billy Daniels, Engelbert Humperdinck, Sheckey Green, and a dozen other show business celebrities.

One afternoon Tommy walked Constance to downtown Vegas where the blue collar trade played. They gambled for small stakes at the Golden Nugget and Benny Binion's. Tommy let Constance shoot the dice at the crowded table there and she almost lost her mind when she won fifty dollars. Other afternoons they played tennis and swam in the huge pool at the Dunes. He was surprised at how well she played, especially when they had a mixed doubles match with a couple from a fancy New Jersey country club and beat them easily in two sets for a ten-dollar-a-man side bet. Constance clutched the money as if it were a thousand. First time she ever played for money. Tommy, I can't lose in Las Vegas.

The four-day holiday was all they hoped for, their wildest dream come true. They made love every night, ate the finest gourmet food and drank the best wines. Tommy stayed fairly even at the crap table, up a thousand or so, down a thousand or so. He would lose his zest for the game after a couple of hours and would take a break and look in on Constance. She had found her niche, played insatiably, her smiling manner captivating her fellow players. From his perch a few feet from her Tom could tell by the amount of chips in front of her and either the look of exultation or faint gloom on her beautiful face whether she was winning or losing. If he saw the forbidding visage, her loser's face, he would reach over in front of her and toss a handful of chips to freshen her bankroll. She would turn in surprise and reward him with a loving look and a grateful smile.

The end of all good things must finally come and the inevitable curtain fell on Sunday. They had stayed up their last night rather late and awakened lazily together with the late morning, searing desert sunshine streaming through the bedroom window. They lay quietly in each other's arms, savoring the memories of the previous three days. They were too contented to broach the unpleasant subject of packing and getting ready to leave Dream City and return to the prosaic environs of New York.

He picked his car up at the long-term parking lot at Kennedy Airport and returned to the TWA terminal to gather Constance and their baggage. He debated briefly whether to drop her off in New York at her apartment and then return home to Whitestone. The debate was short-lived. What was one more night away from home? The lure of another night in the warm comfort of Constance was much more appealing.

They were both dead tired from the frenzied pace of the previous few days and the long plane trip. The shrill blast of the alarm clock on the night table next to the bed woke them up reluctantly from a deep sleep at eight the next morning.

Constance jumped hurriedly out of bed. Tommy just lay there, too tired to even attempt to slap her on the ass.

She came out of the bathroom, dressed, and made breakfast while he showered, shaved, and dressed. He debated whether to call the office or not. Finally decided it would be wise. He was surprised to hear young Frank Donahue's voice answer the phone.

"Hey, Frankie boy, how are you?"

"Jesus, Tom, am I glad to hear from you. Where are you?"

"In the city, about twenty minutes away."

"There's a big meeting of the squad scheduled for later this morning. Something heavy is up. Lieutenant Burke wants us all in here by ten o'clock. Where the hell were you? I called the house Sunday and Justine told me that you were out West on a big case. She seemed surprised I wasn't along. But don't worry, I didn't give you up. The minute I got the drift about the bull-shit hijacking mob I said that you went along with a couple of old-time detectives from the safe and loft squad. How about that story? Am I getting to be as good a bullshit artist as you?"

"Beautiful, Frank. You're even better. I'll tell you later where I was. What's so heavy that he wants us all in?"

"Beats me, Tom. Get your ass going. See you later."

He drove Constance to her office building, kissed her good-bye and proceeded to his favorite garage. He was in high spir-its, tipped Chico, the attendant, a five-dollar bill and whistled as he walked the couple of blocks to the squad office.

Lieutenant Jack Burke sat in the chief's office waiting for Jack O'Keefe, the clerical man, to inform him that all the men were present. His thoughts reverted to the previous Saturday. He had received a long distance call from Chief Moclair telling him to go to an outside telephone and to call him at a number in a phone booth a few blocks from his house. As per instruc-tions, Jack Burke made the call. The chief answered on the first ring.

"Hello, Chief, how are you?"

"Fine, Jack. Are you calling me from a booth?"

"Just as you told me to do, Chief. What's up?"

"Jack, I did just what I said I'd do. I brought down half my cash and yesterday morning I flew up to New York, got the rest of it and flew back in the afternoon. Everything is stashed away nice and cozy for the present. How does that sound?"

"Great, Chief. Good work."

"Jack, I lay awake all night thinking about you and the men. I think it's only fair to let them know my future plans immediately. They've been a good bunch and I think it only proper to give them fair warning so that they can make their own plans. The minute I retire and a new chief comes in they'll be out on their asses without a chance to get set. This way, they'll have a chance to set their course of action, make some plans. Do you agree with me, Jack?"

"A hundred percent, Chief. It's been on my mind a couple of weeks, ever since we had our discussion at your house. Okay, boss, I'll arrange a nice breakfast meeting on Monday and break the news as gently as possible."

"Wonderful, Jack. Take care of yourself. Tell the men to keep it under their hats, not to rush into anything. Now keep this number and we'll communicate this way."

"Fine, Chief. Take care and God love you."

"The best, Jack."

Well, here it is, the moment of truth at last is here. I'm tickled to death to get out of the Job intact. A lovely wife, two great kids, no scandal—a blissful semiretirement ahead with a box full of cash.

Jack O'Keefe popped his head in.

"They're all here, Lieutenant."

All the men were present in the squad room when Tom arrived, the last man in. He greeted all the guys casually except for his mortal enemy, Joe the Boss Marchetti. His ever-sharp sixth sense immediately raised his antennae. Something really heavy was up. And by the doleful look on the guys' faces as they lounged around, what was up didn't appear too promising. He took young Frank Donahue aside and in a very low voice said, "What the hell's going on, Frankie? It's like a goddam funeral home in here. Who died, for Christ sake?"

"Gee, Tom, I'm sure glad you showed up. The meeting is in the upstairs room at Gallagher's Steak House. He's already arranged with Jimmy Clare, the manager, to set up breakfast for the squad at ten thirty this morning. I understand that he also gave strict orders that no one besides the guys in the squad remain in the room after we finish breakfast. Something big is cooking, Tommy. Only Joe the Boss seems to know what's up. I overheard him calling Jimmy Clare about half an hour ago and he was giving him orders as if he were one of the men."

"Jesus, Frank, what the hell could it be? I hope none of the guys are in trouble. You haven't been shaking down any judges or politicians while I was away, have you, Frank?"

Frank laughed. "No, Tommy, I was studying all the time you were away to become a lawyer, then maybe a politician after a while—then I won't have to score the way we do, it will be handed to me."

Tommy laughed. "When you get up there, Frank, I'll be your bag man. Anyway, relax, what happens, happens. Enjoy every day, life is good."

Frank grinned and said, "I'm finally relaxed after three sleepless nights wondering when I'd see your Irish kisser again. Christ, I was worried sick, especially after Justine told me you were out West picking up Mr. Big. What kind of horseshit story did you give her this time?"

A big grin creased Tommy's face.

"C'mon, Frankie, come off it. You didn't expect me to tell her that I went to Las Vegas with the most beautiful girl in New York!"

Frank's eyes widened. "You went to Las Vegas? No shit?"

"I wouldn't lie to you, Frank. But keep it under your hat, no one else knows. And it wasn't such a bad lie I told Justine. I was out West. Frank, I had the best time of my life and from the look of things in the squad room it might be my last fling."

They all trooped in pairs behind the senior threesome of the lieutenant, Joe the Boss and Pete Petersen. They walked the couple of short blocks to Gallagher's and entered through the side service door. They proceeded upstairs to the private dining room where Jimmy Clare greeted each man individually with a friendly handshake. A long table was immaculately set with service for nine people in the right-hand rear corner of the room.

The lieutenant took the seat of honor, the men sat down, and a superb breakfast was served. After the orange juice and platters of sausages, ham and eggs were devoured, a couple of bottles of Remy Martin brandy magically appeared between three steaming pots of coffee. Jimmy Clare and the waiters then vanished from the room. The lieutenant tapped a water glass in front of him with a teaspoon. He arose from his chair and called the meeting to order.

His scholarly, sensitive face seemed more concerned than usual, his heavy tortoise-shell glasses failing to disguise the faint hurt that dwelt in his eyes.

Hesitantly, very softly, he said, "I think the first order of business is for each of us to pour some hot coffee and add a good shot of that fine brandy to it. Everyone agree?"

A low chorus of approval sounded.

The lieutenant raised his pungent cup of coffee and all the men stood in unison and raised their cups to him. Christ, thought Tommy, it's just like one of those old English movies just before the royal guard goes into battle.

With mixed cries of "Good luck lieutenant," "All the best, lieut!" they drank a toast.

The lieutenant wiped his mouth carefully with a napkin, laid his coffee royale on the table, and in a calm voice began his speech.

"I thought it wise to call a meeting this morning before anyone goes on vacation. I assure you that the purpose is for the general welfare of all of us present. I have sad news and I thought it appropriate that we have a good breakfast before you hear what I have to say. Thanks to Jimmy Clare and his staff we were treated and fed like kings.

"Men, I might as well get straight to the point. Chief Moclair is retiring from the police department. It's in the works and becomes effective in a few weeks. The chief and I planned this a couple of weeks back and thought it would be better if we withheld the news until it becomes official. But after some telephone conversations between the chief and me, we thought it only fair to tell you men so that you can make your plans accordingly.

"We are all alone in this room at this table. No other ears to hear what we discuss. I implore you not to mention one word of this, to keep what we say this morning strictly confidential. You men have about three weeks to decide what to do. The chief and I are extremely proud of all you men. You've been very loyal and very competent policemen while under our command. The chief sends his best and regrets that he can't be here to thank you personally. As soon as he retires, I am retiring, going to live out West.

"I'm sure that you all understand when a new chief takes command you will all be replaced automatically. Let's not pull any punches this morning. There are all sorts of rumors going around about a big investigation of corruption in the Job ready to take place soon. Well, men, I don't want to appear before any crime commission or grand jury and neither does the chief. Let's be honest, we've had one helluva run. You men who have your time in I would advise to retire. I will try to place you younger guys in some sort of detail that can utilize your skills. Okay, men, any questions?"

Surprisingly, there were few questions. All their premonitions had been answered. To the old guys, Marchetti, Petersen, Cuccia, and Smith, it was a relief in many ways. They felt the same way about grand juries as the chief and lieutenant. Take the money and run.

Tommy had felt the bad news coming from the minute he entered the squad room earlier this morning. He mentally calculated the time he had left. Another four, five weeks. I better really get my ass rolling and make as much cash as I can while I have the chance. Then what? Justine doesn't think I have a quarter. Knows nothing about the safe deposit box. I'd love to leave her the house and run away with Constance.

The meeting broke up into little groups. He remained seated next to Frank, poured them each fresh brandies.

"Well, rookie, the party's over. What do you intend to do, Frankie?"

"Easy, Tommy. As soon as I'm put back into uniform I'm

resigning. I have about one hundred big ones stashed, have a nice house in Queens almost paid for, and I'll go back to law school full-time and become a lawyer." He laughed. "Someday soon I might be defending crooked cops and outlaw gamblers."

"You better get your degree fast, Frank, because by the time these two rat bastards who are doing all the squealing get finished they'll be a lot of cops needing lawyers."

They finished their tangy, laced coffee and Tom retreated from the table to call Justine on the pay phone downstairs. On the way he passed Lieutenant Burke who was standing, talking to Joe the Boss and Pete Petersen. The lieutenant hailed him, saying, "Don't leave yet, Tommy, I want to talk to you."

"I'll be right back, boss, I'm just going to make a phone call."

He dialed Justine's office number.

"Justine Sloane, please."

"Tommy, it's me. You're such a stranger you don't even recognize your wife's voice. Oh, Tommy, how are you?"

"I'm fine, dear. Everything is smooth. The safe and loft detectives took over the court arraignments and the rest of the technical stuff."

"That's wonderful. Will you be home for dinner?"

"Of course, sweetheart, I can't wait to see you. I'll be home about six o'clock."

He caught the lieutenant's eye as he returned upstairs and Burke walked over to him.

"Well, Tom, what do you think of the bad news?"

"Everything has to end someday, Lieutenant. To be honest, I more or less expected it to happen real soon. I don't blame you and the chief for getting out of the Job. One more thing, speaking for myself and I'm sure the rest of the guys, I loved how above board you spoke this morning. You didn't kick the shit under the rug like a lot of bosses would do. No sanctimonious shit, no apologies. You expressed your true feelings and gave us our options. You gave us fair warning of what might lay ahead and plenty of time to decide what to do. Personally, I think that was damn nice of you and the chief."

"Thanks, Tommy, I appreciate that. It's very nice of you to say those things."

"It's true, boss, from the bottom of my heart."

"Good. All right, let's get down to business. I know the news hit you guys between the eyes, but do you have anything specific in mind?"

"Well, lieut, my first impulse was to resign from the Job. But to be perfectly honest, I love the Job. I have quite a bit to go for my pension, about eight years. I don't know. I'm really undecided, have to think it over real hard."

"The chief and I have spoken about you, feel that you were one of our best men. He can place you in the warrant squad, an arm of special sessions court."

"Sounds good. What does it involve, this warrant squad? I'd really love to make the detective bureau."

"Perhaps later. But the warrant squad is a step in the right direction. You work in plainclothes, pick up guys who jumped bail on misdemeanor charges, things like that. After a year or so you make a hook for the bureau. You have some good friends, you know your way around." He put his arm around Tommy's shoulder. "What do you say? Sound good?"

"Okay, boss, sounds terrific. What's the procedure?"

"You stay real tight, right where you are, until a new chief takes over. In the meantime, through the chief I will contact the warrant squad boss, Captain Bob Keegan. He will take care of you."

"Great, boss, I sure appreciate it."

They shook hands, Tommy waved to Frank and they left Gallagher's and walked down Broadway to Dinty Moore's. They sat down immediately, had a couple of drinks, a light lunch and mapped out their plan of attack for the next few weeks. Frank voiced a little reluctance at being too bold in their last days within the golden confines of Manhattan West. He had a lucrative law career ahead of him, had been lucky to avoid any trouble while he acquired a pretty good bankroll. He wanted to ease out without any pain.

Tommy tipped his glass good luck each drink as they talked, agreed with him wholeheartedly. Right, Frankie, you're right. Meanwhile his conniving brain was churning. In another year or so you'll be a lawyer with a shot at the real money. I'll still be a cop. But in another month there'll be no more splits, no more payrolls. No ten or eleven grand to salt away in the vault. He could live with that, but how about what he pissed away each week just living it up? How was he to afford trips to the moon with Constance? Moët & Chandon champagne and candlelight dinners? Easy! Keep moving, keep hustling, never leave plainclothes. Just play it very cagy. Plenty of scores out there.

He exulted in the lieutenant's promise to place him in the warrant squad. Dressed in civilian clothes. No uniform, thank God. He had dreaded the return to the dreary routine of a precinct cop. The same old shit—domestic quarrels, cop fighters, pain-in-the-ass citizens complaining about you being too rough making an arrest, screaming blue murder because they were victimized and a cop didn't make the arrest.

They parted shortly after two o'clock, agreeing to take it nice and easy the next few weeks until the death knell sounded. Make a few collars apiece for the record, take it real slow on the scores. At least as far as Frankie was concerned. He intended to hustle all the harder. There were plenty of outlaws out there. Ninety-nine out of a hundred never met a Borough West man, spent their waking hours ducking cops. When you grabbed them they usually were scared shitless and came up with whatever they had on them to escape a pinch. Duck soup!

He called Constance at her office and she assured him that she was feeling fine, still exuberant in the flush of the fairy tale trip to Las Vegas. He rang off with a promise to take her to dinner later in the week. He retrieved his car from the garage, decided it was too early to return home to Whitestone. Better give Vince a visit, tell him the bad news. He drove to West Forty-fifth Street and parked his car a few doors from the Candy Mint Lounge, above which Vinny had an office where he conducted most of his business.

He entered the vestibule of the building and buzzed the office on a panel button imbedded in the wall. He identified himself through a voice box on the panel and was buzzed in. Vinny greeted him at the top of the stairs with a bear hug. He stepped back and looked Tom over.

"You sonofabitch, you get darker every time I see you. You look more like a *paisano* than I do. Where the hell did you disappear to this time, the equator?"

Tommy laughed. "I just got back last night from that little town out West in the desert called Las Vegas."

Vinny whistled. "Vegas! You crazy Irish bastard. And just by the cat who swallowed the canary look on your face I bet you took Constance. How'd you get away from taking Justine?"

Tommy's smile was forced, his face became grim.

"Well, I won't have to worry about bullshitting her much longer, Vince, the party's over."

Vinny's face clouded over. His voice was anxious, harsh. "Why? What's up? For Christ sake, no jam, I hope."

"No, thank God. Very simple, Vince. The chief is retiring, the lieutenant is retiring, and so is half the squad. That's all the guys who have their time in. Plus my partner, Frank Donahue, who's resigning to finish law school."

"When does all this take place?"

"In about three or four weeks. But the news isn't all bad, I have one ray of sunshine."

"What's that?"

"The bosses are arranging a spot for me in the warrant squad, attached to special sessions court. Regular clothes, no uniform. Sounds like it might be the nuts—a real hanger. Just horseshit misdemeanor bail jumpers."

Vinny shook his head as if puzzled. Severe voice—"This calls for a drink. Vodka and tonic for you?"

"That'll be fine, Vince."

Vinny walked over to the portable bar in the corner of the office and returned with two tall, icy drinks. They tipped glasses good luck, took long belts of the drinks.

"Tommy, it's hard to believe you're leaving the Borough squad, or Manhattan West as you prima donnas call it. Jesus, Chief Moclair and Lieutenant Burke both retiring. Wait'll Charlie hears about it."

"He'll probably know real soon. The chief is down in Florida and will probably give Charlie a call, knowing what good friends they are. By the way, Vin, what I just told you is strictly confidential. None of us are supposed to breathe a word until it becomes official. Jack Burke warned us so that we could get our act together."

"Damned nice of him. Well, the two bosses had plenty of

class. And don't worry about me saying anything. But there's some good news, eh, still on the tit in the warrant squad. Finish your drink, I'll make us a fresh one. I have something to say to you."

Again they ritually tipped glasses good luck, took deep swallows of their soothing drinks. Vinny spoke first.

"I guess you know, or at least surmised the reasons why the two bosses are retiring. Am I right, Tom?"

"Never a doubt in my mind, Vinny. The lieutenant practically told us why. He threw a breakfast party this morning in the upstairs room at Gallagher's. He told us point blank that he and the chief had no intention of remaining in the Job and being tarred and feathered by some fucking grand jury or crime commission."

"Do you blame them?"

"Are you kidding? Not at all."

"Well, that's what I'd like to talk to you about. It's what I mentioned a couple of weeks ago when you came to the Villa Pompei with Connie for dinner. I'll get straight to the point. As soon as everything becomes official and you get put in the warrant squad, you quit the Job. Vamoose! Out! Fuck the pension, you must be loaded with money by now. Give them some horseshit excuse like your wife is ill or your mother-in-law needs her out in San Diego. Go there for a year or two, take it easy. Then come to Florida and join me in whatever I'm doing. This town is going to blow up. Every wise guy I talk to, the big guys, not the shitheels, feel an investigation coming. What do you say?"

Tommy sipped his drink thoughtfully, spoke hesitantly.

"Well, Vince, that was my first impulse. But I do love the Job. Can't see myself doing anything else. I'd like to go along in the warrant squad for a while then get a hook into the detective bureau."

"But when the shit hits the fan you'd still be vulnerable, still a sure thing to get a subpoena. Every ex-plainclothesman will be called. The same as in Brooklyn in the Gross case. These guys will stop at nothing, you should know that."

While Vinny talked all Tommy could think of was Constance. Go to San Diego, then maybe to Florida. Listen to Justine's church and bowling shit the rest of my life. Never! And no way am I about to leave Constance just yet. He sipped his drink, weighing his answer. Vinny was right, no question. He had to fence with him, not hurt him.

"Vince, you're right as usual. The way they're running New York City it has to go down the tube. But I'd like to try what I said. The warrant squad, then maybe the bureau. I really would like to work on real crime like homicides, stick-ups, rape—all that heavy shit. That's what a cop is made for. Besides, the crime commission or a grand jury might be a year or two away. The two rat bastards are yammering away, we all know that, but it will be a while before the *New York Times* prints all their accusations. They have to authenticate most of their charges and that might take a long while. Besides, we were a supervisory squad over the division squads and kept our skirts pretty clean. I'll take my chances a little while longer. If it looks like it's getting too hot, I'll take off. I promise you that, Vince. Sincerely."

He reached out and grasped Vinny's hand.

"Okay, Irish, you're still as thick as shit. Remember one thing, I love you like a brother and what I said is for your own good. You're a big boy, so take it nice and easy from here in. Watch your ass."

He pulled into the driveway of his house shortly after five with a bright summer sun still high in the deep blue sky. He knew it was much too early for Justine to be home from work. He removed the carryall that contained his suits, slacks, and sport jackets, plus the traveling bag that held his accessories and dirty clothes, from the trunk of his BMW. He carried them into the house, hung them up carefully, and inspected his soiled clothes for any signs of lipstick that might betray his crime-busting story. All clear! I love you, Constance. He put the soiled clothes in the laundry hamper and changed into a sport shirt, slacks, and tennis sneakers.

He made himself a tall vodka tonic and settled into his Barcalounger with a magazine. About ten minutes later the drinks during the day caught up to him and he fell sound asleep. He was awakened by smothering kisses on the lips and the fragrant scent of perfume. Shaken out of a Las Vegas dream he just caught himself in time from saying, "Oh, Constance," loud and clear. He stood up and hugged Justine close. She was so happy to see him she was in tears. He soothed her, kissed her eyes, calmed her down.

"Oh, Tommy, I was so worried about you. I'm so happy you're home I can't help crying."

"Take it easy, babe. Get into something comfortable and I'll make you a drink."

She kissed him with an open mouth and hugged him tight. "Right, sweetheart, I'll be right down."

It was the start of a typically steamy, early August New York day as Tommy maneuvered his BMW through the early morning traffic. He was headed for his new home in the warrant squad. The squad was positioned in the Supreme Court building in downtown New York on Centre Street, a few blocks below old Police Headquarters. His car windows were rolled up tight and the air conditioner kept the interior as cool as the driver. His mind was filled with the events of the last few days he just spent away from home on a big case. A case of Constance Ann Ward.

Three long weekend days as guests of friends of Constance in Southampton, on the tip of Long Island. Very easy on the booze, thank God. Plenty of swimming, tennis, and making love. He felt rested and supremely healthy for the first time in weeks. He chuckled at his further cause to congratulate himself on his good fortune. Justine had also been away for the weekend on a religious retreat with her church bowling group. He had arrived home ahead of her, saving a lot of sharp questioning.

His absences from home were becoming more and more frequent as he invented all kinds of lies and excuses to be with Constance. Sweet Justine was alternately very irritable with him one day, absolutely crazy about him the next day. She never suspected him of any infidelity, just implored him not to work so hard.

The axe fell as predicted almost a month to the day of Lieutenant Burke's funereal breakfast speech. There were no farewell parties, no sad gatherings. The good-byes consisted of a few drinks together and a round of handshakes with best wishes for all future endeavors. The only man with whom Tommy didn't exchange even the faintest amenity was Joe the Boss. The long-nurtured hate still lingered on, both barely able to conceal it when circumstances forced them together in close quarters. A cold war without hope of détente.

He exited from the Queens Midtown Tunnel, turned left towards downtown instead of right uptown to the greener pastures of his former cop home. Yes, the party was officially over.

The four older guys on the squad and the two bosses had escaped with their lives intact. Hefty pensions and plenty of cash securely salted away. Well, maybe not Buster Smith and Joe the Boss. Buster might prefer sitting in a cocktail lounge accompanied by a stunning woman, drinking fine wine and listening to one of his favorite piano players. Joe the Boss, he'll probably stay home and mind his money until he dies. But he'll never die unless God lets him take his money with him.

The three younger guys were philosophical about their transfers. Frank Donahue was very quiet, obviously pleased. His letter of resignation was all written out. He was waiting only for the proper time before he submitted it. Young Auslander, happy to leave rich, was soon to be made a sergeant, had aspirations of rising high in the Job. Jimmy Doran, the youngest, dreamed only of becoming a detective.

And that leaves you, Tommy Sloane, tooling along Second Avenue in your expensive foreign car, soon to embark on a new phase of your law enforcement career. Street cop to radio car cop, to plainclothes cop to warrant squad cop. He had already made a few discreet inquiries from some of his more knowledgeable sources in the Job. The general consensus was that it was indeed a *tit* job, just what he wanted to continue in his hunt for easy money.

He was welcomed into the warrant squad very cordially. Captain Bob Keegan, a good-natured, beefy Irishman, greeted him with a cheery smile and a big handshake. Yessir, Tommy, any man who worked for years under a great man like Chief Moclair has to be a welcome addition to the squad. He was introduced individually to each man. They all seemed equally impressed with the new movie star in their midst, the recent veteran of the fabulous Borough West. The squad consisted of one sergeant, a nice-looking, tall black guy, and five other cops beside himself. The captain excused himself and he was left alone with the men, who actually seemed a little awe-struck by his presence, including the sergeant. The atmosphere thawed out over a couple of cups of coffee and as usual the main topic of conversation was the Job.

Tommy had been in enough situations with fellow cops to know that the role of a newcomer was to listen to all advice, laugh at the inside jokes, in short—act like one of the boys. But he quickly perceived through his smiling veneer that the boys were a lot less effervescent than his former associates. The air of elitism was missing. Polyester suits and sport jackets abounded in sharp contrast to the tailor-made numbers, pure linens, and cashmeres of the old squad. No show-girl talk, no fancy restaurants mentioned. Christ, not even one sign of a hangover.

He listened politely as the sergeant outlined the nature of his duties. There were no arrest quotas, no great pressure, just do the best you can. The city was your province, nail the culprit wherever your information took you. We are responsbile for all persons who jump bail on misdemeanor charges. All shit charges mostly, a far cry from the serious criminals who jump bail on felony charges.

There was one more facet of the warrant squad that made the handsome black sergeant shake his head as he sadly explained it to Tommy. There was a great emphasis placed on locating fathers who had deserted their families. The unfortunate mothers and offspring then became solely dependent on the city welfare program for survival. The sergeant became more intimate and confiding to Tommy as he described how apathetic the men seemed in their attempts to enforce the paternity laws.

In a sad voice he outlined the causes of the almost impossible barriers that confronted the men under his command. The tremendous wave of immigration from the Caribbean and the ceaseless influx of poor Blacks seeking a better life in New York only to wind up in the ghettos was the insoluble problem. Broken, fatherless families were beginning to overwhelm the police and courts who attempted to trace the men who abandoned their families.

The fleeing fathers assumed new identities almost as often as they changed their underwear. The sergeant again shook his head sadly. An almost impossible task, isn't it, Tom? Tom shook his head silently in reply, his face masked in sadness. Tough fucking luck, sarge, my good man. The best news you've given me in your tale of the downtrodden is that I have five boroughs in which to catch up to some bail-skipping purse snatcher or some fucking wino spic or nigger who ran out on his wife and kids. I'll catch one once in a while for you, sarge, old pal, but I'll scalp many an outlaw along the way. Making a score is my goal in life.

Tommy settled into his new duties just as easily as was expected of a veteran cop of his caliber. He picked up his assigned share of bail jumpers and delinquent husbands almost effortlessly. Walt Jackson, the sergeant, and Captain Keegan were well pleased by his good work. They patted him on the back, complimented him freely. He brushed off their praise with his shy schoolboy grin. Just beginner's luck, I guess, sarge, captain.

Meanwhile he was always the good fellow to the other guys on the squad, careful not to alienate anyone by appearing too industrious and making someone look bad. He greeted everyone with a smile, maintained a low profile, evaded occasional invitations to have a friendly drink. He worked alone by choice, but his ready grin and cheerful demeanor soon had him accepted as one of the boys. It was a course of action he had shrewdly mapped out and the accomplished actor and liar he had managed to become over the years simplified his role.

He sized up the warrant squad and his attendant duties in less than a week. He smiled when he thought about it. He was determined to do whatever he had to do in the squad as quickly and easily as possible. He only had to report to the office twice a week to receive his work assignments and make out his reports.

He worked out a quick solution to make himself look good and have plenty of free time to enjoy his favorite pursuits. Scoring money, romancing Constance, enjoying the good life.

To make all of his grandiose plans work, Tommy Sloane had to be a very shrewd cop. Even the God he had long ago forsaken, but whom he occasionally petitioned, would have to admit that Thomas Patrick Sloane was one of the best. His course of action was elementary. The three planks of his work platform were graft, bribery, and corruption.

He would receive the dossiers of his hitherto evasive prey. He would make a phone call to a cop or detective who was the original complaintant and ascertain where the arrest was made and if possible, the neighborhood the culprit frequented. In short order he would get on the trail and spread out tens and twenties like food-store green stamps. He was well aware of the old cop adage that a criminal or wrongdoer invariably returns to his old haunts. Perhaps the really bad guys didn't, but the petty pieces of shit he pursued always seemed to return to their companions in misery. His largesse, which he always referred to as reward money, was quickly accepted and the prey just as quickly apprehended.

There was fortunately little or no courtroom or arraignment procedure to take up too much of his time. Pick the enemy up and bring him to the nearest precinct house and lock him up. The proper authorities would then take over the case and pursue whatever action was deemed necessary.

About a month after he began in the warrant squad a stroke of good fortune hit Tommy. It stood to earn him enough money to more than compensate the loss of the last couple of splits.

The lieutenant in charge of the replacement Borough West squad was a tall, gray-haired man in his late forties named Peter Dowd. He also happened to be a friend of Vinny Ciano's when Pete was a sergeant in the Seventeenth Precinct. Tommy hadn't seen Vinny in a few weeks, but he called him religiously every few days to assure him that all was well in his new post and the outside world. He received a message at the office one morning to call Vinny and they made a date at his office for later in the afternoon.

Vinny greeted him with his usual bear hug and said, "I finally have to send a message to Garcia to get you up here. You Irish sonofabitch, you promised me faithfully that we'd see each other once a week."

"I'm sorry, Vince, but I've really been busy."

"With that horseshit job or Constance?"

A big grin. "Both, and it's not too bad."

"How's it going?"

"Like falling off a log, Vince. A real soft touch. Leaves me plenty of free time to roam around, to do what I want. Picking my spots, making a real nice score here and there. Beautiful!"

"Christ, you'll never leave the plainclothes racket. But, Tommy, be careful, please. Watch your ass, the wolves out there are really beginning to howl."

"Fuck them. By the way, you're getting plenty high class now that you're a big restaurant hot shot. All the wop cops in the Job say, watcha your assa, you know that."

Vinny laughed. "But I'm no longer in the Job. Thank Christ, and I wish you'd get the hell out of it, too."

"Jesus, Vinny, will you stop worrying about me, please. I'm absolutely safe down there. If you turned the pockets of the whole warrant squad inside out you'd be lucky to get a hundred dollars on the table. There's not a quarter to be made unless you're as hip as I am. And the shit we arrest. Christ, half of them I slip a couple of bucks to so they can send out for a bite to eat from the station-house cell. Just give me a couple of more years on this tit job and with the scores I can make throughout the city, I promise I'll quit."

"Okay. Here's the scoop. The boss of the new squad who replaced you guys, Pete Dowd, is an old friend of mine. He stopped by to see me the other day. He mentioned that he was supposed to get in touch with Joe the Boss, but it seems like your old pal went on a trip to Italy. Somebody must have given him a freebee. Anyway, Pete is looking for someone to introduce him to all the 'cousins'. The only experienced guy left around is you. The older guys all seem to have vanished from New York. Anyway, they have a lot of guys on the payroll but feel that they're missing plenty. I suggested that I get you two together and you'd give him the whole layout. He agreed it was a great idea and wants to meet you for dinner tomorrow night."

Dollar signs twinkled around Tommy's brain. He responded with a big smile. "It sounds so good I would like to give you a kiss."

Tommy edged close. "Try me, Vinny, dear."

"Get away from me, you crazy bastard. Get serious for a minute. The meet is set for Friday. That's tomorrow night. At the Villa Pompei. Okay?"

"Fine. But can I bring Constance? We have a date."

"Sure. I'd love to see her again."

The next afternoon Tommy played tennis with some friends in a club near his home in Whitestone. Justine was due to arrive home early from work as she had an important seven o'clock bowling match. He was showered, shaved, and in newly adopted disguise. He still stuck to his undercover bullshit cop story, regaling her with sworn-to-secrecy fabrications of the dangerous cases he was working on. How he had to dress to mix into the areas where they were determined to root out crime. Justine, it's up to our squad to break up the Mob. Over his scrubbed and perfumed body he wore his decoy cop disguise. Old slacks, sport shirt, longshoremen's cap, old windbreaker to fight off the early autumn chill, and to top it off— his old construction worker's shoes he kept as a memento of the poorer days. A pair of expensive Gucci loafers and a carryall with a full wardrobe were in the trunk of his BMW. And if, God forbid, he needed fresh clothes, a full complement of everything was in Constance's apartment.

He was ready to go out the door when she arrived home. He hugged her, wished her luck in her big match, and beseeched her not to worry as she knew he could take good care of himself.

He backed his BMW out of the driveway, waved good-bye to Justine standing in the front of the house. He stopped at a rest area on the Grand Central Parkway about a mile short of the Triborough Bridge and changed to his Gucci loafers and a sport jacket. He discarded the work shoes, cap, and windbreaker into the car trunk. He smiled as he got back behind the wheel of the BMW.

Constance, stunning in a bright red dress and a simple pearl necklace, met him at the door. He kissed her sweetly on the lips and went directly into the bedroom with his carryall over his arm. He emerged a few minutes later in a three-piece pencil stripe blue suit, white button-down shirt and maroon silk tie.

They arrived at the Villa Pompei shortly after eight o'clock and found Vinny at the bar with the new Borough West lieutenant, Peter Dowd. There was a great deal of hugging and kissing during the preliminary introductions. Constance caused lots of appraising eyes and craned necks around the room with her striking good looks. Tommy was quite impressed with Peter Dowd. Everything Vinny said he was. No faker, a real down-to-earth guy. He and Dowd went off to the side of the bar after they ordered their first drink while Vinny entertained Constance. No bones about the good lieutenant. He made arrangements for Tommy to meet a couple of his key men to get all the true "cousins" in the fold starting next week. Tommy also promised to meet the lieutenant one night and introduce him to the real top wise guys. The real bosses, personally. They took to each other right away, became bosom pals by the second drink. Tommy sized Dowd up as much more aggressive than his former boss, Lieutenant Jack Burke. Probably lacked a real key guy, an intimidating force like Joe the Boss to organize things.

Vince sat with the three of them through dinner and as usual it was delicious. Tommy was quiet during dinner, Constance talking more than usual with four vodkas in her. She still captivated everyone and he smiled as he watched and listened to her. The smile was also a sign of his joy over this new stroke of luck. While he ate he was mentally calculating how much he could score taking Dowd around and straightening out some good guys who were on pins and needles waiting to be contacted. Apprehensive as hell about the changeover, the new squad.

The opportunity fell from Heaven. It fit exactly into his new ploy, his future game plan. He had been dropping sly hints in some of the better watering spots around town, as well as to his three trusted stool pigeons, that he was now some sort of supercop. A veiled suggestion that power was invested in him by high authorities to roam the city wherever he wished to stamp out vice and gambling. And at his whim, of course, to make a score here and there if the price was right. It had gone down easily with his two doorman stoolies, who never knew what he did anyway after they gave him good information and he paid them for it. It impressed Willie Baker, his black stool pigeon and chief operative, who now broadened his base of operations.

He buoyantly sipped his wine, talked quietly to Peter Dowd, getting the full rundown on him as the gray-haired lieutenant belted the Scotch and loosened up.

Peter Dowd was obviously a bright, ambitious guy. An ex-marine officer, left college after a couple of years on the G.I. Bill to come into the Job. He had three kids, aged six to fourteen. Had a wife he was crazy about and a nice home on Staten Island. He made no secret of the fact that he loved money. He related to Tommy how he grew up in Brooklyn during the Great Depression. Raised in a cold water tenement flat. Never had shit in his early life. Firmly committed to give his wife and kids the best. The best, you hear that, Tom. You're right, lieutenant, absolutely right. Call me Pete, Tom, no formalities here. Okay, Pete, we'll be good friends from here in. Yessir, the best.

The next week was just like old times. Manhattan West revisited. A class reunion of old college mates. Only most of the mates Tommy introduced Petey Dowd to were former inmates. Graduates of illustrious colleges like Elmira, Sing Sing, Attica, Dannemora, and occasionally Alcatraz. Maybe they never received a degree to hang on their office wall, but ninety-nine percent learned more about making money than if they had graduated from Harvard or Yale.

The first day out Tommy took Petey Dowd's nominated key men on the rounds. A nice Jewish kid named Sy Friedman and another older nice Irish guy named Ray Corley. It turned out to be one of the busiest weeks of his already very busy cop career. He reported early in the morning to the warrant squad, received his work sheet and proceeded to trap a hapless paternity payment evader and a petty thief bail jumper. Once caught, he threw them into a local precinct lockup and went off in pursuit of higher game.

The two new Manhattan West men under his care were only in plainclothes a couple of years and were fortunate enough to move up quickly. They were attached to the tail of a young rising star of an inspector who was made a deputy chief before age fifty. Very unusual, thought Tommy, but a sign of the times. He introduced them around to all kinds of formerly okay places that they missed the first month. All guys who were very anxious to be back again on the monthly payroll.

They stopped for an occasional drink once in a while and the topic of discussion was, as usual, the Job. They were unanimous in their feelings about the deep unrest in the Job. They all cursed the *unholy two*, who according to all reports were clamoring to be heard in public. Rumors abounded. The police commissioner was about to resign. The mayor was forming a crime commission to investigate corruption in the Job. The *New York Times* was soon to explode with startling allegations about the Job. All sorts of ominous predictions.

However, money was money, a vital necessity and as long as it was out there to grab and you got your shot, why the hell not grab it? The attitude of the plainclothesmen was similar to men at war about to face the enemy. Tommy groped for the word to describe it. Fatalistic, that's the word. And fuck the two squealing rat bastards, plus the crime commission. Let the chips fall where they may.

Tommy finished his business with Friedman and Corley in a couple of days and then spent the next few nights in the sole company of Lieutenant Peter Dowd. He introduced him individually to all the top wise guys on the West Side. He made the meets in popular restaurants and fancy night clubs to make it easier to blend into the atmosphere. He tried to arrange two or three of the top bananas to be in one place at the same time. His purpose was to expedite the new alliances as swiftly as possible. Naturally, the top guys were very grateful to Tommy for putting them together with the lieutenant. In case of a major beef they could at least have a sit-down with the boss. In return, everyone was more than generous to Tommy. Hundreds were pressed into his hand by the dozens and at the end of his strenuous week he was surprised at the size of the score he had accumulated. Between the rounds of the spots with the two men by day and his series of diplomatic missions at night with Peter Dowd he tucked away almost ten thousand dollars in his beloved safe deposit box.

To add to his delight, Peter Dowd fell almost completely under Tommy's spell. He was bewitched by his easy manner and the smooth, assured way he handled the top wise guys. He made a promise to keep Tom on the squad payroll for twenty-five hundred a month for at least six months.

The gentle, breezy New York days of early autumn soon changed into the chilling blasts of swirling winds that indicated a harsh oncoming winter. The intervening months had passed as smoothly as the ice on the nearby Central Park skating rink. He picked his spots very carefully to make his scores. A big whorehouse on the exclusive upper East Side. A chemin de fer card game strictly for high rollers on Central Park South. A couple of sneak crap games and blackjack parlors. A dozen or more outlaw bookmakers and number controllers.

The warrant squad was the perfect facade for his activity. The ultimate cup of tea. He had lunch one afternoon with his boss, the black sergeant, Walt Jackson. He secretly exulted when Walt confided in him that he was the Knicks basketball fan of all time. Tom assured him that through his former connections from his Manhattan West days with Madison Square Garden he could get good tickets whenever he wanted them. He paid for them, of course, but he bullshitted Walt that he got them free. This entree removed another stumbling block from his path to further riches. He laid a couple of choice tickets on Walt once a week and if he didn't feel like making the office some mornings a phone call would suffice.

Tommy Sloane was flying high, the world was indeed his oyster as Christmas and the holiday season approached. Vince put him together with a furrier friend of his, Peter Duffy. He bought Constance a beautiful mink coat. All cash, no questions asked.

Christmas was drawing right to the wall, the very next day. The previous couple of weeks had been a hectic but very lucrative period for the self-appointed supercop. He visited all the "cousins," old and new, the top wise guys and whoever else he felt owed him a score. All the Christmas presents were paid for. Constance's, Justine's and his sister Rosemary's and her family. His Christmas present to himself was another five thousand tucked away in the safe deposit box. Euphoria was the word for Tommy as he drove his BMW into New York to meet Constance.

They had lunch at Jimmy Weston's sparkling new restaurant just off Park Avenue on East Fifty-fourth Street. They had already discussed their respective holiday plans so the air at lunch was a happy one. Constance, gorgeous as usual, her new mink coat casually hung over the back of her chair, talking up a storm as they sipped their chilled Chardonnay wine and ate their delicious filet of sole. He intended to spend Christmas with his wife and sister's family and then go to Florida for ten days. Part holiday, part police work, he lied. We have a line on some guy we're looking for who's reported to be in the Fort Lauderdale area. Constance planned to go skiing in Vermont for the holiday week. Some friends from the office were picking her up later in the day and driving up to Mount Snow.

Lunch over, they stood in the cold outside of Jimmy Weston's. Both a little sad. He kissed her good-bye. She gripped him very tight. He felt her tears against his cheek. He hugged her fiercely.

He waved good-bye to her as the taxi pulled away. Gloom enveloped him. Christ, what have I to be sad about? I've got the world by the balls, but I'll really miss her the next couple of weeks. Back to reality. Next on my agenda is my usual Christmas Eve drink with Vinny and then on to Justine at Rosemary and Billy's house. Big family get together. The thought brightened him. He hadn't seen Rosemary, Billy, and the kids in almost six months. He smiled. And the rest of the living relatives. It'll be a nice party.

He decided to drive his BMW over to the West Side. He found some difficulty getting a parking place. New York was filled with last minute Christmas shoppers and trucks of all varieties making late afternoon deliveries.

He finally pulled up in front of the Algonquin Hotel, thankful to find an old friend, Tim Sullivan, the doorman, on duty. Tim was an ex-prizefighter who stood straight and tall despite his over seventy-five years on earth. He slid out of the BMW in front of the hotel and shook hands with Tim with a twenty-dollar bill folded in his hand.

"Merry Christmas, Tim. Up Ireland!"

"Up Ireland always, Tommy. God love you and take good care of you."

"Thank you, Tim. My squad sign is in the windshield. Put the car anywhere you can. What time are you on duty until?"

"Eight o'clock, Tommy."

"Good, I'll be back around seven, Tim."

"Fine, Tommy, see you later."

He walked the couple of blocks to the Villa Pompei where he had arranged to meet Vince. He was greeted with a warmer than usual hug and kiss on the cheek. He reached in his pocket and handed Vince a compact suede box tied by a red ribbon. Vinny took it and looked at him with surprise.

"What the hell is this, some kind of miniature bomb? You know we never exchange Christmas presents!"

"You're a fucking bomb thrower so you should know one when you see it. Go ahead, open it, it isn't a bomb."

"Cartier diamond cufflinks! Are you completely nuts, Irish? Christ, Tommy, they're really beautiful."

"Don't worry about how much they cost. I didn't buy them at Cartier's, that's for sure. They're swag, Vince. I wouldn't bull-shit you. But they're the real McCoy. I got them from Butchie the Booster, the big guy from downtown. You know, one of your fellow *ladrones*."

"Hey, you Irish prick, you're getting to speak good Italian. But remember, I'm an ex-bandit. Now an honest businessman. Tom, honestly, these are too much."

Affectionately, feinting a left jab at Vinny's jaw, Tommy said, "Come off it, Vince. You gave me the Christmas present of all time a few months ago when you put me together with Lieutenant Peter Dowd."

"Still working out great, Tom?"

"Couldn't be better. Beautiful."

"Good. Now the interrogation. What did you give Justine for Christmas?"

"A thousand bucks. She was ecstatic."

"Wonderful! How about Constance?"

"A new mink coat! From your pal, Peter Duffy."

Vinny laughed. "You are a real Irish pisser. I swear, you'll never change."

Tommy laughed. "In the first place, if I ever gave Justine a mink coat she'd have a heart attack. Besides, it wouldn't look good when she wore it over one of her silk bowling shirts."

Vinny shook his head in mock despair, smiled.

"All right, Irish, let's break open the Christmas wine."

They sat at a rear table in the restaurant where Vinny had two bottles of Moët & Chandon ready in silver ice buckets. They toasted each other and had a million laughs as they rehashed the events and their good luck of the year just passed. Their laughter was tempered by the grim prospects of the year ahead, the almost certain forecasts of a huge corruption probe. Vinny vehemently urged Tommy to resign from the Job. He elaborately reinforced his reasons. Get out while the getting is good, for Christ sake. What the hell do you need it for?

The restaurant started to fill and the second bottle of champagne was almost finished. Vinny poured the last two glasses of the delicious wine. They tipped glasses, shook hands real tight, and with their eyes wished each other all the happiness in the world.

About the same time that Tommy was driving to the traditional family Christmas Eve reunion, a vengeance-seeking hoodlum was gaining entrance to Apartment 15C, 398 East Fifty-seventh Street. The ironic part was that not only did Tommy know the pimp who lived in the apartment, but that Tommy was wending his way through the heavy Christmas traffic along First Avenue towards the Queensboro Bridge, two blocks from the murder scene.

Jimmy Wallace was born and raised in Knoxville, Tennessee. He came from a middle-class family and spent two years at Memphis State University. Although scrawny, short, and fearful, he yearned to be a wise guy. He was fond of saying that the only things he learned in college was how to play cards, bet the hot football games, and fuck the best-looking girls.

Up to his ass in debt in Knoxville, he escaped to New York at the age of thirty-five to mend his fortunes. His story about town was that he was a co-owner of a gambling parlor in Knoxville, saved some money, and headed for the Big Town, where the real moolah was. In fact, he had absconded with money entrusted to him as a minor boss in the gambling parlor. On the lam, he was forced to adopt an alias. As he perceived the New York gambling scene, most of the wise guys were either Jewish or Italian. Knowing he could never pass for Italian, he adopted a Jewish name. Now Jimmy Horowitz, he was more easily accepted in gambling circles as a Jew rather than a Southerner.

Jimmy soon hooked up as a bookmaker's runner, developing a loyal, established clientele. Unfortunately, Jimmy possessed the worst human trait a bookmaker can have. He had what is known in the gambling trade as a *big opinion*. He loved to bet a lot more than he loved to book bets. Inevitably, he was soon in the hands of the shylocks and desperately needed additional income to supplement his habits.

Through one of his more lush gambling streaks he had moved in and elaborately furnished a three-bedroom apartment in the high rise at 398 East Fifty-seventh Street. His steady girlfriend, who often financed him, was a seasoned prostitute. She easily convinced him that his apartment was a perfect layout for a whorehouse. Several girls were quickly recruited by his prostitute sweetheart, and in short order Jimmy Wallace, alias Jimmy Horowitz, was in great action. Part-time bookmaker, full-time bettor by day, high-class pimp running a fancy whorehouse by night. His income grew steadily, but so did his habit of betting on losers.

A trim, dark-haired man about forty years old, wearing a black turtleneck sweater underneath a tan, camelhair coat entered through the front door of 398 East Fifty-seventh Street. Teddy Johnson, the doorman, inside the lobby escaping the cold, politely approached him.

"Can I help you, sir?"

"Yeah, I wanna see Jimmy Horowitz in Fifteen-C."

"There aren't any girls up there yet."

"I'm not interested in girls, I just want to say hello to Jimmy."

Johnson rang 15C, talked for a minute, turned and said, "It's all right, you can go up."

The man winked a thank you and walked towards the elevator bank.

Watching the byplay through bleary eyes was a short, husky, Hispanic-looking man. He was half-drunk, falling asleep on a couch in the apartment house lobby. He was dressed in his work clothes, obviously the clothes of some type of construction worker. His name was Raymond Chavez, a construction union bricklayer, working steadily in New York's booming construction business. With overtime, his take-home pay was usually almost five hundred dollars a week. More money than the whole family thought they would ever earn when they emigrated to New York with Raymond as a boy of thirteen.

Raymond Chavez resided in a low-income housing project in Queens. He and his wife, Anita, and their four children lived in a two-bedroom apartment. To run the house and kids Raymond gave his wife two hundred dollars a week. The other three hundred or so Raymond spent gambling, drinking whiskey, and screwing young whores. The younger the better. He had met a tall, big-chested, young prostitute named Cheryl Stanton in Jimmy's whorehouse and had fallen in love. A month later she was still an obsession to him. A few drinks, and he had to have Cheryl. Raymond was patiently waiting in the lobby for the object of his affections to show up.

Cheryl Stanton, Raymond's sex symbol, was a beautiful, dumb nineteen-year-old. Her real name was Sophie Stankowski. Not wishing to become a miner's wife, she left home in the Wyoming Valley in Pennsylvania at the age of seventeen for the high life in New York City. She soon fell under the spell of Jimmy Horowitz and under his guidance soon became an accomplished whore. Along the way she amassed some money, her own apartment and a wardrobe of flashy clothes.

Cheryl came through the main door about fifteen minutes after the trim, dark-haired man. She greeted the doorman, Teddy Johnson, with a kiss, spotted her date, Raymond Chavez, on the couch, shook him awake and took him up to Apartment 15C. She entered the apartment with her own key, heard some loud voices arguing in the living room and took Raymond into the far bedroom.

His erotic fantasies satisfied in the flesh, wide awake now, but a trifle limp from his steamy explorations of Cheryl's statuesque body, Raymond went into the bathroom to relieve himself and to wash up. Cheryl donned a wrap, sauntered into the living room and sat on the end of the couch a few feet from Jimmy. The trim, dark-haired man was visibly very angry, demanding money Jimmy obviously owed him. Right this minute! The scene taking place in front of her was a familiar one to Cheryl. She sat there calmly, not frightened in the least. Plenty of guys before this madman screamed their lungs out, raved and ranted over money Jimmy owed. It was a way of life with Jimmy. He seemed to owe everybody.

Chavez came into the living room. He was dressed and apparently refreshed in spite of his recent sexual exertions. He took a seat on the couch on the other side of Jimmy.

The trim, dark-haired man in the camelhair coat, face contorted in anger, said in a harsh voice, "Look, you Jew cocksucker, you've been bullshitting me for over a month now. You owe me a thousand. Get it up."

Wallace the Southerner, alias Horowitz the Jew, said in a mild, placating voice, "What are you worrying about? I'll pay you in a couple of weeks."

The trim, dark-haired man never answered. He took his right hand out of his camelhair coat pocket and it held a .38 revolver. He put it next to Jimmy's head, and as Jimmy looked up at him in horror, paralyzed with fear, put a bullet into his brain. Not a word, just the sharp, popping sound of the shot. A puff of smoke filled the surrounding air. The would be wise guy pimp slid off the couch like a sack of oats. Blood spurted from his temple. All his debts were now cancelled. He was stone dead.

Cheryl recoiled, screamed in fright. She babbled hysterically, incoherently. Wide-eyed, she fell to her knees, supplicating.

"Shut your mouth, you two-dollar cunt." He extended the muzzle of the .38 and shot her twice in the head. Cheryl slumped face forward. Very dead.

Chavez arose from the couch, horrified, knees shaking, disbelief etched on his face. The trim, dark-haired man pointed the .38 at him.

"Man, please, I have a wife and kids. I didn't see nothin'. I just came here for a piece of ass."

"It's your last fuck, spic." He raised the .38, Chavez backed away, raised his arms instinctively in front of his body as a protective measure. The gunman fired the shot right at him, from about five feet away. The force of the bullet caused Chavez to topple backwards over the end table next to the couch and crash on the carpeted floor. The trim, dark-haired man in the camelhair overcoat casually stepped over his body. He let himself out of the apartment and took the elevator down to the lobby. He exited at the lobby floor and walked nice and easy to the door leading to the street. Johnson opened it for him.

"Thank you, Merry Christmas," said the trim, dark-haired man.

"Take it easy, have a nice holiday," said Johnson.

Chavez regained consciousness. He was in terrible pain. His wound wasn't fatal, the bullet partially deflected off his arm into his stomach. He crawled to the kitchen, raised himself on a chair, used the intercom. He rang the lobby frantically.

Teddy Johnson answered, "What's up?"

"Help me, please, help me. Fifteen-C."

In the parlance of New York detectives, Dick Callahan, detective first grade, Nineteenth Precinct detective squad, caught the squeal. He sat alone at his desk in the third-floor squad room reading a copy of *Time* magazine. He had told his partner, Tony Caruso, to take Christmas Eve off and stay home with his wife and kids.

Teddy Johnson, the doorman, called in the squeal at 8:05 p.m., location, Apartment 15C, 398 East Fifty-seventh Street. Callahan mentally recalled the building. A luxury high rise. Johnson almost screamed over the phone. Two people murdered. One man, one woman. Another male in kitchen, badly wounded.

Callahan immediately called Bellevue Hospital Emergency for an ambulance and morgue wagon. Ambulance right away, morgue wagon no rush. He then called the homicide squad in downtown Police Headquarters. Yeah, Dick, Joe Toomey here. Two murders! Man and woman, another male badly wounded. Shit, I wanted to get out of here early and take my wife out tonight. Okay, Dick, Sam Doucher and I will be up as quick as possible. Yeah, of course. We'll bring a lab guy with us. See you later.

Richard Joseph Callahan. Better known to cops, detectives, bosses in the Job, and assorted hoodlums and thieves around New York as Dick Callahan. Medium-sized, well built, brown-haired, good-looking, forty-eight years old. Former U.S. Marine first lieutenant. Wounded at Iwo Jima. Holder of Silver Star and Purple Heart.

Fully recovered at the close of World War Two, Callahan enrolled at Fordham University under the G.I. Bill. He graduated with honors as a political science major. He briefly debated whether to enroll in law school as a prelude to joining the F.B.I. or to go on the Job. The only question in his mind was which route to take. He was clear on the main issue, a career in law enforcement.

Dick's father, Joseph Callahan, was a highly respected police captain who was forced to retire fairly young because of an almost fatal heart attack. His uncle, Pat, was a lieutenant in charge of the bomb squad. He was killed in the line of duty at LaGuardia Airport while supervising the dismantling of a terrorist bomb.

With many secret prayers and mild persuasion by his father, Dick joined New York's Finest. He satisfied his ambition in life and he loved the Job.

After rookie school he was assigned to the Fourteenth Precinct on West Thirtieth Street. The station house was located in the heart of the teeming garment area, as it was known worldwide. Trucks were parked filled with expensive coats and dresses. Delivery boys pushed racks of designer dresses on wheels along the crowded streets. Thievery was rampant throughout the territory despite the efforts of a flood of local squad and safe and loft detectives.

There were all kinds of fair game for the street thief and the more sophisticated burglars and hijackers. An alert street cop's challenge. Dick Callahan made fifteen felony arrests his first year and a half on the Job. Before he finished out his second year he shot and killed one hood, wounded another, thwarting an armed robbery.

With a slight assist from his father, Dick was soon assigned to the detective bureau, his goal in life. Through his twenty years as a detective he made innumerable solid arrests, solved countless cases, almost all resulting in convictions. He was a methodical, thorough investigator. He was also fearless and incorruptible. The only thing he ever took was an occasional free drink or free meal, plus the annual Christmas envelope as his share of the holiday cash gifts given to the squad detectives by the various bars, restaurants, and night clubs under their umbrella. He took the envelope reluctantly, not wishing to offend the detectives he worked with, not wanting to appear like some chaste, plastic saint.

His first-grade rank entitled him to the same pay as a lieutenant and he thought he was well paid. Besides, Dick was a bachelor, going with the same girl, Kathy, for almost fifteen years. His father had died about four years after he was on the Job. He still lived with his mother in a beautiful, terraced two-bedroom apartment in Sutton Place on the real swanky East Side. He loved his mother, loved the apartment, loved the proximity to his precinct, and sometimes wondered if his old man was one hundred percent honest to wind up with such a lovely place.

Detective Callahan, after making the first two emergency calls, rang the desk lieutenant down below. He reported the crime and asked for a radio car to drive him to the scene.

About ten minutes later Callahan stood in Apartment 15C. He shook his head sadly as he surveyed the carnage. How could a fucking bum do a thing like this? He looked closely, without touching her, at the body of the young girl. She was sprawled face up on the floor. Housecoat open, revealing enormous tits and shapely, long legs ending in a blond tuft of pubic hair. Her beauty ended at her neck. Her bullet-battered face was almost beyond recognition. Bloody, disfigured.

No sad feelings as he looked over the dead body of Jimmy Horowitz. Hung out a lot in P.J. Clarke's. A no-good, half-ass bookmaker who was also reputed to be a pimp. So this nice flat was his whorehouse. Too bad, the fuck got what he deserved.

In the kitchen Teddy Johnson, the doorman, was attempting to minister to the badly wounded man, now known to him as Raymond Chavez. Probably a poor john just up here to get laid.

The ambulance paramedics arrived shortly after Dick made the scene. The homicide detectives and the laboratory man arrived simultaneously with the morgue wagon. The ambulance paramedics carried out Chavez, who had once again lapsed into unconsciousness. He looked bad to Dick as the stretcher passed by him. Hope the poor sonofabitch makes it, lives to give a better description of the killer than this fucking doorman, Teddy Johnson. Keeps repeating. Slim, medium-sized, dark-haired guy. Wore tan coat. You mean overcoat, it's too goddam cold out for a topcoat. Yeah, that's right, tan overcoat. How about a tan camelhair overcoat? That's it. You got it, officer, a camelhair coat.

The next day was Christmas, a bad day for the newspaper business. The *Daily News* carried the crime on page four, the *New York Times* on the second page of the Metropolitan Section. By the third day other just as sensational murders were committed in New York and the massacre on East Fifty-seventh Street became a memory to everyone but Dick Callahan. He brought a police department artist to Teddy Johnson to sketch the face of the killer with the doorman's help. He questioned Horowitz's neighbors in a fruitless attempt to gain some insight into some enemies he might have. He found a hidden address book in the apartment, which contained the phone numbers of a number of prostitutes he questioned to no avail.

He stopped by P.J. Clarke's later the next week and found that Horowitz was a regular there. He was friendly with quite a few cops as well as some of the steady customers who lived and drank the best but never seemed to work. Dick was discreet in his questions, but his initial evaluation of Wallace, alias Horowitz, was confirmed. A bookmaker who also loved to bet and a pimp to boot. Owed the fucking world. But time marched on, other murders and all kinds of crimes occupied the time of Dick Callahan. The double murder was put aside in his file, but someday he hoped he would catch the bastard who did the number on these three people. One good thing, Raymond Chavez recovered in good shape. Dick visited him at the hospital, showed him the sketch and Chavez agreed it was a good likeness. They promised to stay in touch.

Tommy and Justine returned from Florida a couple of days after the New Year rolled in. On the plane coming home Justine squeezed his hand and said it was their best vacation ever. Tommy smiled with false affection. He agreed wholeheartedly on the surface, half-heartedly deep down inside. He had surprised Justine by upgrading their reservation at the Yankee Clipper from a single room to a one-bedroom suite. She was delighted by the expansive accommodations, but voiced worry about the cost. He allayed her fears by explaining that he had received a hefty expense check from the Job to do some investigating in Miami.

He further used that lie to slip away to Hialeah Racetrack for the day a couple of times. He was always sure to run across some New York guys he knew at the track to bullshit and have a drink with; it was an environment he was completely happy in. He hated to admit it to himself, but the truth was that he had to escape from Justine for a while. He tried hard to be nice. Made love to her a couple of times with forced ardor. But Holy Christ, she never shut up talking about her bowling pals, her card games. She also slyly attempted to reconcile him with the Catholic Church. Jesus, like trying to convert Josef Stalin.

The separation from Constance was murder in the first degree. She was constantly in his thoughts, almost never far from his mind. He called her by prearrangement in Vermont on New Year's Eve. He danced, drank, and as the clock struck twelve and everyone kissed each other and cheered, he pretended to be gay, but his heart was heavy. Never again, he silently vowed.

The couple of drinks on the plane coming back gave him a nice lift. He felt like tap dancing his way through the vast airline lobby at J.F.K. Airport. I'm home, Constance.

The next few weeks were filled with all kinds of activity for Tommy. He corralled his usual number of delinquent-paying daddies and busted-out bail jumpers early in the day and prowled the city most afternoons and some nights on the make for a score. A couple of months back he had decided to add another dimension to his pseudosupercop image. For years he had shunned making scores off drug peddlers. Ruled it out— too dangerous, and he hated the shit, anyway. But ever since the Vietnam War got in full swing the New York drug scene expanded so rapidly drug peddlers proliferated. He had heard rumors of some really tremendous scores being made and it opened his eyes and whetted his appetite. With a couple of discreet inquiries he soon found out that even the lower echelon drug peddlers were good for between twenty-five hundred and five thousand a deal.

Why pass that up? Willie Baker, his chief operative, had often urged Tommy to make some drug scores. A piece of cake, Tom, these dudes walkin' around with nothin' but money in their kick.

Willie was thrilled when Tommy subtly confessed that he might have a change of heart. He made a score a week for three successive weeks. Like Willie said, a piece of cake. Look out, Las Vegas! Here comes Constance and her Tommy boy.

They took off for Vegas the last Thursday in January and planned as usual to return the following Sunday evening. Both now seasoned veterans of the crap and blackjack tables, they had another marvelous fling. The friends in Vegas that they had made on their previous trip were just as hospitable and eager to please as before.

To explain his departure from home he gave Justine the usual cops and robbers routine. This time, he bullshitted her that a real heavy case demanded his presence in San Francisco.

The mayor of New York's nerves were jumping. He paced back and forth in his expansive private office deep in the cavernous, time-worn City Hall. He was desperately concerned with some harrowing information he had recently received. The *New York Times* was planning a series of articles on widespread corruption in the police department. Any goddam fool knows there is a certain amount of corruption in all big city police departments. And plenty of other departments besides the police. He had asked some social friends of his to act as intermediaries, men who were close friends to some of the top brass at the *Times*. He asked them to detail the possible ramifications a vilification of the police department would engender. The word came back. A flat rebuff, all the way. No chance. The *New York*

Times prints all the news that's fit to print. An age-old credo. An admirable age-old credo.

Sometimes, perhaps, thought the mayor, as he nervously paced the office, not altogether a wise age-old credo. Shit, that's all I need after the Harlem riots. Jesus, they should never undermine the police department. Not while I'm mayor, anyway. He stopped pacing, looked into the large, mahogany framed mirror on the wall of his private office. It was the fourteenth or fifteenth time that morning he had looked himself over in the mirror.

Yessir, no doubt about it. He was a handsome man. Much handsomer than Jack Kennedy, he assured himself. He once again practiced Kennedy's wide, easy grin and the heartwarming way Jack would raise his hand high to the adoring crowds. That's the way I'll do it when I'm elected President of the United States. He walked back to his desk, began to fume again. He banged his hand hard on the top of the desk. I'll be goddamned if a bunch of crooked cops are going to paint my administration black. Goddam it, I gave up Congress to become the mayor of New York, my stepping stone to my goal in life, the White House. The hell with this nonsense. I'll beat the *Times* to the punch, take the bull by the horns.

He rang for his secretary. Dictated a letter to be hand-delivered to the city corporation counsel, the commissioner of investigation, the Bronx and Manhattan district attorneys and the police commissioner. The letter requested their presence in the mayor's private office at ten o'clock the next morning. The purpose, a conference on methods to handle allegations of widespread corruption in the Job. Get the letter out immediately!

The city corporation counsel, the commissioners of investigation and the police department, and the Bronx and Manhattan district attorneys took their seats at the near end of the long, mahogany table in the conference room adjoining the mayor's private office. The mayor, as befit his rank, sat at the head of the table. He greeted everyone with a firm handshake and a flashing smile. His warm smile. His soon-to-be-president smile.

"Gentlemen, I called this meeting today to discuss a matter openly which I'm sure by now that you are all familiar with. It concerns charges of rampant corruption in our police department. I am sure all of you are aware that the *New York Times* is preparing a series of articles which will, apparently, crucify the police department. They are due to appear shortly and from what I understand are extremely damaging to my administration. I attempted, through some influential friends of mine, to have the *Times* reconsider the articles. I pointed out the havoc the scandal would cause; the breakdown of the already low morale in the department, the undermining of public confidence it would cause. Every conceivable valid argument I could muster. All to no avail. My present information is that it's only a matter of time, perhaps six or eight weeks, before their investigation is finalized and the articles published."

Sad face. The stricken look of ancient Jeremiah, harbinger of doom. He pointed to the commissioner of investigation and said, "Sam, some months back, you sent me a memorandum informing me of some impending trouble. A patrolman and a sergeant were going about making some very serious charges concerning the department. I assigned one of my top assistants to work with you. What happened?"

The commissioner of investigation, a heavy-set, tough-looking Jew in his middle fifties, calmly answered, "Alfred and I heard them out, Mr. Mayor. Not once, but on several occasions. The patrolman looks like a wild man and talks like one. I put him down later as a half-ass psycho. Why he became a cop, I'll never know. He's absolutely paranoid about the police department. In the midst of one of his tirades he would suddenly stop and pose the same question. Three or four times. Why don't they make me a detective? You know why, commissioner? Because I'm too honest, that's why. It's extraordinary, Mr. Mayor, everyone in the Job is a crook except him. Oh, excuse me, there is another honest cop. His pal, the sergeant."

Sam the commissioner chuckled. "There is a way out of this mess, I think. Just appoint the sergeant first deputy police commissioner with the promise of the top rank real soon. One thing he's not too bashful to tell you. He's the only other honest cop in the Job. We tried to have them substantiate their allegations. They had nothing at all that was concrete to present to a district attorney. I'm sure that the Bronx district attorney, sitting on my right here, can tell you that we gave him all possible aid in his prosecution of the crooked plainclothesmen recently within his jurisdiction. The trials where the patrolman in question was the chief witness. Am I correct, Mario?"

The genial, chubby, Italian Bronx district attorney nodded his head and said, "Sam is exactly right, Mr. Mayor. And this guy sure is some kind of head case. Eventually, though, he made a pretty good witness."

The mayor turned to the corporation counsel, said, "Thank you, gentlemen. So far, so good. Have you anything to add to this, Irving?"

"Just listening, Mr. Mayor. I haven't a word to say."

The district attorney of Manhattan raised his hand, caught the mayor's eye. About seventy years old, a gray-haired, stockily built Irishman. A legendary foe of crime. A story-book figure who automatically was elected every four years by a fiercely loyal constituency who had implicit faith in his honesty and ability. The mayor was slightly in awe of the formidable, celebrated district attorney who would send a crooked politician to jail quicker than a top Mafioso.

"Yes, Frank. I'm sure we'll all be glad to hear your views on the subject."

In the deliberate, well-enunciated manner of speaking, common to district attorneys throughout the universe, he said, "Mr. Mayor, if you value my opinion, I think we should ride out the storm. I don't approve of crooked cops any more than you do. But by and large, they are only unearthing petty larceny bullshit that is sure to be blown out of proportion by the investigative reporters. By and large, the police force in New York City do a fine job. To a great extent, they have the utmost respect of the citizenry. Before long, we have the specter of a long, hot summer coming. It's certain we don't need any more riots.

"We kiss the minorities' asses enough as it is and respect for the police force in some areas of the city is diminishing every day. Let's face the issue, look it right in the eye. the The *New York Times* articles will come and go. A week later the average citizen won't remember a goddam thing about it. It'll all blow over, soon be forgotten. There are thousands upon thousands of cops out there doing a superb job. Should we unfairly subject the honest cops to humiliation in front of their friends and neighbors? Once the tar brush is out it spreads over everybody. Once again, Mr. Mayor, don't exacerbate the problem by creating any extraordinary crime commissions or similar bodies. Put up a vigorous front. Make some necessary changes, make some superficial changes. Above all, show the men on the Job that they have your confidence."

The city hierarchy sat back on their chairs. If the present meeting had been held in a crowded arena the applause would have been deafening. But the only applause the district attorney received were the looks of approbation on the faces of his peers when he finished his impassioned speech.

The mayor smiled, his Jack Kennedy smile, said, "Excellent, Frank. I'm sure you know that I will never do anything rash without consulting you."

He saw the police commissioner's hand raised.

"Yes, Harold, go ahead. Let's hear what you have to say."

The police commissioner, an affable, good-natured Irishman, spoke with a slight twang that betrayed his out-of-town birthplace. All the other men at the conference table were native-born New Yorkers. To them, New York was the only city in America. In the world. Any place else, you were camping out. Still, they tolerated the interloper among them. Some even liked him. He wasn't a bad guy. The police commissioner spoke.

"Mr. Mayor, Frank said it all in defense of the men under my command. It's one of the most rewarding periods of my life to be associated with men like Frank and the other gentlemen sitting around this table. Of course, that includes you, Mr. Mayor." A big laugh from the inner circle. He continued, smile off his face, in a grim voice, "The two men who are causing this trouble, who are feeding the *Times* investigative reporters with what we feel are unfounded allegations, in my opinion, are two of the worst type of headline hunters. They have definitive ambitions and don't seem to give a shit who they hurt to realize them.

"For the love of God, in the city where I come from, and in every big and small city in the United States, there are going to be cops on the take. And politicians, judges, prosecutors—you name it. It's almost a way of life in America, as well as the rest of the world.

"The biggest curse, the greatest temptation, to policemen are the stupid, archaic gambling laws. Every year bills are introduced in the legislature up in Albany to legitimize gambling and for some unknown reason never seem to get out of committee.

"Gambling is the cancer, the main cause of corruption among policemen. The public itself wants gambling. The man on the street who bets bookmakers or plays numbers is your average citizen. The major sports, besides horse racing, couldn't function as they do without illegal gambling to heighten the interest in them. Our major issue on the agenda should be to turn the *Times* articles into a vehicle to force the legalization of gambling. To show how far corruption among police would be reduced if gambling were legal.

"Let us examine some hard facts. The average cop with five years or more on the Job takes home about three hundred and fifteen dollars every two weeks. Rookies, a helluva lot less, and those with under five years also much less. Most of these cops have fairly large families. Small kids, families with the wife at home taking care of the house and kids. Moneywise, they're barely getting a little more than families on welfare. Gentlemen, I ask you, would you expect the average cop to turn down a five-dollar bill from a bookmaker or a numbers store, people the cop doesn't think are doing anything wrong? That's a cop's mentality.

"The same cop will defend a citizen's safety with his life on the line if a serious crime threatens. Cops are usually brave men. Good Lord, you have to be a brave man to patrol the streets or ride a radio car in some of the ghetto areas of good old New York City. I'm the police commissioner, with a chauffeur and bodyguard at all times, and even I cringe whenever I visit certain precinct houses in New York.

"That's my perception of the situation, Mr. Mayor. I take the same position as my good friend, Frank here, does. We certainly have to make some internal changes in the department. Give it a face-lift, weed out some of the older top brass. You and the mayors of all the large cities in New York state should talk turkey to the governor and the influential legislators about legalizing gambling.

"Washing our dirty linen in public won't do a damn bit of good.

The last big investigation in Brooklyn didn't change a thing. Two headline-happy assistant district attorneys became supreme court justices and business resumed as usual. I am sure that my colleagues here today agree with Frank and me. Let's not heap any further disgrace upon the Job with televised hearings. We'll have enough with the sensational newspaper disclosures. Once again, to paraphrase Frank, let's ride out the storm."

A hush fell over the table as the police commissioner finished speaking. Looks of admiration were cast his way. Good work, Harold. Fine speech, Harold, I never knew you had it in you.

The mayor again flashed his winning, presidential smile. He stood up, a signal that the meeting was over. He spoke. "Thank you, commissioner, very well put. I'm happy I called this meeting, it's been a good one. I believe we all have been enlightened by yours and Frank's penetrating analyses of current problems existing in the police department. I will not entertain the idea of an independent crime commission without consulting this committee. For the next few months we will keep our project under wraps, meanwhile studying ways to wipe out the rotten apples in the police department. Our committee, which we will make public later, will be called the Miller Committee, in honor of our learned corporation counsel."

About two months later on a Friday morning the handsome mayor was hand-delivered the full contents of the *New York Times* projected articles. This gesture was a perfunctory courtesy usually accorded the city's top-ranking elected official. It was also a calculated, Machiavellian maneuver dictated by the top brass of the *New York Times*. No one ever rose to the top ranks of the *Times* by being dumb.

The *Times* bosses were well aware of the existence of the secret Miller Committee, knew that the mayor had formed this inscrutable panel to forestall any possible criticism of the purity of his regime. The sensational articles were scheduled to begin the next day, Saturday, with a not-too-bad warm-up piece. The bomb was due to fall on Sunday, a multipaged, scathing indictment of the police department. Sunday, when the whole literate world reads the *New York Times*.

How would the mayor handle this journalistic nuclear missile? The mayor's office would be closed for the weekend except for a skeleton force. His first public statement would only coincide with the third withering article, corruption and graft now imbedded in the public mind. One of the early paragraphs in the first article contained a terse sentence.

"The names of the policemen who discussed corruption with the *Times* are being withheld to protect them from possible reprisals."

Goddam those two sonofabitches! The mayor bit his lip as he read the sequence of articles with growing wrath and increasing consternation. Shit, who doesn't know the men responsible for these articles. Every cop in New York does, for one thing. Fading presidential hopes in his mind. It's the same as saying the President of the United States' name during World War Two will be withheld to prevent possible reprisals. Everyone knew who the two informers were. Why not come out with it? Print the names of the Benedict Arnolds!

The mayor grew more vexed, livid, as he read page after page. All that was on his mind as he continued to read was the stigma being cast on his administration. His bright presidential hopes, once so high, were now as crumpled as the fading winter snow outside City Hall, turning into slush as the warm, springlike sun melted it.

He sat back in his chair with a feeling of helplessness. What to do? It was like reading his own obituary. He arose from his chair, paced back and forth, too upset even to practice smiling into the mahogany-framed mirror on his office wall. I'll be a sonofabitch. I heard it was to be a devastating exposé, but I never expected anything this bad. I have to counterattack. My present Miller Committee will never appear strong enough to investigate their counterparts in city government.

Cops, too, were city employees. Newspapers traditionally looked askance at city officials, even of the top echelon that made up the Miller Committee, investigating their fellows. To hell with what my good friends Frank the district attorney and Harold the police commissioner have to say about widening the scope of the investigation. My own skirts are clean and I'm not about to have some crooked cops taint me. Good thing I sounded out my old friend, Phelps Sinclair, at the club last week. He thought an independent crime commission was the proper antidote. Another positive thing. Phelps is dying to cap his legal career as a federal judge. The publicity he would receive as the head of a crime commission would gain him enough recognition for me to obtain his appointment.

He returned to his desk, picked up his private telephone and called Sinclair's law firm. Good, Phelps was in the office. Thank God for snow still left on the golf course or Phelps would never be working on Friday. He came right to the point. Will you head up the crime commission? It will be an honor, Mr. Mayor. Yes, Phelps, you can select your fellow members and staff and I will arrange the budget money. Yes, you have my word. Fine, be in my office at ten o'clock Monday morning for a press conference. We'll call the press conference for eleven and I'll brief you for an hour beforehand. Thank you very much, Phelps.

Well, that's the first step. Too bad about Frank and Harold. From here in I'm worrying about myself. A bit calmer, new game plan initiated, he rang for his press secretary. He dictated a statement to make the last edition of New York's only afternoon newspaper, the *Post,* and the Saturday edition of the *Times.*

"The Miller Committee, headed by our distinguished corporation counsel, was formed three months ago by the mayor's office to investigate charges of corruption in the police department. It consisted of Mr. Miller, the commissioners of investigation and the police department, and the district attorneys of Manhattan and the Bronx. Substantial progress was made, but unfortunately a severe conflict of interest arose. I have decided to disband the Miller Committee. In its stead, I have requested W. Phelps Sinclair, one of New York's most distinguished citizens and outstanding lawyers, to chair an independent crime commission. Mr. Sinclair will be empowered to choose his four fellow commission members and have a free hand in the selection of his entire staff. I am appointing this commission by reason of the powers vested in me by the people of New York. Executive Order Number Eleven."

The crime commission was born.

Frank, the district attorney of Manhattan, shook his head angrily when he received the news. Goddam it, Hollywood Joe should have done what Harold and I suggested. This bullshit should be simmered down, allowed to die out. You can bet it will develop into a three-ring circus, an extravaganza of the worst sort. Too late now, he did it.

Harold was at his out-of-town home having breakfast with his wife, Rita, when he got the bad news. He wasn't too upset, he had seen the handwriting on the wall in his numerous visits to the mayor's office in the last few months. He couldn't miss the anxiety in the mayor's voice, his manner. He was fidgety as hell, constantly questioning him about top commanders in the Job. All good men. Is this guy honest, Harold? How about this guy?

Well, that does it! Good-bye New York City, I had a great time. Pack your bags, Rita, we're going to take that trip to Ireland I promised you. What are you going to do, Harold? I'm going to resign, right now, sweetheart.

Tommy's everyday life ever since the Las Vegas trip was busy and lucrative. After almost eight months on the warrant squad he had his duties down to a science. A few fast arrests a couple of mornings a week, then on to better things. He only occasionally sought information from his two doorman stool pigeons, devoting at least two days a week working on scores with Willie Baker. Some days the chief informant appeared nervous and jumpy, other days overcheerful, talkative, bursting with energy. Tommy studied Willie and worried about his habit.

He questioned him at length one day while having a drink together. C'mon, Willie, don't bullshit me. If you're fooling around with junk, tell me. Willie, as always, dismissed his fears with a pat on the back and a big laugh. C'mon, Tommy, you're my main man. I promised you, man, and I keep my word. I'm off the shit the rest of my life. I'm happy enough with wine, whiskey, and pussy. How else could we make the money we make? How could I keep coming up with these kinds of scores?

No way, if I go fuck up my brain with heroin, man. I'd never shit you, Tom. I'm clean, man, clean.

Thoughts of Constance always served to brush away his vague fears and bouts of self-doubt. He romanced her three, sometimes four days a week. The finest restaurants, night clubs, Broadway shows. Against his wishes, once, the Metropolitan Opera. *La Bohème.* He loved it.

Justine was still the uncomplaining, model wife. He called Vinny a couple of times a week, had a drink with him at least once a week. Vince still was leaning on him to quit the Job.

The first signs of spring were in the air. The welcome sun was losing its warmth as it settled in the west. Shadows were falling around the towering skyscrapers. Tommy had played tennis early in the afternoon at an indoor racket club in Long Island City, a few blocks from the Queensboro Bridge. He debated where to stop for a drink. Jimmy Weston's, Jim Costello's? No, P.J. Clarke's, easy to park my car on that block.

He walked into P.J. Clarke's about four o'clock in the afternoon. It was three days after the mayor had announced the formation of the crime commission. The bar was already crowded. He edged his way towards the back where some of his friends usually stood drinking. Two division plainclothesmen, a detective from the Seventeenth Precinct squad and a bookmaker friend were sitting at a table in the far right-hand corner of the small back room directly off the bar area.

One of them called out, "Hey, Tommy, come over and have a drink."

He walked over, shook each outstretched hand, sat down and ordered a Cutty Sark on the rocks. They all tipped glasses good luck. The bookmaker said, "You showed up just in time, Tom. We were talking about the new crime commission. A real pain in the ass. What's your opinion, Tom?"

A shrug of the shoulders, unconcerned attitude, very laconically—"It figures, doesn't it, with the mayor we got."

One of the young plainclothesmen, a bit in awe of the veteran's reputation, said, "But, Tom, don't you think everyone will be subpoenaed sooner or later. And besides, you do have some sort of special assignment, am I right?"

Tommy ignored the question, replied easily, "First of all, the line organizations in the Job from the P.B.A. on up have filed suit to block the crime commission from holding any subpoena powers. This legal hassle could delay everything a year or two. Secondly, this lawyer, Sinclair, the guy the mayor picked to head the commission, has announced that he will select four more lawyers besides himself as the nucleus. Now we're all sitting here in Clarke's. Among us we've had tons of experience with lawyers. Right, fellows?

"Okay, here's my idea. For the sake of argument, let's say that this guy, Sinclair, is an honest lawyer. He should be honest because he's good and rich. The reason the crime commission may never get off the ground." He paused for effect, sipped his drink. The guys around the table leaned closer.

"For Christ sake, Tom, let's hear it."

"First, we give Sinclair the benefit of the doubt. Let's say he's an honest lawyer. But tell me, men—" his voice rising dramatically—"where the fuck in New York is Sinclair going to find four other *honest lawyers* to round out his commission?"

A loud burst of laughter around the table, Tom joining in. Christ, this guy Sloane is a funny guy. One more round of drinks. Tommy finally got up from the table, shook hands all around, prepared to leave Clarke's. He had a date with Constance at the St. Regis.

The bar was now jammed. He would have to push his way through to the front door on Third Avenue. A hand on his shoulder stopped him. He turned, the guy put his hand out, he shook it. The guy said, "Hi, Tom, how are you? Dick Callahan from the Nineteenth squad."

Tommy recognized him, said, "Oh, sure. I'm fine, Dick, how are you?"

"Never better, Tom." Very casually—"Can you spare a few minutes to have a drink? I think you may be able to help me out with a case of mine."

"Sure thing, Dick, at your service. I am running a little late, but five or ten minutes won't matter. A little Cutty Sark on the rocks, please."

He studied Dick Callahan as the detective tried to catch the bartender's eye to order a fresh drink.

The drinks arrived. Dick Callahan tipped Tommy's glass good luck, big, friendly grin on his face. Underneath the facade of the big grin he studied Tommy's face, just as he had been studying Tommy's actions as he was getting a million laughs at the rear corner table. Supposed to have a lot of balls. Good-looking guy. Dark-haired, nice teeth, face just a little bloated, a few broken capillaries around the nose area. Likes booze, loves broads, dresses real nice. Beautiful three-piece blue pin-striped suit. Expensive-looking camelhair coat. No secret in the Job how this guy lives, how he loves money. Take a hot stove and come back for the smoke. Take the eyes out of a dead man's head. Fits all the classic cop cliches about bandits in the Job. Smooth as silk. Definitely not my type of cop.

"Okay, Dick, what can I do for you?"

"Tommy, I caught the squeal on that double murder case a few months ago. You remember, a Puerto Rican john also got shot. Happened in a high class whorehouse on East Fifty-seventh Street and First Avenue. Just before Christmas."

"Yeah, sure, Dick. I remember reading about it. Killed Jimmy Horowitz, used to come here a lot."

Smiling, nice and easy—"I understand you knew him pretty well, Tommy. Is that right?"

Warily, antennae raised. What's this fuck up to?

"I just knew him from this place. Everybody knew him. He'd love to be a wise guy. Supposed to be a bookmaker, but all he did was tout guys to bet on hot football games."

"He owed you some money when he got shot, didn't he, Tom?"

Surprised, caught off guard. My big fucking mouth when I'm half-bombed. I remember, the day after I came home from Florida I told a few guys at the bar. Sonofabitch! The little prick owed me two thousand dollars when he was sent to his reward. Part of it from football bets and part for a favor I did for his whorehouse.

"You're right, Dick, a few bucks. I gave him some money to

bet a couple of playoff games before I left for Florida. Won both games. I went to Florida the day after Christmas. Didn't know the poor bastard got shot until I read about it a couple of days later in the *Miami Herald*. Cost me a thousand bucks."

Dick smiled. This crooked prick is lying. I heard from a reliable source that he was close to Horowitz, that he was owed two or three thousand. Enough for now.

"You can't trust anybody today, Tommy. Did you know his name wasn't really Horowitz, Tom?"

"Sure. I knew he was originally from Tennessee and his real name was Wallace. Some switch. Jews named Horowitz usually change their name to Wallace." They both laughed.

Dick said, "The world is better off with that pimp bastard gone. I did feel sorry for the young whore and the spic who got shot. I still have the case on my file. He was a pretty big-time pimp, too, wasn't he, Tom?"

Very warily—"I wouldn't know about that, Dick. If I ever thought he was a pimp I'd never have a drink with him."

Christ, I hope this hard-on doesn't know that I got laid there twenty times before I met Constance. On the cuff, too.

Callahan still smiling. You lying fuck, Sloane. Five prostitutes I interviewed said you screwed them and that you were buddy-buddy with Horowitz.

"Tom, do me a favor, please. Enough for today, you're in a hurry. I appreciate your having a drink with me. But give some thought to any enemies Horowitz might have had. Someone he owed a lot of money to, someone he fucked pretty good. It appears to me like a shylock hit. If you come up with something, will you get back to me, Tom?"

"Sure thing, Dick. I know where to reach you. You can get me at the warrant squad in the Court Building. Okay, Dick, thanks for the drink. I'll catch up to you."

Tommy felt vaguely uneasy as he walked west on East Fifty-fifth Street towards the St. Regis. This fucking Callahan is one mean bastard. Those pale blue eyes go right through you. Lock 'em up Dick! Put his own mother in jail if he caught her doing something wrong. Honest Dick. Never took a quarter—bull-shit! Show me a detective who never took a quarter and I'll show you a dead detective.

He shook off his air of apprehension as he entered the hotel lobby. A big smile of joy took over when he spotted Constance. A deep kiss, tight hug. Let me look at you. Wide, toothy smile, beautiful face. I love your mink coat, darling. You must have a rich boyfriend.

Spring peacefully rolled into summer, with no untoward incidents to jar his mode of life. Tommy continued merrily along in his usual weekly routine. He dispatched his warrant squad assignments as quickly as possible. Once every couple of weeks he made an infrequent sojourn to the West Side to handle a good score with information provided by one of his doorman stool pigeons. At least once, sometimes two or three times a week, he worked with Willie Baker.

He balanced his love life with Constance and his home life with Justine almost evenly. He slept with Constance at her place at least three times a week. Their lovemaking only got better and he fell more head over heels in love with her every moment he spent at her side. She was never demanding, accepting the role as the other woman in his life with equanimity. She sometimes hinted at the idea of divorce, but never pressed it as it seemed to upset him.

He arrived home about seven one night during the week to find Justine in tears. A sad letter from her mother who was ailing in San Diego. Would you mind, Tommy, if I flew out and visited her? It would certainly comfort her. I haven't seen her in two years, since she came to visit us.

Absolutely, Justine, by all means fly out to see her. Spend as much time as you have to until she feels better. Two or three weeks, at least. Make arrangements with your office for the time off.

He made all of his plans the next day. The following morning, Friday, he drove her to J.F.K. Airport. The plane was on time. He held her tight, fervently kissed her good-bye.

He drove back to Whitestone to pack his clothes. The day before he had arranged with his sergeant, Walt Jackson, for the next week off. The same day he reached out for Willie Baker, staked him five hundred, told him to work hard, line up a few good scores while he was on vacation. All things were in order as he drove his BMW along the Cross Island Parkway. Ten days in the Hamptons with my loving baby.

W. Phelps Sinclair sat behind a wide, uncluttered desk in his private office on the tenth floor of a miniskyscraper on lower Broadway. It was eight o'clock in the morning and he was, as usual, the first one in the office. W. Phelps was in a contemplative mood as he awaited the arrival of Jeff Halloran, his chief counsel. The W. in front of Phelps was for Willard, he would sometimes explain under duress. He used his first name through prep school at Choate and on through Harvard and Harvard Law School even while he privately despised it. He coveted the name Phelps, the maiden name of his mother, a true aristocrat.

The Phelps family were richer than the Sinclair family and their blood was much bluer at the inception of his parents' marriage. Soon after their marriage his industrious father cured the inequity of wealth and achieved equality on the social scale. Though the family fortunes were somewhat depleted by the Crash of '29 and the subsequent Great Depression, W. Phelps Sinclair, the only heir, inherited a substantial estate.

His law practice developed over the years into a very lucrative one. He maintained two splendid homes. A three-story brownstone on the upper East Side and a five-acre estate in elegant Locust Valley on the North Shore of Long Island. Sixty years of age, at what should be the high point in his life, he felt unfulfilled. A staunch conservative Republican, successive Democratic regimes in the White House had refused even to consider his fondest dream—a federal judgeship. But now he stood at the threshold. Enough publicity should be generated from this rostrum to ensure my dream. But we are bogged down, stalled, need some quick action.

W. Phelps Sinclair was a doer. His mother, Marietta Phelps, was a doer, and his father, Bruce Sinclair, was an exceptional doer. He was intrigued by his appointment to head the crime commission, proud to hear it referred to as the Sinclair Commission. He was appalled by what he learned about graft and corruption in the police department during his brief tenure. He could never understand why a policeman could take money. In his private world of corporate law he never ran across crooked judges, prosecutors, or shady lawyers—well, not too shady.

He was determined to root out graft and corruption in the police department. And with the insights and shocking revelations he had absorbed recently, he knew that his job was very *do-able*. The only word he could think of as he sat behind his desk evaluating his mission was, ruthless. He unconsciously nodded his head, affirming his course of action. Not a chance if they continued to pussyfoot around, afraid of who might ultimately be caught in the web. Ruthless.

Contrary to Tommy Sloane's and a lot of other cops' sarcastic jokes, Sinclair had come up with four hard-nosed, very honest lawyers to sit with him on the crime commission. His next most important choice as chief counsel was an ex-federal prosecutor named Jeff Halloran. About five ten, husky, with dark curly hair. Halloran exemplified what the mild-mannered Sinclair decreed when he decided to become ruthless. Shrewd, ambitious, tightly wired, convinced that he was one of the world's few really honest men.

Halloran vowed to rise in the world to reach whatever future goals an embryonic lawyer aspires to—federal judge, U.S. Attorney General, or, my God, the White House. To be overambitious or overzealous in the prosecution of evildoers was not a stain on the pure of heart. To protect you must play the culprit's game. The malefactor was unquestionably ruthless. The keeper of the flame should be twice as ruthless.

Yes, indeed, thought Sinclair, Jeff is a fine prosecutor, a real good man. The staff of young lawyers and investigators he assembled also seemed to be good, capable men. But something is lacking, we're stagnating. We have to come on stronger. We received a reprieve when the mayor replaced the police commissioner, who had abruptly resigned. Sinclair knew that, if the new commissioner had demanded that the mayor dissolve the commission before he would accept the post, the mayor would have had to accede to his wish. Fortunately, the new police commissioner was a clerical, administrative man. The antithesis of what you would expect as a choice. He seemed so happy to land the job he wouldn't dare upset the apple cart.

Jeff Halloran poked his head through the door of Sinclair's office, interrupting his reverie. He said, "Good morning, Phelps. You wanted me in early, here I am."

"Good morning, Jeffrey. Come in, sit down. There's a lot on my mind I think both of us should talk over."

They discussed their situation in private for about an hour and a half. The only break came when Sinclair's secretary brought them two containers of coffee. Each of them bemoaned their slow start, their lack of progress. The crime commission was slowly but surely fading out of the newspapers and the public's mind. Their initial budget was rapidly depleting. Any hope of fresh money was uncertain unless they soon came up with some sensational, substantiated charges. What to do? We can't fail the mayor and the people of New York. What do you suggest, Jeff?

"Phelps, I've come to the conclusion that we need two more crack investigators. Sharp, merciless guys. We have a few good ones, but we need a couple of real top-notchers. We have only one way to go to dig up hard evidence of corruption. We have to nail some cop real good. Not an ordinary patrolman, we've done that and found they're not smart enough or too scared even to turn a sergeant in. We have to catch a plainclothesman or ex-plainclothesman dead bank. In the act! Threaten to crucify him if he doesn't turn. Once we turn a cop like that around we're on our way."

Sinclair nodded slowly, very thoughtfully, said, "That's the route to go, Jeff. You have my blessing. Hire the two men you want. Whatever you say, goes."

"I won't have to hire them, Phelps, I can get them on loan from the D.E.A., the Drug Enforcement Agency. I worked with them at one time. The only thing I want for these two men are expense accounts. Within reason, of course. These plainclothes cops are like sheep, they love to hang out together. On the West Side it's Gallagher's and Dinty Moore's. On the East Side the main hangouts are Jimmy Weston's, Jim Costello's, and P.J. Clarke's. Clarke's is the main watering place.

"All we have turned so far is the two cops involved in the tow

truck payoffs. Christ, neither of those two could turn a ventril-
oquist dummy and by now we hear no one's speaking to them,
they've blown their cover. We must turn a hip cop who knows
all the mob guys, the pads in the Job, the inner mechanism of
graft. It won't be easy, Phelps, but my guys will give it some
shot." Now, a sly smile—"And boss, they both hate cops."

"Good, Jeff, you have my blessing. Go ahead."

"Great, Phelps, I anticipated that you would give me the
green light. I've already contacted them, they've agreed, and I
arranged permission from Washington to have them temporarily assigned to us."

Sinclair chuckled. "You're an impetuous but good man, Jeff."

Tommy and Constance left the Hamptons at five thirty in the
morning to avoid the heavy traffic along the Long Island Expressway. It had been a marvelous ten days. Long walks bare-
footed along the sandy, flawless, beach; swimming in the
pounding surf, tennis afternoons, cocktail parties at twilight on
vast, breezy patios, dinners in exquisite restaurants—and best
of all—lovemaking unparalleled in the archives of Eros.

He parked the BMW near Constance's apartment house and
brought their luggage up to her co-op. He fixed coffee while
she showered and changed into a white cotton dress suitable
for the office. Finished coffee, she kissed him good-bye and left
for work.

By now Constance's apartment had become a second home
to him. He kicked off his loafers, picked up a magazine and
stretched out on the living room couch. He felt tired, but totally relaxed. He fought off the desire to sleep; he wanted to be
sure to call Walt Jackson, his sergeant, before ten o'clock.

He finished the article he was reading, looked at his wristwatch, got up from the couch, and called Walt.

Everything is fine here, Tommy, take it easy today, come in
early tomorrow morning. Oh, by the way, Tom, you have two
messages here. Same guy called. Said you have his number. His
name is Joe Lenox, says it's urgent. Okay, you got it? See you
tomorrow morning.

Tommy smiled. Called twice, urgent. Willie must be broke

again. Willie Baker, alias Joe Lenox, his code name. Willie loves that secret shit. Must have a good score on tap. I'd love to put him off until tomorrow. On the way home from the Hamptons I promised Constance I would take her to dinner at the Villa Pompei. It would be great to see Vinny and maybe he would reach out for Petey Dowd. Looks like a nice evening shot to hell.

Christ, I'm really enjoying bachelorhood, not having to report home three or four nights a week. Reminds me, I must call Justine on the West Coast this afternoon. Haven't spoken to her in five days. Last call, her mother was getting better. Should be home in your arms next week, sweetheart. Take your time, love. I'm doing real fine, eating sensibly, losing about five pounds. Jesus, I must have screwed ten pounds off in Southampton.

Shit, I better call Willie. I can't let him down.

He called Willie, the Lenox Avenue kid.

"Hello, who's dis?"

"Dat yo' there, yo' bad dude motherfucka." A big grin on his face as he gave his best end-man-in-a-minstrel-show imitation.

"Oh, Tommy, Tommy, my main man. Yo' real funny, soundin' good, man. How's yo' trip? Have a fine time?"

"Great, Willie, just great. What's up?"

"I've got a real hot score on, Tom. Big motherfucka! Top heroin wholesaler, thinks he's gotta license. He moves around ever' few days. Should be a real hanger, man. We have to move on him right away. Like tonight."

"Can't it wait a day or two, Willie?"

"No way, Tom. Trust me. He's gotta go tonight."

"Okay, where and what time do we meet?"

"Ten o'clock. By the big meat market, Hundred Thirty-third Street off Twelfth Avenue. You know, we met dere few times."

"You're on, Willie. See you tonight."

Christ, called back to the front lines the first day I'm back. What a tough life! Well, as Willie would say, to live the good life you must hustle, man, really hustle. He grinned. Not only do I think like Willie, I'm beginning to talk like him.

He stretched out again on the couch to read, eyes heavy. In a few minutes he fell sound asleep. He woke up after one o'clock, bright, afternoon sun streaming into the living room through the parted window drapes. He was starving. He showered, put on a fresh sport shirt and slacks. He walked a couple of blocks west to J.G. Melon, had a couple of beers and a giant bacon cheeseburger. Delicious.

It was a lovely, breezy summer day. He whistled a happy tune as he walked back to the apartment. He called Justine. Everything fine, dear, mother is growing stronger every day. Are you home? No, sweetheart, I'm calling from the office. Of course, the house is all right. Okay, call me next week, give me your flight number and I'll pick you up at the airport. What? Sure, I cut the grass. Good-bye, love.

Christ, I better get home sometime tomorrow and see what's what. The house could be burned down for all I know.

He called Constance. Dinner date is off. Something unexpected came up. Assigned to a big case. I'll wait here, have a drink and a bite to eat with you. Just as well, Tommy, I'm dead tired. See you later, love.

He called Vinny. Yeah, Vince, super vacation, wonderful time. Can't make the Pompei tonight, something unexpected came up. Get hold of Peter Dowd, please, make a date for later in the week. Sure, I promise, swear to God. Thanks, Vince. Yeah, I love you, too.

Willie was pacing up and down, didn't see Tommy when he pulled the car up outside the huge West Harlem wholesale meat complex adjacent to the West Side Highway and the Hudson River. He opened the car trunk and slipped a small .22 caliber Baretta mink in his right-side jacket pocket. He gave a reassuring pat to the snub-nosed .38 caliber detective special on his hip, concealed by his sport jacket. He walked across the street, hailed Willie, greeted him with a big hug. Willie talked a mile a minute. Nervous, jittery. Tom put it down to his anxiety to make a score after two dry weeks. Willie boy loved the good life! Wine, women, and song. Just like you, Tommy. Willie got right to the point. Big spic heroin wholesaler. New dude in town. From somewhere in Florida. I heard Miami. Must be legal wherever it is, the way this dude works. The address. Four seventy-four West 134th Street, right off St. Nicholas Avenue. Third floor, apartment on far left. Has brass knocker on door, big peekhole above the knocker. He don't care if yo' white or black, caters only to peddlers. All colors. Password. Just say Mutt sent me. You got it? Should be good for five grand, easy, Tommy boy.

"Super, Willie. I got it. Let's go."

They drove the few blocks and turned east on West 134th Street. Tom parked, looked around. It was still a fairly nice neighborhood. Quiet at eleven o'clock at night in contrast to noisy lower and mid-Harlem. Willie sat in the car, Tommy got out and walked to number 474. He looked the building over. A six-story walk-up. By the looks of the exterior in pretty good shape. He had a skeleton key but didn't need it. The front door and the vestibule door were unlocked.

He patted his detective special on his hip underneath his sport jacket. He put his hand inside his right jacket pocket, felt the reassuring presence of the Baretta. A large bulb high in the ceiling cast a pale glow over the hallway area. The light receded as he trotted up the long flight of stairs. He could barely see as he reached the second floor landing.

A voice suddenly came out of the dimness. A harsh, guttural voice. "Stand right dere, motherfucka. You goin' up next floor, get some black pussy. You goin' noplace, man, hand yo' cash over or I cut yo' white dick off." A big black guy, with a big sharp knife about six inches from Tommy's throat.

"Take it easy, pal, here's my money."

He had his hand in his right jacket pocket. He squeezed three rounds of the Baretta right smack into the black guy's chest. Pop, pop, pop. Muffled by the coat pocket, like small firecrackers going off in the still, hall landing.

The knife fell out of the robber's hand, he staggered back, a look of astonishment on his face. Tommy kicked the knife down the stairs, ducked behind the big black guy and heaved him down the flight of stairs. His body went thumping down the steps and landed in a loud crash at the bottom.

Better get the hell out of here real fast. Tommy bolted down the stairs, stepped over the body and exited into the street. He walked nonchalantly to his car up the block. Before he entered his car he looked up at 474. A lot of lights were turned on in all the front apartments. He motioned to Willie to shut up and drove nice and easy across town. He stopped the car just off Lenox Avenue, near where Willie lived.

"Tom, for Christ sake, man, what happened? Yo' didn't have time to make the score."

"I got stuck-up on the second floor, Willie. Big, black fuck. Had a knife, looked two feet long."

"No shit, Tom. Whadda yo' know. Can't trust anyone up here in Harlem. You bang him out, Tommy?"

"Bet your chocolate ass, Willie, I put three in him. He should be dead as a mackerel." He turned to Willie, grabbed his shoulder, and in a sharp, severe voice, said, "Listen, Willie, what happened tonight dies with us, you got it? I'm supposed to be on vacation, no way I can explain being up here in Harlem. Especially killing some prick, even if he was a stick-up guy. You got it, mum's the word, Willie."

"Sure, Tommy boy. I forgot it already. I'm glad yo' killed the motherfucka. Ruined our score."

"Good, Willie. Here take a couple of hundred for walking around money. We'll cool it for about a week. Okay?"

"Sure, Tom, thanks a lot. We'll stay in touch."

He drove to the Triborough Bridge. He stopped the BMW at about the center of the bridge in the extreme right lane. He turned his emergency flashers on, got out of the car and looked under the rear of the car as if he had a mechanical problem. He stood up and waited until several cars passed. He removed the automatic from his pocket and threw it high and far. It was his favorite of five unregistered guns that he had seized during his years on the Job.

The next morning he called Walt Jackson, asked for one more day off. Sure, Tommy, but make sure you're here early tomorrow. He straightened up the house, mowed the lawn, cut his sport jacket with the bullet holes in the right-side pocket into a thousand pieces and burned it into fine ashes. He felt a twinge of regret as he watched the tiny swatches of the light blue poplin jacket simmer into ashes. He loved that jacket, thought it looked great on him.

Finished with his chores, he walked a couple of blocks to the neighborhood mom and pop store to restock the refrigerator. He picked up the final edition of the morning *Daily News*. As soon as he reached home he put his food purchases on the kitchen counter and thumbed through the first pages. Page eight, small headline:

Man Found Murdered In Harlem

A man, identified through fingerprints as Alonzo Waters, age twenty-six, no known home address, was discovered shot to death by police late last night in the ground floor hallway of 474 East 134th Street. Neighbors who heard gunshots called police. Fingerprints disclosed that Waters had a previous record for assault and drug crimes. Police feel the murder was drug related and have no suspects at present.

He smiled. Goddam right, a drug-related murder. That whacky, junkie bastard who wanted to cut my dick off saved some spic dealer at least five grand I would have shook him for.

Willie Baker read the news late in the afternoon in the comfy afterglow of a nice heroin fix. He settled down to read the *Daily News*, at peace with the world.

He was startled at first when he read the news. Police feel it was a drug-related crime. Them police sure know their stuff. Bet yo' sweet ass it was drug related. Goddam, this is really bad shit. I have to save this clipping, first time Tom and me ever killed a dude. He took scissors, carefully cut the piece out of the *Daily News* and put it away in the top bureau drawer in his bedroom.

* * *

Early autumn, the prettiest time of the year in New York. Air clean and brisk, crisp to the nostrils in contrast to the humid, smoggy, thankfully departed air of summer. Leaves turning bright gold on the trees scattered incongruously on streets where towering skyscrapers soared towards the blue sky. Football season in full swing. The beloved Giants. An added starter in New York, the Jets. A good team. Should be a great year!

Jeff Halloran sat behind his desk in his crime commission office. In front of him were the two crack investigators he requested from Phelps Sinclair a few months back. His two hot shots had spent a very busy three months. They were digging in pretty good, the weekly reports were getting more interesting. He knew now that he had picked the right guys.

Dominick Stabile, facing Halloran in the chair on his left. Born and raised in Maspeth, Queens, where half the kids he grew up with had fathers or uncles in the Job. Just like Dom had Uncle Rico, whom he adored. But Dominick never grew beyond five foot seven, an inch short of the required height for the Job. He was good-naturedly but unmercifully kidded by his pals. Get a hammer job, Dom. Just a quick whack on the head with a hammer before you take the physical. Guaranteed the bump will add an inch under your curly, black hair. They'll never notice, Dom.

He secretly resented barbs aimed at his stature, but grinned and bore it. He would show these half-ass would-be cops someday. Two years in the army, fifteen months of it in Vietnam, instilled in him a total revulsion for drugs of any kind. After two years of college he was accepted as a trainee in the D.E.A., Drug Enforcement Agency. He soon became a top-notch agent. His secret envy of New York cops turned to actual hatred as he worked on various cases with the elite narcotics squad. The urbane, self-assured, well-dressed detectives completely irritated him. Even though he imagined most of what he felt was ill treatment, he always had a sense of inferiority around them. They were the glamour boys, he was a piece of shit. He'd show them some day.

Frank Kurowski, facing Halloran in the chair on his right. Born in Greenpoint, Brooklyn, a close second to Warsaw in Polish population. His father, Stan, a patrolman for thirty-five years. An attack of polio as a boy left one leg two inches shorter than the other, kept him out of the army, disqualified him for the Job. He knew his father was disappointed in him even though he never mentioned it. All he ever heard his father talk about was the Job. The goddam Job. He quit college after two years to become a trainee in the D.E.A. He'd prove to his father that the horseshit Job should have waived his physical infirmity. He had brains, guts, would make a great cop. He might have been right, for in a few years he became one of the D.E.A.'s top investigators. Now on loan to the crime commission to catch crooked cops. He licked his lips.

Jeff Halloran smiled, looked up from the report he had been reading while his two trusty bloodhounds patiently waited for the master's voice to break the silence. He leaned towards them confidentially, said, "It certainly looks like you two are working hard, are on the right track. And by the looks of your expense accounts here on my desk, if nothing comes of this, you two are having a helluva good time in New York."

Dom Stabile laughed, answered, "Boss, you have to admit, this is some expensive town. Cost you five bucks to take a piss. But mine's not too bad, I'm covering Jim Costello's and P.J. Clarke's. Frank here is in a little more expensive league. Jimmy Weston's, Moore's, Gallagher's.

"But anyway, as we mentioned briefly in the report you just read, Frank and I both agree that we have a logical candidate to turn around. Most of all, if we can catch him dead right. I made some good friends when I worked out of the Washington, D.C. office. One guy in particular, a lieutenant in the personnel office of the navy department. From some conversation I overheard at the bar in Clarke's, I found out our target had been in the navy. My lieutenant pal got me a psychiatric profile on him out of his navy file. It showed plenty of courage, but also a fear of close places, close quarters. Acute case of claustrophobia. No candidate for submarine duty or similar type duty. Are you getting the picture, boss? Just imagine if we nail this guy dead right. The threat of a long period in a jail cell will blow his mind."

"Hmm, sounds good, Dominick. Excellent work. Our guy's name is Tommy Sloane, right?"

"That's correct, boss. Thomas Patrick Sloane, age thirty-six, thirteen years on the police force. A real one hundred percent swinger. A typical New York wise ass cop. Knows everybody. Owners, bartenders, maitre d's, they all kiss his ass like he's the commissioner. Pisses away money like water, real comedian around his pals, keeps everyone laughing. Married, never goes out with his wife. In New York, anyway. Supposed to own a big home in Whitestone.

"Has a beautiful girlfriend, name, Constance Ward. Works as an executive in a big advertising agency. They practically live together in a co-op on East Seventy-fourth Street and York Avenue. Drives a neat BMW, good foreign car. I have no idea who pays for all this—the co-op, car, big house in Whitestone—but this prick lives pretty good.

"But now the good part of the scenario, boss. This guy's getting real careless. He's a lead-pipe cinch to tail. Drinks a lot. Maybe that's why his guard is down. He has a black, or shall I say brown, stool pigeon. The guy won't come into Clarke's, waits outside for Tommy once every few days. They huddle together pretty good, sometimes go across to the back room of Friar Tuck's, opposite Clarke's on Third Avenue. Have a drink, go off together. Boss, we need a good black rookie cop, maybe right out of the police academy. We do a good background check until we come up with the right kid. I want to use a good, black, young cop to tail Tommy Sloane's stool pigeon. Okay, that's me for a while. Frank, you take over."

Frank, soft voice, not as intense as Stabile—"Thank you, Dom. To continue the saga of Tommy Sloane. This guy lives like royalty, boss. Beautiful clothes, expensive foreign car, a gorgeous sweetheart. Spreads money around pretty good, heavy tipper. Like Dominick says, soon as he enters a place they fall all over him. Everybody seems to know him. Hey, Tommy boy, hiya, Tom, plenty of that shit. He drinks booze like it's going out of style, hardly ever shows he had a drink. His girlfriend is a dream, gorgeous. I'd love to take a shot at her myself. He takes her out dancing once or twice a week. Mostly Jimmy Weston's or the Rainbow Room.

"Believe it or not, when they go dancing together they cool the booze, drink a couple bottles of French champagne. Forty bucks a crack. All I know so far is that he works out of the warrant squad in the Job. The office is in the Supreme Court Building. They lock up poor bastards who won't or can't pay child support and misdemeanor bail jumpers. I don't know when the hell he ever works, but it sure isn't very hard duty. This guy is unbelievable. He cashed his pay check in Weston's last week and he and the bartender, Mike, howled laughing when Mike counted out the money. Three hundred seventeen bucks! Two weeks' pay.

"The last bit of news is that he has another stool pigeon besides the black kid. A real sharp young Jew. Works as a doorman at the Hotel Manhattan. I was curious about him. What's a good-looking young Jew kid doing working as a doorman in a hotel? Answer! The kid books a little, obviously does things with Tommy Sloane and also sells pills and other junk to hookers and pimps on Eighth Avenue, where the Hotel Manhattan is. That's about all for now, boss."

Jeff Halloran sat back in his broad, leather club chair. Pensively, hand held reflectively under his chin. Wait'll I see Phelps Sinclair. I sure hit the jackpot. These two guys are all I said they were. Crackerjacks! Tommy Sloane, sounds familiar. Name rings a bell. I'll have Captain Maguire secretly pull his file. Has to be a super hush-hush move. Maguire and Chief Del Vecchio will handle it. Thank God for two honest bosses. Those two sure hate crooked cops. He spoke, "Good work, men. Super. No question you two are on the right track. This guy Sloane looks very vulnerable. I'll get his entire police file, everything he's done since rookie school. Speaking of rookie school, Dominick, a great idea, a sharp black rookie. I'll go one better. We'll get two sharp black kids. The police commissioner will be more than pleased to accommodate me. He's hoping the crime commission will die a natural death. Pig's ass! He'll find out.

"Okay, enough for this morning. I'm very well pleased. Keep up the same amount of surveillance. Remember, easy does it. No rush, let's get this guy Sloane dead right. Scare the shit out of him. He'll turn. Just don't get too inquisitive or you'll blow your cover. One more thing, before I forget. The elite narcotics squad is practically disbanded. Chances are you'll never run into any of those detectives. If you do, bullshit them. You're in New York on a big undercover dope case. Very big, keep it under your hat. Horseshit them, but make a memo later of anyone who might make you as a D.E.A. agent. Okay, fellows, good luck, go to work."

A few days later, Halloran sat in his office looking at a large, manila, Scotch-taped envelope his secretary had just placed in front of him. It was stamped Confidential in bold letters all over the front. He opened it. Good! It contained the police history of Thomas Patrick Sloane from the day he was appointed to the Job.

It soon dawned upon him as he read the file just how Sloane's name rang a bell in his mind. He was a young assistant federal district attorney recently assigned to the budding civil rights bureau. An excitable Spanish lawyer was referred to him. He was bitterly complaining about the savage treatment two of his young constituents received at the hands, or the nightstick, of Sloane. Christ, he smiled, Sloane fractured their skulls, knees, arms, and maybe even their balls. Subsequent investigation proved he acted correctly. Bad kids, one of them stabbed Sloane, who was completely vindicated.

He read on. Plenty of arrests. Killed two Puerto Ricans while evidently aborting a stick-up. Fifteen-minute gunfight, twenty-three shots exchanged. Awarded the Combat Cross. Christ, this guy Sloane could solve our immigration problem.

Five commendations besides Combat Cross for excellent police work. Sounds like a tough cop. Maybe he won't be as easy to turn as Dom and Frank predict. Nine years in the Manhattan Borough West squad as a plainclothesman. To suppress gambling and vice. Suppress my Irish ass. Some juicy pickings on that squad. No wonder he lives so good. By now really used to the high life and too much high life softens them all up. Never been in trouble. Until now, Sloane. Your troubles are just beginning.

Tommy cooled it for a whole week after killing the stick-up guy. He went to work early each morning, carried out his assignments as quickly as possible, and came home early to Whitestone every night. He scanned all the newspapers minutely, but not another word was printed about the killing. What the hell was one more killing up in Harlem!

He explained his absence to Constance very simply. A real big case, love, probably have to go out of town for a few days. Definitely see you next week. I love you too, babe.

A class of three hundred and seventy-five rookies were scheduled to graduate from the police academy the early part of November. There were twenty-one black rookies in the class. Dom Stabile and Frank Kurowski had pored painstakingly over their individual files for many hours. They weeded out the young cops whom they felt unsuitable for the task they had in the offing.

They were looking for a special type of young black cop. He had to possess the qualities of intelligence, dedication, and the street smarts most New York black kids acquire at an early age. He must also come across as an average young man, have no tell-tale characteristics, physical or otherwise, to peg him as a cop. Just another guy that could never stand out in a crowd. A quick-witted, easy kid who could blend into the ghetto areas of New York without causing a suspicious, raised eyebrow.

Their intensive search narrowed down to four rookies. By unanimous agreement, one was outstanding. But we need two young cops, right. Well, let's see if our top guy fills the bill. Chances are the black rookies hang out together at the police academy. Let's see whom he recommends. If it turns out to be one of the other three guys we're thinking about, we take him. Let's get our asses moving, we have to nail Sloane by the first of the year.

They received the green light from Jeff Halloran, who called the police commissioner personally to grant permission to use the rookies. They then arranged to meet their first choice at the apartment they sublet together. They agreed beforehand, no way would he know at present that he was assigned to the crime commission. We'll tell him it's Drug Enforcement Agency work. Big drug ring! When we size him up, okay him one hundred percent, maybe we'll give him the real lowdown.

Their unanimous pick was a slim, five-ten, brown-skinned rookie. His name was Michael Porter and he was twenty-four years old. Michael was brought up in the Coney Island section of Brooklyn, the oldest of four children. His father was a boss in the U.S. Postal Service, his mother a housewife. Nice family. Excellent high school basketball player. Went on to St. Bonaventure's College in upstate New York on a basketball scholarship. Great career on the court, but too small for the pros.

Graduated on dean's list. Major, political science. Has ambitions to study law. Worked for major insurance company after graduation from college. Married to a nurse, childhood sweetheart. No children. Two years after college appointed to police force. Hopes to attend law school while on the Job.

The first meeting was a great success. The two bloodhounds complimented each other on the perspicacity that compelled their choice. Inside of ten minutes it was Mike and Dom, Mike and Frank—no formalities. One helluva kid. They bullshitted him about the impending huge drug bust. He swallowed their story, envisioned a gold detective shield on the horizon. Little by little, Mike, we have to nail the small pushers, one of whom will crack and lead us to the top traffickers. If we break this case, Mike, we'll personally recommend you for the detective bureau. Mike reacted to the carrot dangled before his nose very predictably. Swore his allegiance. Overwhelmed at the prospect of working undercover, generous expense account.

One thing more, Mike, we need another black rookie cop. Any guy in the class you would recommend. Think carefully, has to be a top guy. But similar to you in appearance, can't look too much like a cop. Mike looked at Dom, laughed, baby, have I got a boy for you.

They all laughed. It was uncanny, Mike named their second choice, his best friend in rookie school. And better yet, fellows, both of us hate drug peddlers. See them in school playgrounds, peddling that shit to fuck up kids' minds the rest of their lives.

Vernon Lewis, well built, five-nine. Black skin, broad face. Brought up in Jamaica, Queens. Fine high school football player. Halfback, very fast. Football scholarship to Villanova University, outside of Philadelphia. Fed up with football after junior year, finished college at St. John's University. Major, English. Mother and father dead. Bachelor. Lives alone. Articulate, bright, always wanted to be a New York cop. Maybe someday write as a sideline.

The trap was settling into place. Mike and Vernon just vanished from the rookie ranks of the police academy. Dom and Frank briefed them every day in their two-bedroom sublet in Tudor City, a cluster of distinguished high-rise apartments in an enclave high above the broad avenues on the East Side. Across from the towering United Nations, insular and self-sufficient in old fashioned stores and picturesque restaurants, with landscaped gardens and tiny park, it was an oasis in cement-bound New York.

The ways and wiles of the decoy cop. The art of shadowing their quarry, to be always invisible to the object of their tail. No rush, nice and easy. Have to grab a taxi, grab it. Go in a bar, have a drink, do it. Same goes for restaurants, night clubs, whatever. Every week you'll get your expenses.

One vital thing. No one, you get it, *no one* is to know what you're assigned to. Your family, wife, best friend—nothing. You got that straight? As he indoctrinated the two rookies, studying their attentive faces, Dom figured, what the hell, I'm only lying a little about the soon-to-be gold shields. You never can tell, they might get lucky. Anyway, they're just two innocent rookie cops. In a couple of years they'll smarten up, be like all other cops. Shit, the system will never change. Maybe I'm cynical, maybe I don't like cops, but there's one cop I'm going to give a fucking headache. The big shot, Tommy Sloane.

W. Phelps Sinclair and his right-hand man Jeff Halloran sat down for lunch at the prestigious Lawyers Club. The sumptuous private club was for the elite of the New York Bar, located in the downtown financial district of New York, a short distance from the offices of the crime commission. At Sinclair's request, they were seated at a wall table for two in the rear corner of the room. Complete privacy was the order of the day.

They exchanged pleasantries as they awaited their extra dry Beefeater martinis. They raised glasses, wished each other good luck, sipped their delicious drinks. Sinclair got right down to business.

"Jeff, from what I've read and what you've already told me, you seem to have quite a team out there. I've briefed the mayor, who is very anxious for us to show real progress, promised him that we expect exciting things to happen after the first of the year. The mayor also promised me that he would supplement our budget, which, as you know, Jeff, is running low."

"That's great, Phelps. Good news. You're quite right about my investigative team. They added two black rookie cops to help them in surveillance work and the two kids turned out marvelous. Our main target, the ex-plainclothesman and contract cop around town, Tommy Sloane, is ready for the kill. Like most cops on the take real big, he's gotten careless and very vulnerable. His main stool pigeon is a black junkie who also pushes a little dope on the side. The two rookies know every time he goes to the bathroom, can pick him up any time we give the word.

"He has another stool pigeon, a young Jewish guy who books horses, fixes up guests looking for a girl, and probably sells dope pills to prostitutes. I'm almost certain that Sloane isn't aware of his two stool pigeons' aberrations. He couldn't possibly be that much of a fool. However, we decided to wait until the Christmas holiday season is over to close in. We figure to be ready to go to work on Sloane about the middle of January. How does that sound?"

"Sounds fine, Jeff. Christmas time is not appropriate for proper publicity, anyway. Besides, we don't want to appear too brutal during the season to be merry. Isn't that right, Jeff?"

Jeff laughed. "Very funny, Phelps. All right, let's have one more of those superb martinis and drink to the demise of Tommy Sloane and the crooked cops we hope he'll bring down with him."

Autumn rolled by peacefully for Tommy Sloane. The killing in Harlem had simmered down his activities considerably. He woke up a couple of times in a cold sweat after a wild dream about the brutal encounter. It was always the same dream. He was the victim, the one who got knifed in his dream. The big black robber laughing like a hyena as he grabbed his bankroll and left him bleeding to death on the dark hall landing.

The incidence of the recurrent bad dream, the uneasiness that it caused, puzzled him. It was as if, perhaps, it might come back to haunt him. But he would shrug it off. Fuck him, fuck all stick-up guys. It's either them or me. Better them.

He slowed Willie down to a walk, barely worked with him one day a week, but always making a good score. He tried to avoid Harlem for a while, expressed his reluctance to Willie. Cool it up there for a few months. Willie complained a little, moaned about being broke. Tommy calmed him down, staked him extra after a good score.

He elected the easier midtown West Side route with Manny, his hotel doorman. He was at home on the West Side. Familiar territory, his turf. Manny was amazing, his information foolproof, like taking candy from a baby. A couple of high-class whorehouses, a sneak crap game, and one really funny and very profitable score. A male whorehouse, bossed by a blond, bewigged transvestite, that catered to married guys who came out of the closet every so often to indulge their homosexual fantasies in the flesh. A real solid score. The johns were scared shitless. A big payday!

He finished his warrant squad duties as swiftly as possible, presenting Knicks' tickets to Walt Jackson weekly as usual. Any time he wanted a day off, or two or three, Walt would grant it. Just keep in touch, Tommy boy, in case we need you.

His idle afternoons were spent waiting for Constance in P.J. Clarke's, Jim Costello's, or occasionally with Jimmy Clare at Gallagher's. They usually dined and danced once a week at Jimmy Weston's or the Rainbow Room. He made sure to see Vince at least once a week for a drink, sometimes for dinner.

Vince constantly harped on him to quit the Job. What the hell do you need it for? To get jammed up, you dumb Irish fuck.

Jesus, Vince, lay off, please. I love the Job! Besides, the crime commission hasn't come up with a solid thing. A couple of poor precinct cops for taking a deuce or a fin. Big deal! I hear through the grapevine that their number is up right after the first of the year. Thank God, right, pal? The Job doesn't need those headline happy shitheels trying to improve their station in life by wrecking some poor cops' lives.

And then there was Constance. She grew more beautiful, charming and intelligent every day he spent with her. Still, she was a woman, and to use Vince's favorite expression—sooner or later all women give you *agita*. He was forced to admit to himself that he was right. But it sure upset him when she clung to him fiercely after they made wonderful love and cried, begging him to leave Justine and marry her. He would kiss her eyes tenderly, soothe her, swear that he would until she fell asleep exhaustedly. He silently prayed she wouldn't bring the subject up the next morning.

The Christmas season came with its abundance of envelopes from old cousins and wise guy friends. All very happy to see him. He gave Constance a diamond bracelet. Oh, Tommy, it's magnificent. He didn't reveal, of course, that it was a swag bracelet. Cost him about one fifth of the jeweler's price. Justine received her usual thousand dollars, was overwhelmed by his generosity. He had his pre-Christmas champagne party with Vince, then on to the family get-together with nice presents for everyone.

At the party he sadly broke the news to Justine that he had to go out of town on a big case the day after Christmas. He cursed his bad luck, she held his hand tight and sympathized tearfully. His false sadness turned into instant happiness as he headed his BMW into New York to pick up Constance. They drove to Mount Snow in Vermont, overjoyed to be with each other during the holidays.

Tommy welcomed the New Year in dancing at a Queens night club with Justine and dreaming of Constance in Mount Snow.

It was a typical middle of January day in New York. The winds blew shrilly against the leaded windows of gracious Tudor City apartments. The sidewalks were sheets of ice and the miniature park in the center of the cluster of high-rise apartments was blanketed with a foot of snow.

Five jubilant men were gathered in the snug comfort of Dom Stabile's and Frank Kurowski's flat. In marked contrast to the forbidding cold of the streets below, the atmosphere in the apartment was filled with warmth and charged with the scent of victory.

Though hardly past the noon hour, opened bottles of whiskey stood on the bar in the left corner of the large living room. A broad aluminum tray with a depleted mound of sandwiches was next to the whiskey. Jeff Halloran, Dom, Frank, and their two prize black rookie cops sat around the room, drinks in one hand and a paper plate with napkins and remnants of sandwiches next to them.

Their two victims, whose incarceration was the reason for their jubilation, were certainly not happy and definitely not warm. Willie Baker and Manny Resnick, Tommy Sloane's two top stool pigeons, were safely tucked in cells in the segregated area of the forbidding, time-ravaged Tombs, Manhattan's oldest jail. It was cold in their cells and they sat silently shivering as they awaited their next interrogation by these ball-breaking cops. Fuck Tommy Sloane, get me out of here, each of them was imploring the gods who guided his destiny. Willie needed a fix pretty soon. The kid cop, Mike, let him have a fix before he brought him in. Jesus, that kid a fucking cop! I couldn't believe it when he grabbed me. Where's Tommy? Manny Resnick was asking himself the same question. Where's Tommy?

Jeff Halloran, in an exultant mood, his judgment in his choice of added staff vindicated, offered a toast to his two crack D.E.A. investigators and the two super police rookies who so immensely aided them. He raised his glass, his third Scotch on the rocks of the infant day, and, in the measured tones of a federal prosecutor making his opening presentation for the People, said, "The very best of luck to you men. My personal thanks for the hard work and dedication all of you put in together to make our plan of action a success. I'm especially pleased with the painstaking efforts of you two rookies, which resulted in the quick capitulation of our star witnesses.

"I've had lots of rewarding experiences with Dom and Frank here," indicating his two D.E.A. bloodhounds. He then looked directly at the two black rookie cops, said, "I had some initial doubts about your value because of your inexperience, but you two kids were some surprise. You did one helluva job. My apologies for misleading you when you first joined us. At the time we didn't deem it wise to let you know that you were working for the crime commission. You two must understand that for years there has existed an unwritten code among cops to look the other way at any malfeasance committed by their fellow cops. This is an abominable tradition of the police force that must be stamped out. The mayor implemented the crime commission to begin that task. There isn't room for graft and corruption in the police force and we intend to root out the cancer, to once more make it the shining symbol of courage and honesty the public looks to it as.

"Mike and Vernon, again my thanks. Mr. Sinclair and I will personally intervene with the new police commissioner, and the mayor as well, to see that you two are rewarded with gold shields for excellent police work. You have my word that this will be accomplished before we complete our mission. Now, Mike, suppose you speak first. Dominick has briefed me already in the substance of your investigation, but I'd like to hear your version of the events leading to Willie Baker's arrest."

Mike Porter, self-assured, nice and cool with a couple of Dewar's and sodas warming his belly, said, "It was a real rocking chair, Mr. Halloran. I could have busted him the first week Dom and Frank put me onto him. I picked Willie up less than a week after I started laying on Tommy Sloane. Dom gave me a good description of Willie, so it wasn't hard to figure him out once I saw them hook up. Besides, they laugh and kid around like two brothers when they meet.

"I then tailed Willie to his apartment, One twenty-fourth Street off Lenox Avenue. I rented a room for myself just down the block. I spread a cover story out that I just got back from

Vietnam and was immediately accepted around the neighborhood joint.

"This cat, Willie Baker, is something else. He loves women and booze and he shoots dope. I moved next to him nice and easy and bought a couple of nickel bags of heroin from him. Took me for granted.

"I laid back, waited for further instructions from Dom. I didn't want to blow my cover, be seen around too much. I cooled it for a while, helped Vernon a little with his detail. I only made Willie a few times with Tommy Sloane. Once or twice they'd meet and take right off in Sloane's fancy car.

"Anyway, what happened beyond that is already in my report, which I'm sure you've read, Mr. Halloran. Vernon and I busted Willie Baker two days ago. He's a dead ass junkie, boss, give his old lady up for a fix. He gave Sloane up the minute after I found ten nickel bags of heroin under a hat on a closet shelf.

"But there's one funny thing that came up when I searched the apartment. I told Dom right away. We decided to see what you thought. I found a newspaper clipping in his bedroom bureau drawer. It concerned a junkie murder, happened in West Harlem early last year. I asked Willie why he possessed the clipping. Well, he almost shit. Clammed up, brushed me off. I didn't press him but I called a detective friend of mine, Ray Jenkins. He's in the Twenty-eighth squad. I told him that I was working undercover for the D.E.A., asked him to find out something about the murder. Ray contacted the detective who has the case. No clues, except that a woman who lived in a front apartment in the house where the murder took place saw a small foreign-looking car pull away from the curb a few doors down. She saw this a couple of minutes after the noise of the shots and the commotion in the hall woke her up.

"Right away I began to put two and two together. Vernon and I took Willie down to the Lexington Hotel where Dom and Frank were waiting for us in a suite. I played nice guy, treated Willie the best. I threw a few shots of Jack Daniels in him, let him have a fix, cooled him out pretty good. He opened up. Told me about the junkie killing. Dominick has it all in a supplementary report. We're waiting on you, Mr. Halloran."

Halloran beamed. Christ, what good news! Said, a bit excitedly, "A great job well done, Mike. Marvelous piece of work. We'll do the detective bureau a big favor when we get you men gold shields. Okay, let's relax for a minute. Dom, make us all another drink, please. Then we'll hear Vernon's story."

Vernon Lewis. Articulate, bright, embryo cop and aspiring novelist, he told his story short and sweet.

"Mr. Halloran, this doorman, Manny Resnick, was duck soup to make. For a supposedly top wise guy connection cop, this guy Sloane left himself very, very vulnerable with the stool pigeons he used. I gained access to the Hotel Manhattan very easily, disguised as a messenger boy. There are about a hundred messenger services all over town who employ black kids walking or riding around on bicycles. I guess you see one black messenger kid you've seen them all. I changed clothes every day to be on the safe side, but I guess Manny the doorman is one of those guys who figure all black kids look alike.

"I'm positive he never gave me a second thought. I finally made him and Sloane together, hooked up in a deep conversation. When Sloane left I tailed him to an apartment house on West Fifty-sixth Street, off Fifth Avenue. The same building where we found the madam Sloane was shaking down. Getting the information was easy. Manny was selling qualudes and amphetamines to hookers and pimps like they were jellybeans. A very busy doorman.

"I moved in on him real cool. A few days later I bought some Q's from him, the next day I gave him a couple of bets. Poor Manny, he nearly fainted when I pulled the shield on him. Never made me for a cop. Christ, I thought he would die before we got him to Dom and Frank." Everybody laughed; Vernon was funny.

"You know the rest, Mr. Halloran, it's all there in my report. Manny will tell us anything we want to know about Sloane, we let him off the hook. Manny definitely wants no part of jail. Neither does Willie. They're both dying down in the Tombs. One more thing, Manny's been with Sloane at least ten years. Should have a lot to say."

Halloran's face flushed with pleasure when Vernon finished. "I've arranged for Captain Maguire, whom you four will soon meet, to pick up Sloane tomorrow at his warrant squad office.

We've been assured that he's back home, due to return to work in the morning. His boss, Captain Keegan, has been alerted to make sure he's on hand, thinks it's just some routine matter. We definitely don't want to alarm Sloane just yet. Captain Maguire, once he has Sloane beside him in the car, will instruct his driver to take them downtown to the crime commission offices. We will begin our preliminary interrogation right there.

"As added ammunition we will transport Willie Baker and Manny Resnick from the Tombs to one of our adjacent offices. In the wings, as well, will be Blanche Gordon, the madam Sloane's been shaking down, and Brenda Farrell, the pretty policewoman who posed as one of Blanche's call girls.

"We're going to hit Sloane right between the eyes with what we have on him. No punches will be pulled. Down the line from shaking down gamblers, dope peddlers, and whorehouses—to a possible murder. He'll be looking at fifty years in jail if he doesn't turn, doesn't cooperate.

"Tommy Sloane will tell us what we want to know, do what we ask him to do. He's our key to putting the crime commission on the front page. I'll see you all downtown tomorrow at ten o'clock in the morning."

Tommy whistled a happy tune as he drove through the Midtown Tunnel and turned downtown towards his warrant squad office. He was in high spirits, well rested, felt wonderful. He arrived in the office about nine thirty in the morning. He was welcomed back with handshakes and friendly pats on the back from his fellow cops and sergeant, Walt Jackson. The ski slopes of Vermont and the burning sun of Florida had tanned his face a deep bronze. He was kidded with a few envious jibes—hey, Tom, go undercover in Harlem they'll never make you—hey Tom, you're darker than Walt Jackson—stand next to him, sarge, see's who's darker. Big laughs all around the squad room.

Tommy took the kidding good-naturedly. Smiled, laughed at their jokes, at peace with his private world. He had only one thing on his mind. Finish what work he had to do today and go to Constance's apartment to wait for her to come home and into his arms.

Captain Keegan came out of his office, greeted him warmly with a firm handshake. You look great, Tom. Thank you, captain. By the way, Tommy, I have a message for you, so stay put for a while. A Captain Maguire from downtown wants to see you. Didn't say what it was about. Probably just a routine matter. Thanks, cap, I'll sit here and wait for him.

A faint chill of apprehension hit Tommy's spine. Captain Maguire. What the hell does he want? Maguire. Name rings a bell. Christ, it should. I must have met a hundred guys on the Job named Maguire.

Captain Maguire arrived about half an hour later. Erect carriage, slim, gray-haired. Looked more like an aging Catholic priest than a police captain. He shook hands with Tom, introduced himself. Very cordial. He paid a quick courtesy visit to Captain Keegan. He came out of Keegan's office, suggested Tom put his hat and coat on. Do you mind if I ask where we're going, captain? Downtown! Just like that. Downtown. Tommy dutifully followed the priestly captain, decided it was wiser not to question the motives of a police captain.

An unmarked police cruiser was parked outside the Court Building with an obviously cop-looking guy behind the wheel. The captain walked right to the cruiser, ushered Tommy in first, followed him in. Tommy was beginning to get bad vibes. This is like one of those Russian spy books. The K.G.B. just grabbed me. He was right. Where to, captain? "The crime commission, Fred," said the captain, ignoring Tommy.

Jesus, Mary, and Joseph! The crime commission! Tommy fought the panic aroused at the sound of the dreaded words. Stay cool, be polite, try and bullshit your way out of this. Do you mind if I ask you a question, captain? Go ahead, Sloane. Ice cold. What is this all about? You'll soon find out, Officer Sloane. Just like that.

A frosty silence was the order of the day in the back seat of the car during the short ride downtown to the crime commission offices. Captain Maguire sat upright, very severe face. Tommy slumped back, hand on chin, pretending unconcern. But his mind was churning wildly. What the hell is this all about? As Captain Maguire said—he'd soon find out.

* * *

Jeff Halloran sat behind his desk with a confident air. Dominick Stabile, crack D.E.A. bloodhound, sat in a chair on his right.

Directly in front of Halloran sat Thomas Patrick Sloane. So this was their quarry, the contract champ of the Job, the shakedown artist without a peer. He's putting on his bullshit cool cop act. We'll see how cool he is after he finds out what we have on him.

Tommy was bewildered. The guy on Halloran's right he knew. Hung around P.J. Clarke's, Joe Amoroso. Nice guy, good spender. I'm sure he's a big shot printing salesman. What the hell is he doing here.

Dom Stabile spoke first. "How are you, Tommy?"

"Fine, Joe, how are you?"

Halloran interrupted, fat-cat grin on his face.

"Sloane, a slight correction. This man is Dominick Stabile, not Joe Amoroso. He's an undercover man for the crime commission. And I might add, a damn good one. He was Joe Amoroso, printing salesman, when he was clocking your action around town the last few months.

"Let's get right to the point, Sloane. You are in very serious trouble. Captain Maguire and two New York policemen are in the next room. They are ready to strip you of your shield and gun and book you for several crimes we positively know that you committed."

"Are you trying to scare me, Mr. Halloran? If I'm being accused of any crimes, may I call my lawyer?"

"I am being very factual, Sloane, not trying to scare you. Just hear me out, please. If we decide to book you, yes, you may certainly call your lawyer. We have something else in mind, Sloane. At present, we have not filed any charges against you. We are interrogating you as a policeman, Sloane. A policeman who is sworn to uphold the law. Whether we charge you or not depends on just how you cooperate with the crime commission, of which body I serve as chief counsel. Let me fill you in on just what we know about you.

"We have your two stool pigeons, Willie Baker and Manny

359

Resnick, under police guard in a room down the hall. We have had them under lock and key in the Tombs for two days. They have already told us enough to substantiate charges that could imprison you for a great number of years."

Tommy sat back, stunned, face turned almost white under his deep tan. Willie and Manny locked up! Jesus help me. The old cop saying flashed in his mind. Once a stoolie always a stoolie. These two pricks will bury me to save their own skins.

Halloran couldn't miss the look of dismay on Tommy's face. He's wilting fast, now the home run ball.

"Sloane, there are many serious charges that I think should be easy to prove. Your black pal, Willie Baker, is a drug user as well as a drug peddler. We have him pinned to the wall, a number of direct sales to one of our undercover men. When he blew up, he went all out. He's implicated you in a murder that occurred in West Harlem last year."

Tommy involuntarily bolted upright in his chair. Willie, that black fuck! Started to say something in his own defense. Bit his tongue. Keep quiet. Stay tight.

Halloran, half smile on his face, enjoying the torture, said, "We're aware that the victim was a stick-up guy, a junkie with a bad record. But you were not in that hallway on police business. You were there to make a score. The murder is on the books as unsolved and so far unreported. If reported you'll be lucky to get a manslaughter plea, Sloane. We have a witness besides Willie Baker who saw your snappy BMW pull away a couple of minutes after the shots were fired."

Beads of sweat appeared on Tommy's forehead. He could feel the sogginess in the armpits of his shirt.

Halloran looked hard, straight into Tommy's eyes.

"So much for your pal, Willie. Let's go on to your number two stool pigeon, Manny Resnick. You can sure pick them, Sloane. For a smart guy your brains were in your ass when you trusted these two. Resnick, your doorman informant, is another drug peddler. Mostly pills. He's also half a pimp and a small-time bookmaker. One of my undercover men bought pills from him, bet horses with him, could have done anything with him. Once confronted, put in jail, he gave us a complete rundown on his ten years of service with you. Manny has one helluva memory and he hates jail.

"Manny led us to Blanche Gordon, the madam you shook down for a couple of thousand a year ago. That's her, Blanche Gordon, who pays you five hundred dollars a month for offering her phony protection from the vice cops, another of your rackets. She's right here today with Brenda Farrell, a very pretty policewoman, who you thought was a call girl when Blanche paid you the monthly five hundred just before Christmas. You remember, Sloane, you slapped Brenda on the ass and told her that someday soon you'd like to give her a bang. We have it all on tape, Sloane, every word.

"Sloane, like all crooks, you got careless, too big for your own boots. To put it mildly, we have you right by the balls." He turned to Dom Stabile.

"Dom, go down the hall and bring Baker and Resnick in here."

Tommy sat in his chair, frozen, speechless.

A couple of minutes later Stabile brought Willie and Manny into the room. Willie was shaking, looked like he was ready to cry. Looked sadly at Tommy, said, "I'm sorry, Tommy boy," and let out a piercing wail, shaking everyone up. Dom Stabile grabbed him, hushed him up. Manny was silent, avoided Tommy's eyes, looked like Jean Valjean on the breadline after two days in the Tombs.

Halloran waved to Dom, take them away. He looked at Tom, said, "You want to see more, Sloane, we'll bring Blanche Gordon and Brenda Farrell in here. Then we'll play you the tape. Okay?

"I guess that little scene should satisfy you of just how much we have on you, Sloane. I want your decision right now, Sloane. Get it all off your chest. Just remember one thing, if you decide to cooperate, we call all the shots."

Tommy arose from the chair. His legs were wobbling. He didn't say a word, walked across the office to the window, looked out at the traffic and people bustling through the streets. One horrible thought kept repeating in his mind. Jail! Jesus Christ, jail! Confined to a six-by-eight cell for years. Christ, I even hated to lock guys in cells, always felt sorry for them. Me, Tommy Sloane, a cop, in jail. The stories I heard about the vicious way cops are treated in jail. Spit on, beat up, one poor ex-cop almost got his head cut off. Fuck that, no way it's for me.

What about Constance? What about Justine? Worse, what about Vinny? He'll never forgive me. But the main event is me, Tommy Sloane. What about this? This guy Halloran has me by the balls. Willie, Manny—even Blanche and that good-looking whore. Christ, a lady cop. That's the end! He turned away from the window, walked back to Halloran, voice a little unsteady.

"I guess you win, Mr. Halloran. I'll cooperate with you all the way. But you have to promise me that I won't go to jail."

Halloran jumped up from his chair. Stabile, who had just returned to the room, rushed over and shook Tommy's hand. Halloran shook his hand and said in a triumphant voice, "Great, Sloane, a good decision on your part. You have my word, Sloane, that you will get immunity, will not be prosecuted for your crimes. From now on, you will be in Dom's and his partner Frank Kurowski's hands. They will plot your further course of action. I will be in constant touch, on tap at all times. We will make sure that the secret will be well kept. We don't want a soul, except our inner circle, to know that you turned.

"When you return to the warrant squad just give them some horseshit story about why Captain Maguire wanted you. To identify some photos, anything. Carry on your police duties as usual. Arouse no suspicion. Be very discreet from now on. We intend to give Baker and Resnick pleas to misdemeanors, stash them in Rikers Island for six months. Keep them off the streets so they won't endanger your cover. Sound good to you, Sloane?"

"Sounds pretty good, Mr. Halloran. There's one thing bothering me. I'd hate to turn in a friend. There are loads of guys I can easily nail without hurting someone close to me."

Suddenly harsh-voiced, blue eyes steely, Halloran rasped, "Sloane, forget that friend horseshit. From now on you have no friends. We are after crooked cops, period. You will do as we say or your ass will be right back in a sling. You got that straight?"

Very subdued, contritely—"Yessir, Mr. Halloran."

Tommy and Dom Stabile left Halloran and entered an adjoining room where Dom introduced Tom to Frank Kurowski, his partner. Tommy speedily found out that they were no-non-sense authentic government D.E.A. undercover agents. Very knowledgeable, sharp guys. Now that he was on their team, they were pleasant and friendly enough for him to soon feel comfortable. He dismissed from his mind all misgivings about becoming an informer. He adhered to his old credo—better them than me.

They have me ice cold. I'm as dead as Kelsey's nuts. Might as well get this phase of my life over with and settle down some-where out West. What the hell, I've got over three hundred big ones stashed away in my safe deposit box. Thank Christ no-body knows about that money. Christ, that should give me a helluva start in a new business. I'll find something.

All of this was running around in his brain as Dom and Frank briefed him. Constance, Justine, and Vinny strayed into his mind as he listened to the D.E.A. men. Christ, pay atten-tion, forget everything, concentrate on what these guys are tell-ing me. By all means, stay out of jail.

In substance, it sounded easy. He would be on his own all the way. If he felt a situation called for a backup, Dom and Frank would be right behind him. The tape recorder intrigued him. For practice they wired him up, dismantled the wire, had him repeat the process. Perversely, he was fascinated by the idea of working with a wire.

It was a relatively simple device on the surface, but extremely sophisticated and well engineered. The minute recorder was set in a shoulder holster slung over his t-shirt, resting under-neath his dress shirt, concealed under his armpit. The micro-phone was a tiny disc imbedded in a tie clasp that looked like a small ruby. The mike was connected to the recorder by a length of extrusive wire, finer than human hair.

Tommy donned the fearsome mechanism, engaged Dom Sta-bile in some inconsequential conversation, and almost fainted at the clarity of their words as Dom played the tape back. Un-believable! He had bullshitted girlfriends, sweethearts, his wife, and countless guys on his undercover role. He spun tales of imagined cases he solved with tape recordings so often that he almost convinced himself the bullshit was actual fact. Now the moment of truth was at hand, the real McCoy.

Halloran looked in about an hour after Dom and Frank had finally polished Tommy's tape-recorder routine. He sat and had coffee with them and plotted their future assaults on graft and corruption. There were a few laughs as Tom and Frank discussed some of the eccentricities of a few of the guys who frequented P.J. Clarke's, Jim Costello's, and Jimmy Weston's.

Halloran was pleased to see the air of camaraderie that prevailed in the room. Beautiful! Less than two hours since he capitulated and Sloane is acting like one of the boys. He looked him over as Dom talked. Not a bad-looking guy. Cute as a rattlesnake. I hope I can trust the bastard. If not, I'll cut his balls off.

It was a stroke of luck to get his psychological profile from the navy department. Definitive claustrophobic tendencies. Were they ever right, still, that was many years ago. Sloane has to be some sort of tough guy. Christ, he killed at least three men we know about. Look at him laughing. Has to be one of the most devious bastards of all time. I better brace him up real well, let him know who's boss.

Halloran joined in the general laughter at another of Dom's funny stories. He held up his hand, signaling for quiet. Time to get serious, straighten this guy out. Sharp, federal prosecutor's voice—"Sloane, I'm pleased to see that you're accepting my men so good. However, I must reiterate, this is no fun and games business. We expect you to come across all the way. No bullshit, make-believe stories. Every bit of information you gather must be true, to be able to stand up in court. Don't come up with anything that isn't true just because it sounds good. One hundred percent on the level. Is that straight with you?"

Tommy nodded his head slowly. He was already beginning to hate this Irish prick he had to bow down to.

"We intend to make criminal cases out of whomever you entrap. You'll be subject to severe cross-examination by the defense, so we must have the truth. You do understand that, Sloane?"

"Mr. Halloran, you didn't get me here by chance. All of us here know I'm a professional. For years I've been testifying on the witness stand. I know how to handle a contract, to leave a loophole for the judge when I want to throw a case. I am also an expert at the old zinger, when I want to stick it into some guy's ass. Don't worry about my qualifications as a witness."

Halloran smiled, said, "That's the answer I want, Sloane. Hey, it's almost two o'clock. Suppose I take you guys for a couple of drinks and lunch. Tommy can fill us in a little on what he plans to do."

Well, one step in the right direction. Now it's Tommy.

They lunched in a small, side-street restaurant off lower Broadway. A few Cutty Sark and waters under his belt, Tommy regaled them with sensational tales of scores, pads, cousins, and outlaws. He was now a member of the team, joined in the unholy alliance to bury his fellow cops. At one point, he excused himself to use the men's room. When he left the table the three inquisitors just shook their heads. They couldn't believe their ears nor their good fortune in the target they selected. Tommy Sloane was their man, all right. He was almost too good to be true.

They shook hands good-bye outside the restaurant like old college chums after a reunion luncheon. From here in the agreed-upon future rendezvous was Frank and Dom's Tudor City apartment. Tom was issued keys and told to report there after he finished his warrant squad duties. The recording devices were to be kept there. Tom was to put his recorder on there and remove it there, so that Dom could maintain a secret file of the tapes. Only W. Phelps Sinclair and Halloran, Dom and Frank were to know of Tommy's function in their weaving of the net.

Don't alter your daily routine, Tom. Go to work in the warrant squad as always. Keep up your visits to your favorite saloons. Be very visible. We'll never be seen together. We'll only communicate by either a visit to the apartment or by the unlisted phone there. Pick your spots. We want a half dozen or so underworld guys and as many cops as we can nail. We're bound to turn a few of them. Okay, Tom, that's about it. You have all the scoop on the apartment. Keys, phone number, whatever. Take it nice and easy, stay in touch at all times with Dom and Frank. And, Tom, watch your ass.

He left his three brand-new pals and walked north on Broadway to where his BMW was parked. It was a good walk, over a mile, but he desperately wanted to think things out. The frigid January air cleared his head of the strong Scotch whiskey that helped reduce the tension at lunch. The late afternoon dark clouds hung low, almost blotting out the spires of the taller skyscrapers along Broadway. The threat of heavy winter snow was again in the air.

The dank skies were a perfect match for Tommy's now despondent mood. His moods since arising this fatal day were mercurial, alternating from the highs of anticipation of Constance to the stark realization that he now was the lowest form of cop, a *scumbag*. He trudged along the snowy sidewalks enveloped in gloom.

Jesus Christ, they turned me. What a fucking expression! They turned me. They turned me into a fucking rat. What'll Vinny say once he finds it out? And lots of other guys. I'm supposed to be a tough guy and tough guys don't rat. Yeah, that's right. Tough guys keep their mouths shut and go to jail. Or worse, the electric chair.

Well, I guess I'm not so tough, after all. One sure thing, I want no part of fucking jail. I get chills just thinking about jail and what happened to some poor cops who went to jail. I broke my balls, hustled day and night, took plenty of chances and made plenty of cash. I'll be a sonofabitch if I'm going to rot in a shithouse cell up the river.

The hell with it. I'm glad I turned. Suppose Halloran and his crew put the Internal Revenue on my ass. Then give me a federal bit besides. No, sir. I'll do what they tell me. When it's all over, I'll pack New York in. Go away with Constance, start a new life. I can't worry about Justine, Vinny, my sister, Rosemary. I'm just taking care of myself.

Jesus Christ, why didn't I listen to Vinny? He pleaded with me. Get the hell out of the Job. I was doing too good, too goddam hungry. Jesus, will he be pissed off at me. Maybe no one will ever know. Fat chance, that's just wishful thinking.

He was sitting having a drink when Constance arrived home. She kissed him, asked him to fix her a drink while she changed. He had schemed a good hour before she arrived home just how he would have her do his bidding. He had no intention of confiding one word to her about the crime commission and his recent entanglement. He laughed, kidded, drank, talked about the world in general. Acted as he ordinarily would, waited for the proper opening to broach what was uppermost on his mind. She gave it to him.

"I'm going to fix dinner home, Tommy, it looks like it's going to snow tonight. I have some lamb chops I bought for your homecoming."

She got up from the couch, kissed him tenderly on the lips, ruffled his hair. Husky voice.

"You look wonderful, you bastard, leaving me alone for two weeks while you soaked up the sun in Florida."

He held her face in his hands, tremulous voice—"It won't happen again, love. I'm leaving Justine as soon as I get my affairs in shape."

"No, Tommy, you're not?" Almost a squeal of joy.

"I am, babe, I really am. Make another drink, hold dinner for a while, we'll talk about it."

For the next half hour he poured out the story he had concocted while waiting for Constance. Only thing bothers me, sweetheart, is that she knows that I was left a lot of cash in a safe deposit box by my grandmother. She never trusted banks. My grandfather was a big bootlegger during Prohibition, and she kept this cash in a vault. Justine knows about the vault, but not exactly how much. It's in both our names and she has a key, although she's never used it.

Suppose you rent a safe deposit box, I'll be your brother, and we'll transfer the money as soon as possible. I'll leave a few thousand in my old box just in case she wants half the money when I ask her for a divorce.

Oh, Tommy, sure we'll do that. It was your grandmother's, it's your money. Any time you say. I'll make the arrangements tomorrow.

Two days later all of Tommy's ill-gotten gains was transferred from his safe deposit box in Queens to Constance's newly acquired one in her New York bank. As planned beforehand, Constance glibly introduced Tom to the young bank executive as her brother, explaining that they both wanted a joint safeguard for some important family documents. Of course, Miss Ward, Mr. Ward. No problem, pleased to accommodate you. No problem. Pay the fee. No questions asked. Sometimes banks were wonderful.

Earlier in the morning, Tommy removed most of his money from his safe deposit box. It was in bundles of ten thousand. All in hundred dollar bills. He stuffed twenty packages into an old school briefcase, a battered memento of his Bishop Molloy days. The amount caused the briefcase to bulge perceptibly and, not wanting to arouse any alarm or suspicion in Constance, he took off to New York with two hundred thousand dollars.

Constance waited outside the bank vault chamber while he placed the two hundred thousand dollars in the friendly confines of the deep steel box. Outside the bank, she kissed him a quick good-bye and grabbed a taxi to her office. He had arranged the morning off with Walt Jackson, pleading pressing family business. How true, he mused outside the bank. Might as well transfer the rest of the cash.

He hopped into his BMW and sped over the bridge to his own bank once more. He removed the remainder of the money from his safe deposit box. Twelve more packages, one hundred twenty thousand dollars, went into the briefcase and two packages, of ten thousand and one of five thousand were stuffed into his camelhair coat pockets.

He drove to his home in Whitestone and secreted the twenty-five thousand dollars from his coat pockets to a hatbox on his closet shelf in the master bedroom. Just in case, a little emergency stash. He then drove back to Constance's bank in New York, was given a cheerful "Hello, Mr. Ward" by the bank vault guard, and lovingly placed the remainder of the money in the deep steel box. He slammed the box shut, turned the key, and breathed a sigh of relief.

Mission accomplished, thank God. He sat behind the wheel of his BMW, a heavy burden lifted from his shoulders. Let them find my fortune now. He looked at his watch, eleven fifteen. Two hours to go before I report to Tudor City. I could sure use a drink. He drove as if by radar straight to J.G. Melon. The front door was locked. He saw B.J. the bartender, knocked on the window and was let in with a hearty handshake. Have a drink, Tom. You bet. Same, Cutty on the rocks? Make it a double, B.J. Coming up, Tommy boy. He sipped the mellow Scotch contentedly, the blood again flowing warmly through his veins. Life was once again worth living. His hard-earned money was safe and sound.

The Tudor City apartment soon became more a part of his police life than the warrant squad office. Dom and Frank rehearsed Tommy endlessly in the procedures to be used in the sting operation that lay ahead. The tempting gainful propositions and leading questions to be asked to forever entrap the corrupt. To reveal their venal greed into the slowly winding coils of the well-hidden tape recorder.

Once he was pronounced skillful and devious enough for battle they planned a very arduous schedule for Tommy. Ever the vigilant government agents, they insisted the government share in the spoils that Tommy's efforts would result in. They explained to him that a bribe offered to any type of police officer was a federal offense. As Tommy listened to this startling news, he silently thought of what a simple way that would be to wipe out organized crime. Christ, in about two weeks half the F.B.I. and federal district attorneys would be out of work.

Their argument was that the U.S. Government had aided the crime commission in many ways. Money, undercover men from their own agencies, and access to forbidden secret files. It was only proper that the U.S. Government should be rewarded with their share of the catch. Of course, it wasn't mentioned what sensational headlines the publicity-hungry federal attorneys would garner in prosecution of prominent underworld figures.

Tommy listened, nodded affirmatively, meanwhile making silent reservations about whom he would attempt to entrap. No way was he going to implicate the real big shots of the underworld. He knew that he would have to migrate to Alaska or North China to avoid getting his head chopped off.

He went into his act after a few days of training. His ploy was a simple one, devised strictly by himself, drawn from his long years of experience. A veritable army of gamblers and wise guys knew him personally. They regarded him as a friend, a benevolent protector of their illicit enterprises for years.

His story was almost foolproof as he had been playing the role for some time. He was one of four plainclothes cops on a new citywide supersquad, set up by the mayor's office. You know, Tony, Sonny, Mikie, Leroy, Carlo—to investigate all this corruption horseshit.

He spread his story around various parts of the city, never overworking a particular area. He made a meet with his intended victim, confidentially assured him that he would never be bothered, and casually pocketed the hundred dollar introductory fee that was eagerly pressed into his willing hand.

Dom Stabile and Frank Kurowski were flabbergasted when the tapes were played back. You're some number, Tommy, a real winner. We could sure use a guy like you in the D.E.A. Big grin, maybe I'll take you guys up on it, must be *some* scores to be made there. The only flaw in the operation was the lack of the real name of the victim. The gamblers and hoodlums caught in the net were all named Louie the Gimp, Irish Mike, Harry the Jew, Cheech, or the like. Some of them probably couldn't even remember their Christian or Jewish names, they were so used to their nicknames.

Discreet cross-checking with police and government files, plus photographs, soon identified them properly and Tommy was finally pulled off that facet of the investigation. Eleven unsuspecting friends of Tommy Sloane were culled from the incriminating tapes and readied for eventual indictment.

Dom and Frank reported their findings to Halloran and stressed the value of Tommy to the investigation. Their chief was pleased with the initial results. He did have some reservations. There's not one top underworld big shot on the list. Why not? Sloane claims he doesn't know the top bananas. Anyway, they stay in the background, aloof from the everyday operations. Well, maybe we can break one of these guys and reach the higher-ups.

Halloran became just a bit tight-lipped. Dom, what about crooked cops? When are we going to start getting solid evidence on some of Sloane's friends on the police force? Tommy has started already, boss, nice and easy. He's one smart sonofabitch. He's spreading the word that he's the contact for a really big high-roller floating crap game. À la Las Vegas! We should have some progress by next week. Good, Dominick, get his ass into high gear. Mr. Sinclair wants to hold the hearings by early spring. No problem, chief.

Tommy continued to live pretty much the same life as an informer as he did ordinarily. A sorrowful and major difference was that he no longer was making his cherished scores. He incurred some expenses making his almost daily rounds and was allowed to submit an expense sheet. A sheet that was invariably subjected to minute scrutiny. $108.75? Why so much, Tommy? He would flush and feel like screaming out—for Christ sake, I used to give $108.75 in one night to singing waiters out in Rockaway!

However, he kept quiet, bit his tongue, scrupulously itemized his extravagance. The veiled threat of jail always hung over his head, especially when confronted by Halloran. I hope you understand, Sloane, that you do as we say. We call the shots here, not you. Yessir, Mr. Halloran.

He chafed under the pressure, got his back up a couple of times. Just to keep in practice and have a few extra dollars in his pocket to wine and dine Constance, Tommy made an occasional secret shakedown. One in particular was heart-warming and very profitable. A high-roller horse room in the Seventies on Park Avenue. A real rocking chair, smooth as silk, fifteen hundred. He received the tip innocently while in the middle of a group of his drinking pals in Jimmy Weston's. A young Wall Street broker described the layout perfectly. Carelessly thrown-about tips like this came easily to Tommy. Well dressed, with his urbane manner he blended chameleonlike into a few such groups, no one realizing for a moment that he was a cop. Certainly not a cop interested in any gambling bullshit, only real, important crime.

He arranged his free time almost equally between Justine and Constance. Constance was up in the clouds about his plans for divorce and their eventual marriage. A couple of times he was tempted to confide in her his present precarious situation, but always rejected the idea. He made love to her, caressed her afterwards, held her close, her head on his chest while he mapped out their future together with his fingers crossed. What the hell am I going to tell her when the shit hits the fan?

Christ almighty, common sense dictates that I have to be exposed someday soon. That Irish prick, Halloran, keeps breathing down my neck. Make sure you get concrete evidence, Tommy, we need the whole truth. You will be subjected to rigorous cross-examination on the witness stand. You bet, with the whole world looking on. No question, the moment of truth is coming soon. Jesus, everyone will know I'm a stool pigeon.

Fuck the world, I want to get off. Yessir, off to the great wide West with my loving baby, Constance. Justine, well, er, I'll take good care of her. Only fair after sixteen years of marriage. I have to admit, she was a good wife. Vinny! What'll I do about him? How the hell will he take it? Christ, I get a blinding pain over my right eye just thinking about Vince. I've only called him twice in two months. Bawled the shit out of me last time I called. What to do?

Six weeks later.

Jeff Halloran and W. Phelps Sinclair sat having lunch at Michaels Of John Street. It was a gracious, deceptively large restaurant in the heart of the financial district, a few short blocks from Sinclair's Wall Street law office. Their first dry Beefeater martini was already stirring their blood, their juices enlivened with the warm glow induced by the delicious drink. Their shared euphoria had started with their short walk in the unexpected balmy weather. The lukewarm, gusty breezes blowing through the stunted side streets off lower Broadway were a welcome herald of early spring.

They were both in an exuberant mood, matching the sunny

skies New Yorkers had long awaited. Their mission was coming to a climax. Their debt to the people of New York would soon be cleared, the police force free of graft and corruption. The ensuing headlines that would damn the police would surely propel Sinclair to his cherished goal of a federal judgeship. Halloran, twenty years junior to Sinclair, nursed higher ambitions of public office. In the future, perhaps, dear God, the United States Senate.

They exchanged inconsequential conversation along their walk and through the first martini. Inquiries of the family's well-being, their golf handicaps, and their mutual friend the mayor's presidential hopes. The second martini came, dry and crisp. They tipped glasses reverently. Halloran quickly got down to the nitty-gritty.

"Phelps, I asked you for lunch today because I've put together something which I believe will meet with not only your approval, but with your whole-hearted support. The plan is very controversial and I reserved my answer until I discussed it with you. Phelps, it's a bonanza, the chance of a lifetime."

Sinclair smiled, a bit vacuously. The second martini in Michaels would make Rodin "The Thinker" smile.

"Get on with it, Jeff. What's the great surprise?"

Halloran cleared his throat, said, "Phelps, I've been approached by some higher-up TV executives to televise the forthcoming crime commission hearings." Halloran failed to say that he had mentioned at a party at his country club that the crime commission, long thought dead, was about to unfold some sensational exposures. At his table was the TV biggie who went for the bait. He pressed Halloran further and gave him a commitment if Halloran could clear it with Sinclair.

Halloran let Sinclair digest this juicy morsel, continued, "We've had further talks and the TV people seem to be enthusiastic. They need a time span of a month or so to arrange their schedules and assign the desired personnel. What's your opinion, Phelps?"

Sinclair was a trifle stunned, his brain racing. Television! Oh, how wonderful! He immediately conjured up the image of Estes Kefauver, the racket-busting senator of the early fifties. Good heavens, I've been told a few times that I resembled

Estes, an old friend. Now almost twenty years later I'll be Senator Kefauver reincarnated. He spoke excitedly.

"Jeff, I think it's a marvelous idea, simply marvelous. How in the world did you arrange it?"

"It wasn't easy, Phelps, just luck and some hard work. Fortunately, I play golf with some top executives in the TV world. A big help. But Phelps, a few obstacles have arisen that I think you can handle."

"Go ahead, Jeff, what are the problems?"

"The new police commissioner is dead set against the idea. He's trying to persuade the mayor to kill it. My source at police headquarters said that the P.C. screamed bloody murder at the mere idea of television. I'm sure that Frank, our esteemed district attorney, won't look with favor on our television concept when he learns about it."

"Jeff, you carry on with your plans. Don't worry the mayor, I'll personally overcome any objections that he might have. We'll make sure to give him a little air time and lots of credit. He'll love that. Fine, Jeff, just fine. Now give me the latest rundown on exactly what we've got to offer the public."

"Phelps, this cop Sloane is a gem. And I don't exactly mean a diamond in the rough. He's good-looking, a great dresser, and the best actor of the century. Sloane has produced evidence on tape, solid enough for indictment of about thirty men. I believe about twenty are currently policemen. I curtailed him for a while. We only have street and vice cops ready for indictment. I plan to have Sloane entrap a boss. First maybe a squad lieutenant who might later crack and implicate an inspector or perhaps a deputy chief. Do you agree, Phelps?"

"Excellent idea, Jeff. Fine thinking."

"One more obstacle before we order lunch. We have this cop Sloane undercover so deep no one has the faintest inkling that he has turned. We must reveal his identity in a few weeks. Certainly a week before we go on TV. He's the worst sort of crook and I don't care one bit if anything should happen to him. However, I think to cover ourselves we should put him under the protection of federal marshals. More or less like the Alias Program."

"Splendid, Jeff. I'll arrange protection for Sloane even

though he doesn't deserve it. Good, Jeff, let's order our lunch. I'm starved."

The following day Tommy arrived at the Tudor City apartment rendezvous about one o'clock. He was in a high mood after a dynamite night spent with Constance. They had dinner and danced at the Rainbow Room, continued on to Jimmy Weston's to drink another bottle of Moët & Chandon and dance until almost closing. They made terrific love upon returning to Constance's apartment, slept late as neither had to get to work early, and capped their miraculous episode with the best lovemaking of their lives in the morning. She made breakfast and over a second cup of coffee urged him to get started on his divorce plans. He looked at her worshipfully, said he sure would, and wondered how the hell she was going to accept what lay ahead for him.

What the hell, it'll be all over soon and I'll be in her arms forever. He let himself into the apartment with his own keys. Uh oh, look who's here? Mr. Halloran, himself, with his federal D.A.'s face on.

Halloran, Dom, and Frank greeted their star cop-catcher very cordially. They were engrossed in playing back some of the more incriminating tapes, everyone getting a big laugh out of some of the funny things heard on the playbacks. A sudden thought hit Tommy. You can bet your ass these poor cops won't laugh when they hear the tapes.

The atmosphere was very congenial. Tommy was laughing, happy, still in the afterglow of Constance. Halloran hit him by surprise, like a low blow straight to his balls. He looked directly at Tommy, his voice suddenly harsh, tough prosecutor intonation.

"Tommy, I came here especially to talk to you today. I understand you're very friendly with Lieutenant Peter Dowd, the boss of the Borough West Squad."

On your guard, Tom, this guy Halloran is getting cute again. He shrugged noncommittally, said, "Well, I know him, Mr. Halloran, but I wouldn't go so far as to say I was very friendly with him."

Halloran shook his head in exasperation, said, "Tommy, I've

warned you a couple of times, don't try and bullshit me or you'll be on your ass in a Tombs cell before the day is out. I know goddam well that you're friendly with Dowd, see him regularly for a drink together. I'm also concerned that we haven't caught one Borough West man in the net. You have nailed a few division men who come under the overall supervision of the Borough West. How come no Borough West men? Could it be a show of loyalty to your ex-alma mater?"

Tommy looked at him, hate in his eyes. I'd love to shoot this know-it-all Irish fuck right between the eyes. Ah shit, what's the use? He has me right by the balls.

He answered in a humble voice, face downcast.

"It's not that way at all, Mr. Halloran. The Borough guys are too shrewd. I thought they might make my story for a phony—all bullshit. A top guy wanting to run a floating crap game would certainly contact one of them. Why the hell would he need me? The division guys are a different breed, they figure that I'm still well connected in the Borough West. That's how they fell so easily for my scam."

Halloran, listening intently, fingered his chin. Dom and Frank sat by wordlessly, not daring to interrupt the boss. The relentless bounty hunter continued, "It sounds plausible, Sloane. Maybe someone else might go for your story, Sloane, but don't you understand that we've had you *tailed* constantly. Our reports show that you've met Peter Dowd several times, had drinks with him, acted like the best of friends.

"Our present plans are to have the crime commission open hearings within a month. Sloane, I don't deny the fact that you've done some excellent work. We've nailed a good number of cops and quite a few hoodlums. But let's fact it. Sloane, we have not nailed one boss. Just suppose, for instance, we implicate a well-hung lieutenant like Peter Dowd—he in turn might lead us to his deputy chief inspector. The golden boy of the Job. Chief Driscoll. Handsome, photogenic, bachelor, very bright, forty-four years old. A real-life glamour cop. Privately, we have information that the only reason he will never steal a railroad car is because he could never lift it.

"C'mon, Sloane, the goddam West Side is still running wide open and you know it. From Greenwich Village to West

Harlem. Let's cut out the shit, Sloane. Get that tape recorder on and bring me Lieutenant Peter Dowd. We'll take over from there. That's an order, Sloane, get moving."

Tommy was seething with rage as he walked up to East Forty-third Street and turned left to Second Avenue, the escape route from Tudor City. Christ, I really need a drink to calm me down. He stopped at one of the boy meets girl bars on Second Avenue where he was sure no one knew him. It was three o'clock in the afternoon and the saloon was almost deserted. Good. No jokes, no barroom levity today.

He ordered a double Cutty Sark on the rocks, water on the side. He sipped his drink and silently cursed the first day he met Jeff Halloran. That no good Irish bastard. He was also pissed off at Dominick and Frank for not coming to his defense. Those two no good fucks. Pat me on the ass one minute and stick it into me the next minute. Those crime commission pricks. A bunch of rats, two-faced bastards.

He finished his drink, felt a shade better about the world, and ordered another. He sipped the second drink slowly, thoughtfully. What the hell's the sense worrying? If it's between me and Peter Dowd, better it be Peter Dowd. All this shit will be over in a month, anyway. I'll take my cash and run away with Constance. She can always get a good job and I can start some kind of business. What about Justine? Too bad, Justine, I can't worry about you.

He went to the wall phone in the rear of the bar, dialed Lieutenant Peter Dowd's number. Hi, Pete, this is Tommy. How about a drink? Yeah, it's a little important. Good. Kean's Chop House at five o'clock. See you, Pete.

Later the same evening. Tommy Sloane lay stretched full length on the long couch in the living room of Constance's apartment. He did not expect her until a bit later. She had told him when she left late this morning that she had some important clients in town and would probably be detained. He was peaceful in his solitude, head propped up by two large pillows

377

as he contemplated his day. A tall Scotch and water was in easy reach on the cocktail table next to him. He had dozed fitfully for about an hour and awakened with a throbbing headache. Two aspirin and a strong Scotch on the rocks eased the pain.

His thoughts were filled with the hour and a half he had earlier spent with Peter Dowd. Jesus Christ, Peter fell into his trap like a cub lion separated from his doting mother. Pete went for his trumped-up crap game hook, line and sinker. What a fish! The faithful little recorder tucked away in the shoulder holster under his armpit was one busy sonofabitch for the hour or so they drank in Kean's.

Tommy smiled, pleased with himself. He liked Peter Dowd, but tough luck, Pete. He had to keep Halloran happy to save his own ass. Wait until he plays this beauty back tomorrow. That will keep the Irish bastard satisfied. I think I'll hit him for a couple of weeks vacation as a reward. Walt Jackson will surely okay it. I'll see if Constance can arrange at least a week. I'll bullshit Justine. Super idea!

Tommy reached for his Scotch on the cocktail table, took a long belt. He reviewed the cocktail hour with Pete. A high roller floating crap game. Great idea, Tommy, I love it. The guys running it one hundred percent? Two hundred, Pete. You say so, I go along, Tommy boy. You say they have three locations ready to go on my side of the borough? That's the word, Pete. Perfect, Tom.

Okay, Peter, then I can go back and say that you gave me the green light? Absolutely, Tom. How much will it cost, Peter? For a good pal like you, Tom, I'll be reasonable. I want you to look good, make a nice score. Thanks, Pete. Okay, what's the number? How about fifteen hundred for me and the big boss and fifteen hundred for the men?

Sounds very reasonable, Pete. Great, Tom, when will you get back to me? A day or two, Peter.

The few Scotches he had with Tommy added to the few he had before he met Tom certainly loosened Peter's tongue. Tommy grinned in reminiscence. Tommy, I can't believe it, it's going so great. My kids will never see a poor day. I have plenty socked away for their education. They'll never have to break their ass the way I did. The same with my wife, Margaret. Anything happens to me, she and the kids are set for life. There's nothing like making a lot of cash. I owe a lot to you, Tommy, you were a big help getting us started in the Borough West.

Tommy reached out for his drink, took another nice belt. Poor Peter, you'll sure have a lot to answer for when that Irish prick Halloran goes to work on you. And your matinee idol boss, Chief Ray Driscoll, won't be smiling into the cameras on his way to the crime commission. Too bad, boys, better you than me. Wait until I play this tape back tomorrow for Halloran, Frank, and Dominick. I guarantee they'll all come at once. A triple orgasm! He laughed.

Tommy settled back comfortably in the broad leather lounge chair in the living room of the Tudor City apartment. His solemn face never betrayed his amusement as he watched the growing exultation registering on the faces of Halloran, Dom, and Frank as the fatal tape unwound. It was incredibly damaging to Peter Dowd. How in the name of Christ would Peter ever wiggle out of this trap? The insidious tape at last whined down to a halt.

Halloran broke the hush in the room, big grin on his Irish face.

"Tommy, it's unbelievable. I knew you could do it. This is the final nail in the coffin of the New York cops. We've got this crooked Lieutenant Peter Dowd by the balls. I can't wait to see his face when we confront him with this tape. He's going to drop dead. We'll offer him no choice. Either Dowd gives up his movie star deputy chief or we'll put his ass in jail for five years. Terrific work, Tom, absolutely terrific."

Tommy stood up, preening at Halloran's compliment. Tremendously pleased with himself, a tough job well done. His turn to break into a big grin. Halloran's calling me Tommy again. Means he now loves me. Okay, Tommy, be humble, jerk this guy Halloran off a little. Get that two-week vacation while he's in a good mood.

"Thanks a lot, Mr. Halloran. Honestly, sir, I never thought he would go for my act so easily." Another bullshit lie. He knew in his heart that Peter Dowd completely trusted him. The only reason he kept him off his list was because he really liked Pete. Besides, Vince was responsible for putting them together, for his getting so close to Pete. Jesus Christ, Vince! I sure hope he doesn't get wind of this. Shit, what else could I do?

Halloran, Dom, and Frank sat quietly discussing the implications of the damaging tape, their next set of moves. They had the one big fish they needed, had him dead right. Their future strategy remained to be mapped out. Halloran turned to Tommy with a benign, big brother smile. I'd just as soon this devious bastard get the hell out of here, not hear about our future plans. He said, "Tommy, you can leave now if you wish. You've done some great work. As a matter of fact, why don't you take the rest of the week off?"

"Great, Mr. Halloran. Thanks a lot, real nice of you. By the way, Mr. Halloran, I've been under a lot of pressure the last few months. I'm very tired, sleeping very badly. I'd sure love a couple of weeks vacation. It looks like you're ready to wrap up with the crime commission hearings to be held inside a month from now. I assume you'll really need me then. I'd like to be rested and fresh when I testify. You know, in a good frame of mind. How about it?"

Halloran paused, deliberated his reply. I sure don't want this wise-ass crook to know I plan to have the hearings on network television. Who knows? He's liable to chicken out, take it on the lam. The crooked prick must have a bundle stashed somewhere. But what choice do I have? I'll make his vacation conditional. Give him a couple weeks off, when he returns I'll put him immediately under the protection of the U.S. Marshals. The Alias Program. When I have him safely under guard, I'll reveal his identity. I'll then call a press conference and break the news about the open TV hearings. We should get spectacular press coverage long before we appear on TV. Good old Phelps Sinclair will love the idea.

"You want two weeks off, right, Tommy? It's fine with me but I'll have to clear it with Mr. Sinclair. I'm sure it can be arranged. However, there must be certain conditions. I must know exactly where you are at all times. You do understand why, Tommy? Exactly where, at all times."

"No problem, Mr. Halloran. I'll call Dom and Frank collect every day. That sound okay?"

"Sounds good. Okay, you can leave now, Tommy. Once again, a great piece of work."

Tommy went directly home, already beginning to scheme an excuse for his projected ten-day vacation with Constance. He had drinks and hors d'oeuvres ready for Justine when she came home from work. She was thrilled by his consideration, overjoyed when he said they were dining out, and over-whelmed when he announced that he was home through the entire weekend. He glibly explained to Justine that his heavy case load had lessened for a few days in preparation for a really heavy assignment out of town.

Actually, Constance earlier in the day had informed him that she had to spend the coming weekend with her boss at his Connecticut estate. The big clients who were in town would be his guests and he insisted that she be there as well.

Tommy spent the next three days with Justine. He treated her royally. He took her out to dinner every night, made love to her twice, and couldn't believe how much he enjoyed her. She was really a great girl. And so completely naïve. She sure went for my story about probably having to leave for Georgia next week. Heavy case, Justine, probably take eight to ten days to wrap it up. Just be careful, please, Tommy, don't get hurt.

It was going to be rough on her when he broke the sad news that he was divorcing her. But let's face it, I'm totally in love with Constance, nothing is going to deter my future with her. We'll start life anew together. Where? Only his pagan god could answer that.

He knew deep down that it would be a murderous ordeal to take the witness stand against the guys who trusted him. Christ, especially Peter Dowd. Vinny? Oh, God, how badly he'll take it. He'll never forgive me. Losing the best friend I have in the world. Well, tough luck, Vince, I'm not going to jail for anybody.

I'll testify and when I'm finished I'll pack in the Job. When the shit hits the fan I'll break the sad news to Justine. She can have the house and I'll lay another twenty-five grand on her. Shit, the least I can do after sixteen years with her. I'll submerge for a while, resurface somewhere under a new identity. Dom and Frank assured me that it would be a cinch. There's a hundred guys at least in the informant program, leading normal lives under an alias. As soon as I'm settled I'll send for Constance and part of the cash. We'll make it, baby.

All this was going through Tommy's mind as he drove his BMW to New York on Monday. He foresaw no problem with Walt Jackson about taking his vacation. Later in the day he would book reservations for him and Constance at Doral Country Club in Miami. Miami was still alive this time of year. Plenty of night life. They would both love it.

After her Connecticut business trip, Constance joined Tommy in Florida. The Doral Country Club proved even better than their advertising brochure claimed it to be. They played tennis every morning, swam in the Olympic-sized pool in the afternoon, and dined and danced every night. To break the routine they enjoyed dinner and dancing at the Palm Bay and Jockey clubs a couple of nights. It was a fabulous trip. Miami and Miami Beach was like a fairyland to them. They made love every night, slept in each others arms, and made all sorts of grandiose plans for their future together.

Tommy's high spirits were slowly waning. The vacation was coming to an end. As the final day neared, he tried to tell himself to discuss his precarious personal life with Constance. She was certain that he was a hero cop, a dedicated foe of crime, a faithful servant of the people. He had assumed the pose of a top crimefighter, an undercover man without a peer. Regaled her with outrageous stories of his feats in combatting crime. He had bullshitted Constance almost as much as he bullshitted Justine.

Happy and smiling on the surface, his heart was as dark and heavy as the jet stream of the plane that swiftly cut through the skies on their return to New York. As promised, he had called Dom and Frank a few times. Nothing new. Have a good time,

Tommy, relax. Yeah, relax my Irish ass. He turned in his seat, looked at Constance, asleep next to him. Beautiful tanned face, eyes closed in tranquil repose. How tranquil will she be when the balloon bursts? When she found out the guy she loved was an informer? A stool pigeon? Or the label in the Job—a scumbag?

Thursday, four days later. An overcast, gloomy, early spring afternoon matched Tommy's somber mood. Tommy again sat in the lounge chair in the living room of the Tudor City apartment rendezvous. But he sat poised on the edge of the chair, worried, sick to his stomach. Halloran, Dom, and Frank were present. They all seemed unconcerned, an attitude that heightened Tommy's irritation. Dom mixed everyone a drink. Halloran, as usual, had the floor. He said, "Well, it had to come some time, there's no use bitching about it. The word is definitely out that Sloane has turned, that he has been our chief source of information. It's spread around the city like wildfire. I've already arranged for a team of U.S. Marshals to guard Tommy twenty-four hours a day. From now until the conclusion of the hearings, and possibly for sometime afterwards, Tommy, you will be under guard around the clock."

Dom and Frank nodded their heads in agreement. Tommy didn't say a word. Halloran continued, "When did you get the first inkling, Tommy, that you had blown your cover?"

"Some inkling, Mr. Halloran. Yesterday morning about ten o'clock, I received a phone call at my warrant squad office. I didn't recognize the guy's voice. Anyway, he practically screamed into the phone. Called me every kind of rat bastard, rotten scumbag. Promised they'd blow my fucking head off before I got a chance to bury anybody. I was a little shook up, but I cooled it around the office, left early. I then called Dominick and told him about the phone call. Today I reported to my office as usual. Every guy there turned his back to me, wouldn't say a word to me. Treated me like shit. Even my sergeant, Walt Jackson, snubbed me completely. I got out of there fast. I called Dom again and he told me to drive home, pack some clothes and come to Tudor City. Here I am, Mr. Halloran."

"Well, it's unfortunate, Tommy, but it had to come sooner or later. The hearings are scheduled two weeks from today." Halloran walked over to the bar, freshened his drink and said very laconically, as if he were telling the time of day. "We really are running a bit tight—we have loads of work to do. Mr. Sinclair wants everything pitch perfect when the crime commission hearings are televised on network TV."

Tommy, momentarily shocked, exploded out of his chair. He shouted, "Television? Oh, no, for Christ sake, I'm not going to be on television? You're only kidding, Mr. Halloran, aren't you?"

Sharp voice, again the tough prosecutor—"I'm not kidding, Sloane, just stating facts. The mayor and Mr. Sinclair have made all the arrangements—" another bullshit lie. Halloran continued, his voice harsher.

"The crime commission hearings will be televised to give the citizens of New York a broader view of the widespread graft and corruption that currently infests the police force. The mayor and Mr. Sinclair are in accord. That's it, Sloane."

Tommy sat down, hands held to his face. He was stunned. Christ, what Halloran just said can't be true. But it was true. He would be up there on national TV squealing his head off. Be marked forever as a stool pigeon. Fuck it, I won't do it. He blurted out, "No good, Mr. Halloran, no way I'm going on national TV. Forget about it. I don't give a good fuck what you do to me. Get yourself another boy."

Halloran's face reddened with anger. In an icy voice, with barely controlled anger, in almost strangled tones, he said, "Sloane, you listen to me. I warned you once and now I'll warn you for the last time. We have everything we need by now to make our big splash. We'll go on television with or without you. But you better make up your mind right now to do the fuck what I tell you to do. If you refuse, you'll be handcuffed and thrown ass over head into a cell in the Tombs. When I finish up adding all the charges pending against you, they'll throw the goddam key away. From now on, keep your mouth shut. You do as I say, period. Is that straight enough, Sloane?"

Oh, God, would I love to put a couple of shots into this Irish prick. But he's got me dead right. I sure as hell want no part of the Tombs. Humbly, contritely—"I'm sorry, Mr. Halloran. It's just the whole idea of being on TV shook me up. You know, caught me by surprise."

Dom Stabile broke in with a humorous attempt to soften the tense atmosphere in the living room. He said, "C'mon, Tommy, you're a born ham actor. You'll be a big hit on TV, maybe get a movie contract out of it."

Dom's remark caused a somewhat strained laugh, but a laugh, nevertheless. Temporary peace was restored.

The unholy four spent the next few hours making plans for the annihilation of the New York police force. They were methodical, as if they were strategic planners in a war room plotting an invasion of an enemy country. No doubt about it. The crime commission hearings were going to be a brutal extravaganza. Two weeks before the big show. Get your tickets ready.

One more disquieting note remained to disturb Tommy. Halloran casually mentioned that he had summoned Lieutenant Peter Dowd to appear at the crime commission offices at ten o'clock the next morning. This sonofabitch Dowd is a real money-hungry cop. You can bet your sweet ass that he'll crack once I play that tape back for him. And men, if he ever leads us to handsome Ray Driscoll, the glamour boy deputy chief, we'll be the TV hit of the year.

Peter Dowd had a very bad Wednesday night. He had arrived home about eight o'clock, had a couple of drinks with his wife, Margaret, and picked at some pieces of chicken curry she had heated for him as a late supper. Over their drinks, he kept the conversation with Margaret light and humorous. He maintained a serene veneer, but a sharp pain over his right eye almost caused him to wince occasionally.

The events of the day were very unsettling to Peter Dowd. All afternoon and through the drive home over the Verrazano Bridge to his neat two-story home in New Dorp, Staten Island, he was almost in a daze. His mind kept reverting to one incident. Chief Driscoll was away. He was in his office. Ray Corley, one of his top plainclothesmen, poked his head through the door.

I've got some bad news, boss. Sit down, Ray. What's up? Boss, this will kill you. Tommy Sloane, our great pal, is the chief informer for the crime commission. Oh, no, Ray, you can't mean it. Boss, I got it dead straight, right from the feed-box. Checked it out downtown. He's gone bad, boss. It's all over the Job already.

When did he turn, Ray? A couple of months ago, from what I hear. Wore a tape recorder, trapped a zillion guys. Ray, have you or any of the men talked to Sloane lately? Thank God, boss, none of us have seen him since last Christmas. Good, Ray, good news. Stay far away from the prick, Ray. Keep your ears open.

He went to bed with Margaret about eleven o'clock. He tried to read, couldn't concentrate. Margaret, as usual, fell asleep almost immediately. He patted her ass fondly, kissed her bare shoulder. What a wonderful woman! He got up very quietly, went downstairs and made himself a very strong, straight drink of Scotch. Put it on the night table next to him. He finished it off in three long swallows about five minutes apart. Felt numb, eyes heavy. Finally asleep. He awakened still tired, looked at his watch. Good Christ, only one thirty. He went downstairs, re-filled the glass of Scotch. Lying awake in the dark, he rehashed the conversation with Ray Corley. He knocked off the Scotch in two long belts. The fiery liquid seared his throat but he remained quiet. The alcohol began to work, his brain began to dull, his mind stopped hallucinating. He clutched Margaret for dear life and finally fell asleep.

He was wide awake but pretended sleep as Margaret arose to the shrill sound of the alarm clock. For the twentieth time since he received the bad news he reassured himself—Tommy Sloane would never double-cross me. He's too good a friend of mine. Tommy Sloane? Who would ever believe he'd turn stool pigeon?

Thursday morning Peter Dowd arrived at his Borough West office atop the Eighteenth Precinct about eleven o'clock. He wore sunglasses to shield the haggard look in his eyes. Christ, I hope there's no more bad news today, I can't go through another night like last night. Two full glasses of Scotch before I got to sleep. First time I ever needed two jolts like that to make me sleep. No booze today, that's for sure. Get home real early, maybe take Margaret out to dinner. Chief Driscoll still away.

The police commissioner. Great choice. Ray Driscoll was a real collar ad, a Hollywood version of a police chief. A real nice man, though. God bless him.

He sat behind his desk looking over the daily reports. His clerical man knocked, opened the door, announced a visitor to see him.

A good-looking, slim black kid came into his office. Very polite, shook hands, flashed his shield.

Officer Mike Porter, Lieutenant, attached to the crime commission. Forgive me for not calling beforehand, but I was ordered to keep my visit very confidential. Mr. Halloran, the chief counsel for the crime commission, would like to see you in his office at ten o'clock tomorrow morning. Sure thing, fine, Porter, thanks for being so discreet. Tell Mr. Halloran that I'll be there. Ten a.m., right? Thanks again.

Lieutenant Peter Dowd went through the motions the rest of the day, like a zombie. He lunched alone at Gallagher's. A couple of drinks and a small steak cheered him momentarily. Jimmy Clare, the manager, stopped by. Bought him an after-dinner drink, picked up his check. Peter protested. Forget it, lieutenant, you're one in a million, the least I can do.

He arrived home about six o'clock. Had a drink with Margaret and dinner with her and the kids. He kissed them all when he left the table. Oh, God, how I love my wife and kids.

He sat down to read a book on his enclosed porch. Margaret watched TV in the living room, the kids were upstairs doing their homework. Finished, they each came down and kissed him good night. Margaret finally switched off the TV, kissed him good night. I'll be up soon, dear.

He sat back in his armchair on the porch, the book in his lap, still on the same page he had started a couple of hours before. One thought kept revolving in his mind. His life was over, finished. That fucking, double-crossing scumbag Tommy Sloane has me dead right on his tape recorder. I went for his crap game bullshit like a real sucker. Holy Christ, fifteen hundred for me and the boss, fifteen hundred for the men. Then all my horseshit later about how good I was doing.

Christ, that sonofabitch Halloran will crucify me tomorrow morning. I hear he's a merciless prick. I just can't face the disgrace. How can I explain this to Margaret and the kids? Thank God she knows where all the cash is and has access to it. The house is nearly paid. The relatives, the neighbors? How can I face them? The way everyone looks up to me around here. They'll find out I'm nothing but a crooked cop, a crooked police lieutenant.

Well, the hell with everything. There's only one thing left for me to do. He walked to the hall closet off the living room, took his .38 caliber snub-nosed detective special off the shelf, reached in the corner behind an old hat for the bullets. He put two in the barrel of the pistol. Spun the barrel, one in the chamber ready to go. One next to it, just in case.

He walked into the spotless kitchen, taking along a half-filled bottle of Scotch. He poured a water glass full of Scotch and sat down at the kitchen table. He took a long swallow of Scotch, sat back, meditated, hand on chin. He got up, crossed the room to the kitchen counter and picked up a pencil and scratch pad. He sat down again, took another long swallow of Scotch, looked at the gun on the table next to his glass. A fit of silent rage seized him. If only I had you right in front of me, Sloane, I'd put one right in your scumbag head. Too late!

He wrote his farewell note.

Dearest Margaret,

   Forgive me sweetheart, for what I am about to do. I have no other choice. I love you and the children more than anything in this world. Just remember, my darling, everything I did was for you and the kids.

I love you,
Peter

He drained the last of the Scotch. A sudden rush of tears rolled down his cheeks. He put the .38 caliber, snub-nosed detective special inside his mouth. He pulled the trigger and blew his brains out.

Dick Callahan knew that it was going to be a long night. He got up out of the living room chair, put on his gun, suit jacket, topcoat and hat and walked the few city blocks from his mother's Sutton Place apartment to the Seventeenth Precinct. He waved to the sergeant behind the desk and a couple of cops on the main floor and went up the stairs to the detective squad room.

He hung up his topcoat and hat, sat down and put his feet up on the desk. It was almost two o'clock in the morning. He could not erase the sad events of the previous day from his mind. The same, morose refrain kept banging away at his brain.

Poor Peter Dowd, poor Margaret and the little kids. The weekend had been a nightmare. The woeful wake held in a small funeral home in Staten Island. The long lines of men and women—friends, neighbors, fellow cops—waiting in grief-stricken silence for their turn to offer a last prayer.

Dick Callahan's heart wrenched with pain as he recalled dear, desolated Margaret, clutching young Peter's hand, as she stood beside the closed coffin receiving the tearful hugs and kisses of the mourners. Her face stark white, etched with deep lines of bereavement. Trying so hard to be brave beside the cold, closed coffin that sealed off the shattered face of her only love.

The grim, vengeance-filled faces of the thousands of cops in full uniform who saluted the coffin as it was carried from the church to the hearse for its long journey to Holy Cross Cemetery in Brooklyn. No, Dick, not the Veterans Cemetery on Long Island. Peter wanted to be buried in Holy Cross. Right near his mother and father. He bought a plot there. That's where I'll be buried. Right next to Peter. Her tightly held emotions splintered. Wracking sobs. Oh, Dick, I wish I could be buried next to Peter tomorrow. Oh, God, please take me!

Callahan looked up at the gray white squad-room ceiling, his eyes filled with tears. Jesus Christ, of all the guys, Pete Dowd. What a sweetheart of a guy. What fun they had as young marines in boot camp in Le Jeune. Two hip, New York Irish kids. After officers candidate school, they parted. Never saw each other until the war ended with both of them first lieutenants. Once more their paths crossed. In rookie school, both on the Job together.

Poor Peter. Ambitious, dying to get ahead, loved money. Opted for the plainclothes route. His kids were going to have the best. Margaret, I'll make sure she has everything she ever wanted.

Poor Peter. Now's he dead, six foot under. Well, I hope the fucking Sinclair Crime Commission pricks are all satisfied.

And that scumbag Sloane. Big man about town. Sharp dresser, foreign car, all kinds of broads. Couldn't take the heat. Soon as he got nailed he gave everyone up. I'm glad I was an honest cop. In their own way, all cops are honest. These fucking muckrackers should try being a cop for about a week. Poor Peter. That squealing sonofabitch Sloane.

Callahan thought about the last time he met Sloane. In P.J. Clarke's, right after that pimp and whore murders. And the spic john got shot. Sloane knew that pimp, Horowitz, who got shot. He got a little nervous when I asked him what he knew about Horowitz. Finally admitted the pimp died owing him a thousand. Fucking liar, I hear he bragged it was two thousand. Sloane wore a camelhair coat that night in Clarke's.

Dick got up, went to his file cabinet, ruffled through it. Ah, here's the composite. Shit, it looks a little like Tommy Sloane. In fact it looks a lot like Tommy Sloane. Here's the john's phone number. My *amigo*, Raymond Chavez. I will call on you soon, *señor*, and show you a picture. It may not be exactly this picture I hold in my hand, but a picture you might recognize that from what I hear will be all over the front pages next week. Maybe even on television.

Callahan felt a lot better. He put the composite sketch back in the file, put on his hat and topcoat and walked home. He crawled into bed, the pain of the last few days fading from his mind. He had his first good sleep in four days.

Tommy Sloane was chafing at the bit, a bundle of nerves. He looked longingly out the bedroom window of the twelfth-floor suite of the midtown hotel where he was under guard. The new team of two U.S. Marshals was in the living room talking in low tones. The teams changed daily, all of them polite enough, but Tommy sensed an air of hostility towards him. Under the skin they were all cops and cops universally hate cops who rat.

Too bad, thought Tommy. But five days of this under protection shit was wearing on his nerves. He had called Halloran yesterday to protest. Stay put, Sloane, do as you are told. The hearings commence next week. If some friend of Peter Dowd's sees you walking around he's liable to put a couple of shots in you. We need you alive. In a few weeks you'll be your own man, go where you want. Okay, thanks, Mr. Halloran.

Every time he heard the name, Tommy involuntarily shuddered. Peter Dowd? Why the hell did the dumb fuck kill himself? Too goddam bad. If he couldn't stand the gaff he never should have been a plainclothes lieutenant in the first place. And he was a money-hungry prick. Tough luck, it wasn't my doing that killed him, it was his own imagination.

One good thing, the papers haven't printed my name yet. Only make reference to a former plainclothesman who is reputed to be the chief informer!

But, shit, every cop in the Job knows that it's me.

Constance. I wonder how she'll accept the news. God, do I miss her. I hope it wasn't my imagination, but she sounded a little cool on the phone this morning. Thinks I'm in Atlanta, Georgia on a big case. Balls, I'm in custody of the U.S. Marshal's office. Six blocks away from her office.

Justine. They gave me the okay to see her tonight. Bodyguards driving me out. I'll bullshit Justine they're two safe and loft detectives. Need some fresh clothes, dear, on another big case.

He again looked out the window on the traffic below, the busy streets crammed with people. New York! How I loved you. What have you done to me?

The unmarked government cruiser pulled up in the driveway of Tommy's home in Whitestone. It was just past six o'clock in the evening and darkness had set in. The two U.S. Marshals told Tommy that they preferred to wait in the car. He emerged from the rear seat lugging his carryall containing a couple of suits and a small travel bag filled with soiled clothes. He asked them to give him half an hour. No problem, Tommy, take your time.

The minute Justine opened the front door he realized something was radically wrong. Justine looked stricken enough, but one look at the tear-stained face of his sister, Rosemary, standing in the living room, handkerchief held to her mouth, confirmed his worst fears.

Justine looked ten years older than when he left her a week ago. She attempted to speak, choked up, and burst into fresh tears at the sight of him.

He put on his bravado act, threw his carryall and bag on the living room couch, spoke very gruffly.

"What the hell's the matter with you two? This is some kind of greeting I'm getting in my own home."

Justine wiped her red-rimmed eyes. She answered in a strangled, halting voice.

"My girlfriends were here on and off over the weekend. You know, Tommy, a few of their husbands are policemen. Oh, Tommy, all the years I was married to you I thought you were such a good person, such a good cop. How blind I was. I should have known from the way you threw money around that you had to be a crook. That's right, Tommy, you're a hoodlum and a crook. And now you have that poor lieutenant's blood on your hands. It was on account of you he shot himself. The lies you told me about your big cases taking you out of town. You were with your whore girlfriend all the time, practically living with her. Constance Ward. That's her name, so don't lie to me."

He stood facing her as if paralyzed. He looked to his sister Rosemary, beseechingly. Please, say something kind. She turned away from him, eyes filled with contempt. Jesus Christ, now the whole world hates me. Every cop. Every wise guy. Now Justine and Rosemary.

"Just where the hell did you get all this information?" Angrily, assuming a bold front.

"Please, Tommy, don't even ask. Twenty people called, at least. I couldn't put the phone off the hook 'cause I was waiting for your call. And look what I worried about. A crooked, two-timing hoodlum who couldn't be satisfied with a good wife. The man I worshipped is the worse sort of bum."

Tommy flushed. "And you, Rosemary, how do you feel about me?"

Rosemary opened her mouth as if to speak, uttered a

screeching wail and flung herself on the couch, sobbing as if her heart would break.

He shook his head. I can't bullshit my way out of this mess. That's the end of the dutiful husband horseshit. The show is over, might as well end it right now. He motioned to Justine to follow him upstairs. They entered their bedroom. She was still crying, very softly. He removed a hatbox from the closet and put it on the bed. He removed the twenty-five thousand dollars he had stashed underneath the hat inside the box and tossed it towards Justine.

"Look, Justine, I'm in deep trouble. There is no use arguing about it. I'm not even going to deny anything. Believe me, at this stage of my life you're a helluva lot better off without me. Take this, it's twenty-five thousand dollars. Hide it somewhere until you are ready to leave New York. I promise I'll sign my share of the house over to you.

"I would never leave you destitute after being your husband over sixteen years. I'm sorry, Justine, it's all my fault. You've been a good wife. Maybe it's for the best. You get the divorce. I promise that I'll pay any legal fees involved. If you go back to San Diego, at least you'll be in good financial shape.

"That's it, Justine. Let me pack some clothes. Those guys in the car outside are two U.S. Marshals who are bodyguarding me. Next week I have to testify on network television. I'm branded a rat, Justine, but I'm a sonofabitch if I'm going to jail. It's either me or them, Justine, better them. That's the way it is. I'll just be a few minutes packing. Good-bye and good luck, Justine."

Jeff Halloran took every precaution necessary to ensure the safety of his star witness. For the week before the TV hearings were to start, he had Tommy Sloane safely cached in a government house in Arlington, Virginia, just across the Potomac River from Washington, D.C.

The stage was set, the drama about to unfold. Tommy, not due in New York until later the same night, sat glued to the TV set at two thirty in the afternoon, the first day of the crime commission spectacular. He was a nervous wreck, trying to keep his composure in front of the two stone-faced U.S. Marshals who were his bodyguards.

The opening day star was Jeff Halloran. The funereal setting was the ornate assembly room of the New York Bar Association. The dark-stained walls were embossed with stern-faced portraits of long-deceased honest bastions of the bar. Faces that by some miracle might shed sorrowful tears at any suggestion that the human race was frail enough to be tainted by the lure of dirty money!

Lights, camera, action! Halloran was center stage. Dressed immaculately. Face solemn, reminiscent of the young altar boy he used to be. A faint, peacock strut as he bowed to his peers and collected his thoughts and notes. A cordon of reporters sat nearby, eagerly awaiting his vitriolic accusations, ruthlessly prepared to tell the world by wireless and print of the thievery extant in the New York City Police Department. John Barrymore, that most revered of actors, could not have managed a better performance.

Halloran began deliberately, slowly painting the portrait with the scrupulous eye for detail of the immortal Rembrandt. The cadence of his voice enraptured his audience. He brushed the canvas with a light touch, his voice grew increasingly strident as he attacked with ponderous strokes that evoked a black portrait of immorality. His initial charge ran the gamut from soft tones to condemnatory shrieks that summoned memories of the Redemptorist Fathers conducting mission week. Chilling memories of the hellfire and damnation sermons that scared the piss out of any young Catholic kid shepherded to the mission by a temporarily sanctified father.

Halloran promised forthcoming testimony that would reveal the unholy alliance among cops and gamblers, dope peddlers, crooks—up to shakedowns of legitimate business men. His damning homily appalled his listeners, many of whom hoped it was false. A TV viewer of Halloran's excoriation of the police would surely flee at the sight of a blue uniform on the streets of New York. Perhaps into the arms of a rapist, thief, or mugger. A much safer haven than the Boys in Blue. The Finest now graphically depicted by Halloran as the Worst.

Halloran was thoroughly enjoying his greatest hour, to vault him shortly to high public office. He enumerated vivid instances of graft as he strode back and forth before the sober faces of the five *totally* honest lawyers who comprised the crime commission. He drew deeper into his black bag of tricks to titillate further his already fascinated audience. He played a few reels of tape recordings to punctuate his peroration. Lurid, sickening tapes.

Halloran concluded his scurrilous invective with the promise of more to come. The next day of the hearings he promised to unveil his chief witness. A fallen policeman who had now seen the light. A man, caught in the unavoidable web of corruption, who had turned in hopes of restoring honesty to the police force.

A certain Patrolman S., whom by tomorrow will be revealed in full identity. Patrolman S. has worked ceaselessly beside our own undercover men to authenticate the patterns of corruption on the police force. This now reformed policeman has participated in every conceivable insidious form of graft and corruption. Our chief witness tomorrow will delineate the vast scope of depravity existing in all levels of the department.

Halloran, now growing a trifle hoarse, turned halfway toward the majestic members of the crime commission, sure that his face was in good camera angle. In hushed, reverent tones. Reminiscent of Socrates's plea before the Athenians. Yes, citizens, Patrolman S. will be right here in the witness chair to testify before the dedicated members of the crime commission. Men who selfishly served at the behest of His Honor the Mayor, to clean up this cesspool that has been created over the years.

Halloran paused, raised his eyes in evangelical pose and walked out of camera range for the first time in two hours. Mercifully, his scathing speech was finished.

Tommy wished he were anywhere else in the world except the back seat of the government car driving him back to New York City. Visions of Samoa, Fiji Islands, Outer Mongolia danced in his head. Anywhere but the road that led to his uncertain ordeal the next day.

The U.S. Marshal driving and his partner next to him in the front seat only engaged in sporadic conversation during the long drive. They ignored Tommy completely. He sat quietly in the back seat, reflecting upon Halloran's virtuoso TV performance earlier in the day. The cold-blooded air of his body-guards was indicative of how lawmen throughout the country reacted to Halloran's vilification of the Job.

A cop was a cop, whether he was a U.S. Marshal or a deputy sheriff in Butte, Montana. All cops despised anyone who vilified a fellow cop, especially when the accused had no chance to defend himself. Halloran caustically condemned the entire New York Police Force on network TV without chance of rebuttal.

The government car reached the Tudor City apartment rendezvous about ten o'clock at night where Dom and Frank were eagerly awaiting him. They greeted Tommy, their star witness, with the enthusiasm worthy of his celebrity status. Their friendliness was in marked contrast to the frigidity of his recent U.S. Marshal bodyguards. A few drinks later, settled comfortably in a club chair amidst the welcome, congenial atmosphere, he began to shed his apprehension.

The two D.E.A. men were obviously pleased that their work of the last six months was reaching a successful climax. Dom and Frank in turn rapturously praised Halloran's afternoon debut on TV. He was great, wasn't he, Tommy?

Yeah, sure, Dominick. He was excellent. Secretly, Halloran's posturing only confirmed what Tommy felt all along about him. He was strictly full of shit, would climb over anyone to further his own ambitions. But no use getting controversial, keep your mouth shut. Too late now, the show will soon be closing. After tomorrow my balls will finally be out of the wringer.

Yessir, another couple of weeks in good old Arlington, Virginia and then I'm off to somewhere with a brand new identity. When things cool off and I'm settled down, I'll send for Constance. In a couple of quick moves I'll transfer my cash. With three hundred thousand under my belt, I'll get into good action in nothing flat.

The thought of Constance caused a sharp pang. Christ, I haven't spoken to her in over a week. Dom has assured me that I'll get to see her over the weekend. I wonder how she's going to accept what I've done. What I've done? Bullshit! Let's face it. I'm a stool pigeon. Jesus Christ, it's a helluva lot better than my going to jail for ten years. Oh, Constance, sweetheart, I'll make it all up to you.

Dominick jarred him back to reality. One more drink for the road, Tom, then to bed. Mr. Halloran wants you nice and fresh for tomorrow.

Tommy, Halloran, Dom, and Frank were together in a small office adjacent to the assembly room of the Bar Association, the setting for the televised crime commission hearings. Halloran almost gushed over Tommy when he arrived, friendlier toward him than he had been in months. You look great, Tom, everyone treating you good? Fine, Mr. Halloran. Glad to hear it, Tom, it'll be all over for you after today for at least a month. Of course, we'll need you to testify before the grand jury when we go after our indictments. Sure, Mr. Halloran, I understand.

Tommy understood, all right. He had been positively assured that after the indictments he would enter the government Alias Program. A brand new identity in a brand new town, far away from New York. With my love, Constance, by my side and plenty of cash. So today I will bury everybody, Mr. Halloran. Shoot!

Halloran schooled him assiduously for the couple of hours before the hearings were to commence. He carefully rehearsed the answers to the questions he would later put to Tommy before the cameras. He stressed that Tommy answer in the vernacular. Accentuate, Tommy, the words cops and wise guys use. Pad, juice, score, hat, bagman, cousin, outlaw—that's the stuff. Refer to the hoodlums by the names the cops knew them as. Gimp, Tony Cheesecake, Big Cheech, Spanish Johnny, Jamaica Sam, Richie Irish—you get it, Tom?

Halloran's coaching of Tommy was a shrewd maneuver. The words and names rolling off his tongue would add a definitive authenticity to his sordid tale. There wouldn't be left an iota of doubt in the minds of the TV viewers and zealous press that the truth was being revealed. The innermost details of the long-guarded system, the unholy pact between cops and denizens of the underworld. The public loved crime shows. The picturesque patois of the gambling world. Tell it like it is, Tom—ice, fix—you get it, Tom? Testify just the way it will roll off the tapes. Good boy, Tommy, go get them.

The answers down pat, the jargon to be spoken imbedded in his mind, Tommy was ready for center stage. Halloran warmed up the audience just as the opening act stand-up comic does in preparation for the entrance of the star.

Voice suddenly very grave. He wished he could have shouted, a big hand for the star of our show. But in hushed tones, turning to the members of the Crime Commission, he said, "I call the next witness, Patrolman Thomas Sloane."

There was a buzz of anticipation from the closed audience as Tommy strode purposefully across the lush broadloom carpeting to the witness chair. He was dressed in high fashion for his debut on camera. Three-piece blue pencil-stripe suit, white button-down shirt, maroon tie, and his ever-present black-tassled Gucci loafers. Now at last onstage, his inner fears were cast off and the ham actor lurking inside his psyche soon took over.

One appearance. Make it a good one, Tommy, and Halloran and these saintly sonofabitches on the crime commission will take the best of care of you.

W. Phelps Sinclair posed the explosive question.

"Besides your own group, your own friends, Officer Sloane, tell us what you know about other groups, other division, borough, and headquarters plainclothes squads. Do you know for a fact that almost everyone participated in the pad, as you refer to it?"

Answer by Sloane. "Everyone, to my knowledge."

"Everyone?"

"Yessir, everyone."

The next hour, Tommy Sloane put on a masterful performance. The jargon, the nicknames of the underworld gave his testimony a stark reality. It was impossible to doubt one word, so easily and fluently did he delineate the mechanics of the system. It was as if a young Dr. Spock was lecturing to a group of young mothers on the care and upbringing of children. This was it, right from the feedbox. When he finished there wasn't a sound in the Circus Maximus. The lions had once again emerged victorious, all the Christians were dead. The assembled audience, the press, the TV viewers hated to believe what they just heard. But really, that young cop was so convincing, so knowledgeable. It must be true!

The televised hearings had a profound effect on the people of New York. They saddened the hearts of many natives who admired and loved their policemen. They served to further enrage their disconsolate opposites who despised all policemen. There was one note of unanimity the hearings struck. The New York cops were bound together in equal loathing for His Honor the Mayor for permitting the shameful spectacle and the chief informer, Tommy Sloane, for sustaining it.

Two vital people in Tommy's life sat focused on their TV sets in their respective living rooms about two miles apart.

On Sutton Place, detective Dick Callahan intently watched with a hatred that grew almost unbearable by the minute. The bile rose in his throat at the well-dressed, good-looking visage of Tommy Sloane having his field day in front of the camera. In turn smiling, smirking, rolling his eyes deprecatingly as he spewed his calumny.

The born-again actor reveling in his role on screen as he destroyed the Job that had treated him so well. The Job he had once sworn to uphold. The Job that Dick Callahan loved!

The leer, the big grin as he recounted odd bits of corruption, it all infuriated Callahan. The prick is killing the Job, the same Job he got rich with by violating every rule the ordinary street cop lived by.

Smile, you rotten squealer, smile, you thieving fuck. One sure thing—Peter Dowd isn't smiling in his grave in Holy Cross Cemetery. But you won't be smiling long, you no-good, yellow piece of shit. Tonight, I will call my newest best friend, Raymond Chavez, the john who refused to die in the whorehouse shooting.

Raymond, my *amigo*, does the sketch I showed you of the perpetrator resemble the cop I asked you to stay home and watch on TV today? Yessir, you fucking disgrace to the Irish, I'll nail you to the cross. I want to see you smile when I slap the handcuffs on you. Too bad, Sloane, I hate to do it to a cop, but you're indicted for murder one.

Dick Callahan switched off the TV. Enough garbage for the day. He went into the kitchen, made himself a drink. The strong Scotch soothed his jumpy nerves. Another long swallow.

Getting calmer. The inner rage was ebbing. Callahan's turn to smile. First smile all day.

Constance, twenty-two city blocks north in her apartment on York Avenue, was in turn fascinated and horrified as she watched Tommy's act on TV. Her suspicions, which had begun a couple of weeks before, were now being confirmed. It had happened a couple of times since Tommy went to Georgia on that big case.

By now she was used to the V.I.P. treatment always accorded her as Tommy's sweetheart. At lunch with an office colleague in Rose's, the brush-off was unmistakable. Practically ignored by Frank, the maitre d' and Paul, the owner. Barely acknowledged at dinner with a client in Jimmy Weston's. George, the maitre d', Jimmy Weston, very cold.

It was all in sharp contrast to the effusive greetings she was used to when accompanied by Tommy. Constance was puzzled, hurt. And worse, no word from Tommy for almost two weeks. Very, very unusual. Then the two phone calls yesterday. The first one, a strange voice. Constance Ward. Yes? Honey, make sure you watch TV tomorrow afternoon and find out what a piece of shit your boyfriend is. What? Who's this? Hung up.

A bit later, Tommy. Bright, cheerful, sounds like he hasn't a care in the world. See you over the weekend, darling. I can't wait.

It was like a bad dream. Her Tommy, her love, looking so handsome. But telling all those terrible stories about the police force. My God, I loved him because he was such a great cop. Such a great guy. Oh my God, now he's actually being an informer. I can't stand it.

Constance switched the set off. Tears were rolling down her cheeks. My hero, the man I want to marry, spend the rest of my life with. She threw herself on the bed, sobbing. Tommy, come home soon. Tell me what's wrong.

The next evening after Tommy's testimony. About seven o'clock.

Detective Dick Callahan and Raymond Chavez sat in a booth in a bar and grill in Astoria, Queens, a couple of blocks from

Chavez's home. A broad smile lit up Dick Callahan's face as he sipped his tall Scotch and water. He repeated, for the third time. "You're sure, positively sure, Raymond, that Tommy Sloane is the man who shot you?"

"Mister Callahan, the minute I saw his face on the TV I recognize him. Almost the same as the picture I helped you make. That's the sonofabitch who shot me and killed Jimmy and poor Cheryl."

"You must understand one thing, Raymond. You're going to have to take the witness stand in open court and identify Sloane. You're not afraid it might embarrass you in front of your wife and kids? You know, the whorehouse bullshit, all that stuff?"

"No way, Mr. Callahan. My wife already forgave me. I want to get even. That fucking guy Sloane tried to kill me. Shoots me in cold blood, then he laughs. Now it's my turn. I hope he gets the electric chair."

Callahan grinned, nodded, said, "We'll do our best, Raymond. Now remember, keep all this strictly to yourself. Don't tell anyone, not even your wife. I'll be in touch with you when the district attorney wants you to testify before the grand jury."

"I'll keep quiet. I'll do anything you say, Mr. Callahan. Thanks for the drinks. I'll be a good witness, don't worry."

At almost the exact hour, in the living room of Constance's apartment, Tommy Sloane sat in a chair facing his sweetheart. He had his third full Scotch on the rocks in his hand. He had been speaking almost nonstop for almost an hour. Constance sat cross-legged on the couch, dressed in a navy blue robe. Her eyes were red, her flushed, swollen face wreathed in sadness.

He leaned toward her confidentially, tried to sound very convincing, lying through his teeth.

"But, hon, you just don't understand the whole thing. It's not as bad as it seems with all the TV hoopla. I hated what I was doing but I just couldn't buck the system. I went along with the rest of the guys. Sure, I admit it, I made a lot of money, took graft. But it was either take the money or go back to uniform up in Harlem. Or even worse, get busted out of the Job."

"Oh, Tommy, come on, I'm not as absolutely näive as you think I am. I watched the way you threw money around. I saw plenty of shady-looking characters cozy up to you, send bottles of wine over to our table. But all those lies you told me. Why did you lie to me so much?"

His face assumed an injured look of innocence. He looked right into her eyes, lied, "But sweetheart, you don't understand. All that garbage I was forced to testify about yesterday happened a couple of years ago. A long way back before we met. I have been assigned to some really big cases the last year or two. I swear, love, honestly."

Doubtfully, still suspicious, in a soft voice, she said, "Oh, Tommy, it's so awful. What happens to us now? You've told me over and over that they framed you, would send you to jail unless you cooperated. That's true, isn't it, Tom?"

In a sincere voice, face downcast, almost tearfully, he lied, "That's the story, sweetheart. Three cops I trusted set me up, squealed on me. I had no choice. Go to jail or cooperate. I could never leave you."

"What about your wife? What about our future?"

"I've already had it out with Justine. It's all over. She has agreed to file for divorce. My situation will be over in another month at the most. Why don't you go away somewhere? Florida, California, anywhere. Wait for me until I get finished. Then we'll get married and I'll go into some sort of business. Make a fresh start."

"Quit my job? Oh, Tommy, what about the money all this would cost? What will I live on while on while I wait for you? You know I only have a small income. Without my salary it would be impossible."

Real big smile. Money softens up all women.

"Babe, money is the least of our worries. Sweetheart, we have over three hundred thousand dollars salted away in the joint safe deposit box we opened in your bank."

Eyes wide, incredulously, almost gasping.

"Three hundred thousand dollars! Oh, my God, Tommy, I never dreamed it was that much money. I'd have died if I ever knew."

He stood up, walked across to her, leaned over and kissed

her. Her lips were cold. He tried to force his tongue inside her mouth. She pushed him away, said, "Oh, Tommy, please. Much as I love you, not tonight. Besides, dear, I just got my period. I hurt all over. When will you be back? Maybe we can get away together?"

Tommy flushed, a little abashed by her rebuff. He collected himself, checked his anger. What the hell! This all has to be some shock to her. I'll bullshit her along. She'll be my old Constance in a week or so. But I'm off to Arlington, Virginia, tomorrow. Goddam it. I won't see her for at least a couple of weeks. Wait, a good idea!

"Sweetheart, suppose you take off for Washington, D.C. for a couple of weeks. Check into the Mayflower, a great hotel. I have to be there on some government case I was instrumental in. I'll be able to see you every night. Suppose you go to the bank and take five thousand out of the safe deposit box. That'll hold you for a while."

"Tommy, it's all so sudden. My job, my career. All up in smoke. And you, how I'm worried about you. There's bound to be a lot of hate for you. Some crazy cop might try to hurt you."

He laughed, the old bravado returning.

"Don't ever worry about me, sweetheart, I can take care of myself." He looked at his watch. Running late, Dominick and Frank outside waiting. "Look, I have to go now. I'll call you tomorrow. Please do as I say starting Monday. Quit the job. Take whatever cash you feel you need. We'll have plenty of money to start a new life."

She stood up, kissed him tenderly, led him to the door. She kissed him a little more deeply as she let him out. Promised she would do as he said. It just might take a bit longer. I'll see you in Washington soon, darling.

Constance locked the front door, stood momentarily staring at it. Went into the kitchen and made herself a tall Scotch and water. She settled back on the couch and reviewed the last hour and a half with Tommy. Shook her head. No way will I give up my career. I love my job. God, when he kissed me it was almost as if he were a complete stranger. I had absolutely no feeling for him. And I lied to him for the first time. I really am not having my period. But I couldn't stand the thought of him touching me tonight. Maybe I'll get over it, love him again.

Oh, God, how I loved him. But the image of him on television repels me. My Tommy, my hero. A low life crook, informer, cheap hoodlum. She took a long pull on her Scotch. God almighty, three hundred thousand in that vault. I'll have to go to the bank and count it before I go to work. She took another swallow of Scotch, threw her head back. My God, three hundred thousand dollars!

The crime commission hearings dragged along for another week. They featured a few scruffy-looking tow truck operators, a couple of frightened uniformed cops whom Halloran had turned and a couple of embittered ex-policemen who had been long fired from the Job previous to the formation of the crime commission. It was all rather boring and downhill after the startling, vivid, tape-punctuated testimony of Tommy Sloane.

The press and public interest began to wane after about ten days and Halloran finally brought the proceedings to a merciful halt.

Tommy was once again sequestered away in the safe house in Arlington, Virginia. He had been in contact with Halloran only once since he left New York over a week ago. Halloran had assured him that he would rush the necessary paper work leading to the eventual indictment of the hoodlums and policemen whom Tommy had implicated. He would require the presence of Tommy before a grand jury in about a month.

The guard rules were ironclad. Under no circumstance was Tommy allowed to leave the safe-house compound. This austere edict nullified any hopes that he might rendezvous with Constance in nearby Washington, D.C. He spoke to her often by telephone, reassuring her that the ordeal would soon be over. He was annoyed that she still held her job, but she promised to give notice the minute some concrete plans were made for their future.

He chafed under the monotony of the interminable days, the constant supervision of the U.S. Marshals. He took long walks during the lovely spring days, enjoying the lush greenery of

Virginia, missing Constance terribly. At night, he read himself to sleep.

His cordon of bodyguards were polite enough, but remained aloof, distant toward him. He brushed off the reason—never testify against a fellow cop—kept to himself. Conversation limited, Tommy by nature an extrovert, retreated into his shell. Soon, dear God, this too shall pass.

While Tommy waited in galling loneliness for the days to pass before his summons to New York to conclude his crime commission role, Detective Dick Callahan was a very busy man. His mission in life was the head of Tommy Sloane and he was unearthing every nail that could place him in his coffin.

He worked day and night until he finally located five prostitutes whose names he had originally gleaned from the secreted black address book he found in Horowitz's apartment. All five knew Tommy Sloane as a frequent visitor to the whorehouse. All five had sexual relations with him at least once. One, a tall, leggy brunette named Laura Osborne recalled being present when Sloane threatened to blow Jimmy's head off over some money he was owed.

Callahan was extremely cautious about the new composite of the alleged assailant as described by the victim who lived, Raymond Chavez. He took Joe Toomey of homicide out for a drink. He gave him a copy of the new composite sketch. This is up to date, Joe, burn the other one in your file. Joe took one look, whistled. Beautiful, Dick, beautiful. How did you manage this?

Callahan replied with a knowing wink. The less said the better. You agree, Joe. Positively, Dick. Just keep that in your file in case you're called. I want to convict this scumbag Sloane so bad I can taste his blood. Callahan figured there was no use telling Joe Toomey how a homosexual he had befriended a few times, a fashion illustrator, drew the sketch to minute specifications.

Callahan was in constant touch with his good friend Joseph Keating, assistant D.A., homicide bureau, as he assembled his evidence. Keating was a long-time veteran assistant D.A. who had been in charge of homicide for many years. Gray curly hair. Slim build. Six feet tall, one hundred and seventy pounds.

Fifty-eight years old, twenty-five of them as assistant D.A. Well respected, with a deep voice that still retained the slight accent of his native borough of the Bronx. Graduate of Fordham University and Fordham Law School. Father was a New York patrolman for thirty years.

Joe Keating loved good cops, especially ones like Dick Callahan. He hated hoodlums, especially murderous hoodlums. Lectured widely in favor of the death penalty.

Callahan had approached Joe Keating a few days after Tommy Sloane's testimony shook New York. He was very interested, assigned two of his own investigators to work along with Callahan. Chavez and the five prostitutes were interrogated for hours. Keating was convinced that the state had an excellent case.

About two weeks into his latest sojourn at Arlington, Virginia, Tommy was informed by one of the U.S. Marshals that they were ordered back to New York the following day. Tommy, assuming it pertained to the start of wrapping up the pending cases, was elated. He received what he thought was good news about two o'clock in the afternoon.

About the same time that Tommy received the news of his return to New York, Jeff Halloran arrived by prior appointment in Assistant D.A. Joe Keating's office. Halloran's face was red with agitation. The sight of Dick Callahan calmly sitting next to Keating helped inflame his already considerable anger. They exchanged the usual amenities very briefly. Halloran, his face contorted, his voice almost a shout, demanded to know what the hell Keating and Callahan were trying to pull? What the hell is all this couple-of-years-ago murder case all about? Do you people understand that all the hard work of the crime commission would go down the drain if Sloane were ever indicted? What jury would ever believe a man indicted for murder?

Halloran's hysterical harangue was swiftly squelched by Dick Callahan. In a steely voice, Callahan shot from the hip.

"Calm down, Halloran. You're not scaring the shit out of any crooked cops now or grandstanding in front of the TV. Just shut your fucking mouth for a few minutes and listen to me. You're goddam lucky Mr. Keating and I don't indict you for suppressing evidence of a murder. Do you think your asshole D.E.A. buddies are the only good investigators in New York? They wouldn't make a patch on a good New York cop's ass. You had evidence of another murder committed by Sloane while on a shakedown up in Harlem not too long ago. Am I right, Halloran?"

Halloran's face paled. He flinched as if slapped in the face. That goddam black kid, Mike Porter, I made a detective. Had to come from him! Jesus, these cops stick together.

Callahan knew he had him by the balls.

"You want me to continue, Halloran? To name names and dates? Halloran, why don't you stick your cop-hating act up your ass and go back to Wall Street with your shithead friend, Sinclair. There are still plenty of good honest cops around, Halloran, and I'm one of them. I'll match my life against yours any day in the week. Even on TV where you are a real star. In the meantime, get the fuck out of here before I throw you out."

Halloran's face blanched. One look at the set of Dick Callahan's jaw caused him to turn abruptly and scurry out of Keating's office.

Keating and Callahan broke into a fit of laughter when the door slammed. Keating wiped his eyes, said, "Dick, that was the highlight of my career as a D.A. You sure put that showboat bullshit artist in his place. Okay, the fun's over. Let's get back to work, lay out our plan of action."

Tommy arrived in New York City late that night and was quartered in a midtown hotel along with his ever-present U.S. Marshals. He immediately called Constance, who answered in a sleepy voice, and reassured her that the end was in sight. Soon, darling, this will be all over and we'll be together the rest of our lives. She didn't sound overenthusiastic on the phone, but he dismissed her apparent lack of warmth as due to being awakened from a sound sleep.

The next morning, to his surprise, Tommy was taken to the Manhattan District Attorney's office rather than the U.S. Attorney's office where the U.S. Marshals usually led him. They sat him in a room about twenty-five feet long and fifteen feet wide. The right wall of the room was covered entirely by a huge mirror. Several other men who looked like policemen entered the room and took seats on either side of Tommy. He was completely ignored and a bit mystified, but he just sat there in silence waiting for someone to page him.

The four men seated around Tommy were indeed policemen. The huge wall mirror was what is known in police circles as an X-ray mirror. On the other side of the mirror was Detective Dick Callahan, Assistant D.A. Joe Keating, a police stenographer, Raymond Chavez, and the five prostitutes who were formerly call girls for the long-deceased Jimmy Horowitz.

The wounded john, Raymond Chavez, and the five prostitutes immediately identified Tommy Sloane. Chavez identified him as the gunman, the prostitutes as the man who frequented the whorehouse, and Laura Osborne further identified Tommy as the man who threatened to blow Jimmy Horowitz's fucking head off over some money owed.

Tommy was taken to lunch by the U.S. Marshals, still in the dark as to what was happening to him. He kept his composure but deep inside he was worried sick. Something was up, and it was getting more apparent by the hour that it wasn't good. The scene in the room with the wall mirror, surrounded by four beefy-looking guys who never said a word, looked like some kind of setup. What the hell was going on? Not one word from that goddam fink, Halloran. Where is he?

It was three o'clock in the afternoon. Tommy sat reading a paper. One of the U.S. Marshals put his head in the door, said Mr. Keating wanted to see him. He entered Keating's office and to his amazement Dick Callahan was sitting on Keating's right. The contemptuous look on Callahan's face aroused a chill along Tommy's spine. What the hell is this hard-nosed fuck doing here? It didn't take too long to find out.

Keating pointed to a chair in front of his desk and Tommy sat down. He was thankful to be sitting down because he might have fallen down at Keating's next move. In a controlled voice, expressing no emotion, Keating read him his rights. The Miranda decision. Anything you say can be held against you—you have a right to remain silent. You may contact an attorney.

Tommy sat rigid, not believing what he was hearing. Jesus Christ, this can't be over that nigger I shot up in Harlem that night with Willie? Holy Christ, Halloran swore that all the past shit would be forgotten. Where the hell is Halloran?

Keating finished. Tommy, very politely, said, "Mr. Keating, I haven't the slightest idea of what I'm being charged with. I was promised immunity by Mr. Halloran in return for my testimony. If I'm accused of any crime, what is it? I'd like to know what the charges are so I can contact my attorney."

"Sloane, you are being charged with the murder of Jimmy Wallace, alias Jimmy Horowitz and Cheryl Stanton, plus the attempted murder of Raymond Chavez. The following information will be given to your attorney. Approximate time of crime and premises where the crime was committed."

Tommy kept a straight face, but an immense feeling of relief came over him. Thank God, not that Harlem bullshit. What a lot of crap this is. All Callahan's doing. No doubt about it. Shit, I remember when Jimmy and that big whore got knocked off plain as day. Christmas Eve before last. I was with Vinny all day and with Justine and the family all night. Read about it the next day in the Sunday News. I can account for every minute. He said, nice and easy, "If you don't mind, Mr. Keating, I'd prefer to remain silent until I have my lawyer with me. I can only tell you that this is a big mistake."

"Fine, Sloane, as you say. For the present, you will remain in custody of the U.S. Marshals until we need you further. We will advise your attorney when to have you available."

Tommy thanked Keating, looked Callahan directly in the eye and walked out of the room. His brain was whirling. The only lawyer he could think of to call was his old pal, Abe Pearlstein. Abe was a pretty good criminal lawyer, knew his way around. He called Abe's office and left a message to call him at the hotel. Urgent!

Abe Pearlstein contacted Tommy about five o'clock and was sitting in his hotel room about an hour later. A bottle of Cutty Sark Scotch, ice cubes, and a pitcher of water was on a table near them. They both had half-filled drinks in their hands and wasted no time getting down to business.

"Tommy, once more, you're positive that you had nothing to do with this crime, are completely innocent?"

"No way, Abe, as God is my judge."

"I called Joe Keating, got the dates and time. Christmas Eve about a year and a half back. I remember those murders 'cause I knew Horowitz. That prick wasn't even a real Jew. Christ, we Jews have enough trouble without a pimp like him taking a Jewish name."

Tommy laughed for the first time all day. He said, "That's him, Abe, a real hunk of shit. I knew him well, but I sure didn't kill him and that broad. But Abe, I don't trust Dick Callahan. He'd send his own mother to the electric chair."

"You can say that again, Tom. He's some tough cookie. I have a good idea, Tom. Would you be willing to take a lie-detector test? You know that there's no indictment yet. We just might stave it off before it goes to the grand jury."

"Abe, I'll take fifty lie-detector tests. I swear on my dead mother, I had nothing to do with killing those people."

"Good boy, Tom. By the way, you mentioned you had plenty of alibi witnesses."

"I've got a dozen, Abe. Vinny Ciano, my best friend, whom I was with until after seven o'clock. By the way, you mentioned the crime took place between seven-thirty and eight-oh-five at night. Christ, I just thought of something. I got my car from Big Tim Sullivan, the doorman at the Algonquin Hotel at about seven-thirty. Perfect. Tim'll verify that. Then I drove to Queens to meet my wife and take her to our annual Christmas family reunion."

"That sounds good, Tommy. I have an ex-cop to do my preliminary spade work for me. Name is Frank Owens, a real good man. You give me the names of all your alibi witnesses and Frank will interview them. Maybe we'll run them through Keating before the grand jury acts. Frank will also arrange the lie-detector tests. I suggest we take two, one independent of the other."

"Sounds great, Abe. I'm getting more relieved by the minute."

"Speaking of relief, Tommy, one more thing. This is going to cost money."

"How much, Abe?"

"Let's say ten thousand for starters. Okay, Tom?"

"Fine, Abe. I'll arrange it for you in a day or two."

Events moved swiftly and inexorably toward the ultimate fate of Tommy Sloane. He got things moving early the next day. He was confident, anxious for a quick vindication. He called Constance, was very wary on the phone, told her to call his lawyer, Abe Pearlstein, and give him some of the papers in the box she and her brother kept. She sounded alarmed, but got the message. You sure you're all right, Tommy? Fine, sweetheart, it'll be all over soon. Abe met him later in the day, told him that she gave him the ten-thousand-dollar retainer. Lovely girl, Tom, you're a lucky guy.

The following day Abe returned with Frank Owens, his ace investigator. Tall, slim, good-looking guy in his late fifties. Former first-grade detective. Bright guy. Frank arranged for Tommy to take two separate lie-detector tests, both with polygraph people with impeccable credentials. Escorted by the usual two U.S. Marshals, Tommy went through the rigorous examinations and passed with flying colors. Everyone close to him was jubilant.

Abe called Jeff Halloran immediately after receiving the results of the tests. Tommy is innocent, Mr. Halloran, what are you going to do about it? Halloran said it was wonderful news, they'll never indict him now. Congratulate Tommy for me, Mr. Pearlstein. That was the last they heard from Jeff Halloran, Sinclair, the D.E.A. men, or anyone else connected to the crime commission.

The day after the good news about the lie detectors came an avalanche of bad news. Frank Owens, Abe Pearlstein, and Tommy sat in the living room of the hotel suite. They all had brimming glasses of Scotch on the rocks in their hands. They all needed a drink, Tommy especially. He was stunned, face pale, as he listened to Frank Owens's recital of his most recent spade work.

Tommy, unbelieving, almost spluttered, "You mean to say, Frank, that Vince practically threw you out of his office?"

"Tommy, he's evidently a nice guy. I just called him, said I was an ex-cop, wanted to talk to him. He was very cordial at first, couldn't be nicer. I then explained my reason for seeing him. You know, to establish the time element for your alibi. Tommy, he almost exploded the minute I mentioned your name. He cursed you, said he would rot in hell before he would help you. Called you, among other names, a rat scumbag. He showed me the door saying he hopes you wind up where you put Peter Dowd. I don't have to go on, do I, Tommy?"

Tommy just shook his head. Vinny, how we loved each other. Look what it has come down to.

Frank Owens, in an even voice, continued, "I got out of there quick, Tom, and decided to go to the Algonquin, inquire about how to reach Tim Sullivan, the doorman. Well, now you know. Tim Sullivan dropped dead of a heart attack outside the hotel about three months ago. Where do we go from here, Abe?" Looking inquiringly at Pearlstein.

Pearlstein's face almost registered as much despair as Tommy's. He sipped his drink thoughtfully, said, "Well, maybe the lie detector tests and the statements of Tommy's family will cause Keating to drop the case before it goes to the grand jury."

Tommy just listened, not saying a word. He knew deep down he was doomed. All these years he had the world by the balls. Now the tables had turned. It started the night he shot the stick-up guy in Harlem. Everything seemed to go downhill from that day on. He should have listened to Vince. Take the money and run. He was too hungry for his own good. Now the world, Constance, Keating—has me by the balls.

Abe Pearlstein argued his case in the privacy of Joe Keating's office. It was all to no avail. Sure he passed the lie-detector tests, Mr. Pearlstein. This guy Sloane is such a skilled liar he could pass a million tests. But lie-detector tests are merely a guideline. As you know, Mr. Pearlstein, they are not admissible in a court of law. I'm sorry, sir, we are presenting our case to the grand jury this afternoon. Thank you for coming, Mr. Pearlstein. Thank you for your courtesy, Mr. Keating.

Dick Callahan and Joe Toomey from homicide picked Tommy up at his hotel at ten o'clock the next morning. They shook hands with the two U.S. Marshals and told them that from thereon Sloane was in custody of the People of New York. Tommy was handcuffed by Callahan and taken out to a waiting unmarked cruiser car.

They drove directly to the nearest precinct to the courthouse. A crowd of photographers and reporters were waiting outside the precinct house and they could hardly negotiate the short distance from the car to the entrance of the precinct. Tommy kept his head high as the cameras blinked and popped all around him. Reporters besieged him with questions. He just smiled, his brave smile, he hoped.

He was at last, after being fingerprinted, mugged, and cursed at by a few station-house cops, arraigned in supreme court. Two counts of murder, one of felonious assault. No bail.

Tommy spent the worst six weeks of his life waiting to come to trial. For security reasons he was placed in Queens County Jail, a branch of the city penal system that was supposed to be cleaner, safer, and more livable than any other branch jail.

His horror of jail was soon confirmed by the conditions of his imprisonment. He was only allowed an hour walk a day, couldn't eat the jailhouse food, and could only sleep on the rocklike cot when he was exhausted. He lost twenty pounds, and looked almost emaciated the day he was finally brought to trial.

He was so elated to escape from the tiny cell for a day he was almost happy to be on trial. Billy Walsh, his brother-in-law, delivered his clothes daily for his court appearance.

The trial was an almost foregone conclusion. The whores paraded in all their call-girl regalia to the witness stand and described his antics in Jimmy Horowitz's whorehouse. Laura Osborne gave her damaging version of the argument he had with Jimmy over the money owed. She drew a gasp from the packed courtroom when she clearly enunciated Tommy's threat—"pay me the money you owe me or I'll blow your *fucking* head off!"

Raymond Chavez was a devastating witness. He arose in the witness chair and practically screamed as he pointed at Tommy. He's the man who shot me when I begged for my life. For one hair-raising minute it seemed as if he would leap from the witness chair to the defendant's table and try to strangle Tommy. A very venomous scene, not wasted on the jury.

Abe Pearlstein did his best. He couldn't shake the saucy, onstage manner of any of the call-girl witnesses. Cross-examining Raymond Chavez for any length of time was a potential disaster. Abe Pearlstein shrewdly dispatched him from the witness chair in short order.

Abe gave it a game try for the defense. He martialed his coterie of relatives to substantiate Tommy's Christmas Eve reunion party alibi. Justine, in the throes of divorce, flew in from the Coast to help Tommy. Rosemary, Billy, Aunt Marge, Aunt Kitt, Uncle Frank, and all the rest made excellent witnesses to prove Tommy could not be in two places at once. He was definitely at the party when the shootings occurred.

Tommy, after much soul-searching by Abe, took the stand in his own defense. A crucial error. Billy Walsh delivered his best outfit. Tommy, ever the ham actor, was too sartorially perfect, conveyed the image of a thief rather than a poor humble policeman. Resplendent in a gray three-piece suit, blue button-down shirt, dark tie, and his beloved Gucci loafers. Looking lean and handsome after the recently lost weight, he was almost too cocksure in his initial skirmish with the veteran D.A. But Joe Keating, the skillful old warrior of numerous courtroom battles, gradually destroyed Tommy. His preliminary gentle questions veered sharply.

"Tell me, Sloane, you are an admitted crooked cop?"

"Yes."

"You've been a master shakedown artist, a thief, a crook throughout your career on the police force. Am I correct?"

"Yes."

"You admitted to Detective Callahan and several other people that the victim, Jimmy Horowitz, owed you money. Is that correct?"

"Yes."

"How many people have you killed, Sloane?"

"Two in the line of—"

"I didn't ask you that. How many people have you killed, Sloane?"

"Two."

"You sure it wasn't three, Sloane?"

Abe Pearlstein was jumping up and down, objecting strenuously. He was reprimanded by the presiding judge. His Honor John X. McHale. Overruled, Mr. Pearlstein. Overruled, Mr. Pearlstein. The good judge was just short of Joe Keating's chief assistant.

Tommy at last climbed down from the witness stand, the ordeal over. The confident, sharp-looking man who was first sworn in bore no resemblance to the poor, shaken guy who left with a defeated look on his face. The look of a beaten man.

The jury was only out a bit over two hours. Abe Pearlstein, Tommy, and all the relatives knew that it was all over. Gloom and disaster were in the air. Abe attempted to cheer Tommy, to raise his spirits. We can't miss on appeal, Tommy, we'll get a fair shake upstate from the Court of Appeals. Tommy listened with half an ear.

He sat, head in hands. It's all over. How can I spend the rest of my life in prison? Oh, Vince, how could you desert me when I needed you so? You could have saved me, Vince.

And Constance? What's going to happen to her? To us? Oh God, I loved her so.

The end was anticlimatic. The bailiff poked his head into the room. The jury's in, Mr. Pearlstein. Abe led Tommy before the bench.

Judge McHale. "Mr. Foreman, have you reached a verdict?"

The foreman. Stocky, blue collar type.

Cleared his throat, responded in a hoarse voice. "Yes, your honor. Guilty on all counts."

GREENHAVEN CORRECTIONAL FACILITY IS located in Stormville, New York. It is in the Hudson Valley area, not too far from the famous town of Poughkeepsie. Greenhaven is a maximum-security prison in every sense. It was originally built as a federal prison in 1939 when the United States stood on the threshold of World War Two.

The original purpose of the severely structured, remote prison was to house projected defectors from military service as well as present members of the armed services who committed serious crimes.

Greenhaven was a harsh, tough prison. The inmates sweltered in summer, froze in the winter. It was divided into four tiers of cell blocks and two recreational yards—one for A and B Blocks, one for C and D Blocks. A high interior wall separated the two yards.

Greenhaven contained the usual rehabilitative prison shops that didn't rehabilitate anyone, a school, and a series of work gangs. The gangs, referred to as the W.P.A. in honor of the Works Project Administration of the Great Depression, did the various repair and cleaning jobs inside the walls. The usual inmate population was well over two thousand, and consisted mostly of convicts who were serving long sentences. There were much better places in the world.

Tommy arrived in a van manacled to a pretty nice black guy. It had only been about a two-hour trip from the state receiving prison at Sing Sing to his new home, Greenhaven Correctional Facility. He piled out of the van with the other inmates who were transferred with him. A guard unmanacled their hands.

He rubbed his chafed hands to help restore the circulation. The cuffs had been clamped real tight. Another subtle way to let you know you're a prisoner, a resident of the Joint.

Tommy gazed around his new surroundings. High gray walls with intermittent gun towers encircled the yard where he stood. Very forbidding-looking. Jesus Christ, twenty-five to life! How the hell am I ever going to make it in this forsaken place. Over sixteen years to go before I even meet the parole board. If I ever live that long in this fucking zoo.

He was finally led to a cell in B Block. He had his duffel bag containing his toilet articles and a few paperback books. He still wore the state clothes he was issued when he arrived at Sing Sing. He put his toilet articles on the sink and lay back on the cot that was his bed. The cell had a sink, a toilet bowl and a set of earphones attached to the outlet in the wall behind his bed. The cot was much more comfortable than the one he had spent the last two months sleeping on in Queens County Jail.

He reflected upon his last visits in Queens. Constance crying bitterly, he assuring her that the conviction would never stand up. We have the best appeal lawyer in the country, sweetheart. Be patient, love, you know I'm innocent.

His thoughts turned to Abe Pearlstein and Bruce Ehrhardt, his new lawyer handling the appeal. Twenty-five thousand up front! I hope he's as good as they say he is. Thank God for Constance. Good old Abe. Thinks it's her money. Good thing, else these lawyers would take my balls off. What's the difference? If only I beat them on appeal.

The following day a guard came to his cell and said he was wanted in the warden's office. The warden was a nice guy. The two of them sat together having coffee like old friends. I feel sorry for you, Sloane. You bucked the system, became an informer. Well, it's your problem, Sloane. If you were an honest cop you'd never be here. You're absolutely right, Mr. Warden.

How do you feel about working in prison, Sloane? Gee, warden, if I don't do something I'll go crazy. Have you any enemies you know about who are incarcerated here, Sloane? Not that I know of, warden. Suppose, Sloane, I keep you segregated for a few weeks to see how the land lies. We have a network of informers here in prison. I'll see if there is any danger waiting for you when you go into population. How does that sound, Sloane? Very nice of you, warden. Just give me enough books to read, sir, and I'll be happy.

Tommy, gradually getting over his claustrophobic traumas after a few months in jail, was slowly going out of his mind in the segregated area of Greenhaven. The boredom was insufferable. He stayed aloof from the other inmates who were secluded there. He considered himself a cut above his neighbors in the cell block, classifying them in his mind as professional stool pigeons. He rationalized his own behavior under fire and found it acceptable. He was given no other choice, he had to turn.

He was in constant touch with Abe Pearlstein and Bruce Ehrhardt, his two lawyers. His hopes for a reversal on appeal were buoyed by their letters and his spirits rose accordingly. He had two separate and equally tearful visits. One with his sister Rosemary and one with Constance. The stark atmosphere of the visiting room, the heavy perforated wire they talked through, made for a depressing scene. He asked them both to wait until he sent for them before they decided to visit him. He reassured Constance through almost daily letters that his conviction was sure to be reversed and that they would live happily forever after.

He requested an interview with the warden and asked him could he be given a job in the prison. The warden said that there didn't appear to be any animosity in the prison population toward him. He asked Tommy would he like the hospital, kitchen, or school to work in. Tommy, a lover of the outdoors, said he would prefer one of the work gangs. He explained that he once was a construction worker and maybe might make a good addition to a yard-repair group.

The following week Tommy was transferred to one of the W.P.A. gangs and put back into B Block. About sixty percent of the crew were black guys. Tommy was quickly accepted and settled into the daily routine of repairing broken pipes, painting walls, and various other face-lifting jobs around the slightly aging prison. He went into the yard every day for recreation period, playing basketball with the young black guys and enjoying the workout. He was sleeping well at night once again. His body was healthy and he worked and played a little ball through the hot summer, anxiously awaiting the fall term of the court of appeals when his motion would be on the calendar.

He made few friends. The guards, or hacks as they were called, were friendly enough to him but not too friendly to cause any raised eyebrows. He was the only cop in the Joint.

Most of the New York inmates gave him a wide berth, not even acknowledging him in the yard or at work. He was fairly close to some of the black kids he played basketball with. They kidded him, called him Old Man Whitey, and applauded him when he made an exceptional move or shot in the basket. Tommy was making the best of a bad situation, a situation that he knew from his latest lawyer reports could very possibly end in his freedom within the next few months.

It was a blistering hot Saturday afternoon in early July. It was a long afternoon recreation period in A and B Block yard. The sun-blanketed yard was filled with inmates. Some were lifting weights, others playing baseball or basketball, still others walking back and forth in pairs, and many groups gathered around long tables enjoying a feast. The tables were all spoken for and referred to in prison jargon as "courts." Protocol demanded that you never approached a court unless first invited or you were a very good friend of one of the members.

Paulie Ippolito was the head man of his court, referred to in the prison as the Downtown Guys Court. Paulie was an underboss in the downtown family, a highly regarded man in Greenhaven prison. Fifty-two years old, stocky, muscular build, thick gray hair, a year to go on a five-year bit for his part in a stock swindle.

He was in deep conversation at the end of the table with Larry Infante and Freddie Torrio, two of his underlings on the court. Two guys who would attempt to vault over the prison wall if Paulie ordered them to.

"This is how it is. I got a visit from my cousin Tony this morning. You know this cop who came in the Joint a couple of months ago. This guy named Tommy Sloane. The Irish guy, always playing basketball with the shines. I got the word on him. He used to be a hundred percent guy, everybody trusted him. But he turned stool pigeon for the crime commission, wrapped up a lot of our friends. Got wired up, bullshitted them, nailed ten or fifteen guys and about fifty cops.

"Anyway, they stuck it up his ass on a murder rap. The word is out that it might get reversed. A real shit case. Anyway, the boys are worried. He can still testify if it gets reversed and send a shitload of guys to the can.

"Here's the story. Big Angelo and Richie Irish from the West Side want him handled in the worst way. No fucking up, deadsville, you get it? He's in the W.P.A. gang. I've been keeping tabs on him. Two good shine friends of ours are in his gang. Bootsie, the big black guy had the numbers in South Brooklyn with us, and Little Jeff, the scar-faced kid. Good kid, we got loads of swag from him downtown.

"It should be a cinch to hit this rat Sloane. He stays away from white guys, hangs out mostly with shines. Larry, you get hold of Bootsie and Little Jeff. Tell them it's a must. Angelo wants this stool pigeon fuck belted out. All the way. There's a good score in it for them and Angelo will see that they're well taken care of when they get out of here. They're both due to go home soon, can use a good score. Start working on it right away, the two of you."

A few days later Larry Infante, Paulie's courier in Greenhaven, laid the proposition on Bootsie and Little Jeff. Larry reported back. No problem!

Two days later Larry had the whole rundown. He told Paulie to get word to Angelo to leave twenty thousand dollars up front with Dave the Indian at his bar in Brownsville, Brooklyn. We'll see Angelo when we get home. Little Jeff is due home in September, Bootsie in November. Larry grinned as he told Paulie their exact words. We'll take care of it. This sucker will soon be gone, man. They also asked you to give Angelo their best regards.

Bootsie and Little Jeff, skilled practitioners, planned the hit as carefully as General Rommel planned his campaign in Africa. Just as Paulie said, there was no rush. The rewards would be great when they hit the street a few months later. They wanted to be absolutely certain that Angelo and Richie Irish would be well pleased. They were top-drawer guys on the outside and were in a position to put Bootsie and Little Jeff into instant good action.

They recruited a husky weight lifter named Derrick, who had forearms like tree trunks. Their next recruit was a sinewy, mean-faced Puerto Rican named Rafael, reputed to have knifed at least ten guys on the outside. Their fee was to be five thousand dollars each. Like most prisoners, they were dead broke, and the promised sum seemed like a million dollars. The four of them became much friendlier toward Tommy over the next ten days. Tommy recognized this as a further sign of acceptance and responded to their overtures gratefully. Good morning, Tom, hiya, Tom. Hey Boots, hey Jeff—whadda you say?

Getting the proper weapon to Rafael was easy. A butcher knife was smuggled out of the huge prison kitchen and was honed down to such a fine point it could penetrate a steel door.

The date was set. The plotters had waited for a guard the convicts called Old Harry to be on duty the midnight to eight shift. He was close to sixty-three and due to a muscular disorder hobbled around very slowly; he was just being allowed to put in his time for maximum pension. Everybody liked Old Harry, a veteran hack for almost forty years.

The piercing ring of the morning wake-up bell at six o'clock roused the prisoners out of their dreams of pretty girls, maroon Cadillacs, fancy clothes, and noisy night clubs. They wearily washed, shaved, and brushed their teeth in the real-life spartan confines of their tiny cells. At six thirty the long line of cell doors were automatically sprung open by electronic impulse. The men slowly emerged from their cells to stand about in groups for a minute or two before the call to line up in pairs for their march to breakfast in the mess hall.

Tommy came out of his cell in a happy mood. He had dreamed all night of Constance—playing tennis, dancing, walking the beach—a lovely dream. He looked back on the dream as a good omen of things to come. His cell was almost at the rear of the tier of cells. Guys stood around exchanging a few words, awaiting the signal to pair off for their march to the mess hall.

Bootsie and Little Jeff were facing Tommy, big smiles, asking him did he have a good sleep. He never had a chance to reply.

Derrick, the weight lifter, was directly in back of him. He clamped his tremendous right forearm under his chin in a mugging hold, pressing hard against his larynx. In the same motion he clasped his broad left hand across Tommy's mouth. He uttered a strangled, gurgling sound, the air stifled in his throat. He was helpless, strength rapidly draining, couldn't scream.

Rafael did his job well. He balanced himself against Derrick's strong left arm and stabbed Tommy repeatedly in the back. The stilletolike knife plunged through his body as if it were butter. It was all over in about a minute.

The piercing bell rang again. Line up for the mess hall. The convicts in the rear who saw what happened were too terrified to open their mouths. They just stepped over Tommy's body and continued their march. Rafael threw the knife through the bars of one of the front cells. Old Harry hobbled along at the head of the line, good-naturedly chatting with the prisoners up front.

A tier clean-up man assigned to mop up the area outside the cells discovered Tommy's body. He ran up close, took one look at the spreading pool of blood under the body that was lying face down, turned, and started screaming for a guard.

The warden shook his head sadly when the principal keeper gave him the bad news. Tommy Sloane—ex-vice cop, ex-chief witness for the crime commission—doing twenty-five to life for a double murder. Stabbed to death in my prison. Jesus Christ, stabbed, I'll say he was stabbed. They cut the poor bastard's insides into ribbons. Too bad, he didn't seem like a bad person. At least he died quickly.

Well, my skirts are clean. I placed him in segregation for his own protection. He pleaded to go to work and enter the prison population. Tough luck, Sloane, you can't buck the system.

===➤ *Epilogue*

THE WARDEN RELEASED THE NEWS of Tommy's murder to the press late Friday evening. It made page four of the late *Daily News* on Saturday as well as the late editions of the *New York Times*.

It also made a lot of cops in New York very happy, the happiest of all, Dick Callahan. Now he'll be right where I wanted him, six feet below with Peter Dowd.

It also brought a lot of tears to the eyes of Rosemary and her husband Billy. As next of kin, Rosemary was notified first. After her initial hysteria, she asked the prison authorities if Leo P. Quinn, the family undertaker, could pick the body up on Sunday. She tried to notify Justine, but Justine's mother explained that Justine was away on a sailing trip with a new friend and couldn't be reached.

Constance read the newspaper story dry-eyed, never shedding a tear. It was as if an immense burden was lifted from her shoulders. She had grown to despise the occasional visits to Tommy in prison. Actually dreaded them. She loved Tommy as her hero cop; her handsome, funny, charming sweetheart. Her greatest love. He appeared docile, subdued, almost obsequious when she visited him. The murders they framed him for. Or did they frame him? The lies she caught him in. I don't think I could ever have married Tommy, even if he were freed. But the story has one happy ending. I have two hundred and seventy thousand dollars left in the safe deposit box after paying those lawyers. It was a great trip, Tommy, and you left me at the altar in good shape. Well, I won't feel too guilty now about having a drink with that good-looking new account executive in the office. Good-bye, Tommy.

Rosemary and Billy stood beside the flag-draped closed coffin in the left wake room of the Leo P. Quinn Funeral Home. There were only a few floral wreaths, all sent by relatives. The funeral home hours were from two to five in the afternoon and seven to ten at night. A couple of aunts and uncles came during the day to pay their tearful respects.

The funeral mass at nearby St. Sebastian's Church the next day was a simple ceremony and mercifully brief. Rosemary made one concession to Tommy's memory—an organist and a young Irish tenor to sing three songs that she knew Tommy loved—"The Rose of Tralee," "Galway Bay," and "Danny Boy."

Tears streamed down her cheeks as she recalled the wonderful nights they spent years ago in the rented family cottage in the Irish section of Rockaway. How they all loved to sit with a drink and listen to the beautiful Irish ballads. Especially Tommy.

The church was almost empty, only a scattering of the usual old men and women in the back pews who daily prayed for their ultimate salvation. Rosemary and Billy clutched hands tightly as the priest performed his rituals on the altar. The tenor's clear, sweet voice filled the hallowed church as he sang his final song, the heart wrenching lyrics of "Danny Boy."

Enraptured by the song, Rosemary was suddenly startled by the sounds of muffled, spasmodic sobbing a few rows in back of her. She turned slightly, cast a covert glance. Only tight, curly black hair was visible behind clenched fists hiding his face as he knelt against the back of the pew. It was Vinny!

Yes, it was Vinny, crying his heart out as he listened to "Danny Boy"—flooded with memories of all the great days and nights he had with Tommy. Oh, Tommy, I loved you more than the brother I never had. Jesus Christ, Tommy, why did you let those rotten bastards turn you, make you a rat? You, Tommy, the bravest guy I ever knew, all the balls in the world. Why? Why?

The strains of "Danny Boy" brought back all the good days, the weekends he and Connie spent with Justine and Tommy in Rockaway. It seemed like only yesterday. Touring all the Irish bars, listening to the singing waiters and occasional customers sing the haunting, lovely songs of Ireland. How Tommy's eyes glistened when a young waiter sang the ballad of "Kevin Barry." Tommy explaining, a little bombed, eyes teary, the story of the young I.R.A. revolutionary, Kevin Barry. The fucking British hung the kid, Vince, because he wouldn't reveal his friends.

Oh, Tommy, you were so like those Irish guys you loved to talk about. Shoot-out Tom, tough Tommy Sloane—and you had to end this way. Why, Tommy? Why?

The mass was over. The priest gave Tommy's body inside the casket his final blessing. The funeral home employees carried the casket down the church aisle to the waiting hearse outside. Rosemary and Billy stepped out into the aisle to follow the procession. Vinny intercepted her almost immediately, crushed her in his arms, both sobbing heart-brokenly.

Outside the church they regained their composure enough to finally speak.

Rosemary said, "Oh, Vince, it was so nice of you to come to the mass for Tommy. I know how much he loved you. And Billy and I really appreciate it so much. Will you come to the cemetery with us? It's Calvary, only a short ride from here."

Vinny cleared his throat, just about managed to speak.

"No, thank you, Rosemary. I couldn't face that but I had to come here this morning, in spite of everything. Rosie, you know how much I loved Tommy."

He halted again, all choked up, fought back another on-slaught of tears, continued, "It's all my fault, Rose, all my fault. I made him go into the Job, schemed to get him into plainclothes. That's why he's lying out here in a coffin. Tommy could have been anything, now he's dead. I just came today to tell you how sorry I am, Rosemary. It's not Tommy they're burying today, I buried him seventeen years ago when I made him go on the Job."

Vinny hugged Rosemary, kissed her again, shook Billy's hand and walked towards a car with a chauffeur at the wheel waiting down from the church.

The funeral cortege took off. Two limousines following the hearse carrying Tommy's body to Calvary cemetery. Rosemary and Billy, arms around each other, in the first car, and Leo P.

Quinn, the third, with Father Andrews in the second car to say a few prayers at Tommy's grave for the repose of his soul.

There was no motorcycle escort preceding the hearse carrying Tommy's coffin for he was no longer an ex-cop. No, no motorcycles ahead for the coffin of an ex-convict. And worse, an ex-cop turned scumbag—the worse epithet a cop could use.

The hearse and the two limousines wended their way very slowly through the narrow streets of Queens. Tommy's last ride was surely not in the Fast Lane he loved to travel in, the way he loved to live. Soon Father Andrews would say the final prayers at his grave, hopefully to somehow bend God to look kindly on Tommy.

Tommy Sloane needed all the prayers he could get.